Laura Dean Keeps breaking up with me

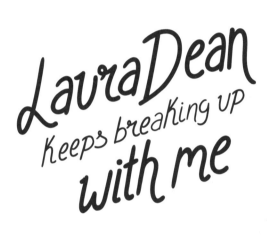

MARIKO TAMAKI

Laura Dean
keeps breaking up
with me

ROSEMARY VALERO-O'CONNELL

:01

First Second

New York

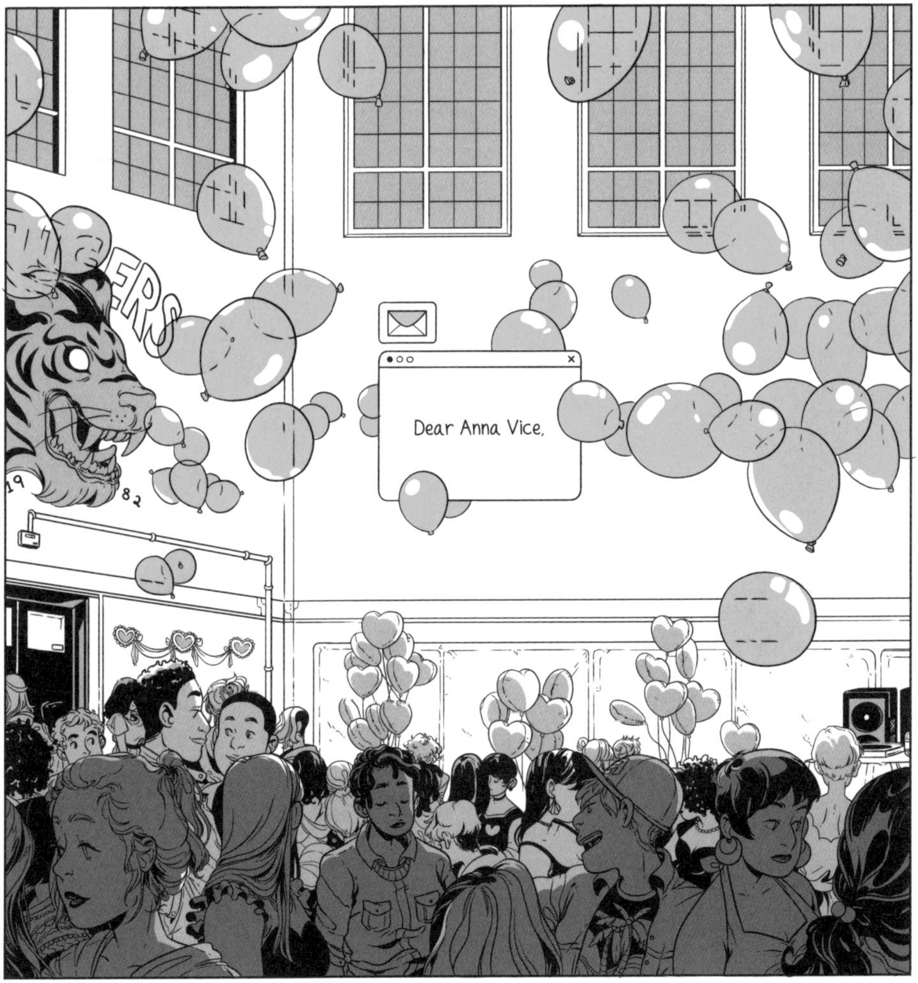
Dear Anna Vice,

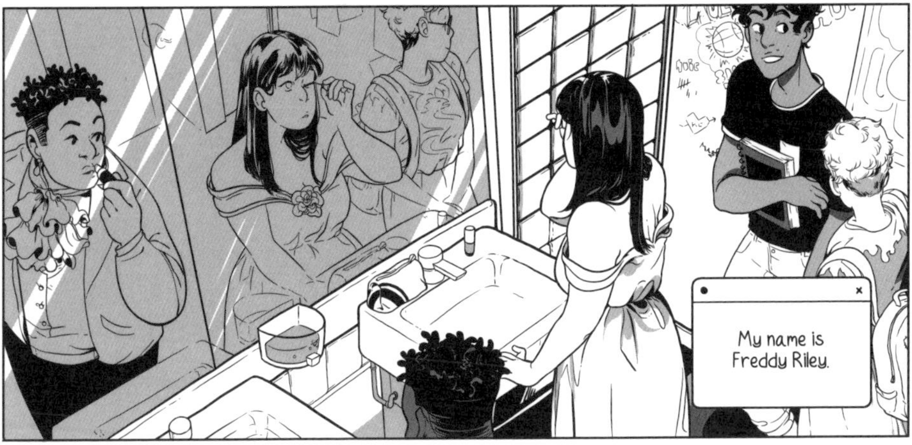
My name is
Freddy Riley.

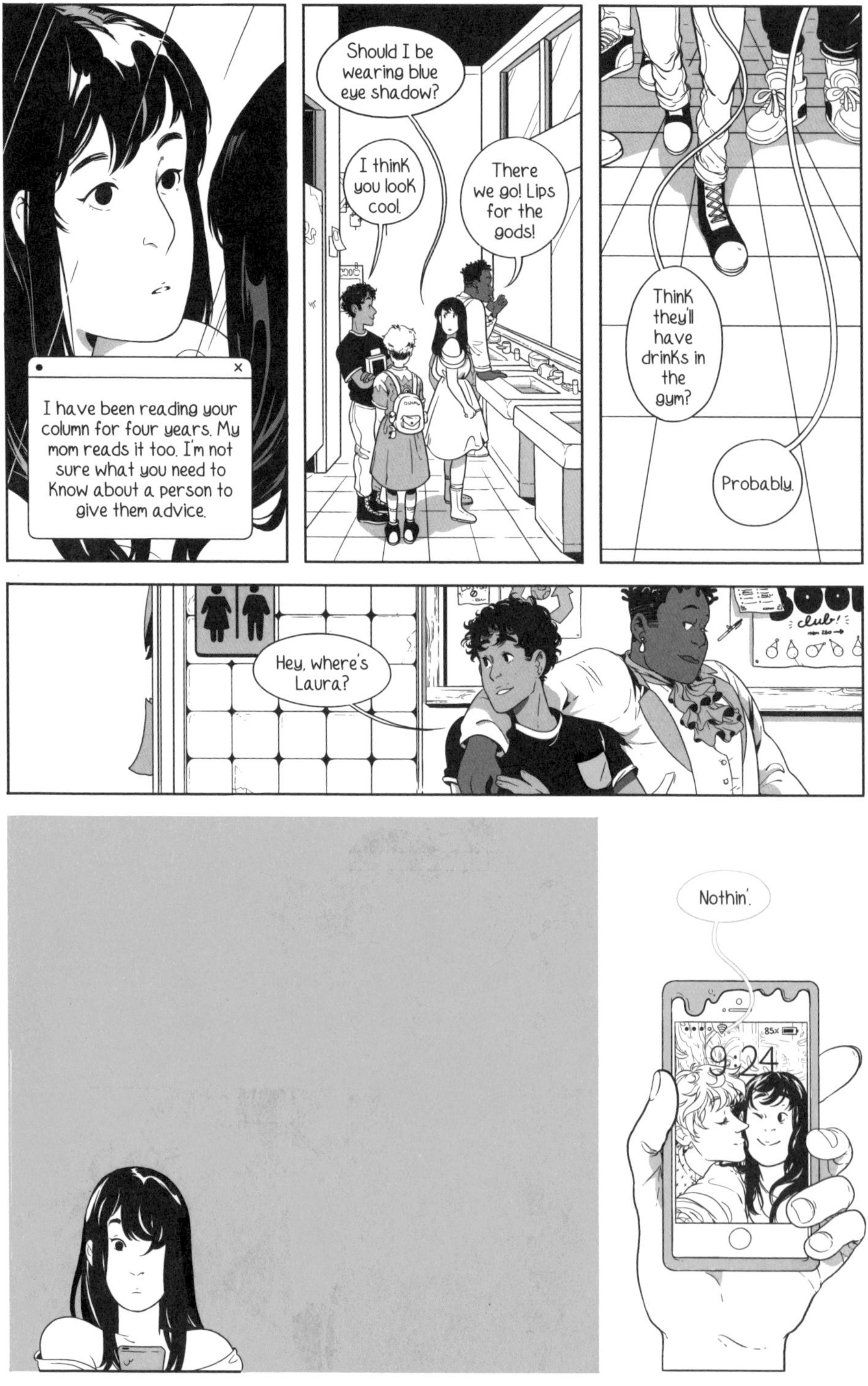
I have been reading your column for four years. My mom reads it too. I'm not sure what you need to know about a person to give them advice.
Should I be wearing blue eye shadow?
I think you look cool.
There we go! Lips for the gods!
Think they'll have drinks in the gym?
Probably.
Hey, where's Laura?
club!
Nothin'.
9:24
85%

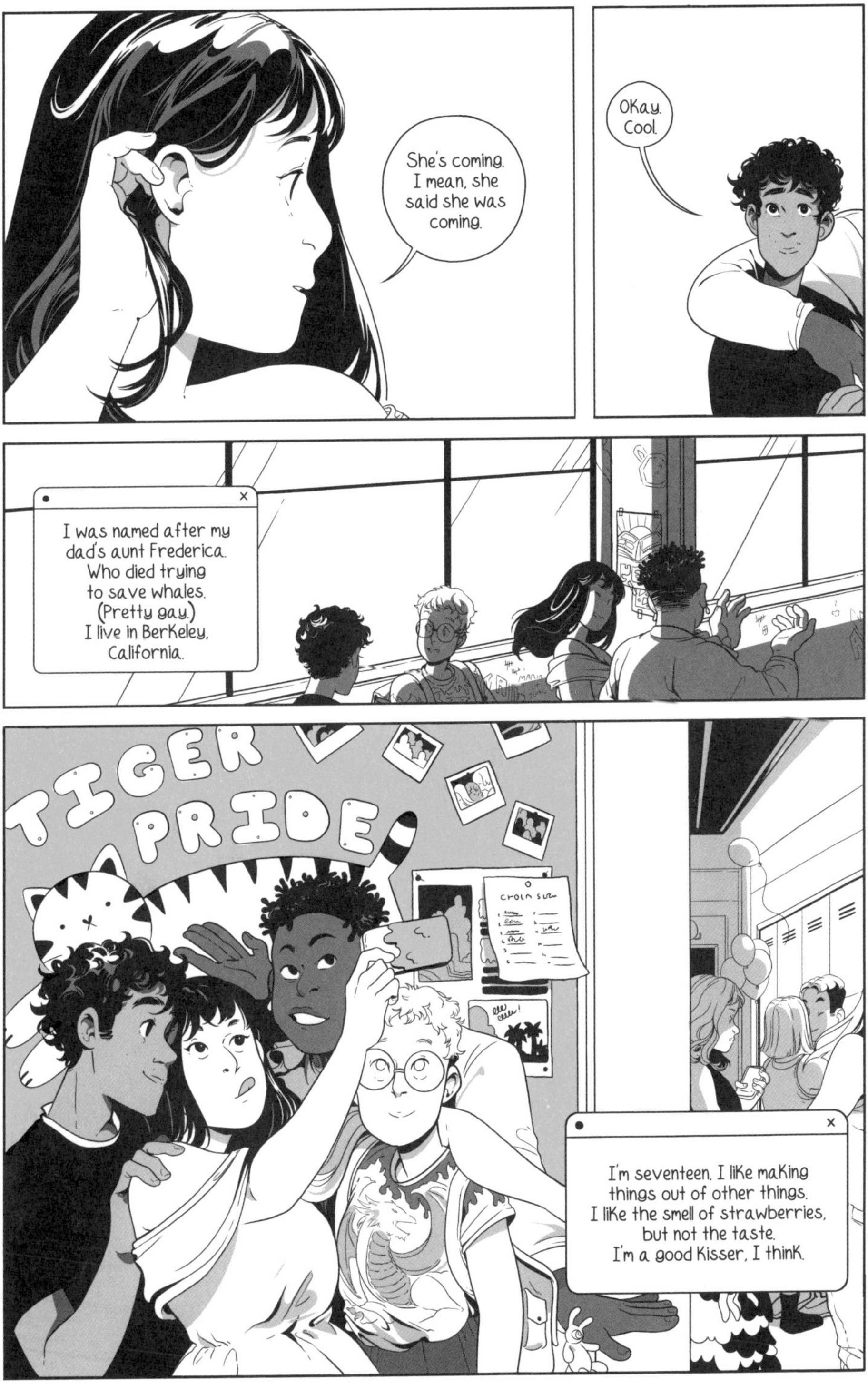
She's coming. I mean, she said she was coming.
Okay. Cool.
I was named after my dad's aunt Frederica. Who died trying to save whales. (Pretty gay.) I live in Berkeley, California.
TIGER PRIDE
I'm seventeen. I like making things out of other things. I like the smell of strawberries, but not the taste. I'm a good kisser, I think.

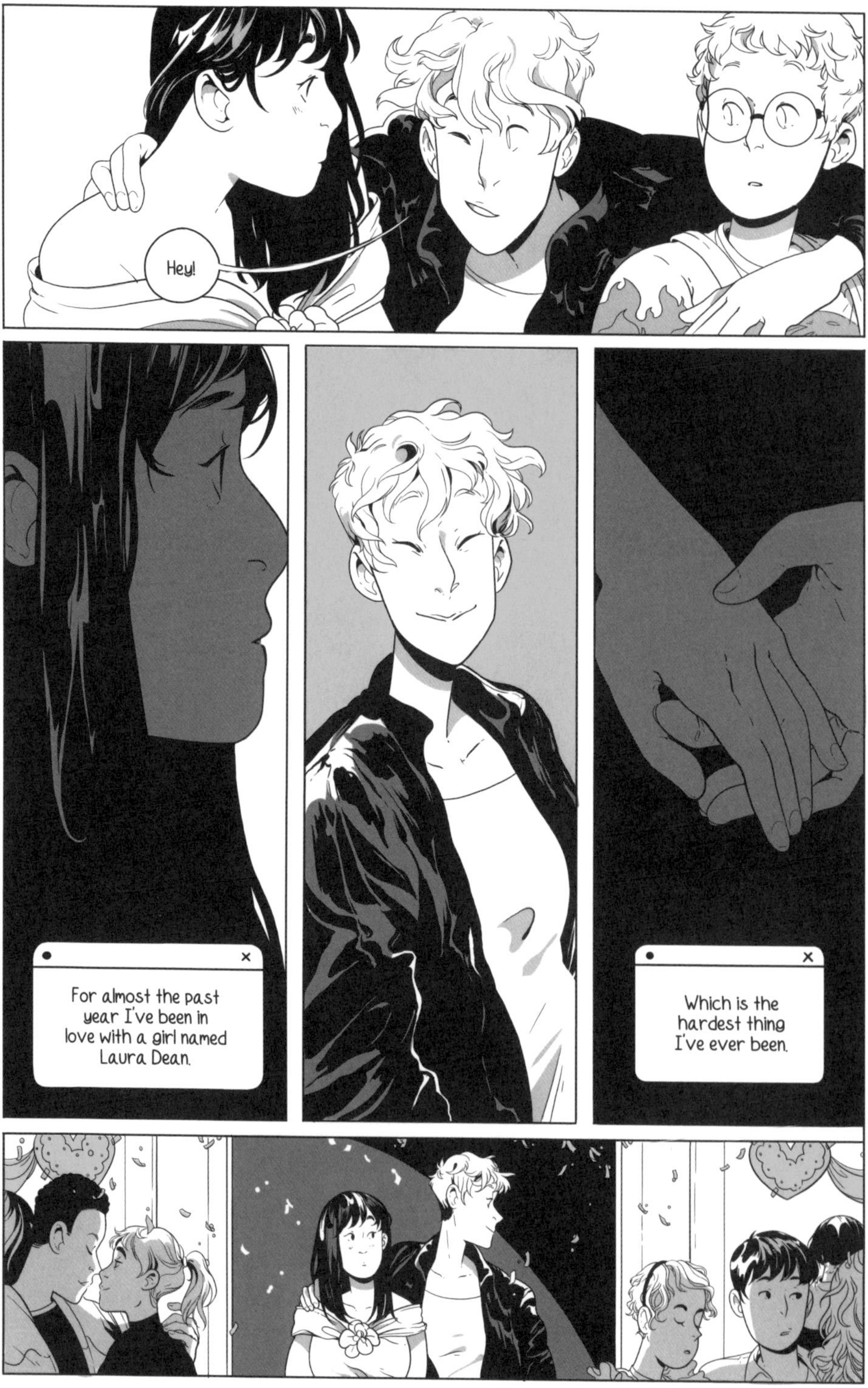
Hey!
For almost the past year I've been in love with a girl named Laura Dean.
Which is the hardest thing I've ever been.

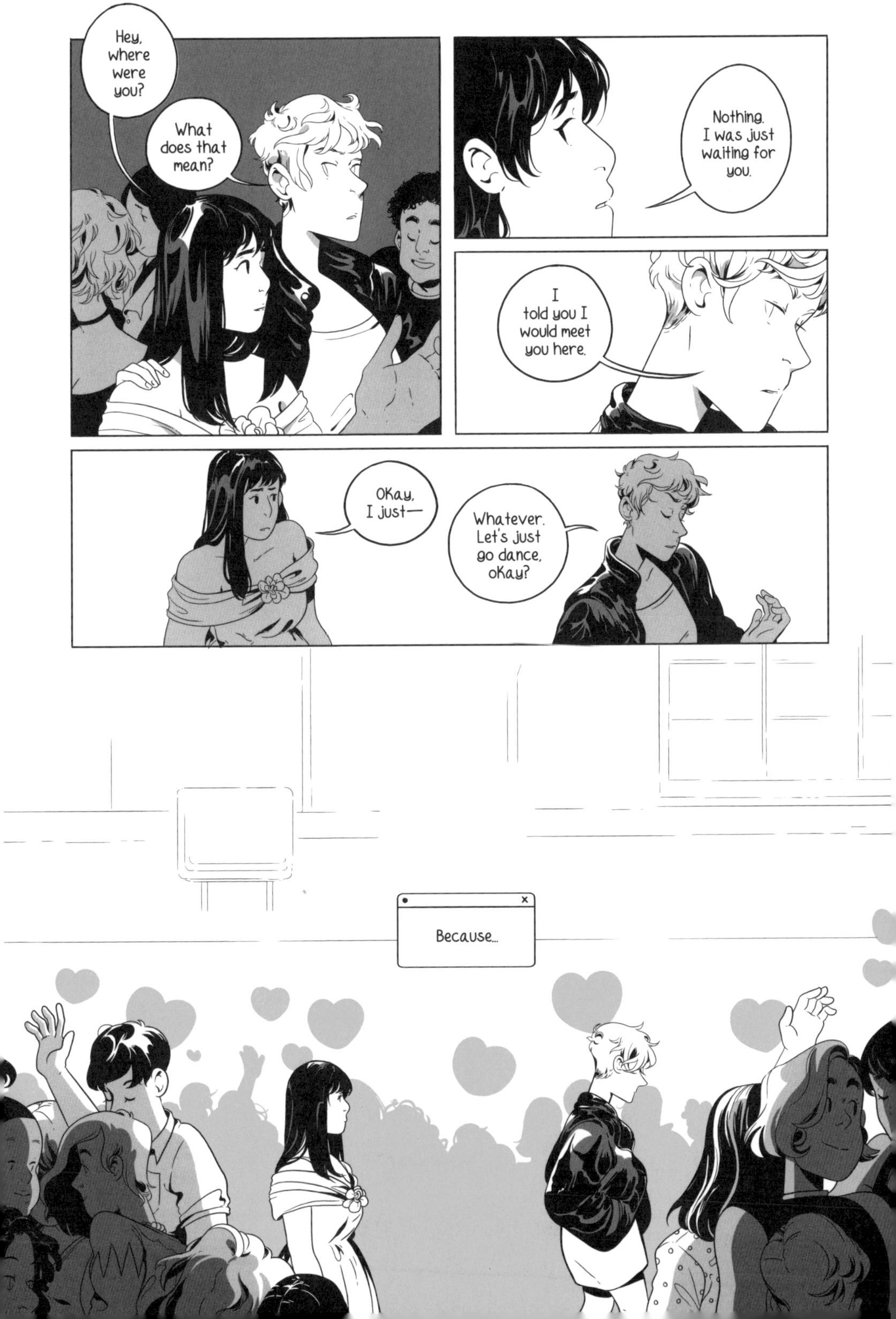
Hey, where were you?
What does that mean?
Nothing. I was just waiting for you.
I told you I would meet you here.
Okay, I just—
Whatever. Let's just go dance, okay?
Because...

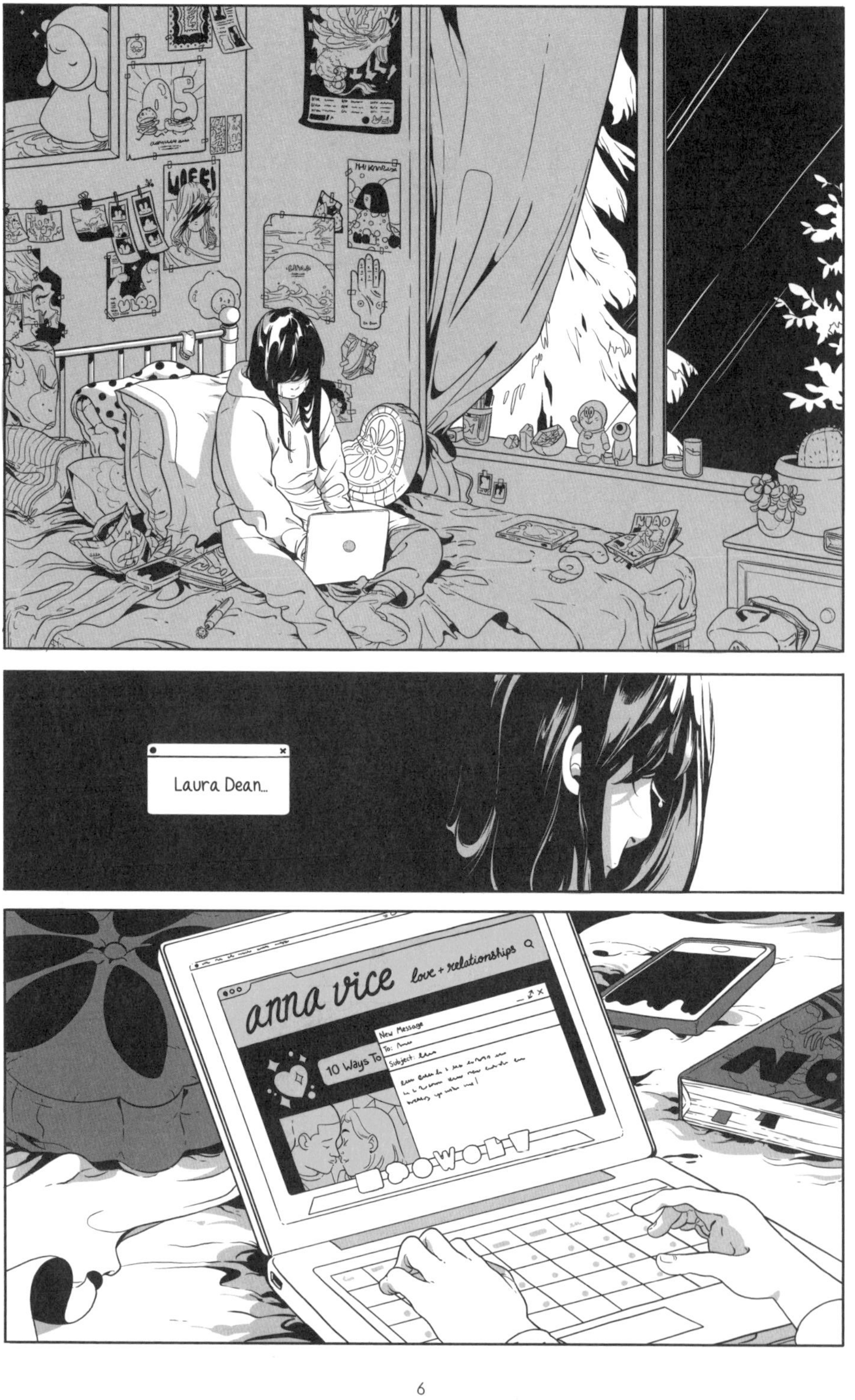
Laura Dean...
anna vice
love + relationships
New Message
To:
Subject:
10 Ways To

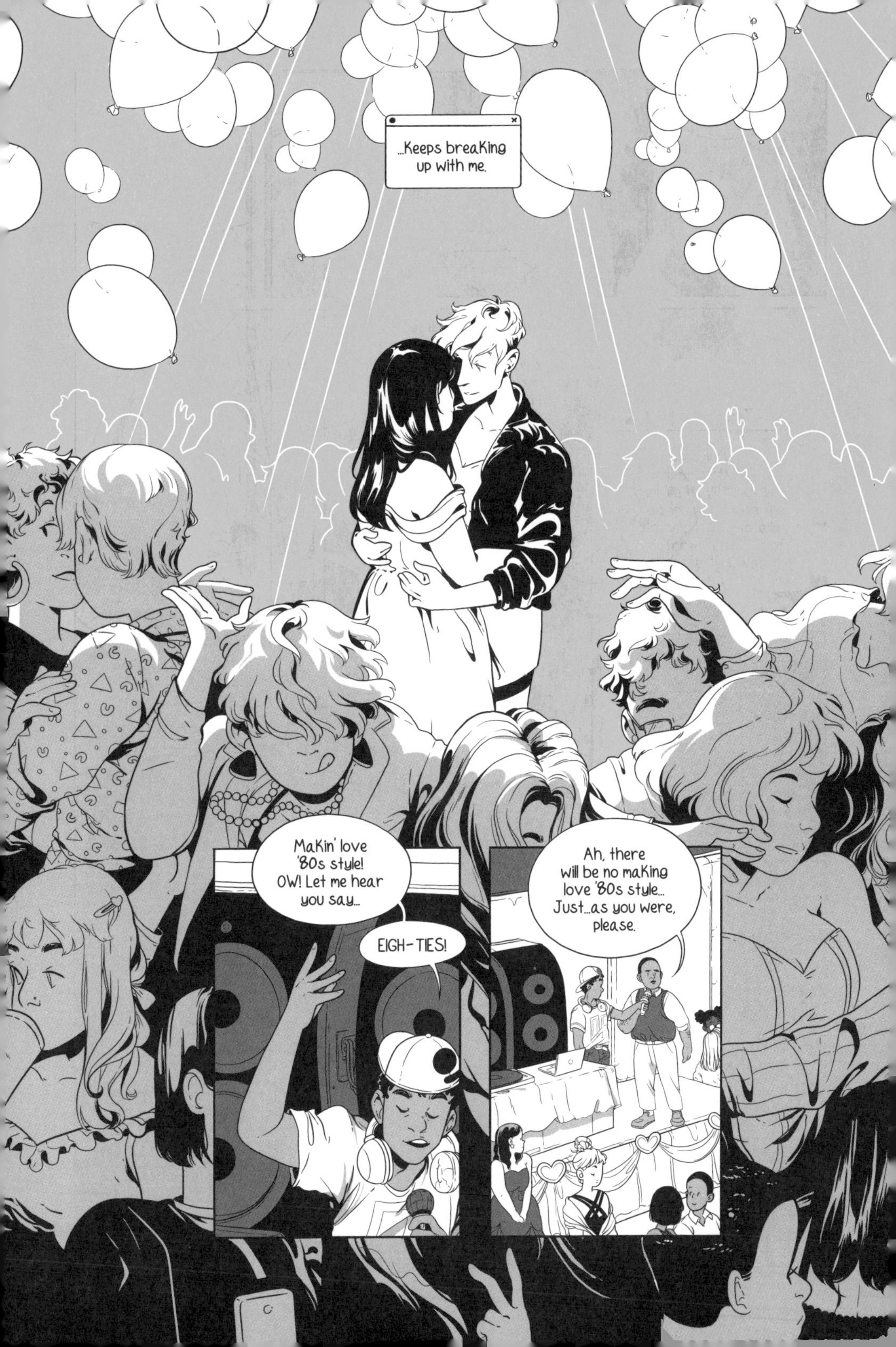
...Keeps breaking up with me.
Makin' love '80s style! OW! Let me hear you say...
EIGH-TIES!
Ah, there will be no making love '80s style... Just...as you were, please.

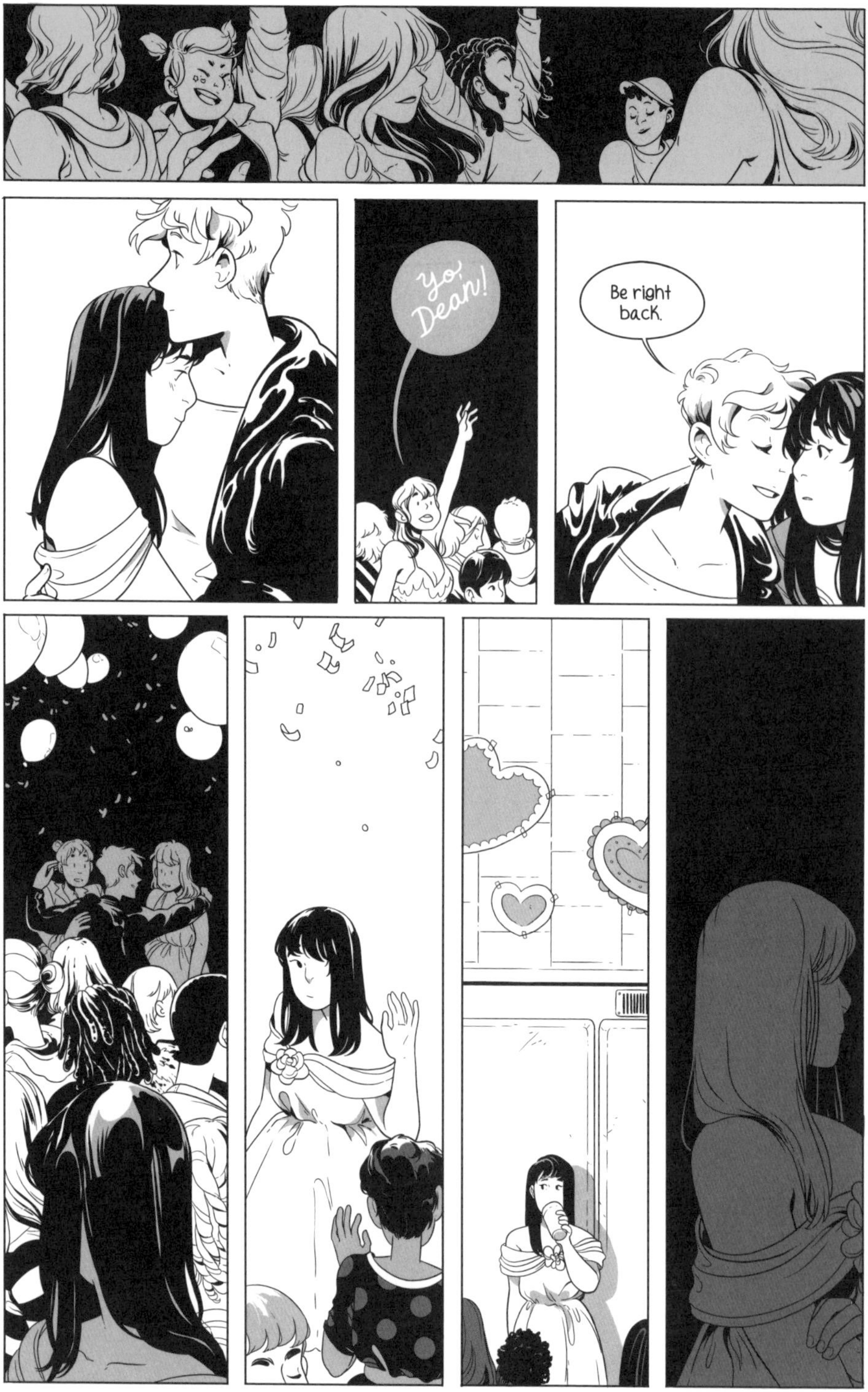
Yo, Dean!
Be right back.

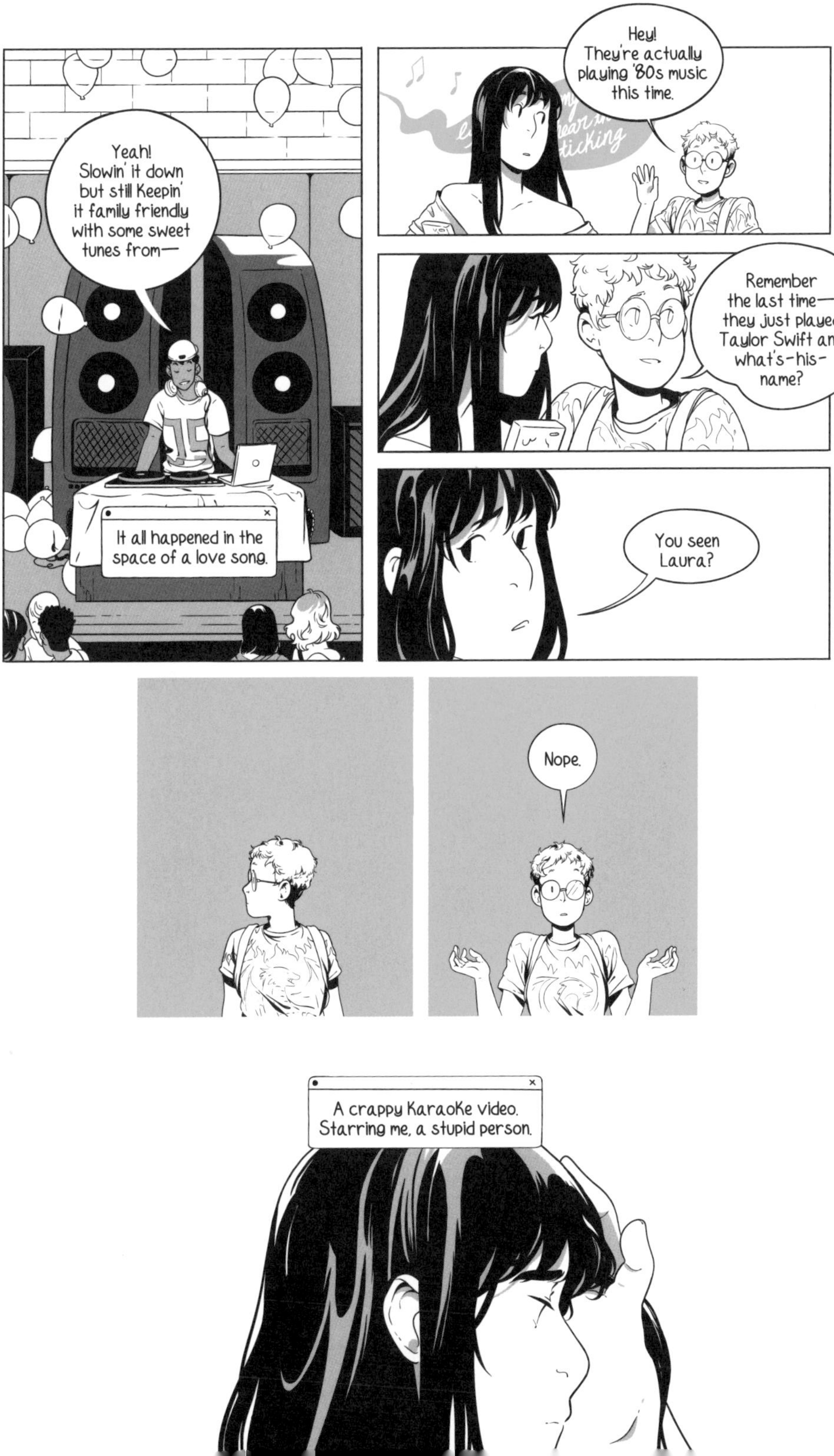

Yeah! Slowin' it down but still Keepin' it family friendly with some sweet tunes from—
It all happened in the space of a love song.
Hey! They're actually playing '80s music this time.
Remember the last time— they just played Taylor Swift and what's-his-name?
You seen Laura?
Nope.
A crappy Karaoke video. Starring me, a stupid person.

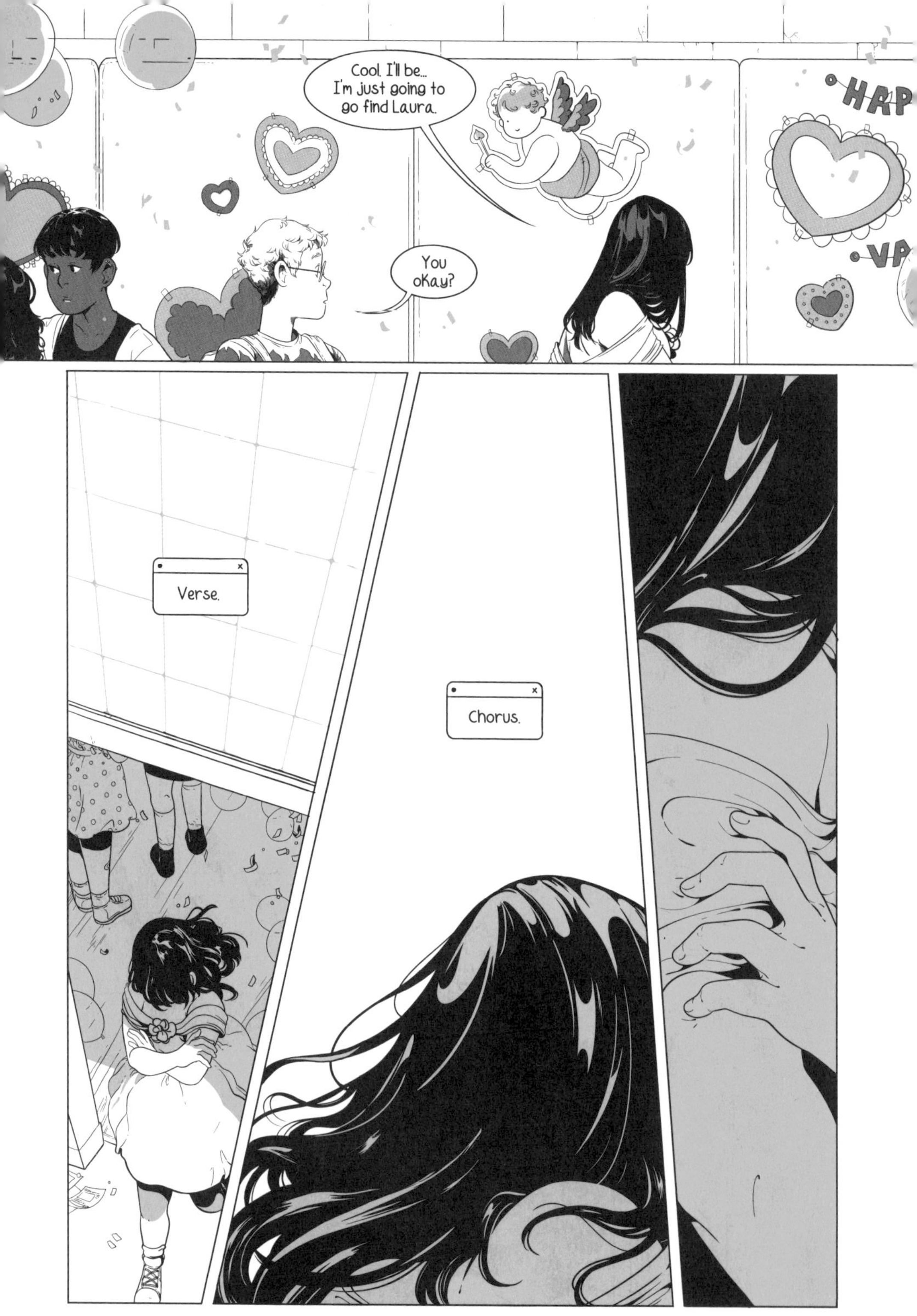
Cool. I'll be...
I'm just going to
go find Laura.
You
oKay?
HAP
VA
Verse.
Chorus.

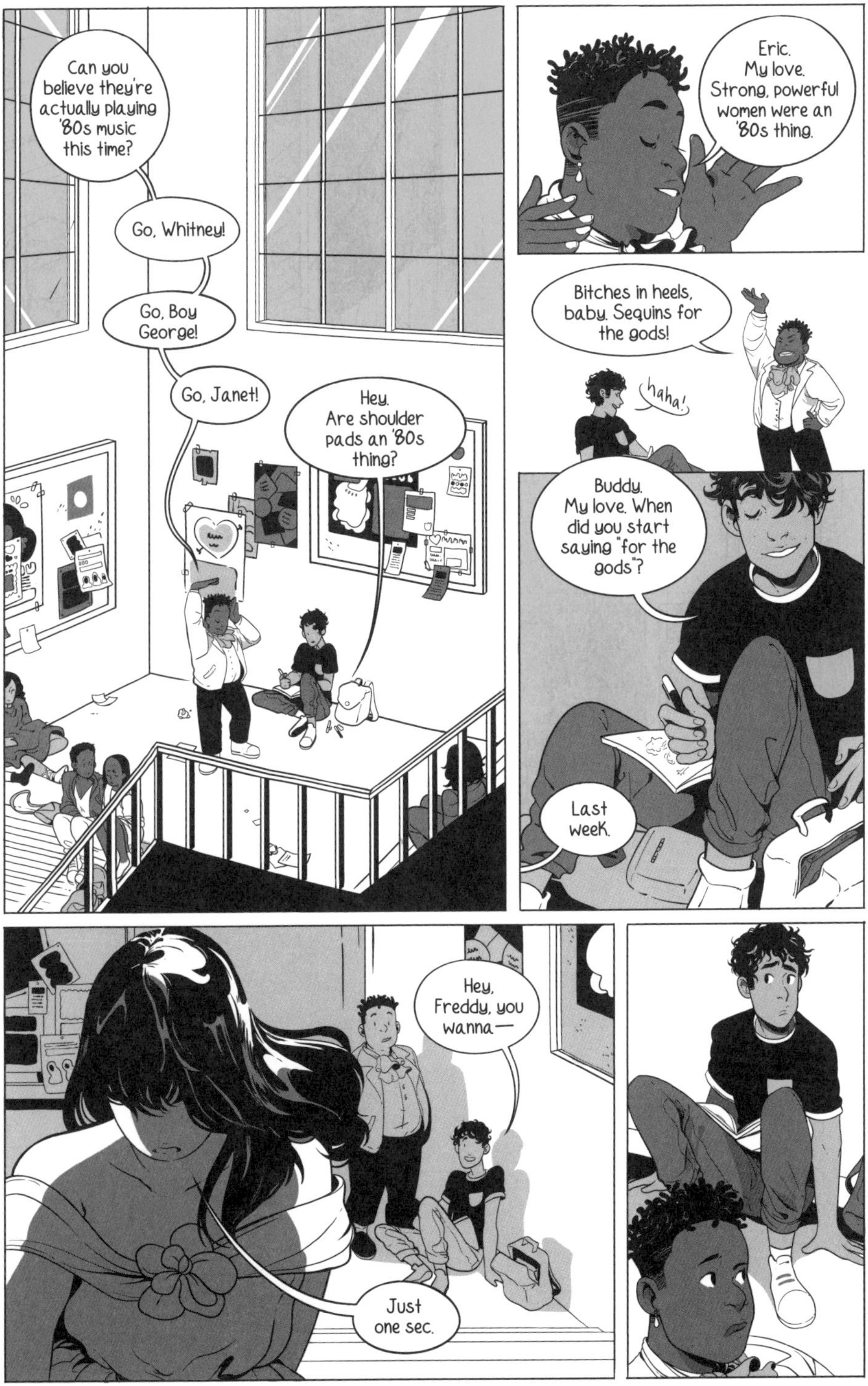
Can you believe they're actually playing '80s music this time?
Go, Whitney!
Go, Boy George!
Go, Janet!
Hey. Are shoulder pads an '80s thing?
Eric. My love. Strong, powerful women were an '80s thing.
Bitches in heels, baby. Sequins for the gods!
haha!
Buddy. My love. When did you start saying "for the gods"?
Last week.
Hey, Freddy, you wanna—
Just one sec.

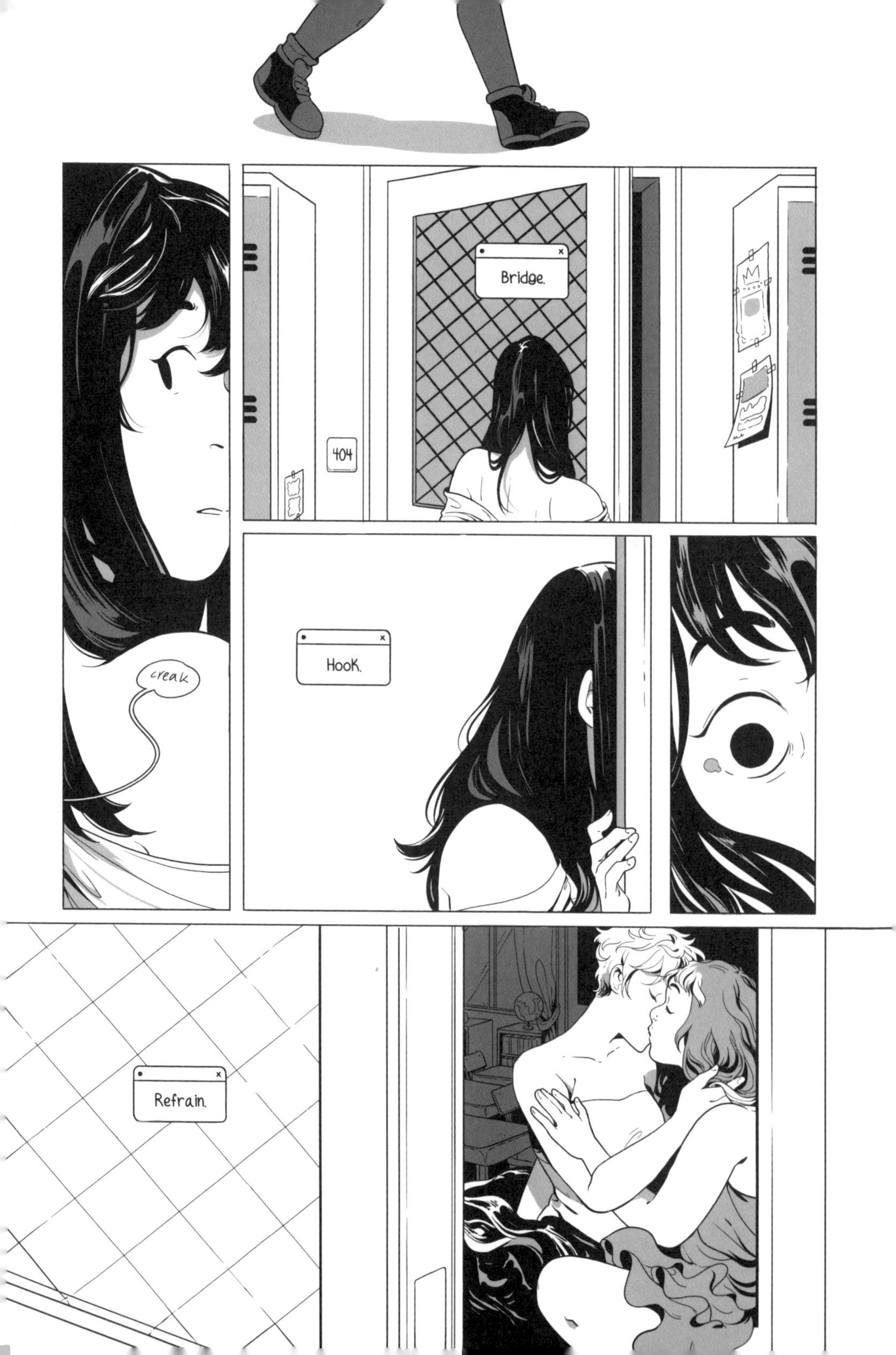
Bridge.
404
creak
Hook.
Refrain.

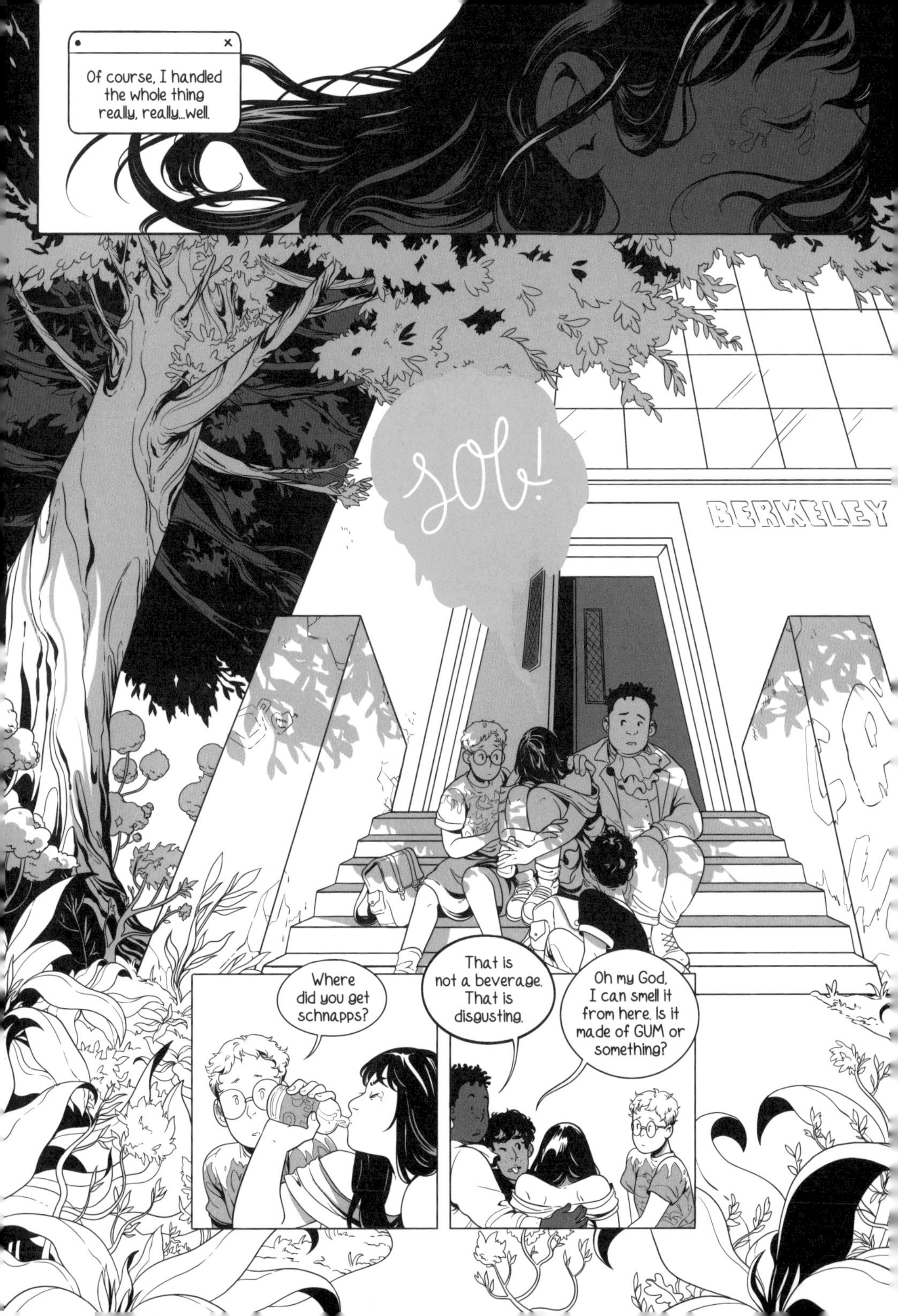

Of course, I handled the whole thing really, really...well.
SOB!
BERKELEY
Where did you get schnapps?
That is not a beverage. That is disgusting.
Oh my God, I can smell it from here. Is it made of GUM or something?

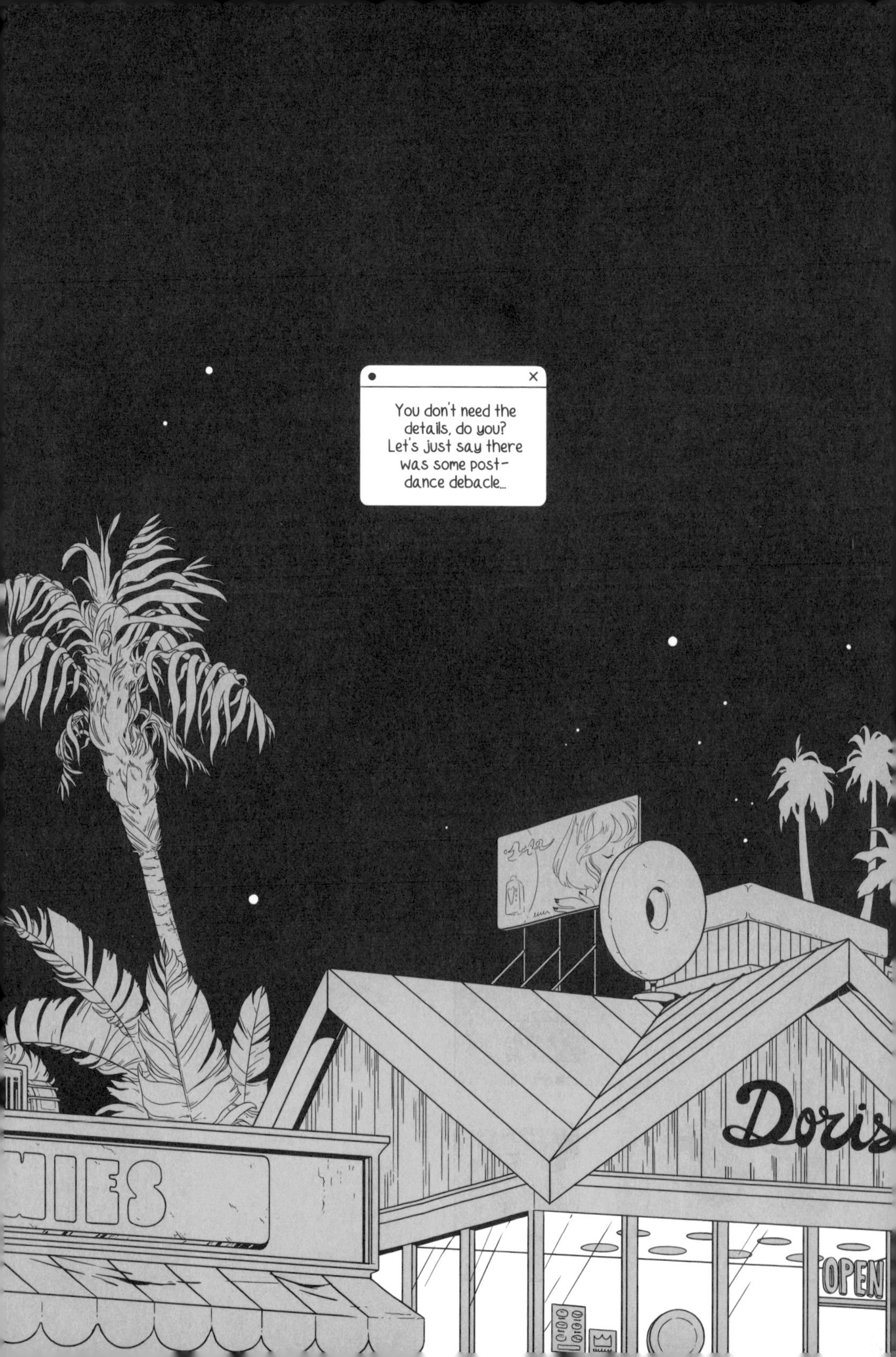
You don't need the details, do you? Let's just say there was some post-dance debacle...
MIES
Doris
OPEN

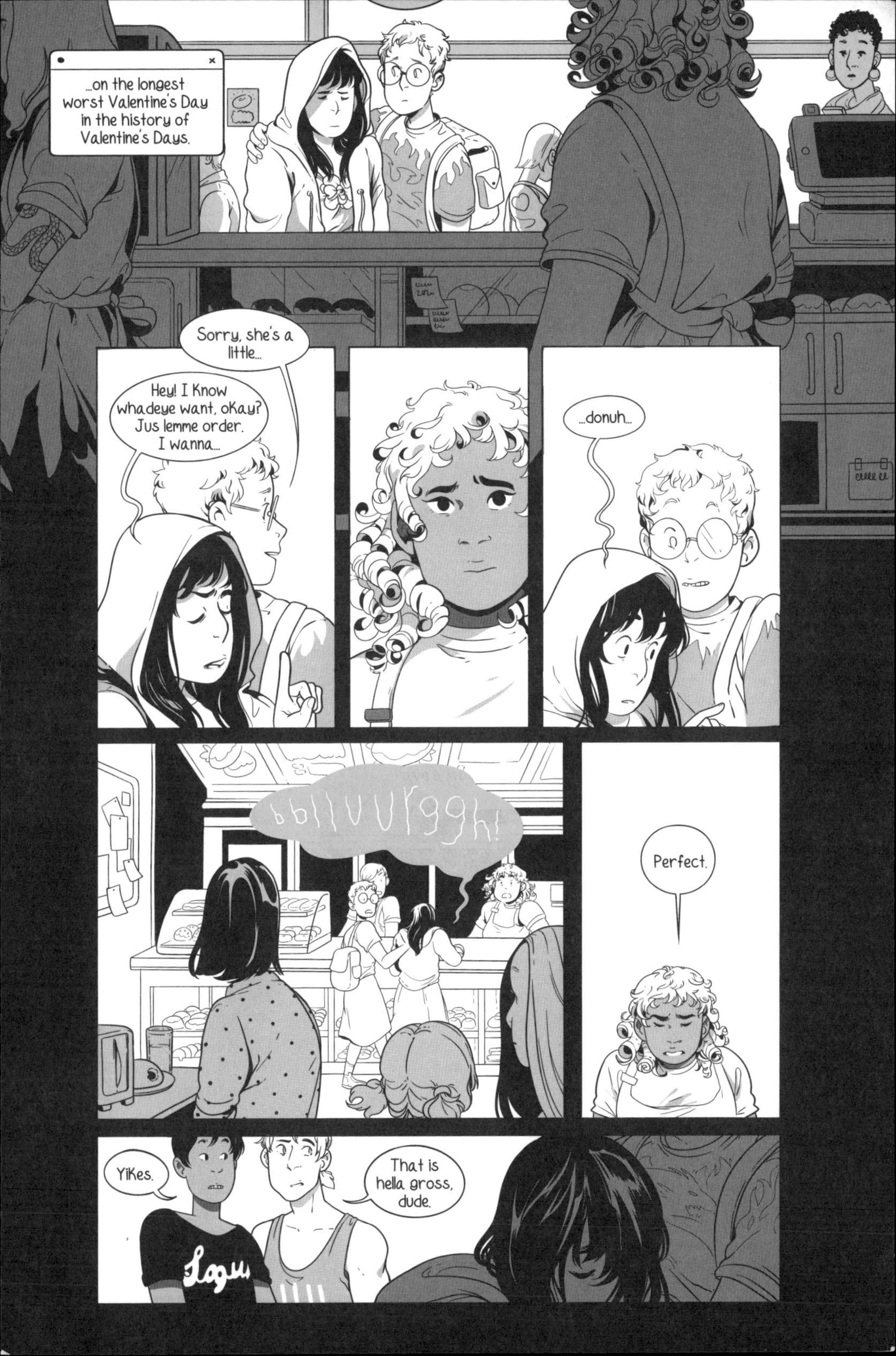
...on the longest worst Valentine's Day in the history of Valentine's Days.
Sorry, she's a little...
Hey! I know whadeye want, okay? Jus lemme order. I wanna...
...donuh...
bblluurgghh!
Perfect.
Yikes.
That is hella gross, dude.

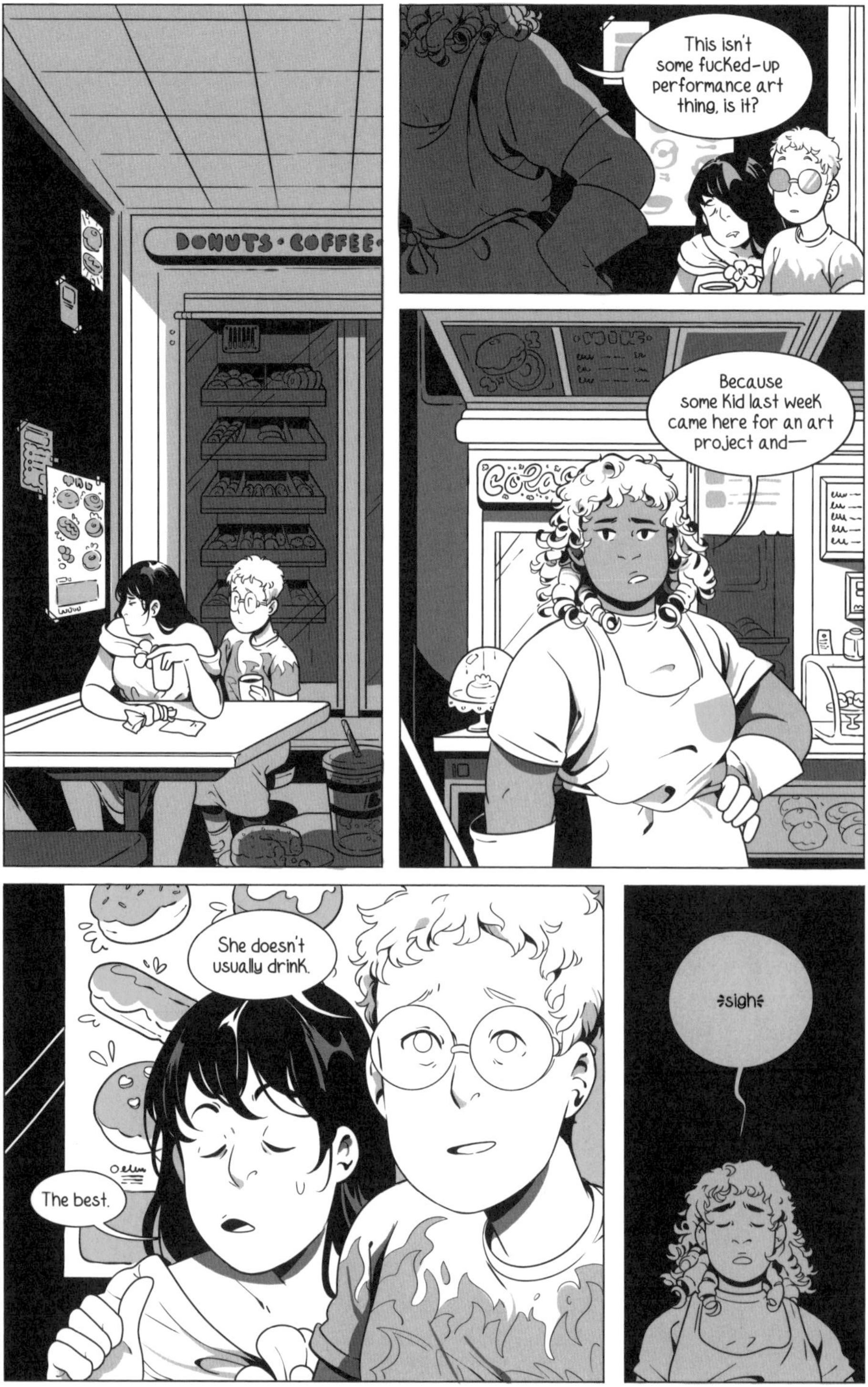
DONUTS • COFFEE
This isn't some fucked-up performance art thing, is it?
Because some kid last week came here for an art project and—
She doesn't usually drink.
The best.
sigh

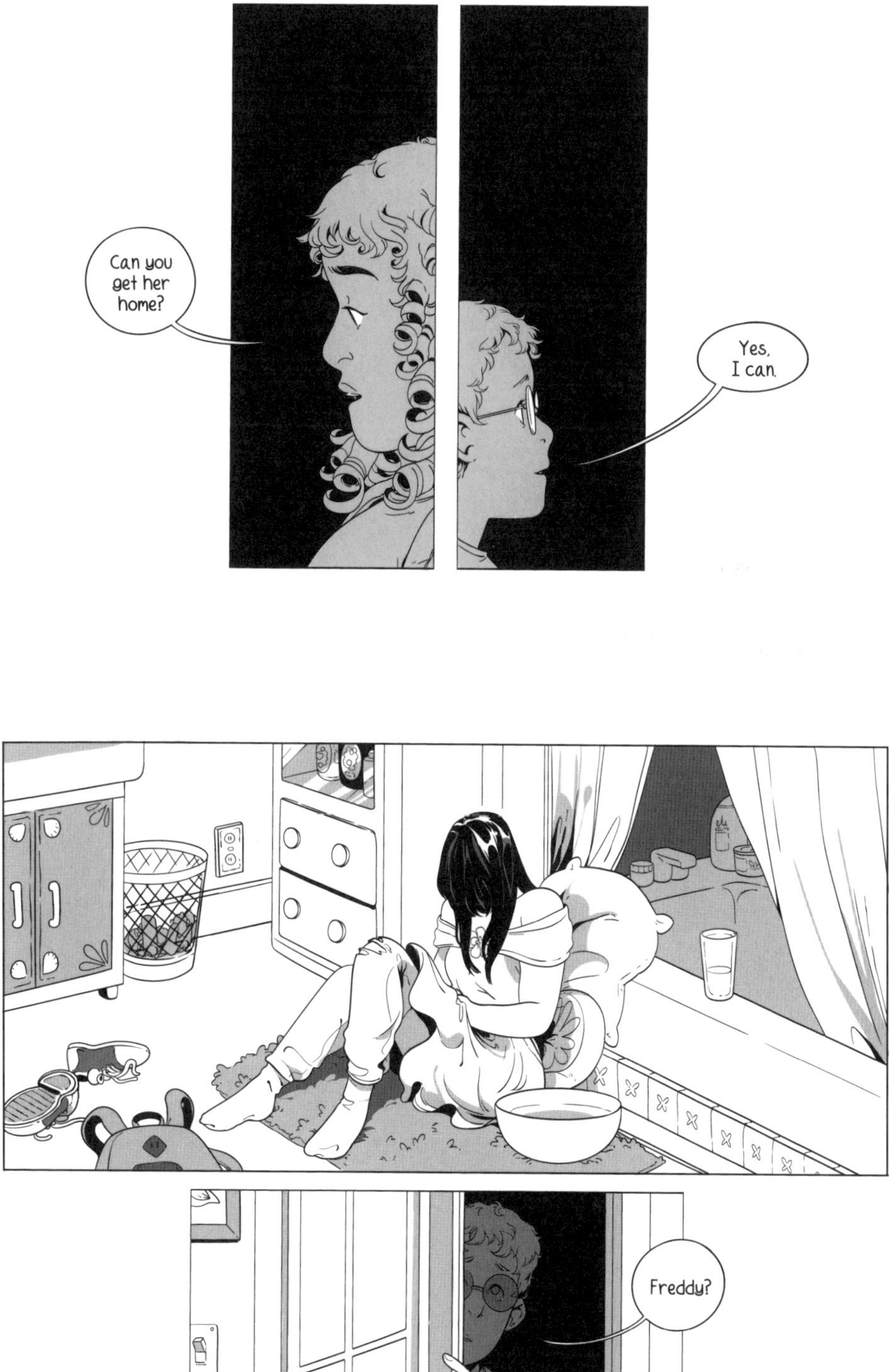
Can you get her home?
Yes, I can.
Freddy?

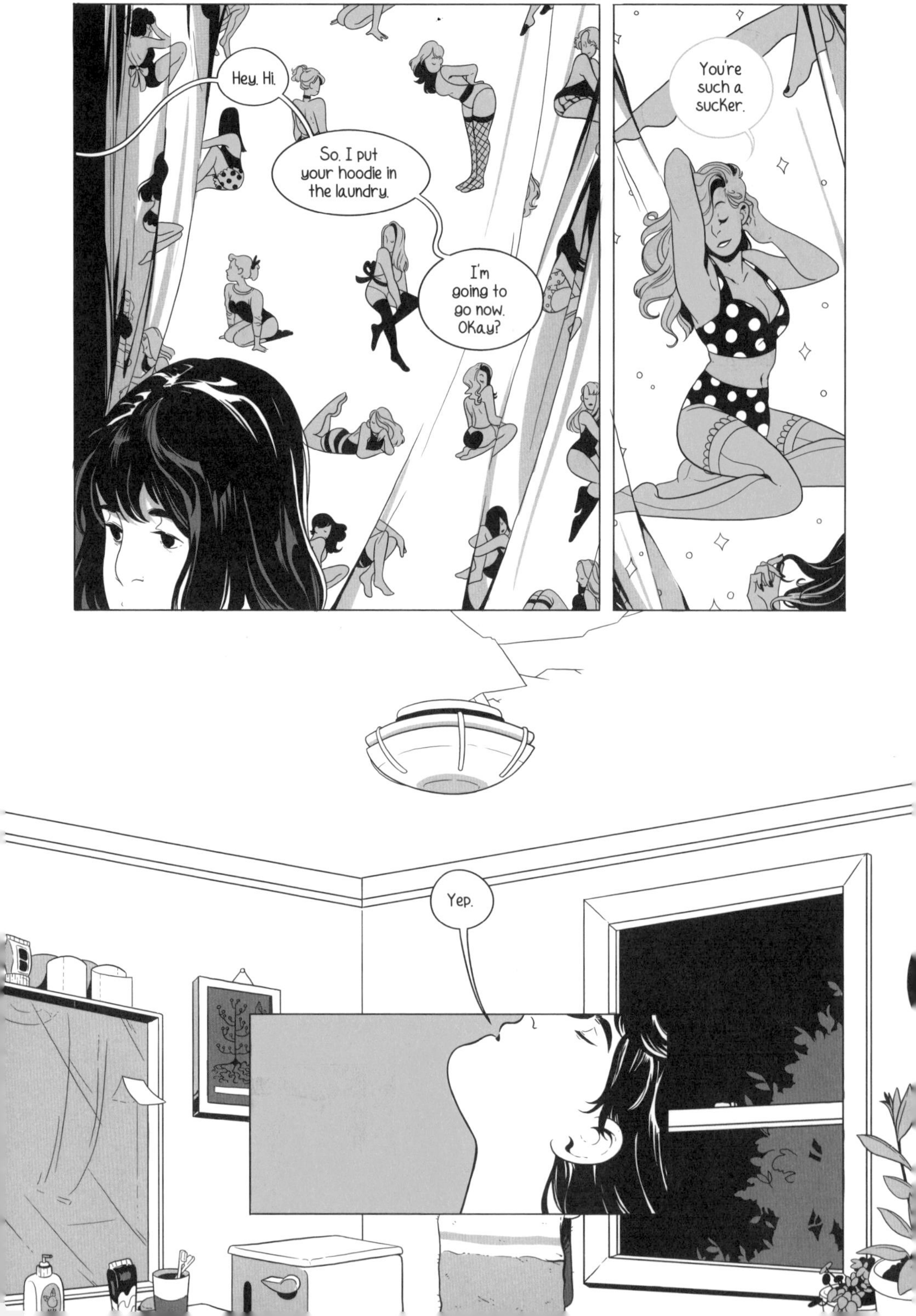
Hey. Hi.
So. I put your hoodie in the laundry.
I'm going to go now. Okay?
You're such a sucker.
Yep.

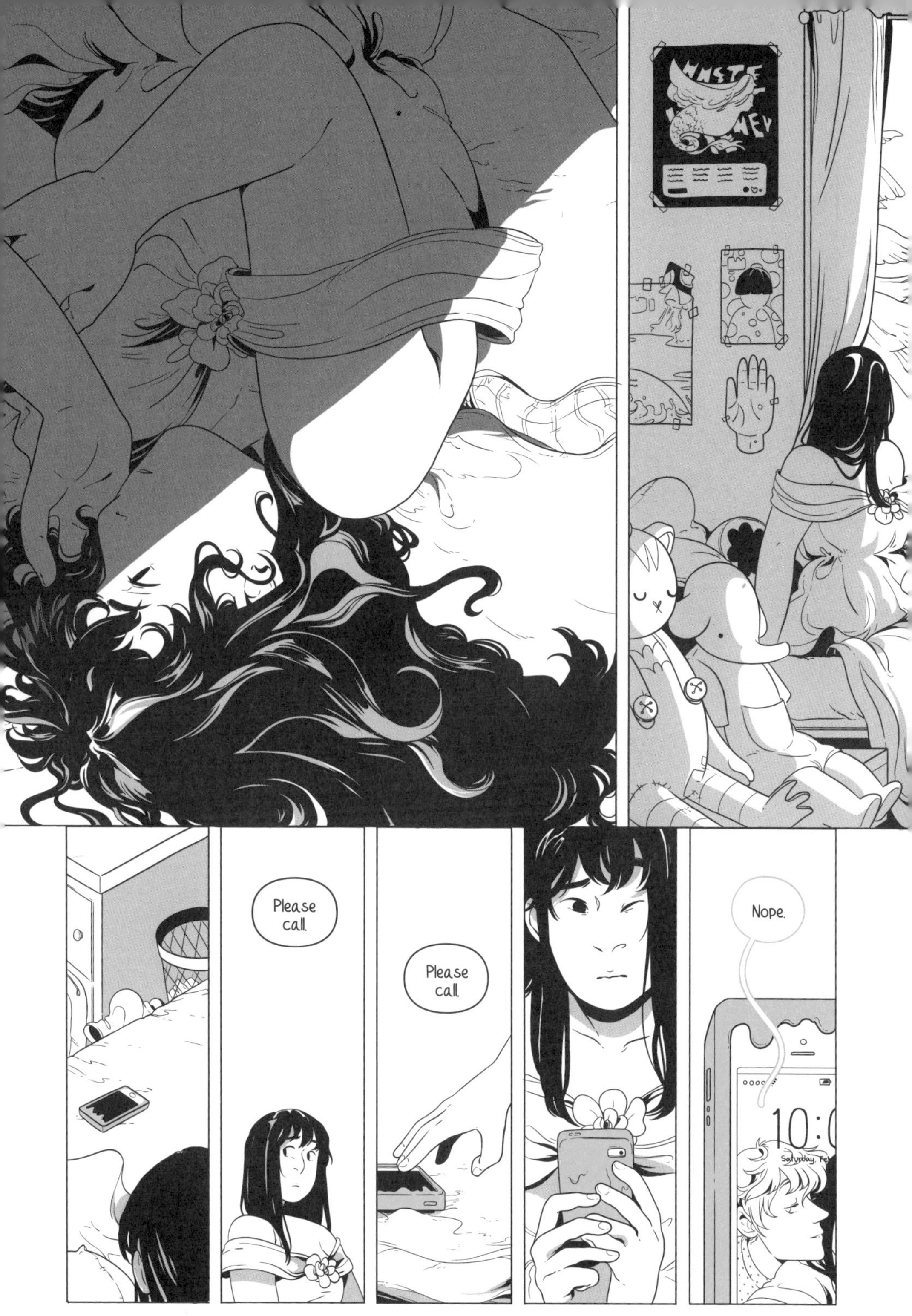
Please call.
Please call.
Nope.

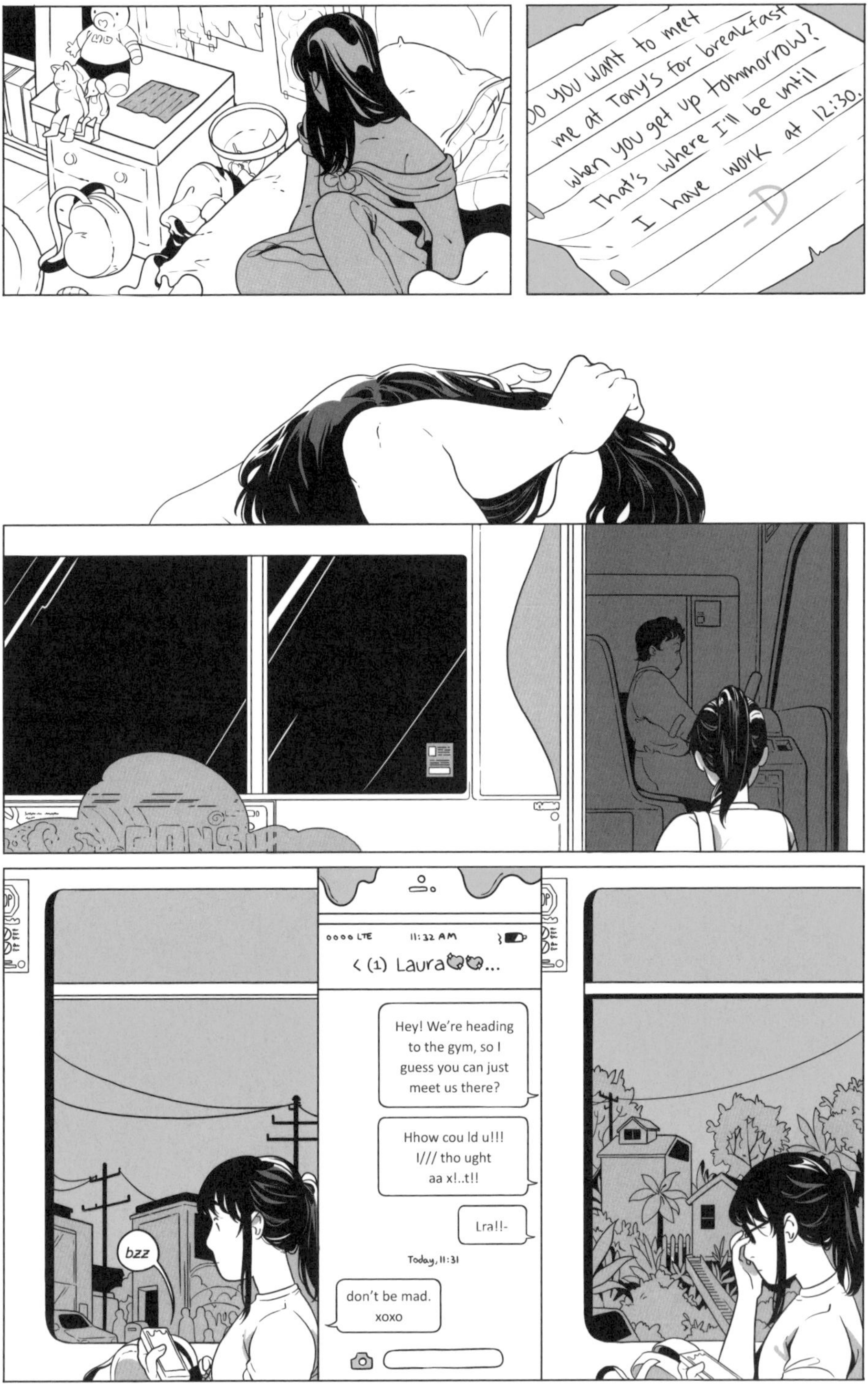
Do you want to meet me at Tony's for breakfast when you get up tommorrow? That's where I'll be until I have work at 12:30.
-D
bzz
0000 LTE 11:32 AM
< (1) Laura
Hey! We're heading to the gym, so I guess you can just meet us there?
Hhow cou ld u!!! I/// tho ught aa x!..t!!
Lra!!-
Today, 11:31
don't be mad. xoxo

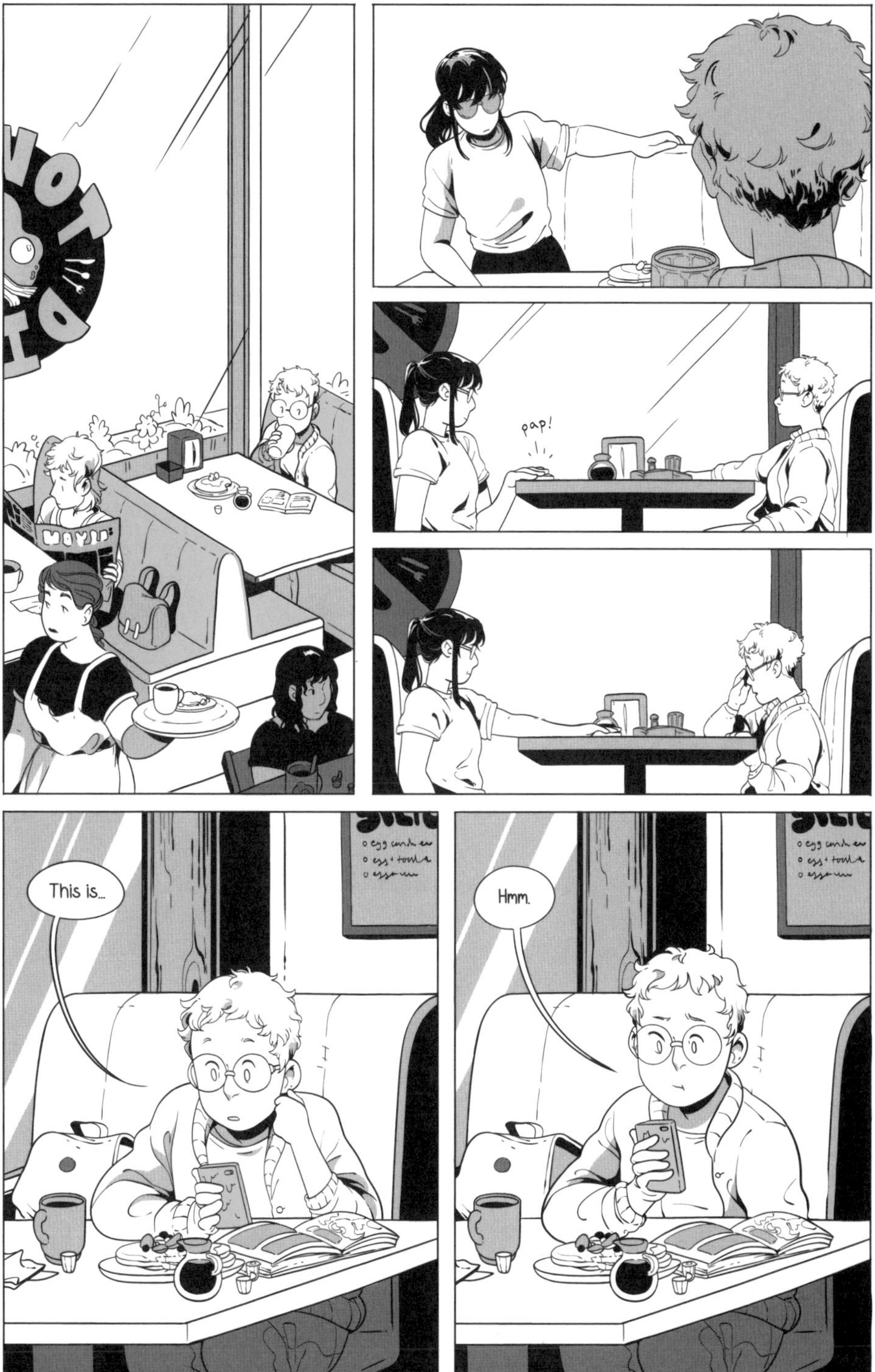
pap!
This is...
Hmm.

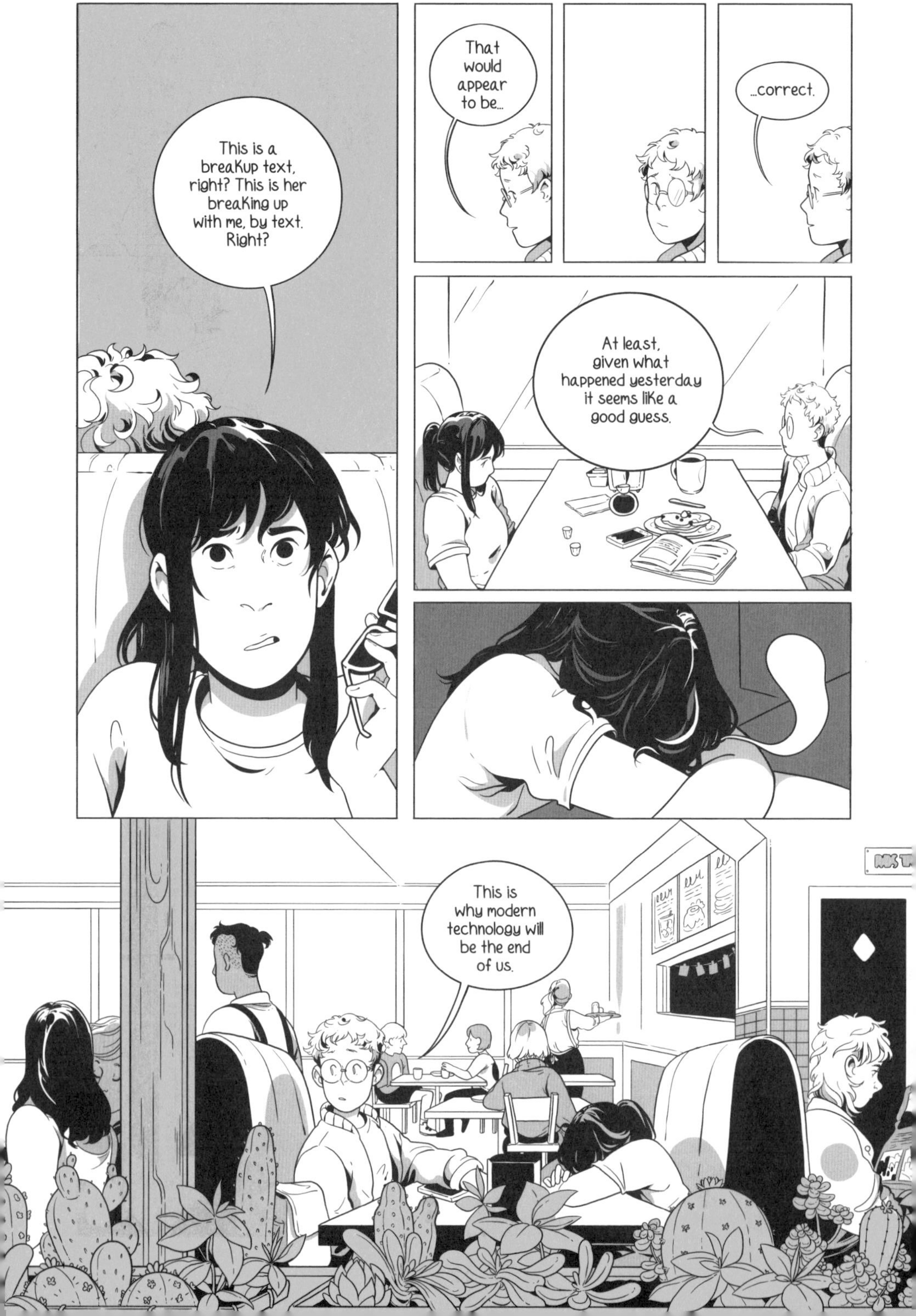
This is a breakup text, right? This is her breaking up with me, by text. Right?
That would appear to be...
...correct.
At least, given what happened yesterday it seems like a good guess.
This is why modern technology will be the end of us.

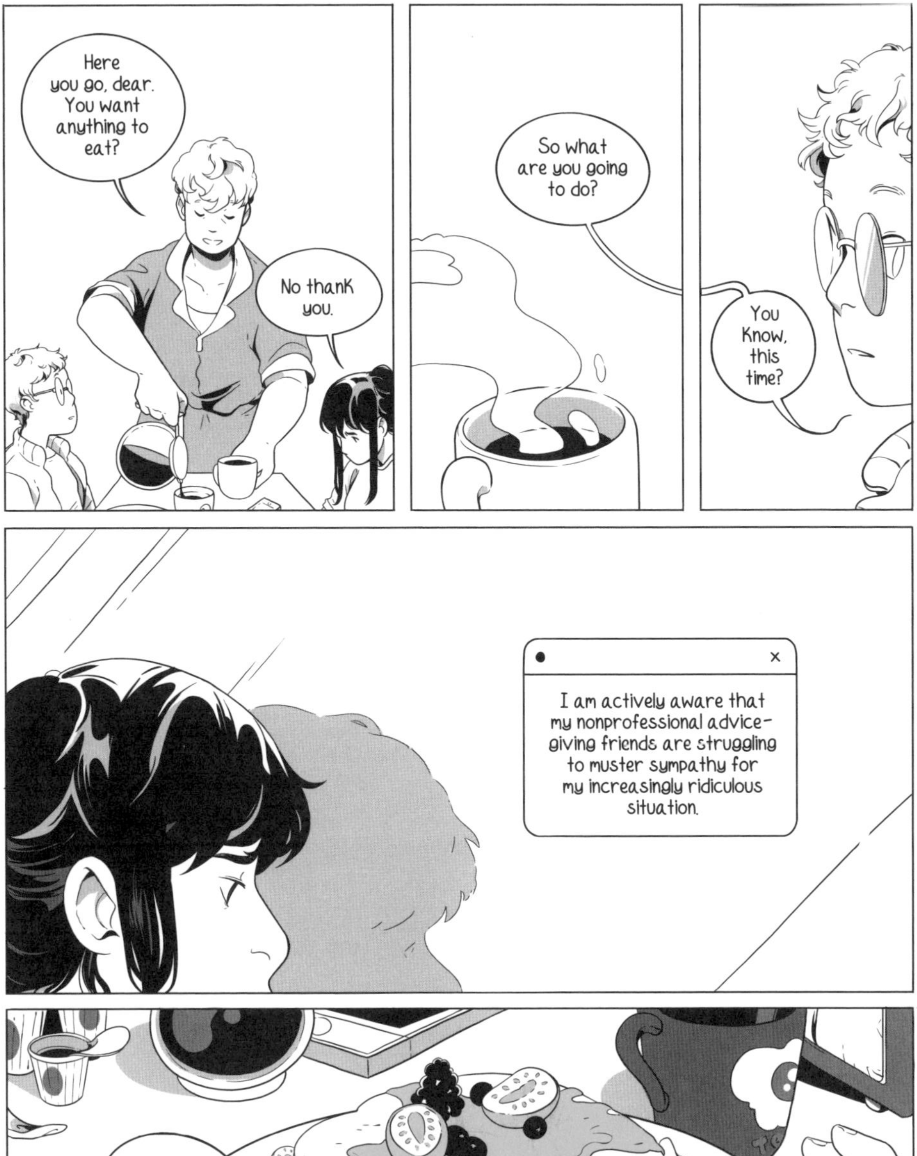

Here you go, dear. You want anything to eat?
No thank you.
So what are you going to do?
You know, this time?
I am actively aware that my nonprofessional advice-giving friends are struggling to muster sympathy for my increasingly ridiculous situation.
You want some?
For my love of a girl who has broken up with me, now, three times.

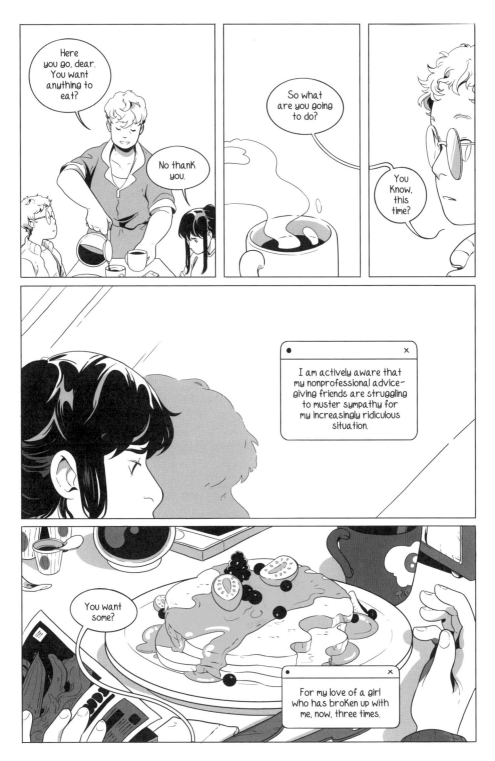

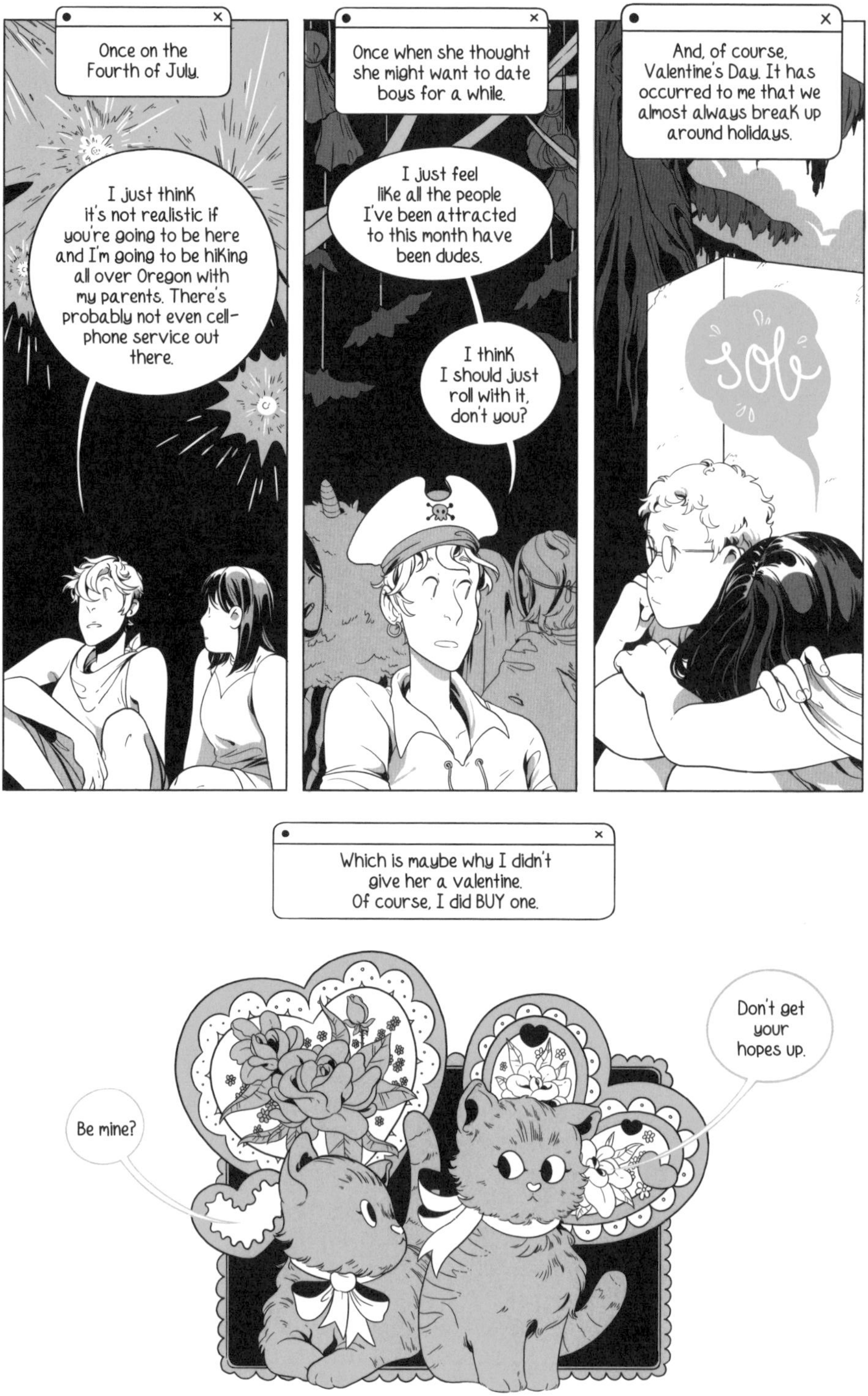
Once on the Fourth of July.
I just think it's not realistic if you're going to be here and I'm going to be hiking all over Oregon with my parents. There's probably not even cell-phone service out there.
Once when she thought she might want to date boys for a while.
I just feel like all the people I've been attracted to this month have been dudes.
I think I should just roll with it, don't you?
And, of course, Valentine's Day. It has occurred to me that we almost always break up around holidays.
sob
Which is maybe why I didn't give her a valentine. Of course, I did BUY one.
Be mine?
Don't get your hopes up.

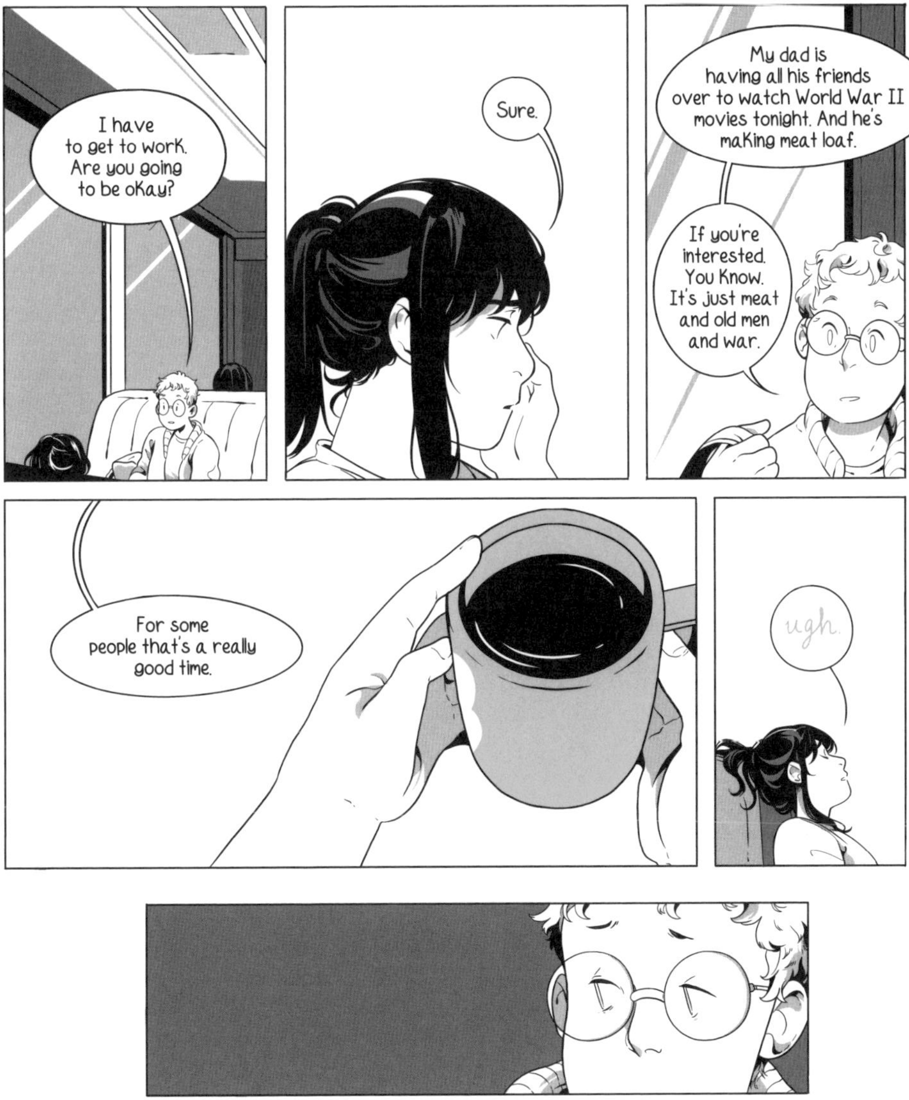
I have to get to work. Are you going to be okay?
Sure.
My dad is having all his friends over to watch World War II movies tonight. And he's making meat loaf.
If you're interested. You know. It's just meat and old men and war.
For some people that's a really good time.
ugh.

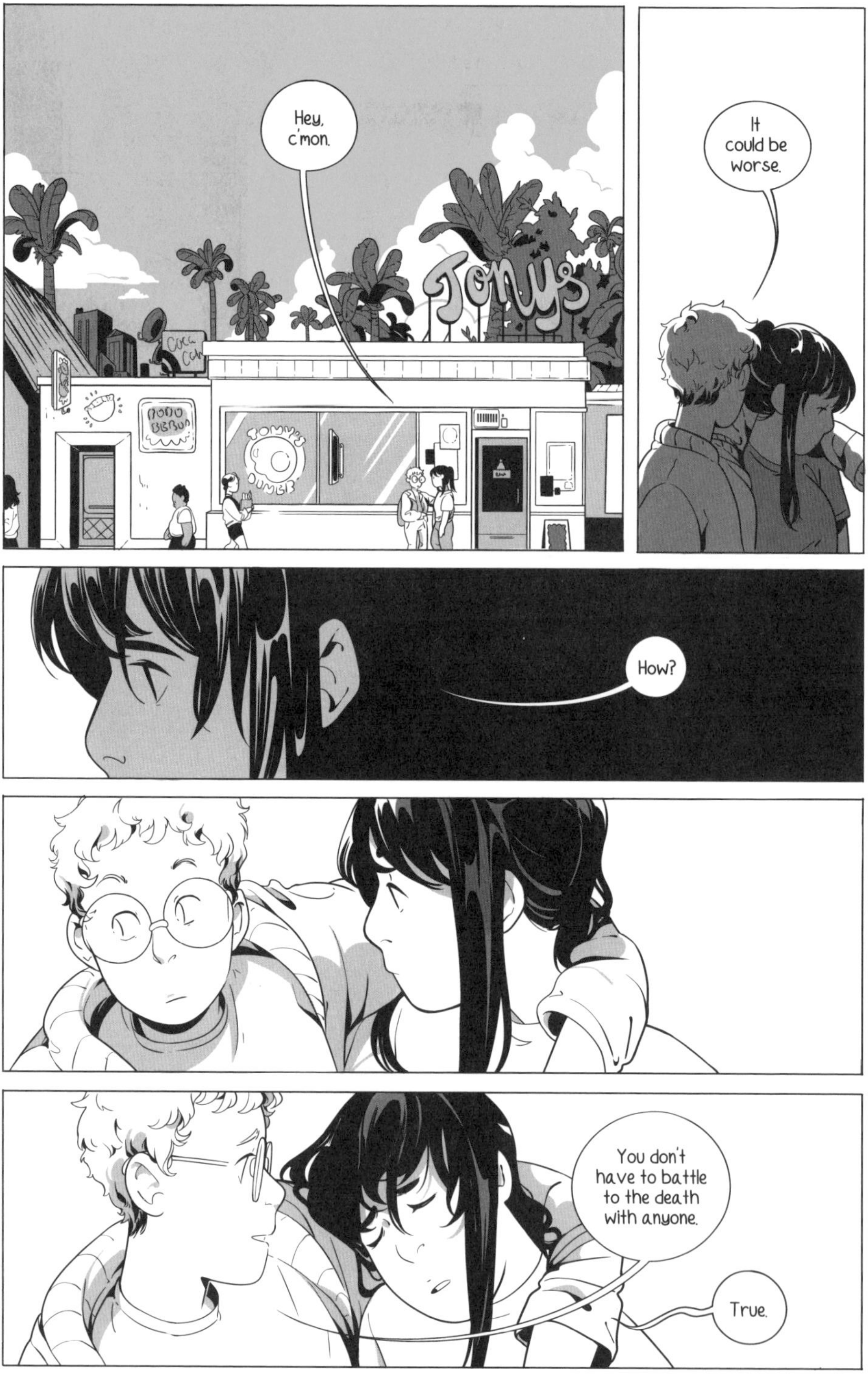
Hey, c'mon.
Tonys
Tommy's Dumbe
It could be worse.
How?
You don't have to battle to the death with anyone.
True.

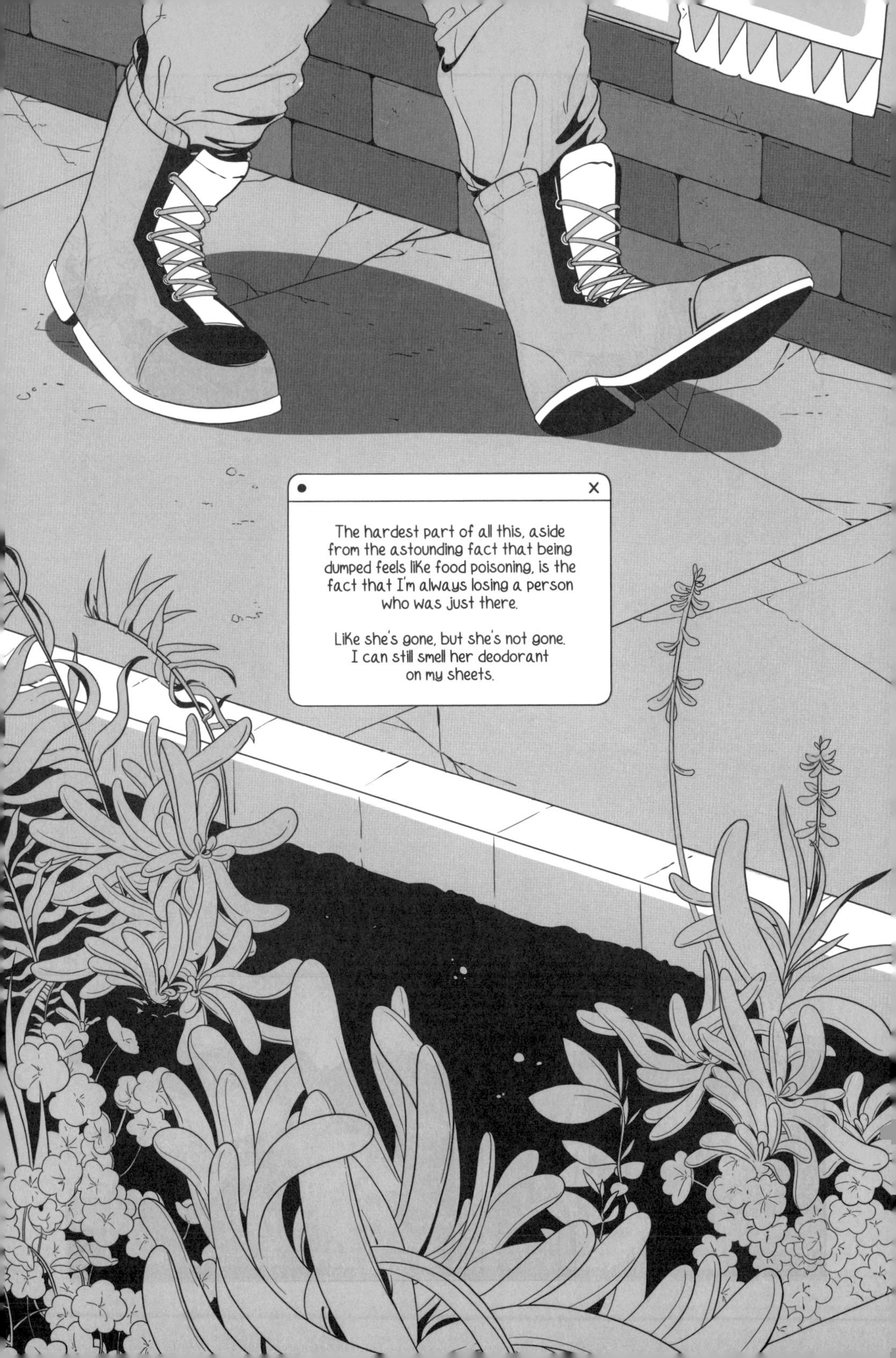
The hardest part of all this, aside from the astounding fact that being dumped feels like food poisoning, is the fact that I'm always losing a person who was just there.
Like she's gone, but she's not gone. I can still smell her deodorant on my sheets.

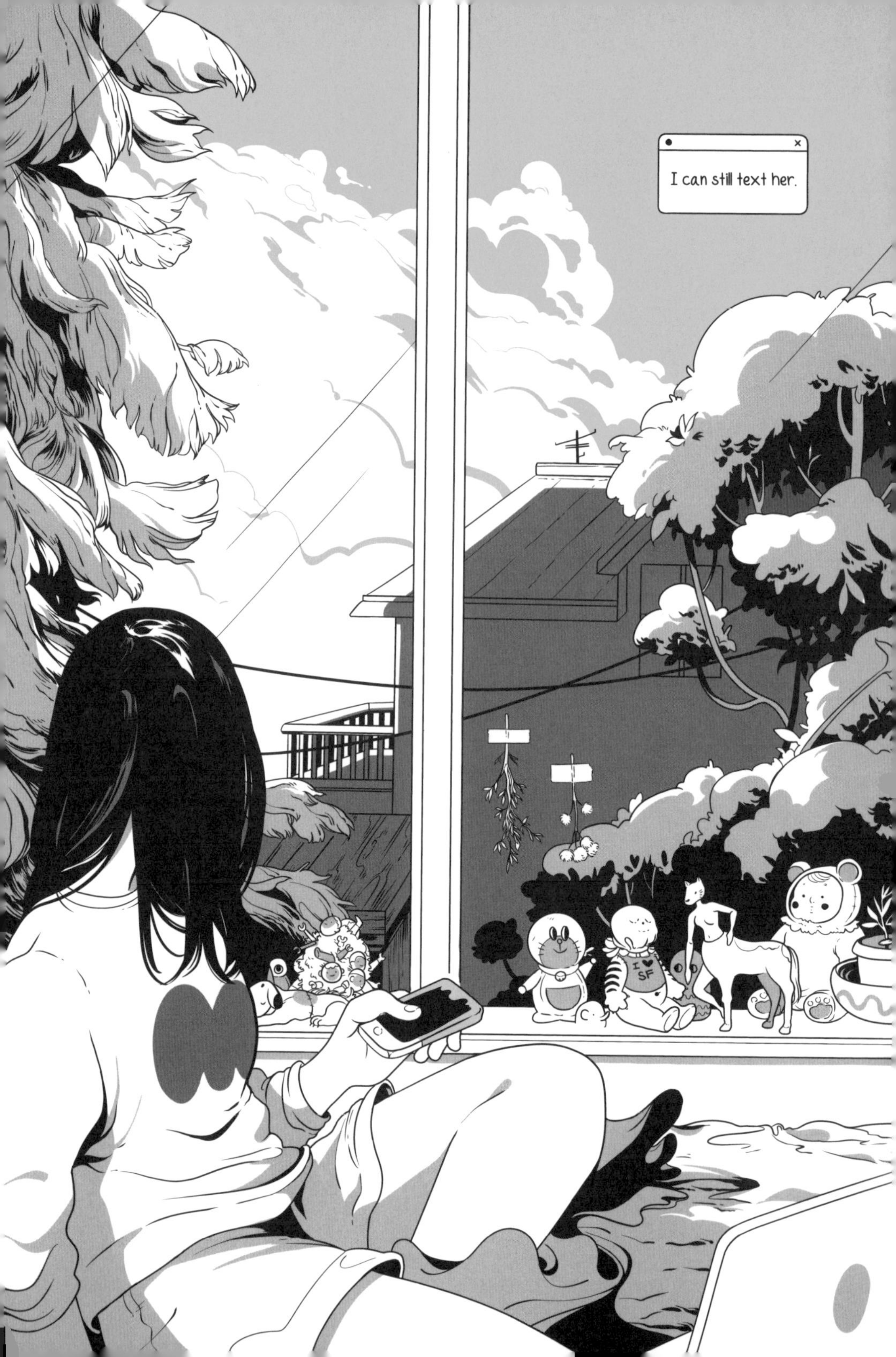
I can still text her.
I ♥ SF

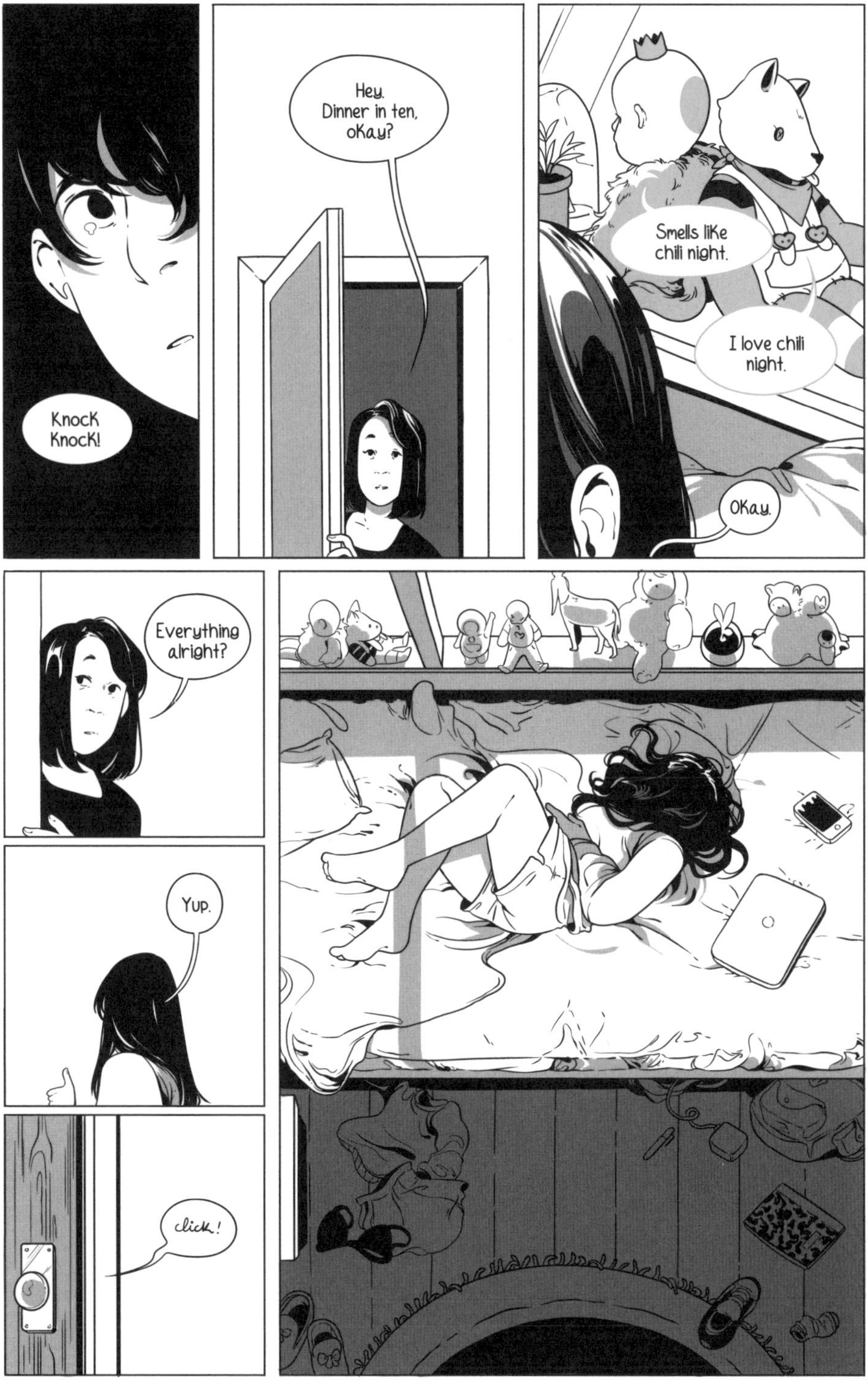
Knock Knock!
Hey. Dinner in ten, okay?
Smells like chili night.
I love chili night.
Okay.
Everything alright?
Yup.
click!

Of course, I Know there are LGBTQIA activists out there who fought for centuries for me to have the right to fuck up like this.

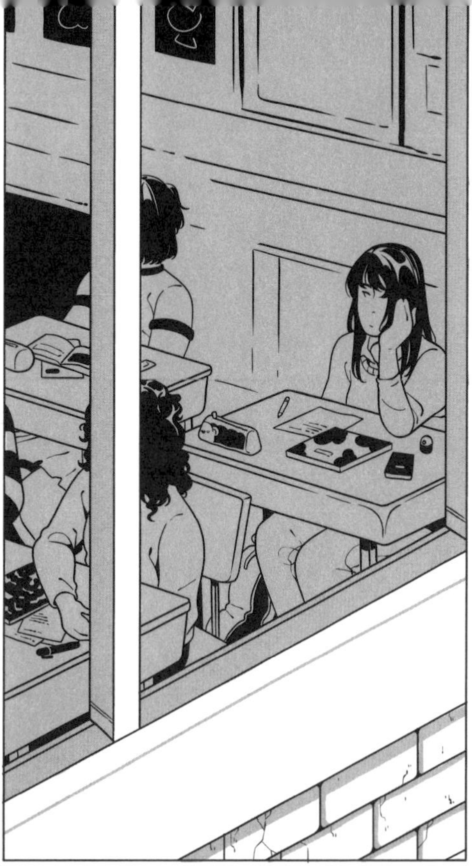

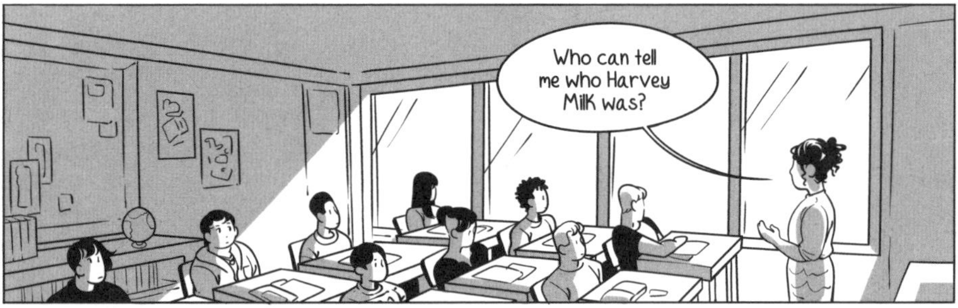
Who can tell me who Harvey Milk was?

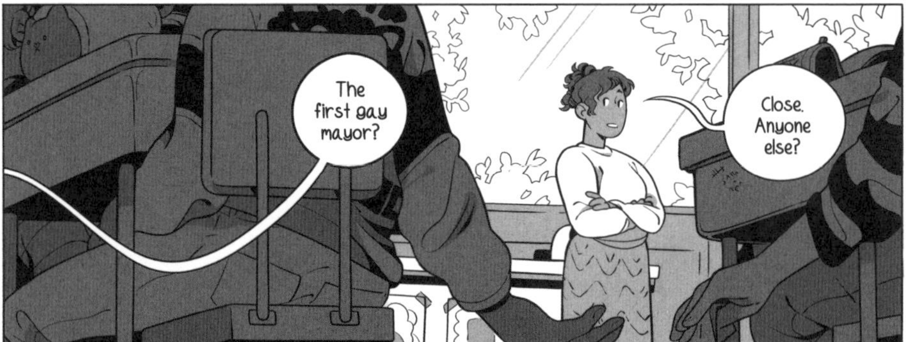
The first gay mayor?
Close. Anyone else?

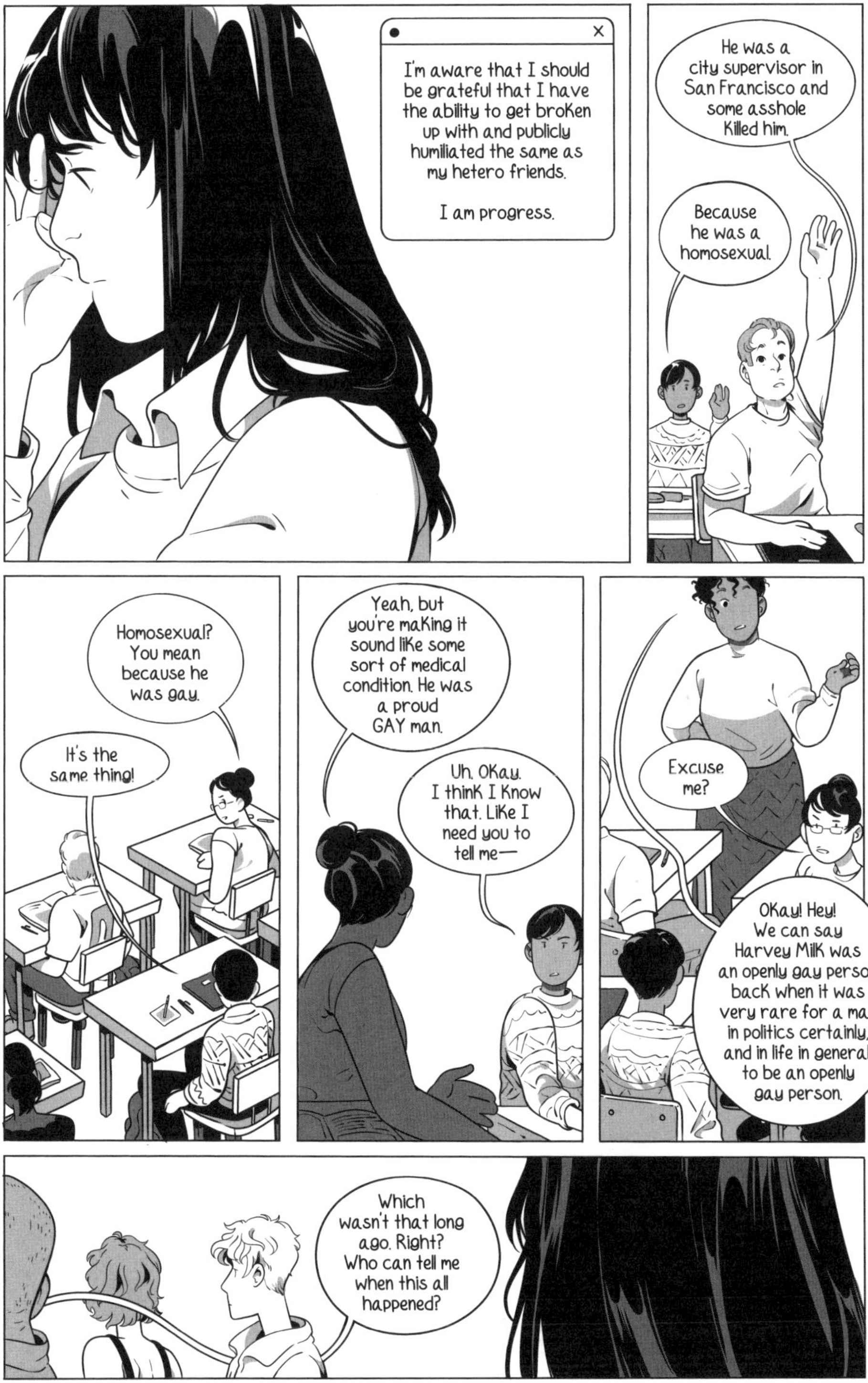
I'm aware that I should be grateful that I have the ability to get broken up with and publicly humiliated the same as my hetero friends.
I am progress.
He was a city supervisor in San Francisco and some asshole killed him.
Because he was a homosexual.
Homosexual? You mean because he was gay.
It's the same thing!
Yeah, but you're making it sound like some sort of medical condition. He was a proud GAY man.
Uh, Okay. I think I know that. Like I need you to tell me—
Excuse me?
Okay! Hey! We can say Harvey Milk was an openly gay person back when it was very rare for a man in politics certainly, and in life in general, to be an openly gay person.
Which wasn't that long ago. Right? Who can tell me when this all happened?

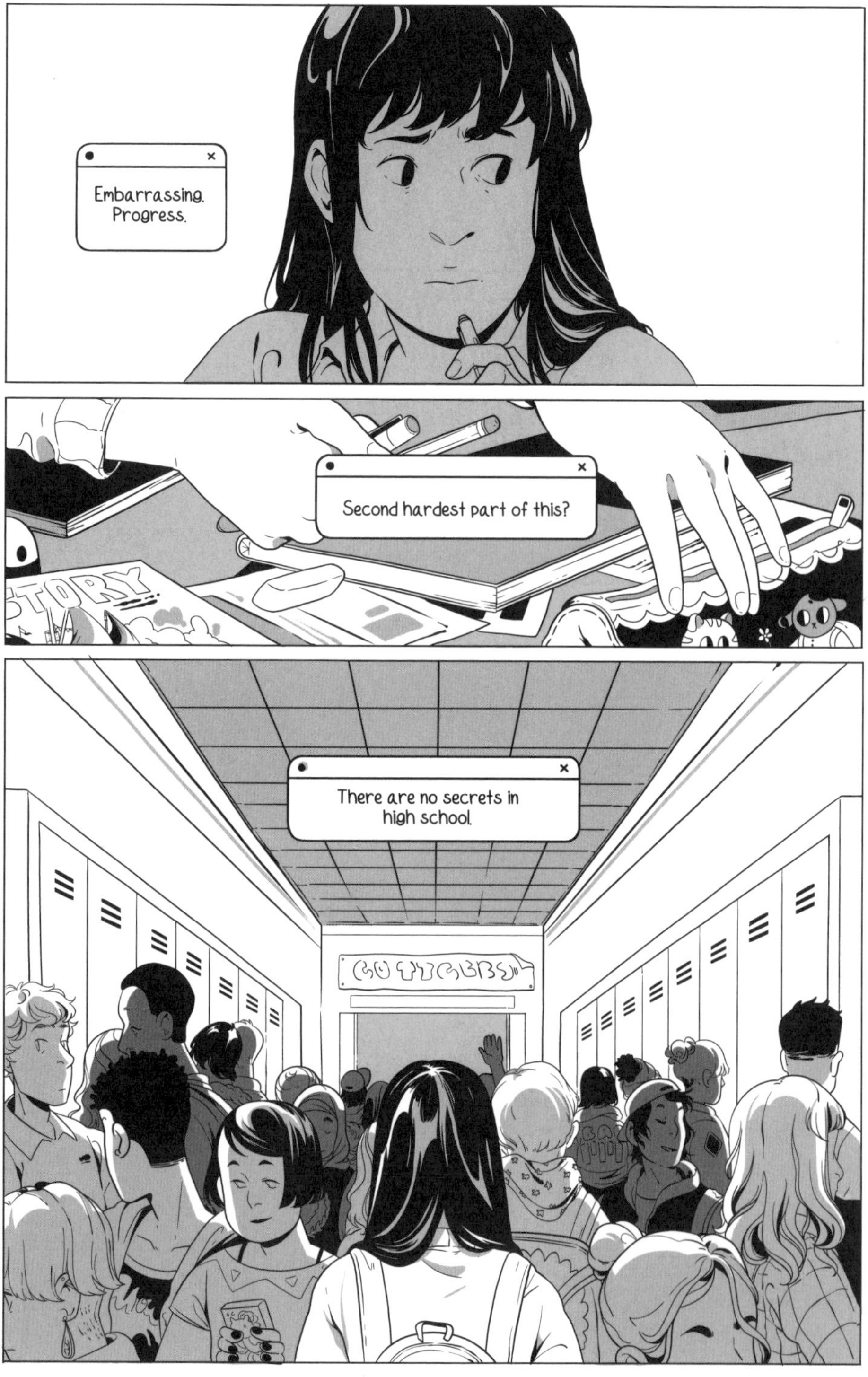
Embarrassing.
Progress.
Second hardest part of this?
There are no secrets in high school.

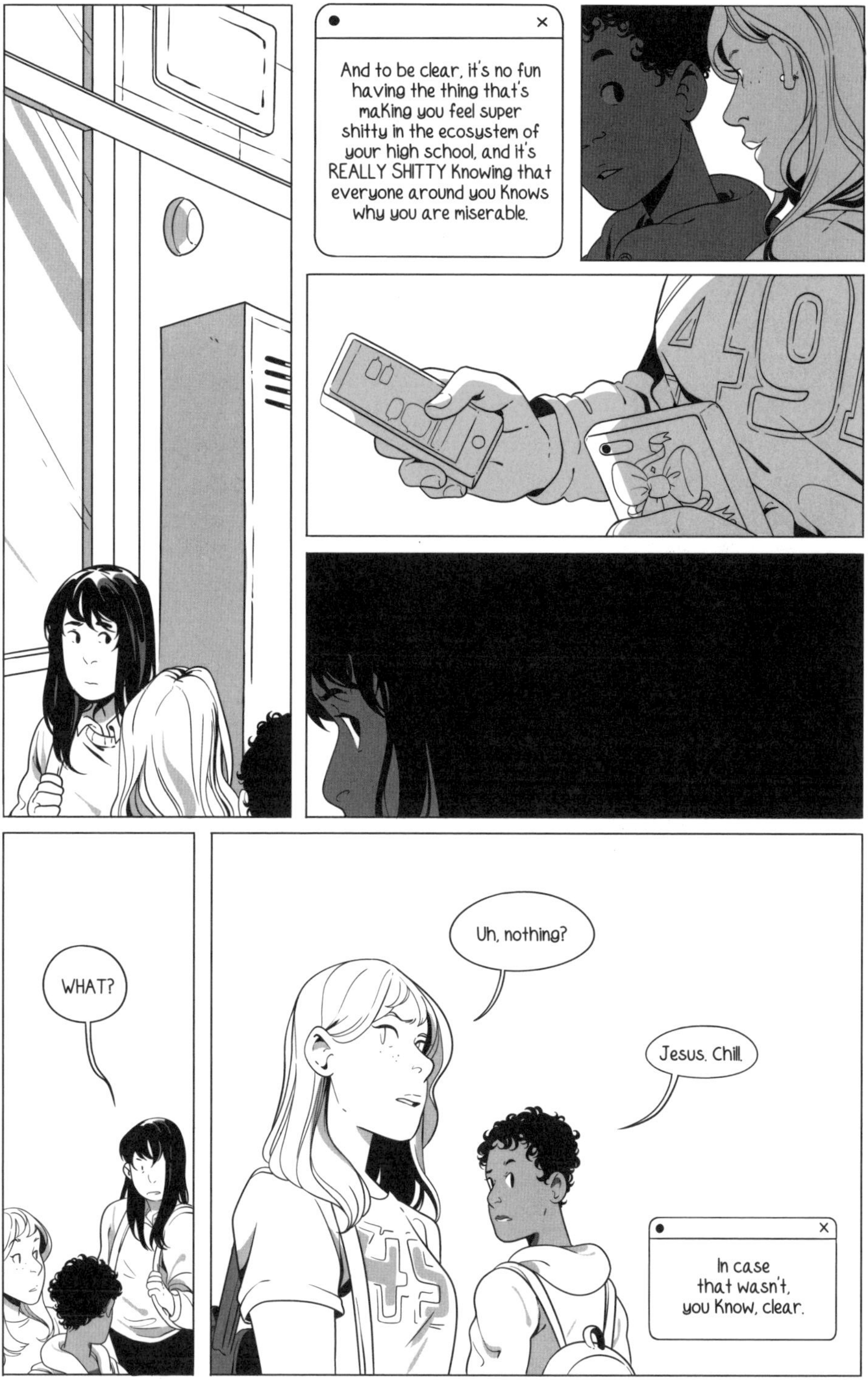
And to be clear, it's no fun having the thing that's making you feel super shitty in the ecosystem of your high school, and it's REALLY SHITTY Knowing that everyone around you Knows why you are miserable.
WHAT?
Uh, nothing?
Jesus. Chill.
In case that wasn't, you Know, clear.

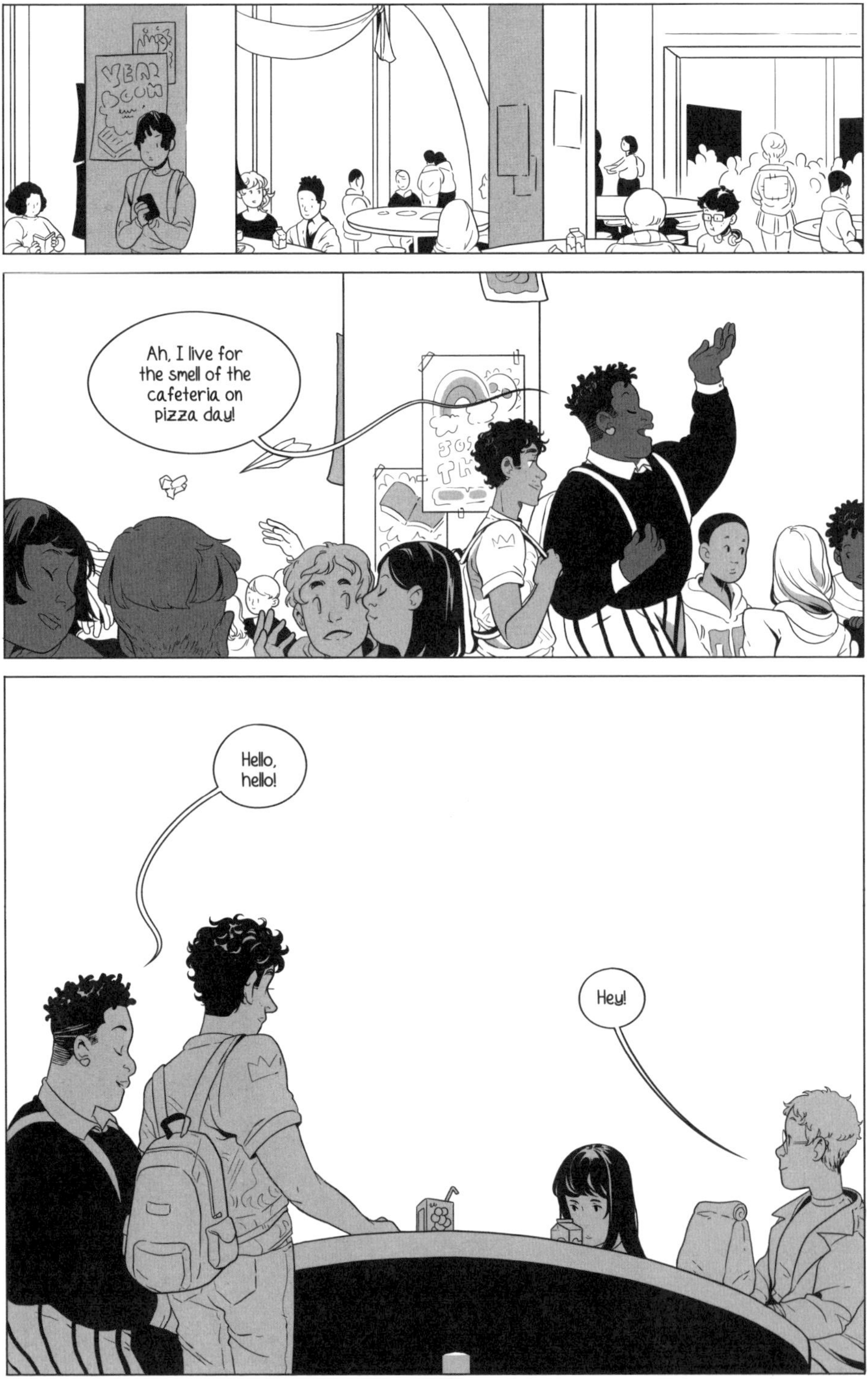
Ah, I live for the smell of the cafeteria on pizza day!
Hello, hello!
Hey!

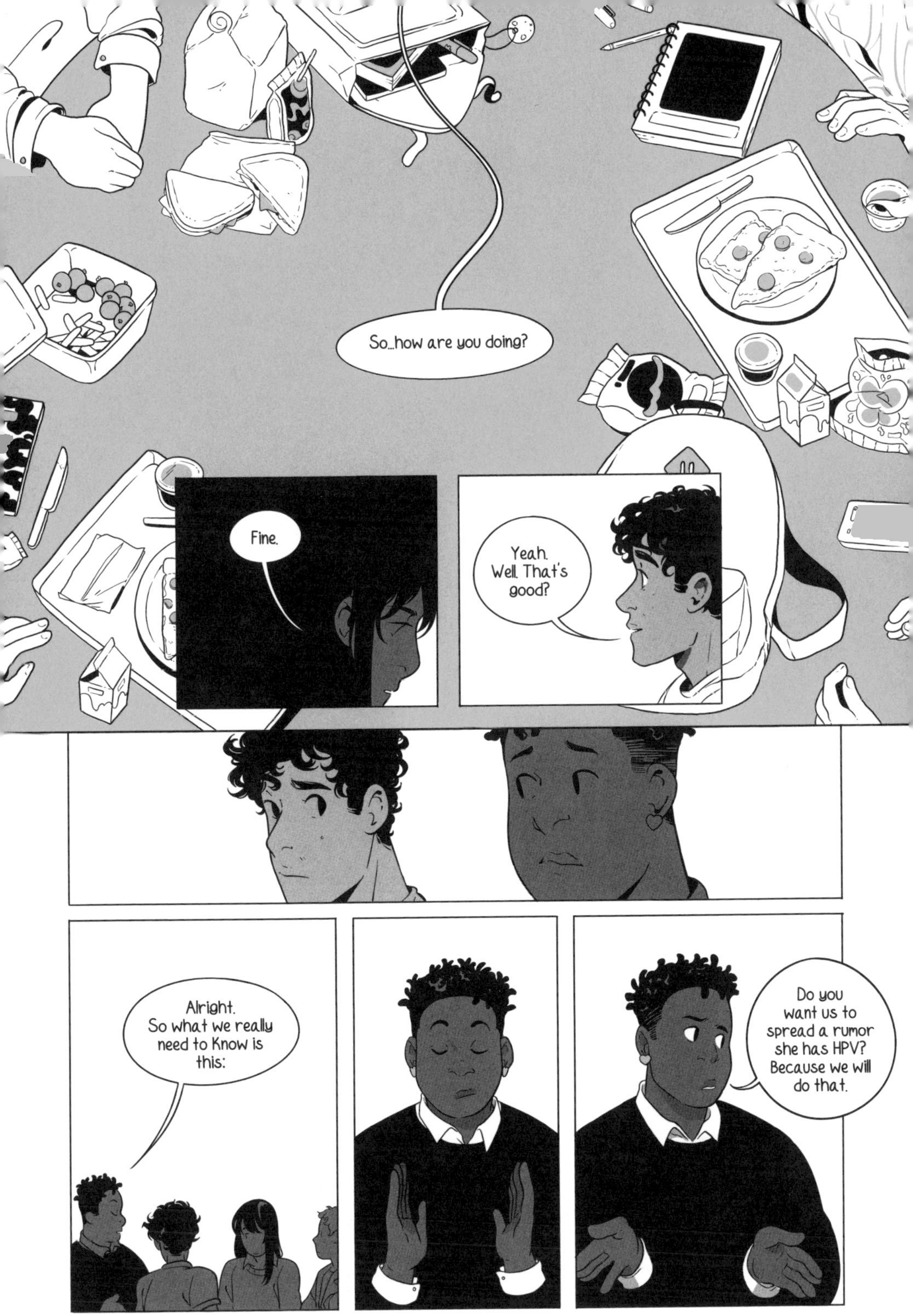
So...how are you doing?
Fine.
Yeah. Well. That's good?
Alright. So what we really need to Know is this:
Do you want us to spread a rumor she has HPV? Because we will do that.

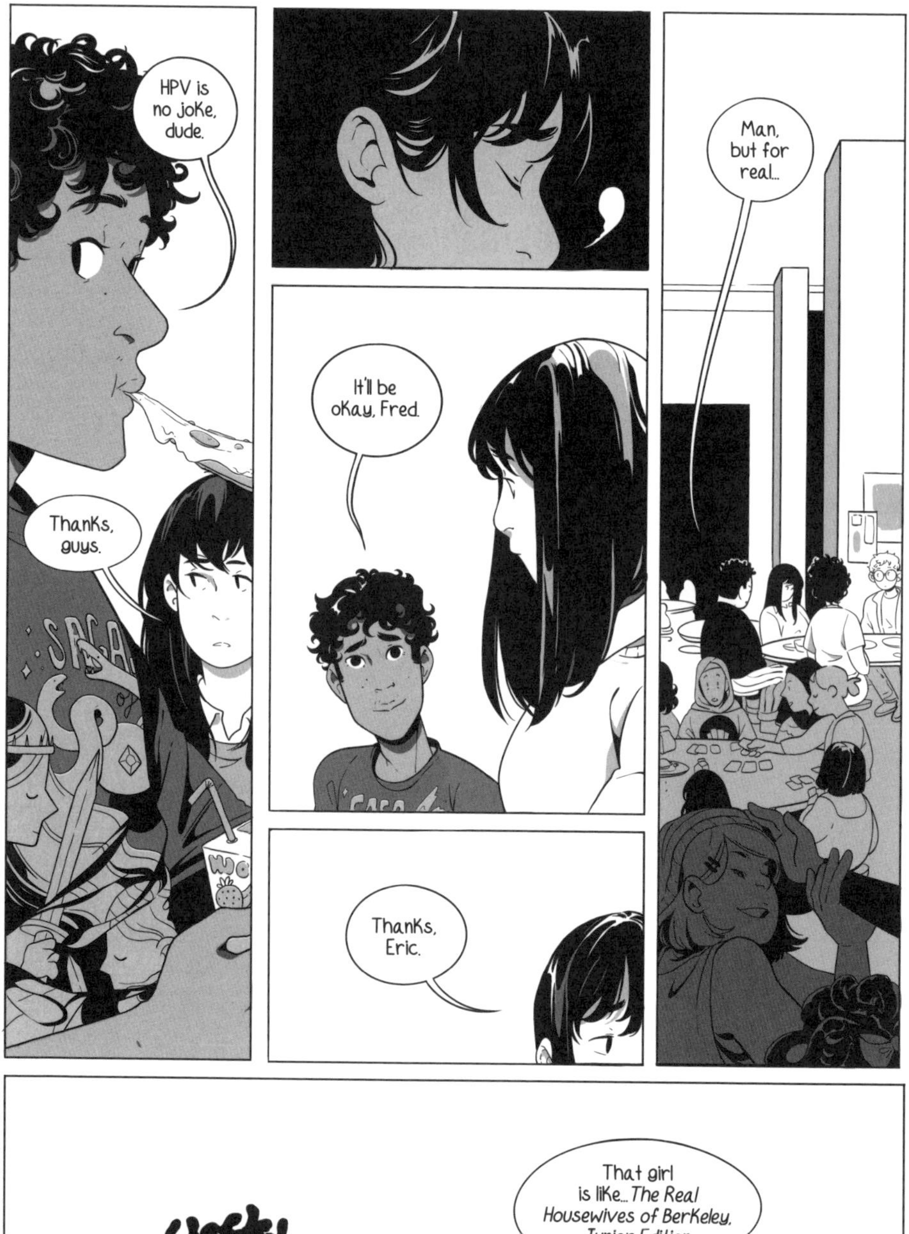
HPV is no joke, dude.
Thanks, guys.
It'll be okay, Fred.
Thanks, Eric.
Man, but for real...
That girl is like... *The Real Housewives of Berkeley, Junior Edition.*

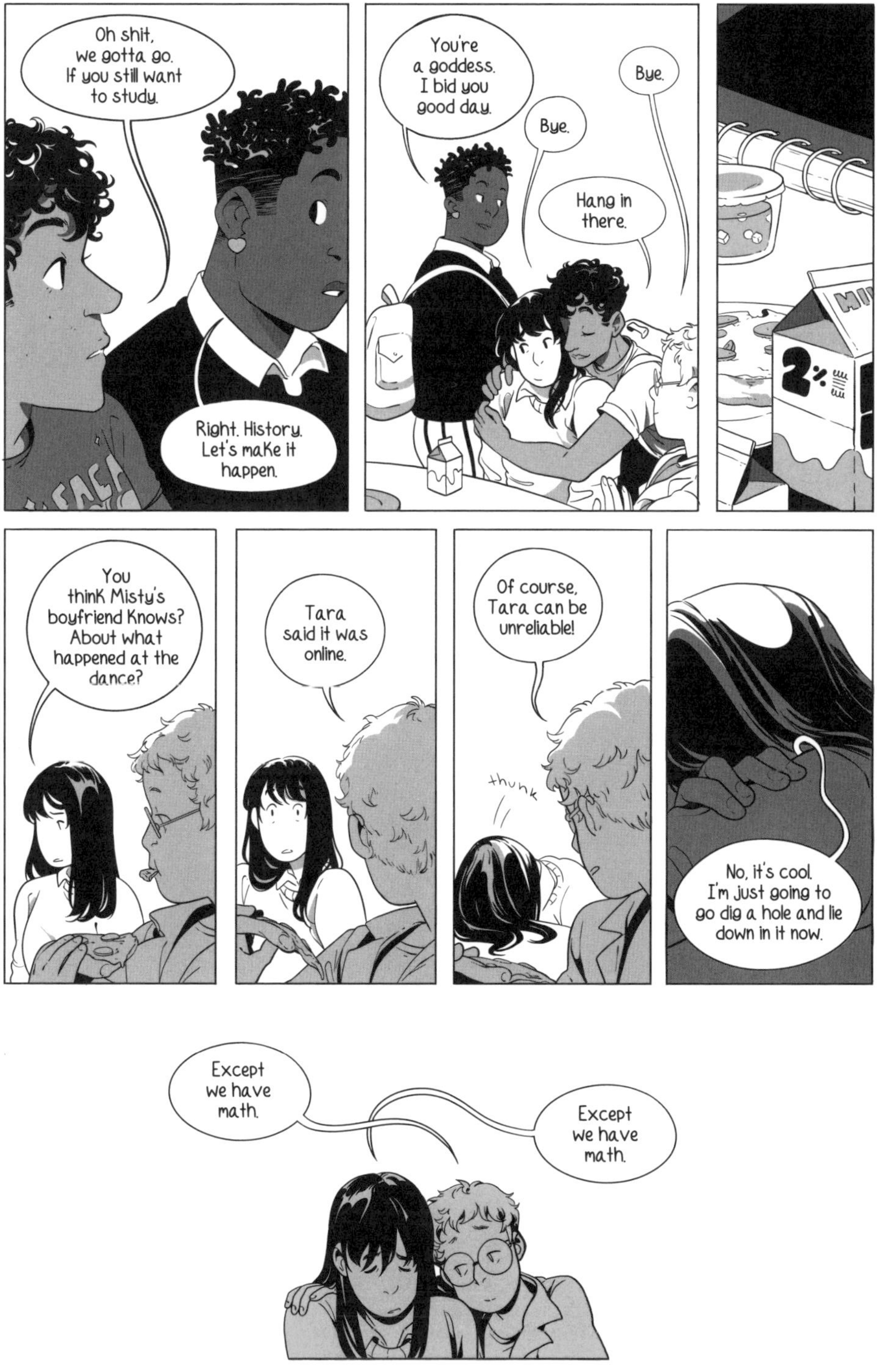
Oh shit, we gotta go. If you still want to study.
Right. History. Let's make it happen.
You're a goddess. I bid you good day.
Bye.
Bye.
Hang in there.
You think Misty's boyfriend knows? About what happened at the dance?
Tara said it was online.
Of course, Tara can be unreliable!
thunk
No, it's cool. I'm just going to go dig a hole and lie down in it now.
Except we have math.
Except we have math.

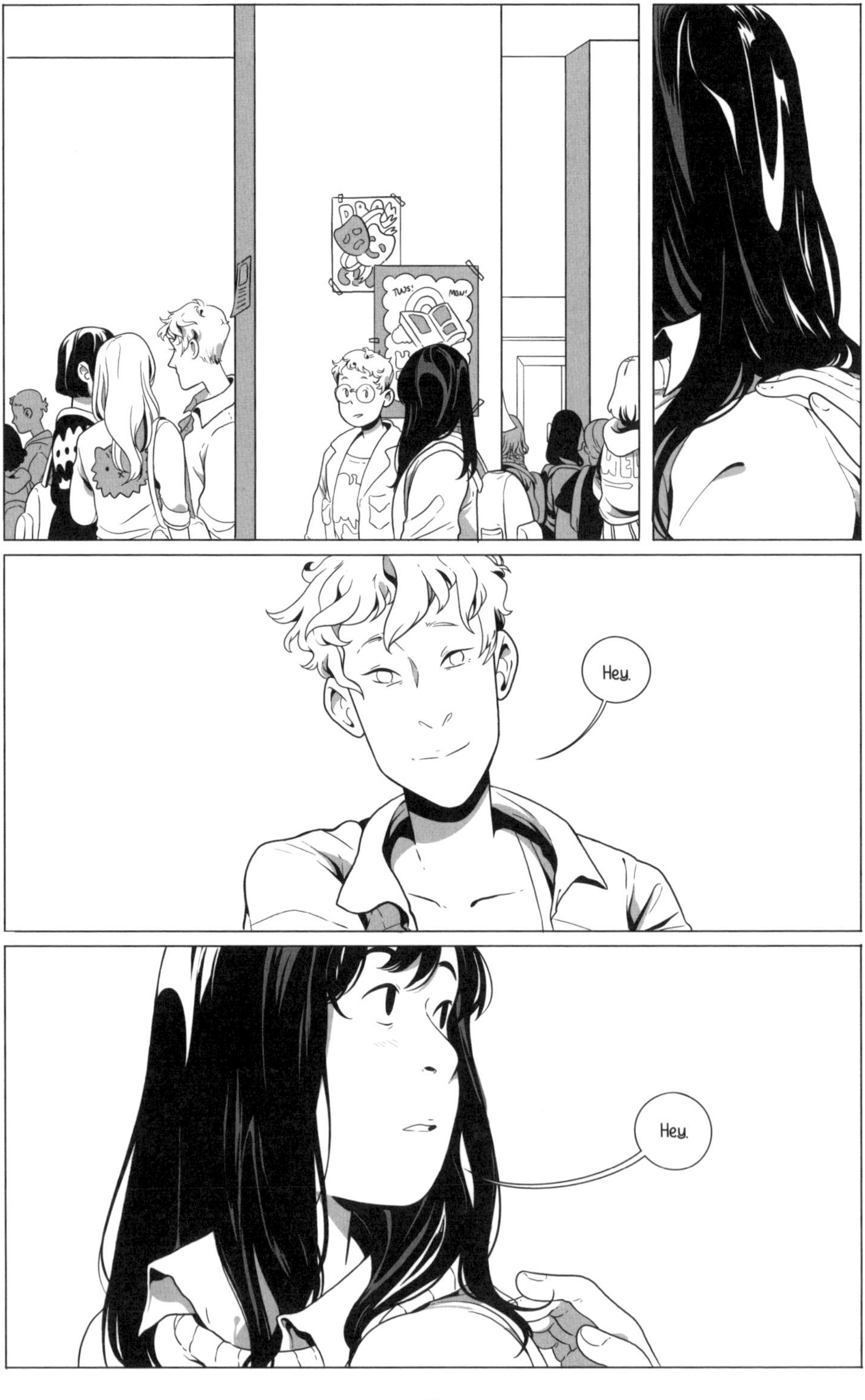
Hey.
Hey.

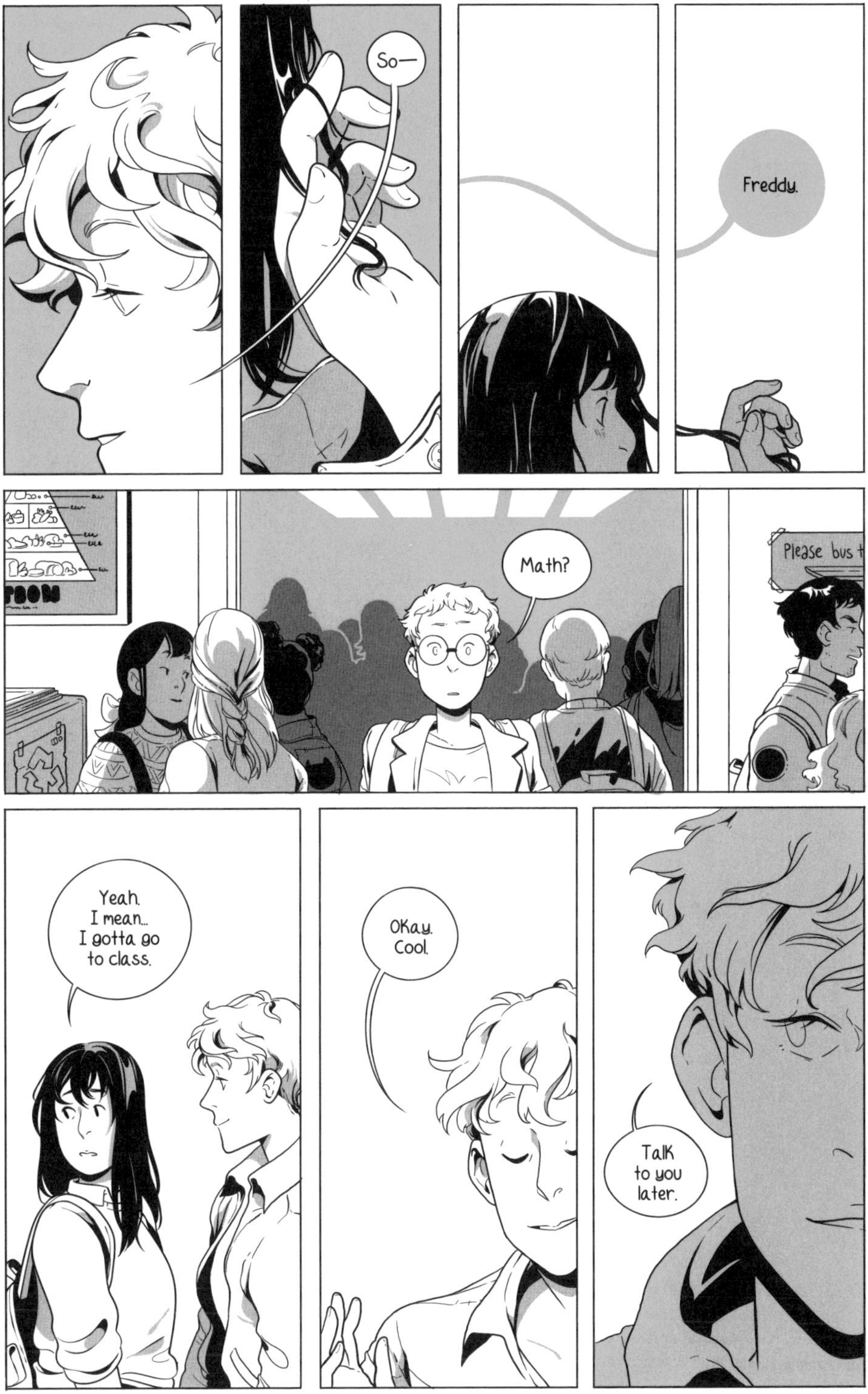
So—
Freddy.
Math?
Please bus t
Yeah. I mean... I gotta go to class.
Okay. Cool.
Talk to you later.

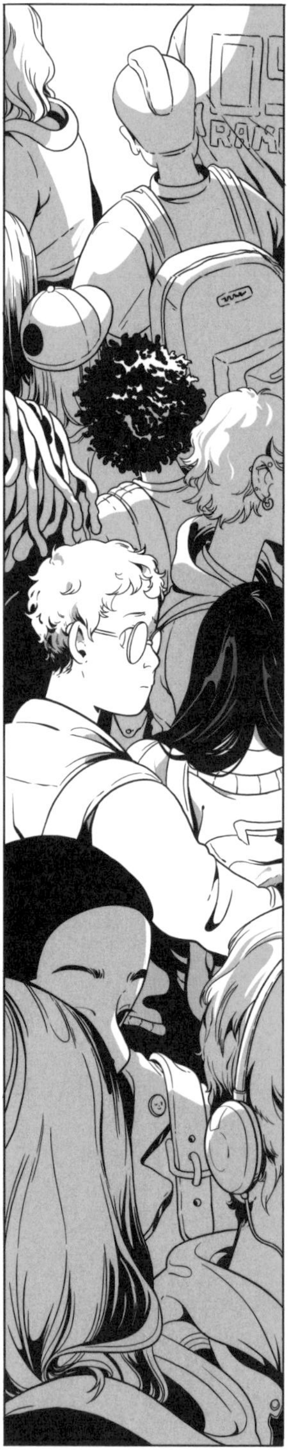

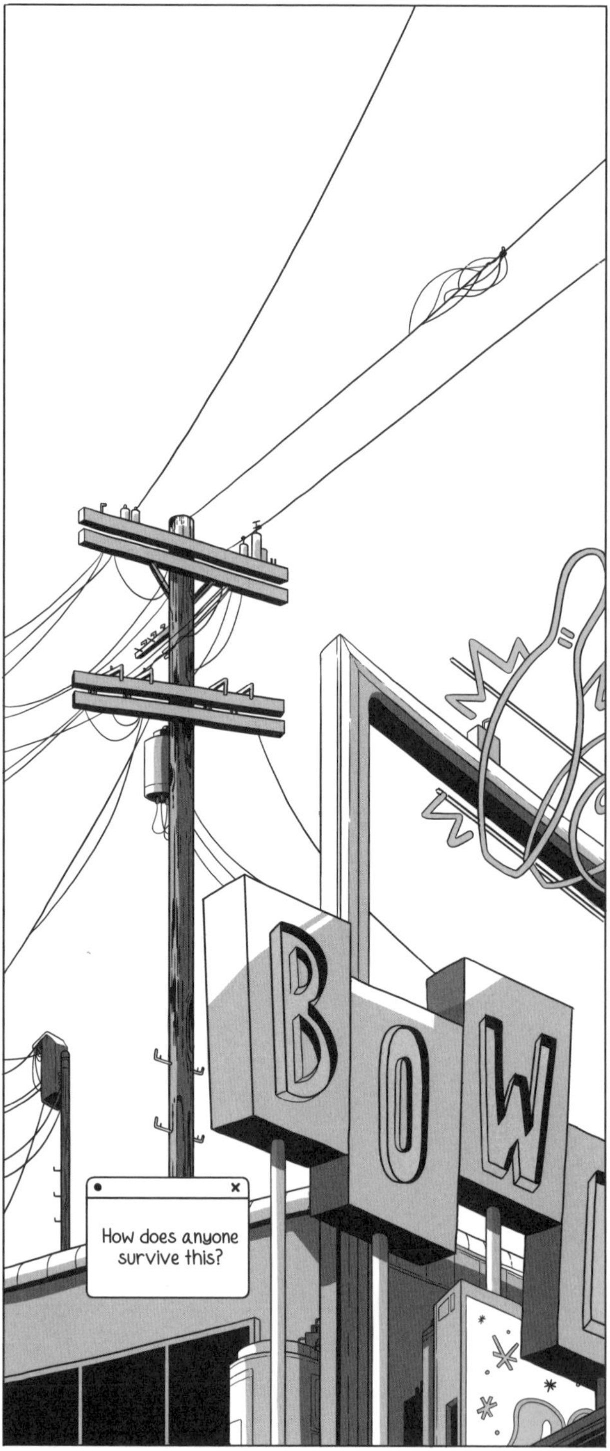
BOW
How does anyone survive this?

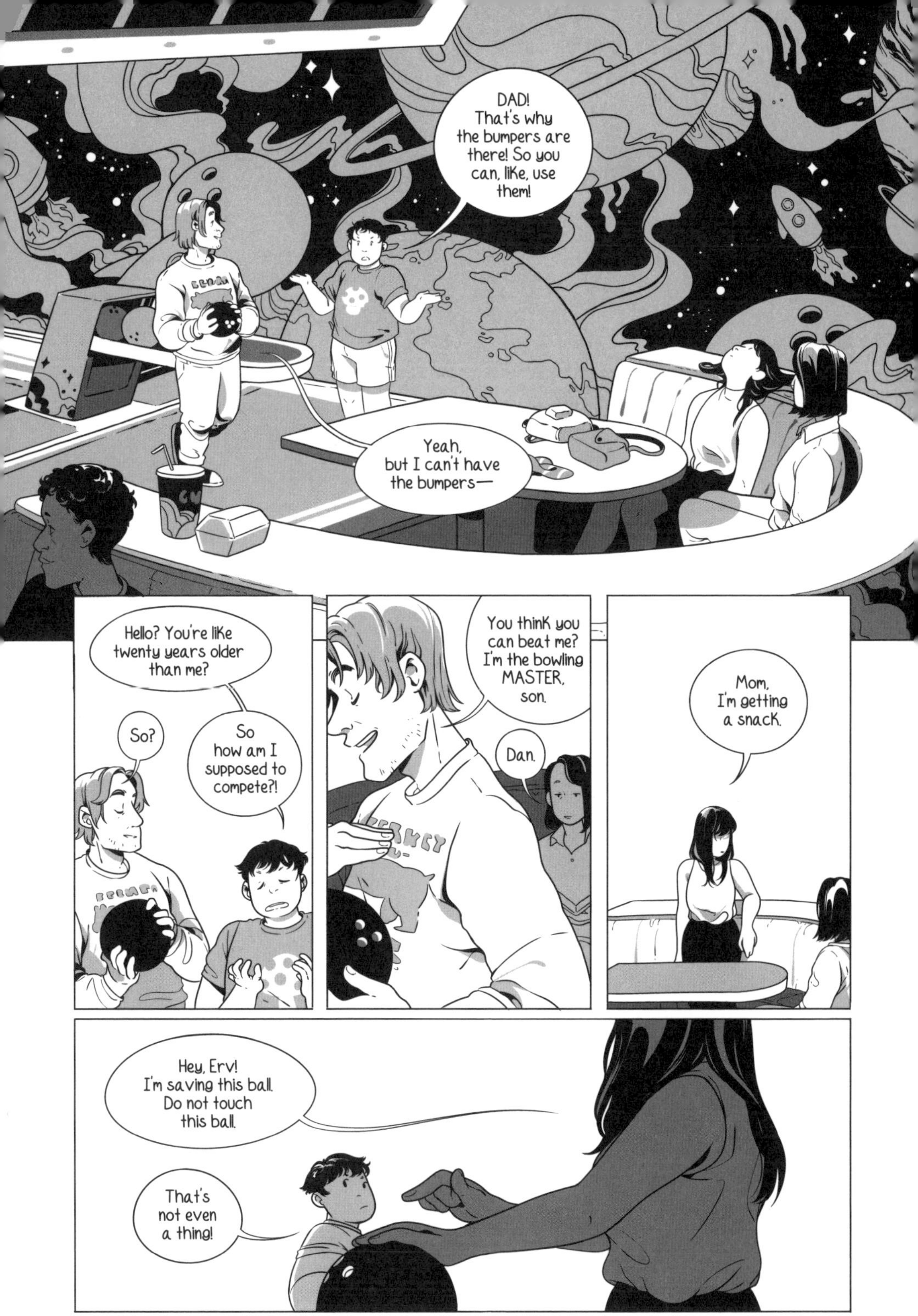
DAD! That's why the bumpers are there! So you can, like, use them!
Yeah, but I can't have the bumpers—
Hello? You're like twenty years older than me?
So?
So how am I supposed to compete?!
You think you can beat me? I'm the bowling MASTER, son.
Dan.
Mom, I'm getting a snack.
Hey, Erv! I'm saving this ball. Do not touch this ball.
That's not even a thing!

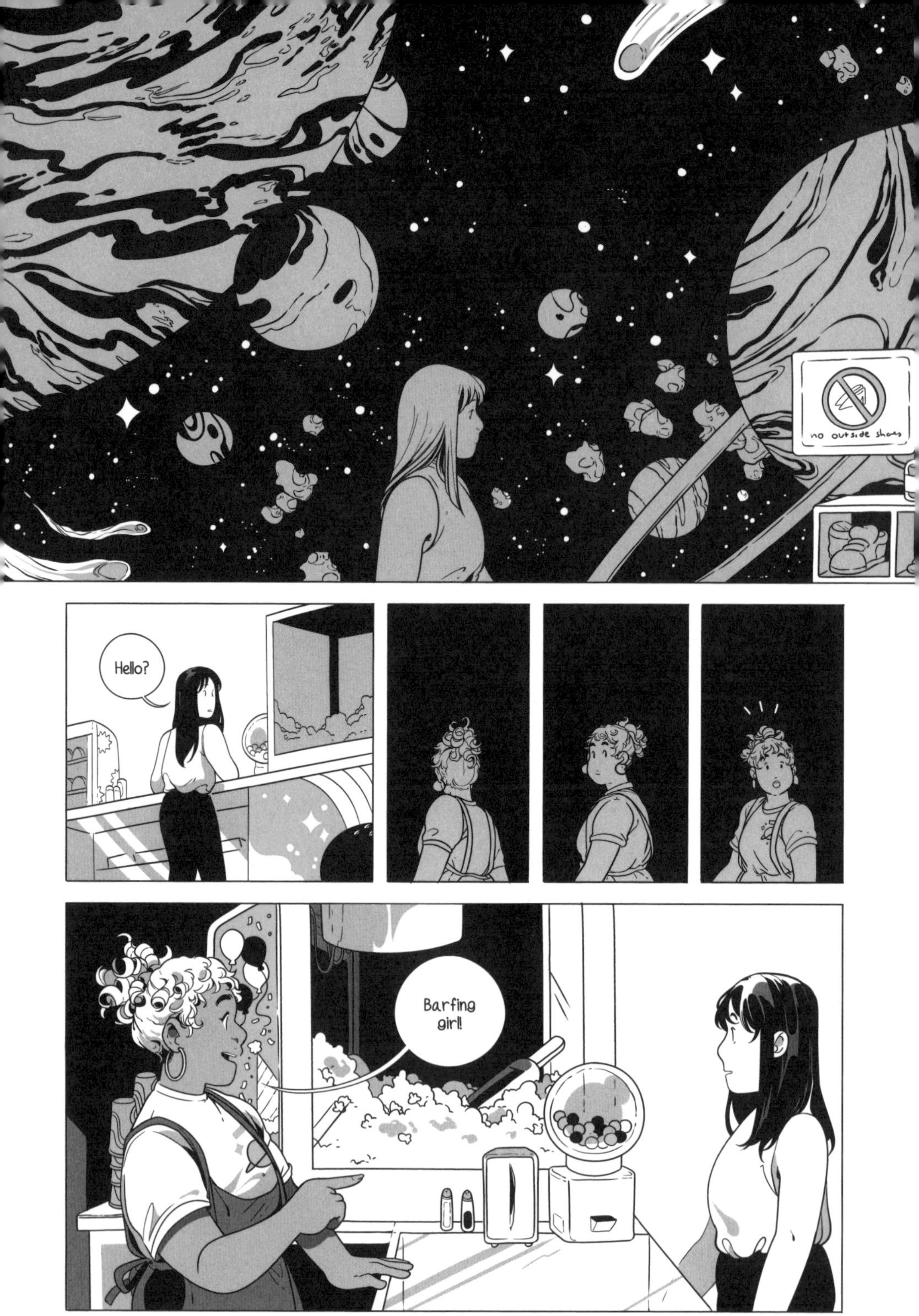
no outside shoes
Hello?
Barfing girl!

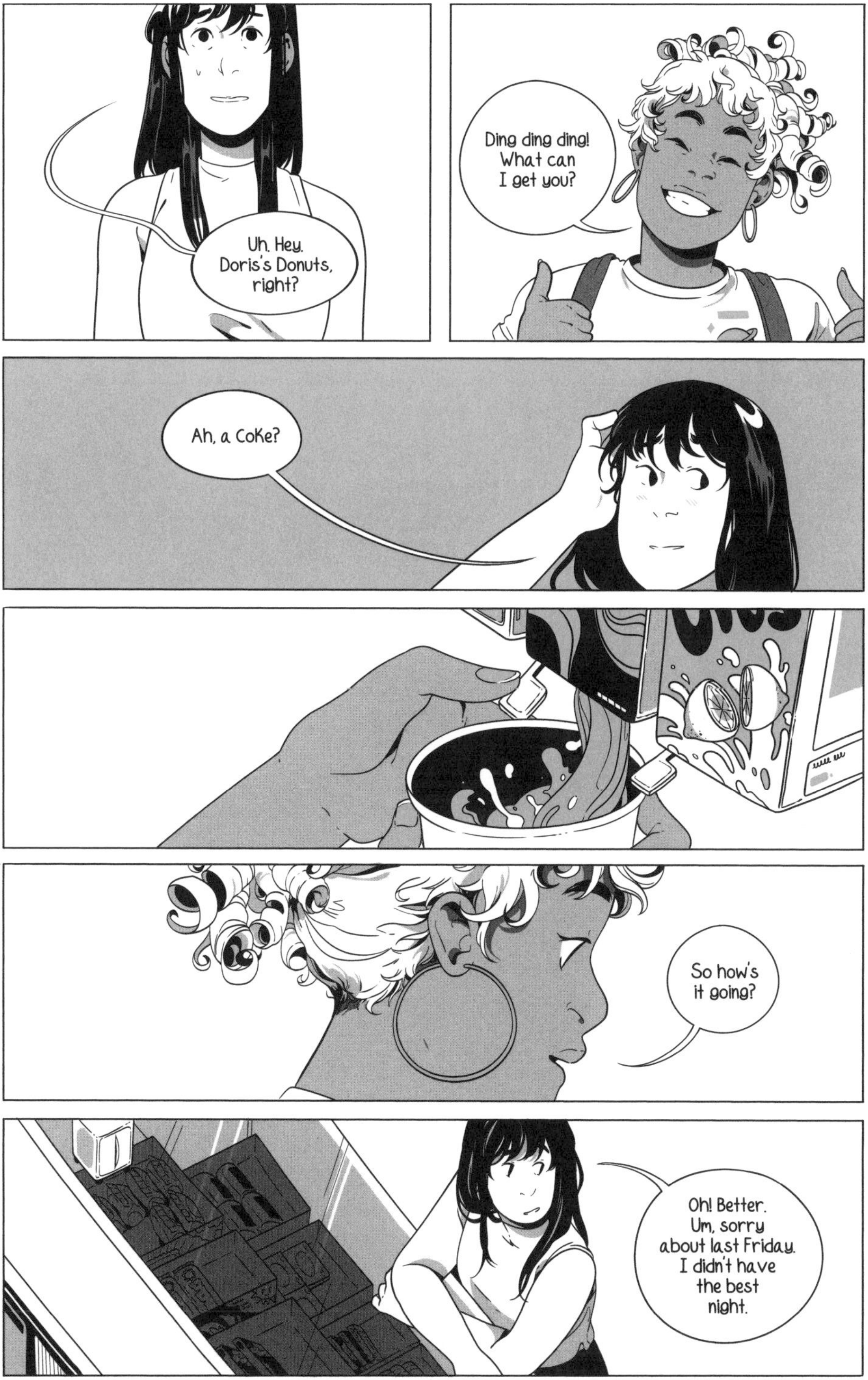
Uh. Hey.
Doris's Donuts,
right?
Ding ding ding!
What can
I get you?
Ah, a CoKe?
So how's
it going?
Oh! Better.
Um, sorry
about last Friday.
I didn't have
the best
night.

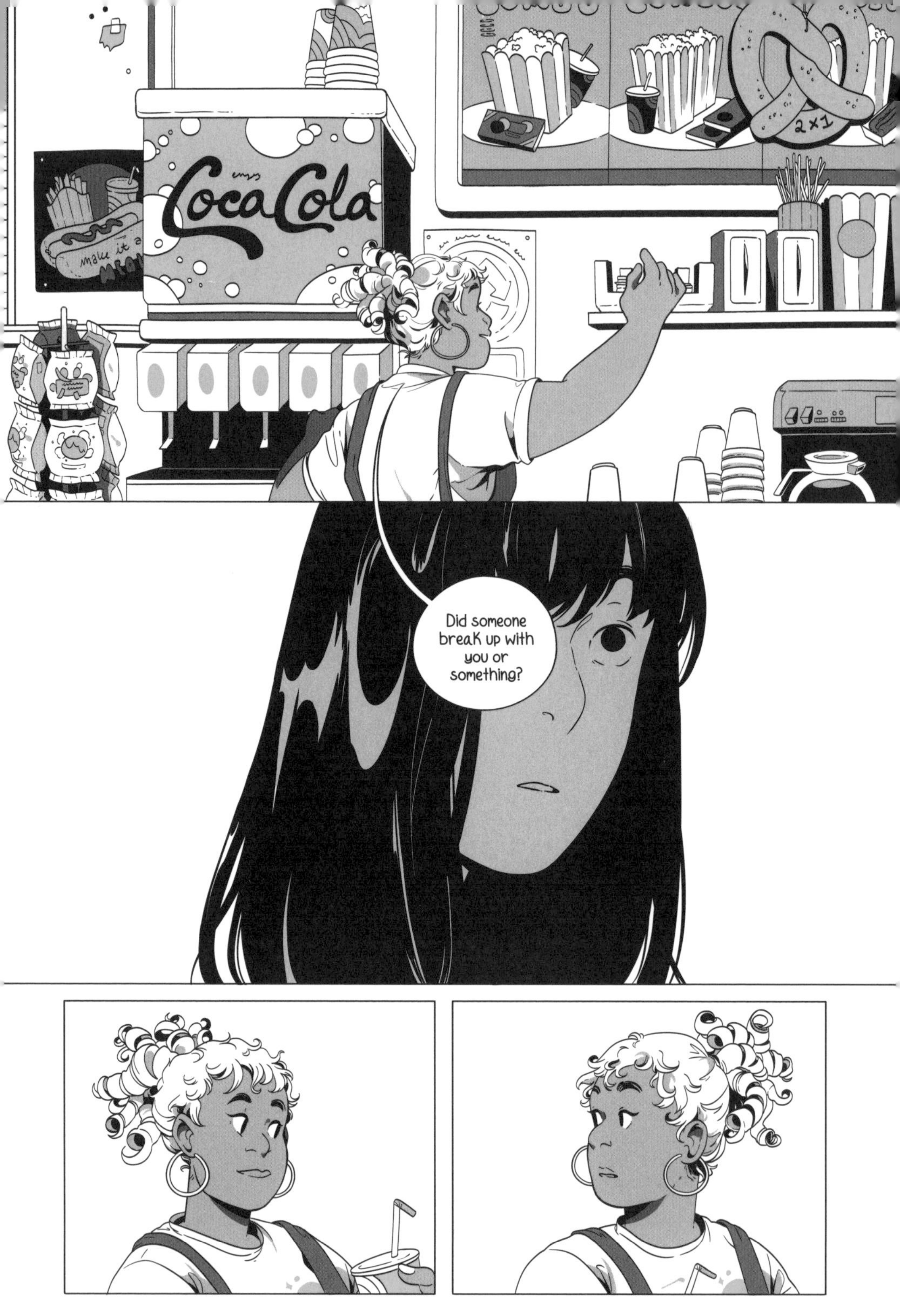
Coca Cola
2x1
Did someone break up with you or something?

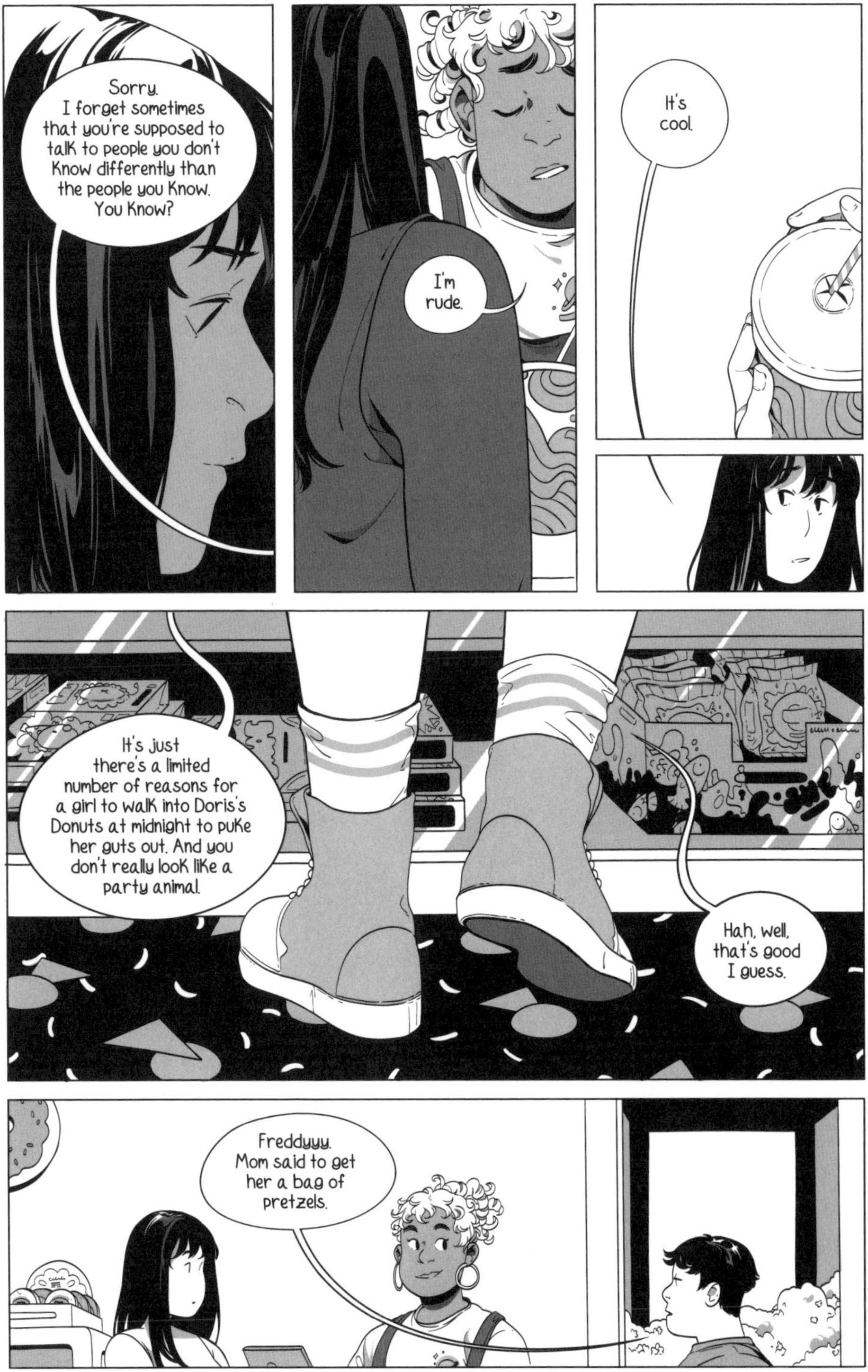
Sorry. I forget sometimes that you're supposed to talk to people you don't Know differently than the people you Know. You Know?
I'm rude.
It's cool.
It's just there's a limited number of reasons for a girl to walk into Doris's Donuts at midnight to puke her guts out. And you don't really look like a party animal.
Hah, well, that's good I guess.
Fredduuu. Mom said to get her a bag of pretzels.

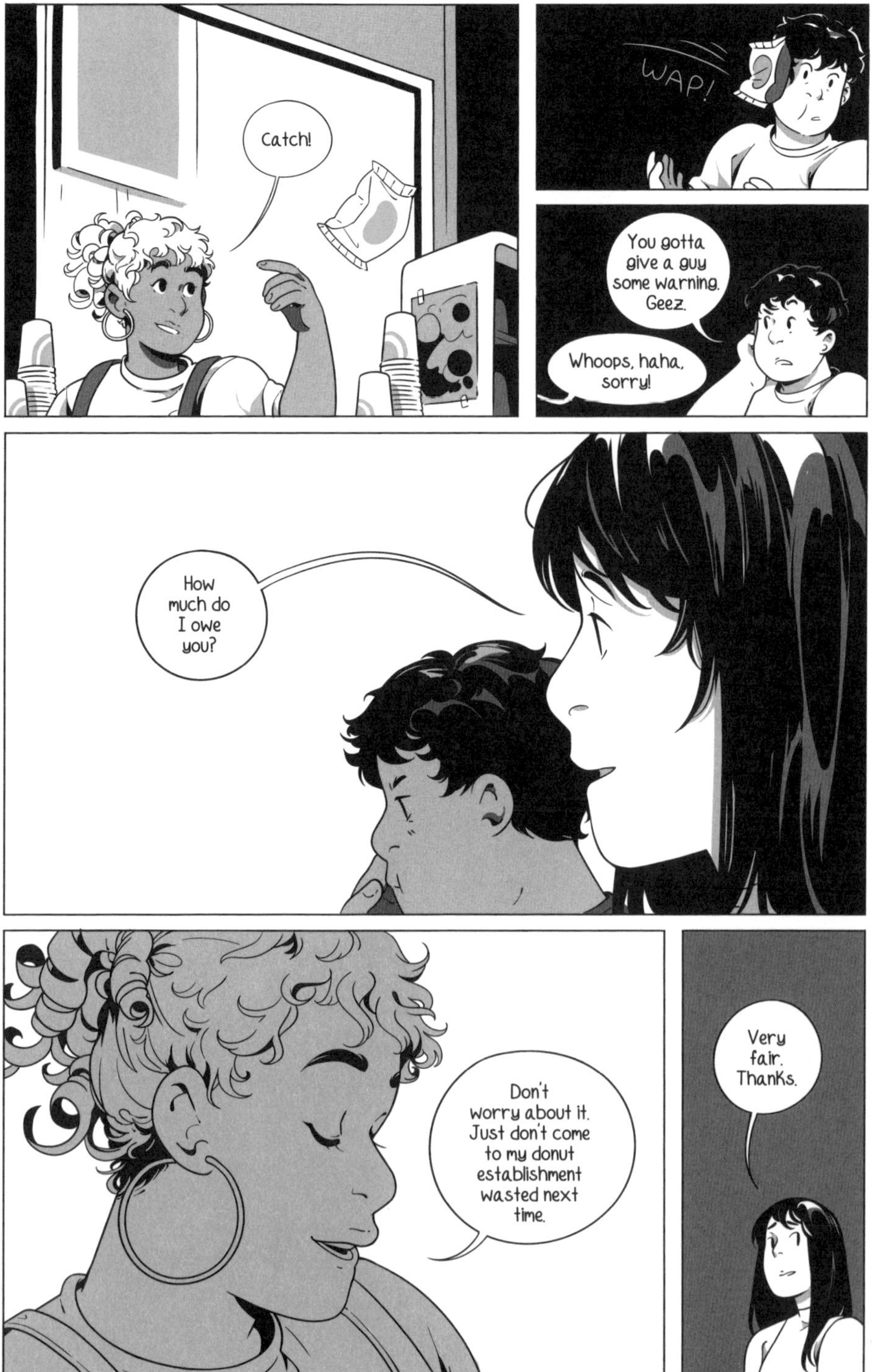
Catch!
WAP!
You gotta give a guy some warning. Geez.
Whoops, haha, sorry!
How much do I owe you?
Don't worry about it. Just don't come to my donut establishment wasted next time.
Very fair. Thanks.

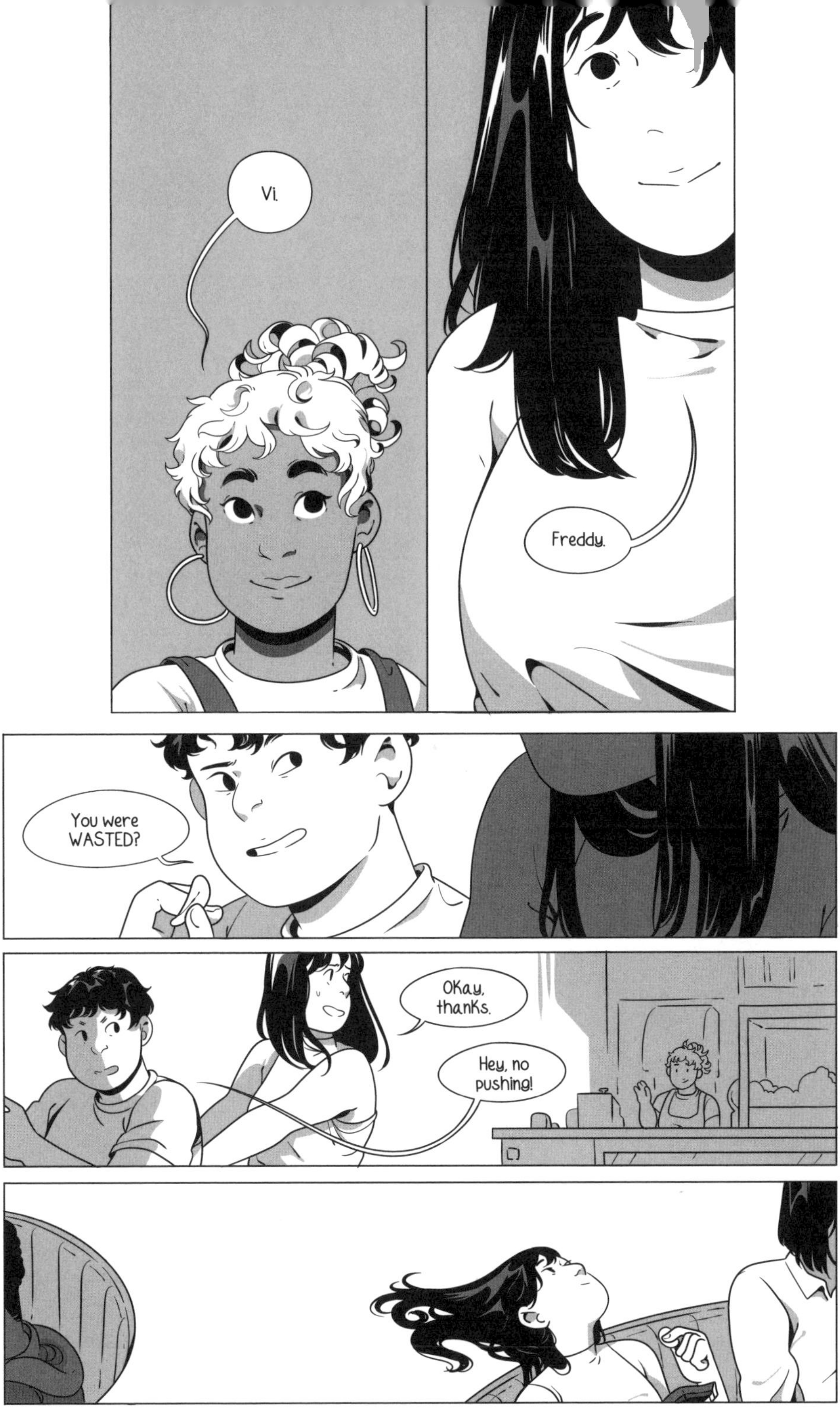
Vi.
Freddy.
You were WASTED?
Okay, thanks.
Hey, no pushing!

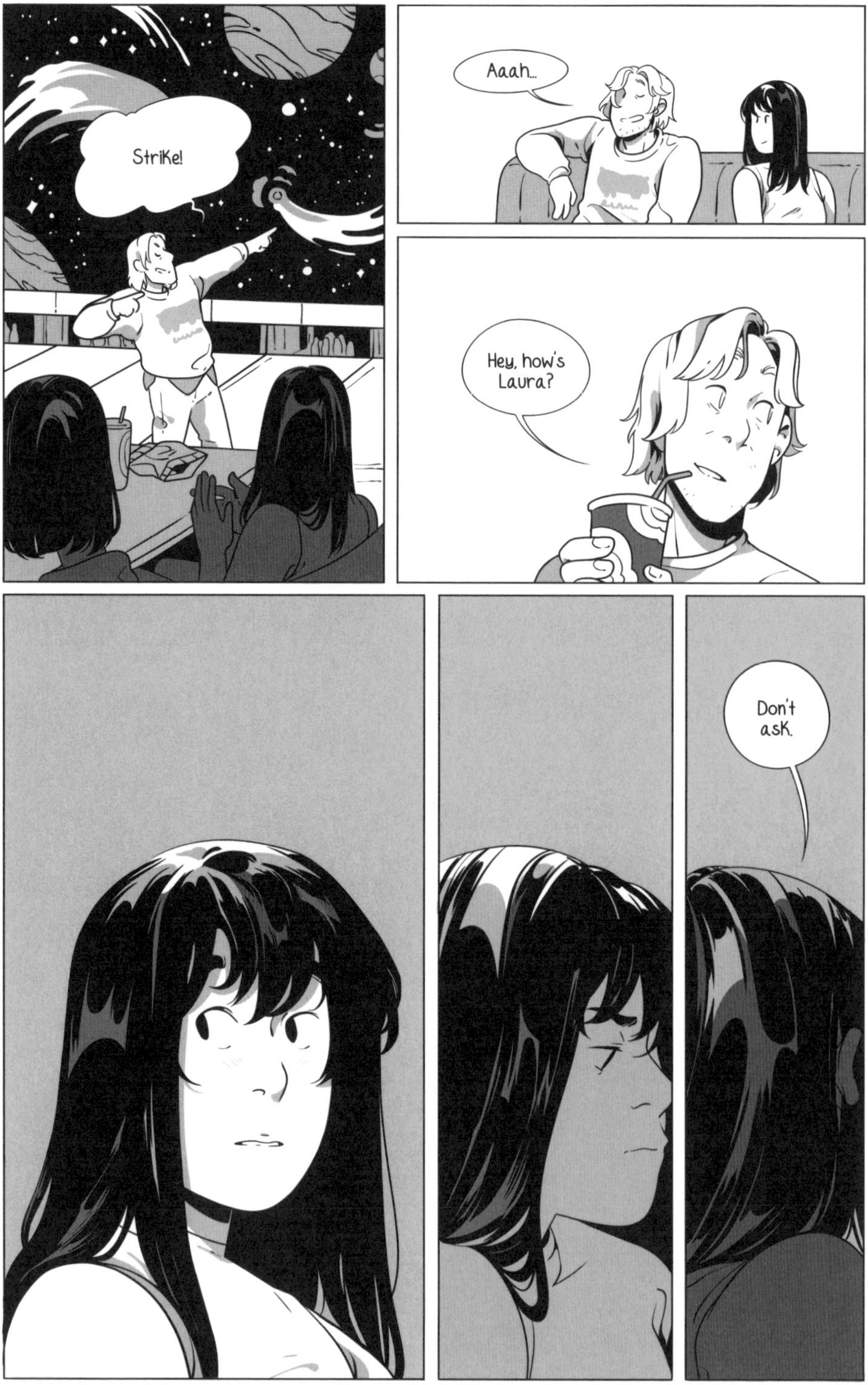

Strike!
Aaah...
Hey, how's Laura?
Don't ask.

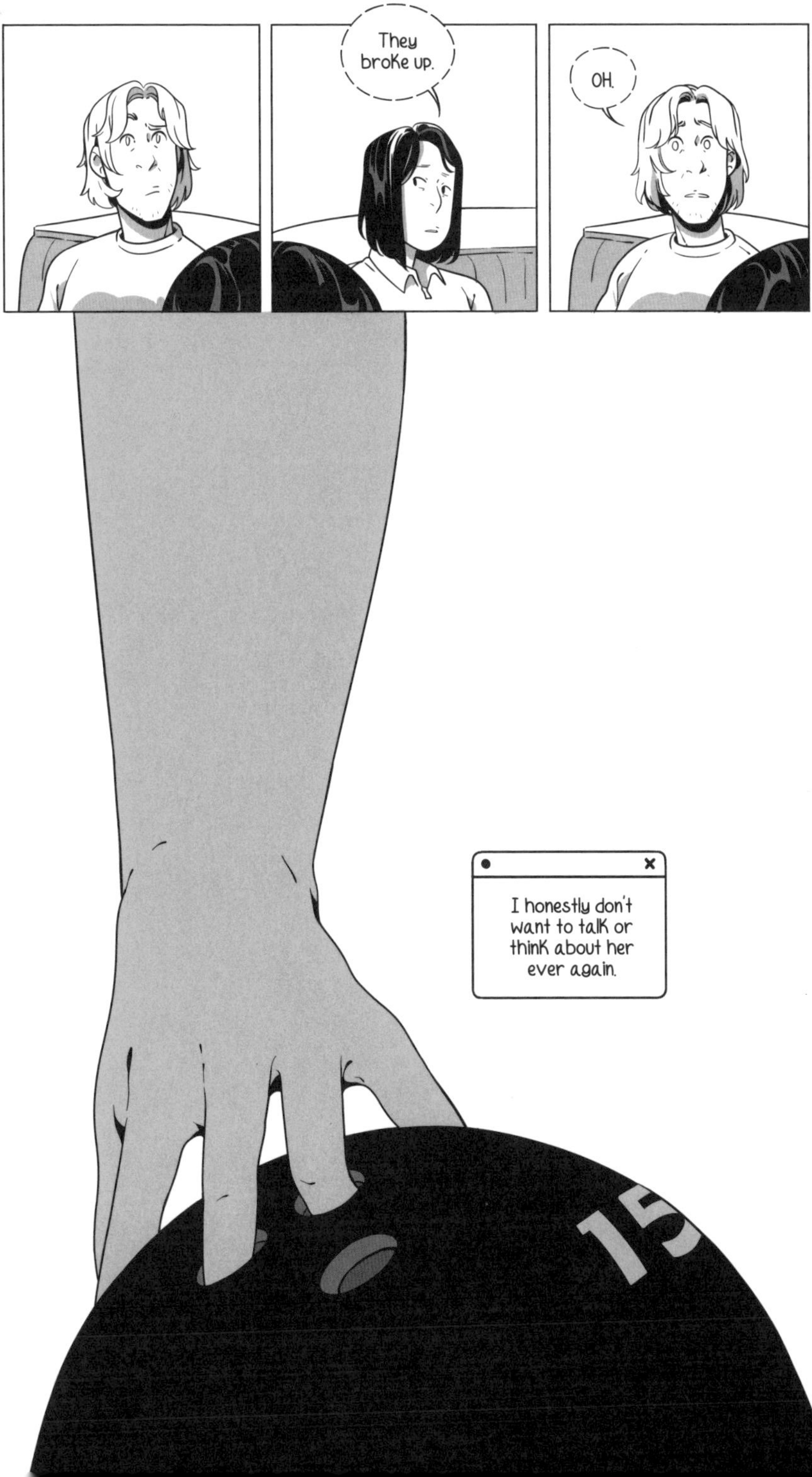
They broke up.
OH.
I honestly don't want to talk or think about her ever again.
15

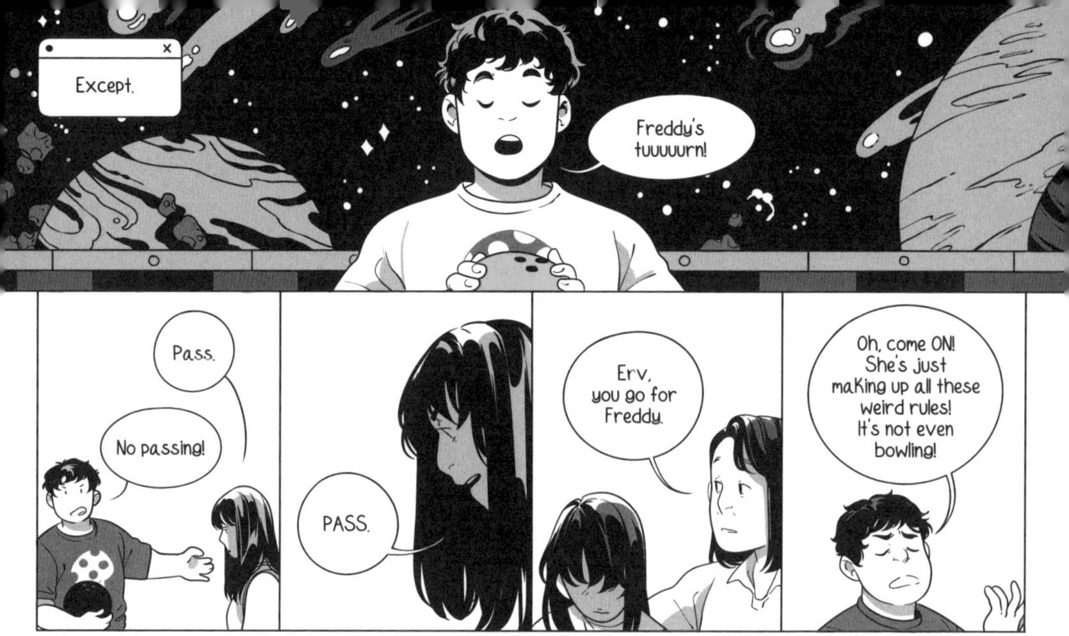
Except.
Freddy's tuuuuurn!
Pass.
No passing!
PASS.
Erv, you go for Freddy.
Oh, come ON! She's just making up all these weird rules! It's not even bowling!

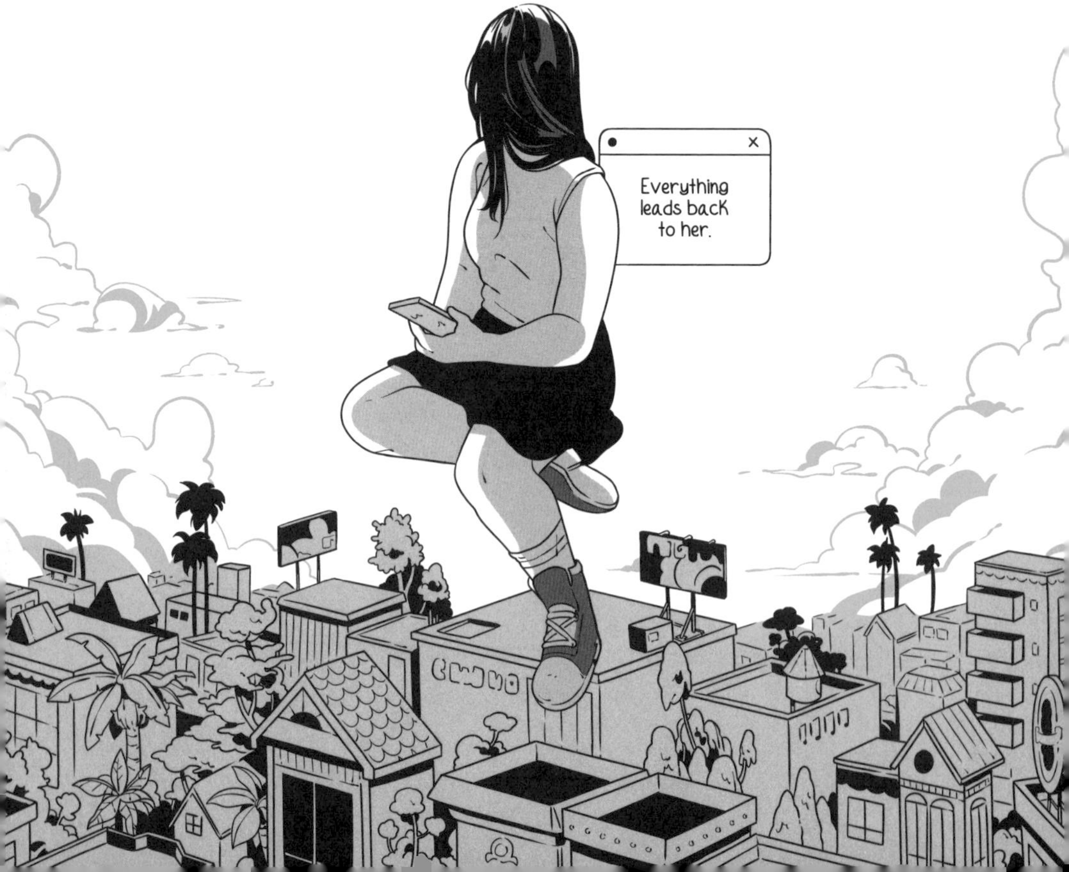
Everything leads back to her.

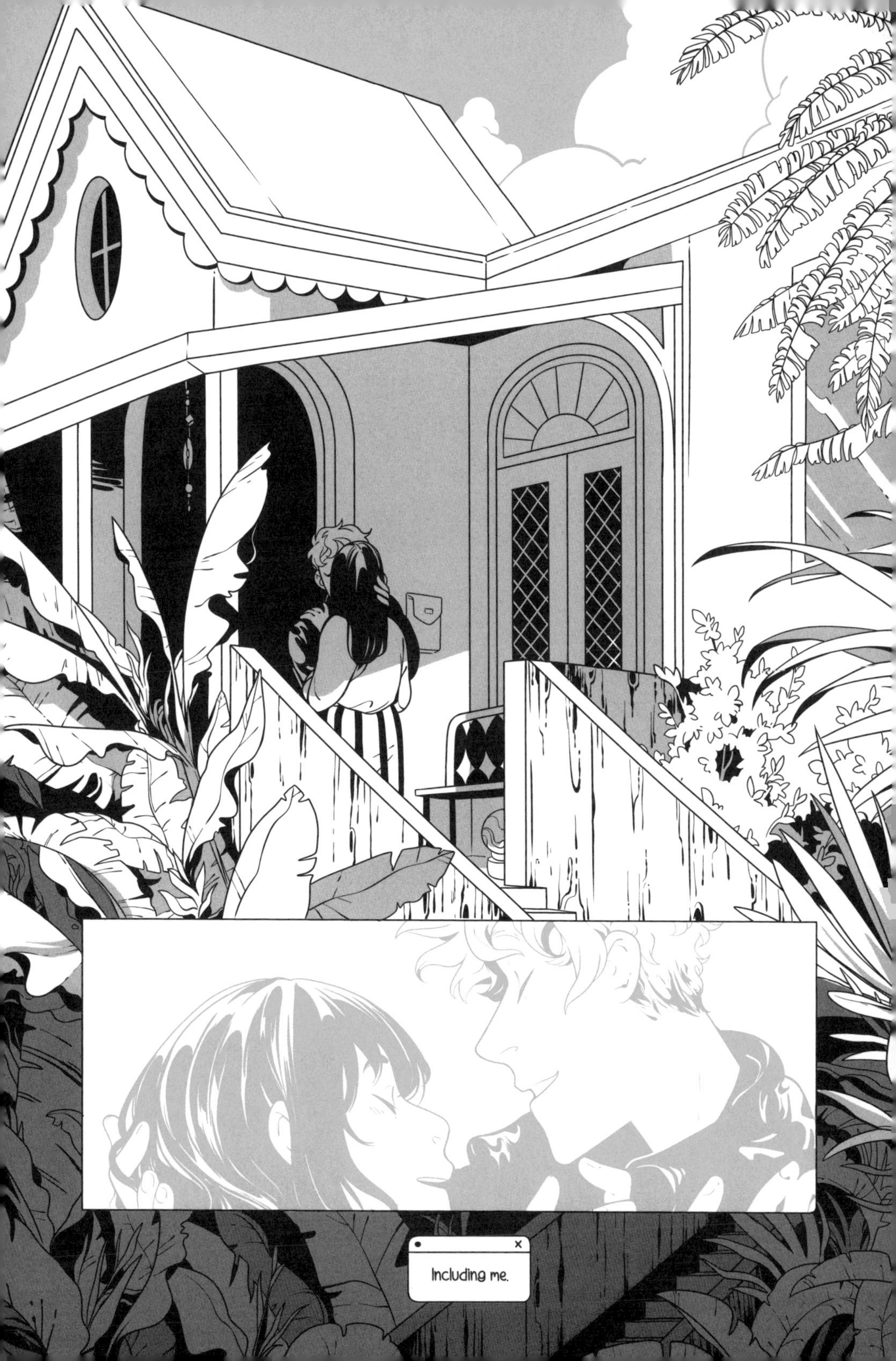
Including me.

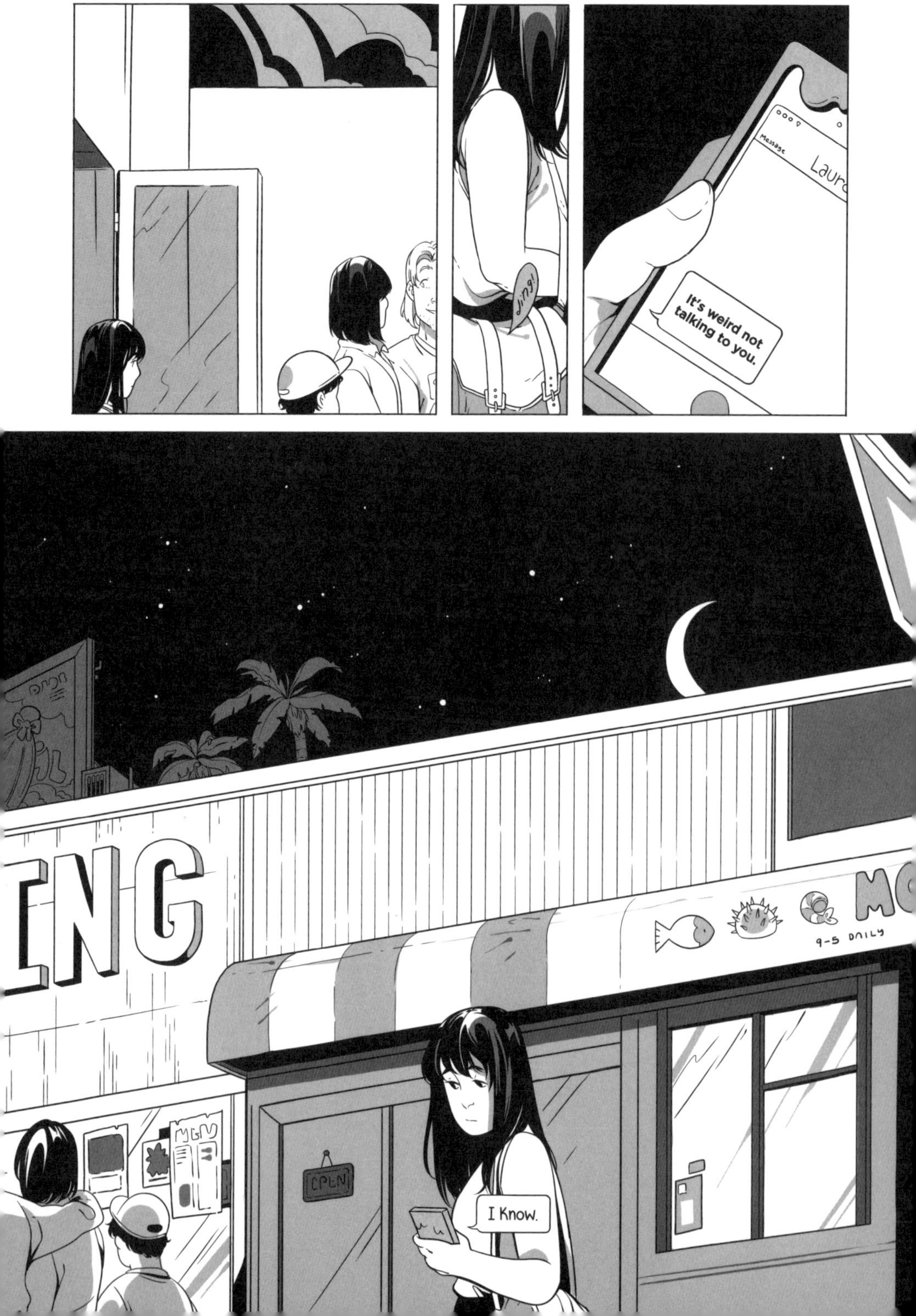
Ding!
Message
Laura
It's weird not talking to you.
ING
9-5 DAILY
I Know.

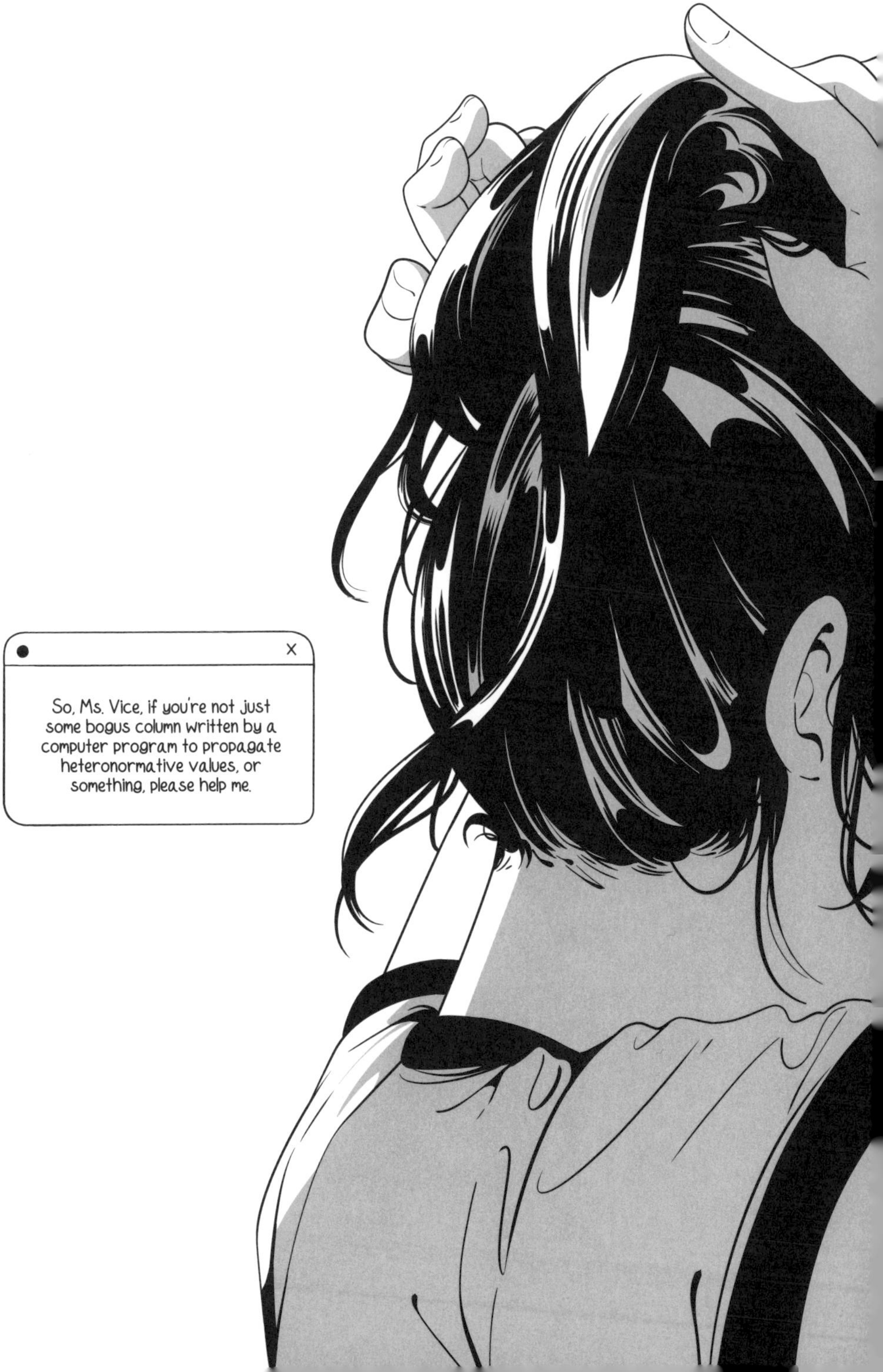
So, Ms. Vice, if you're not just some bogus column written by a computer program to propagate heteronormative values, or something, please help me.

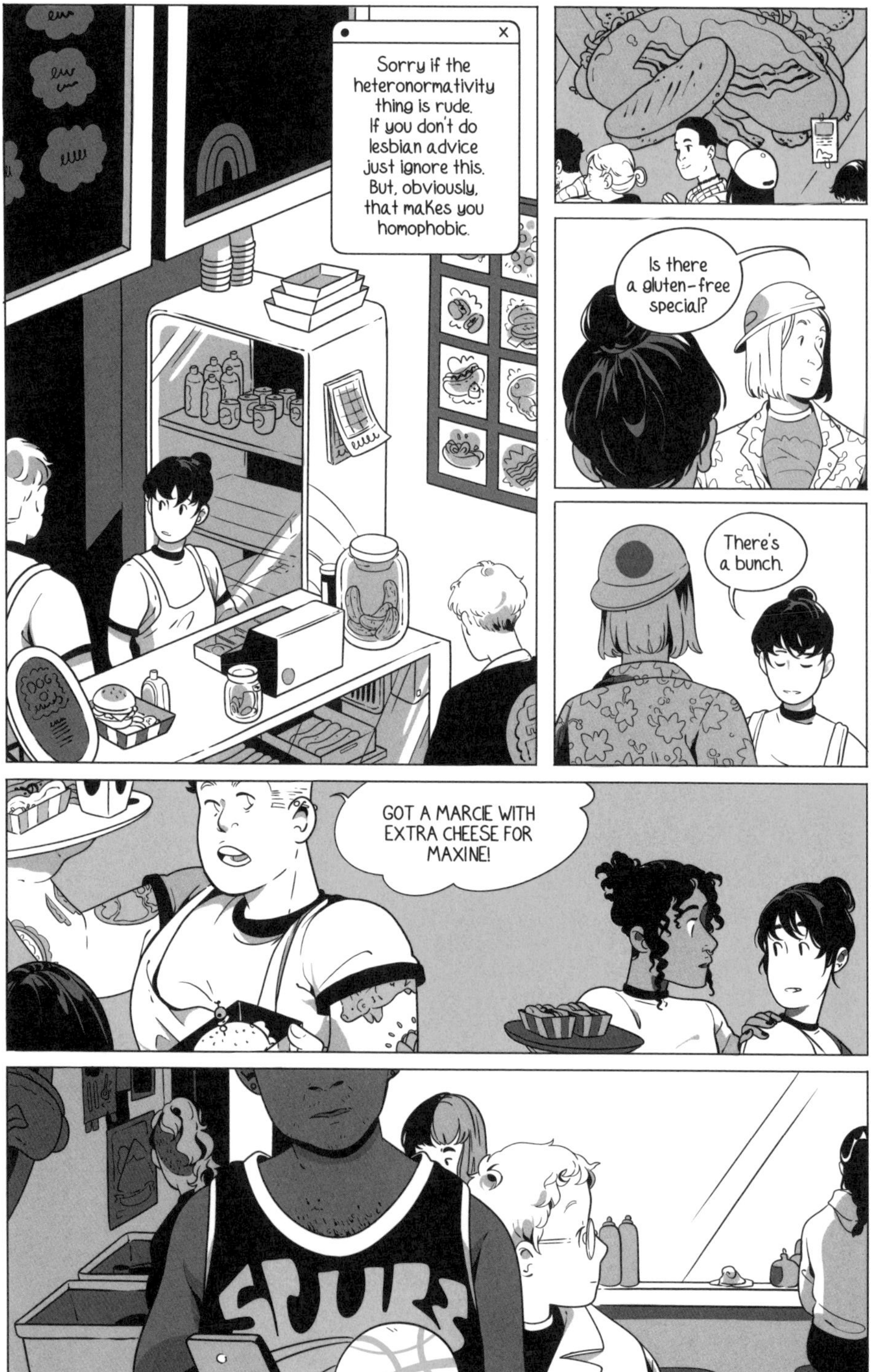
Sorry if the heteronormativity thing is rude. If you don't do lesbian advice just ignore this. But, obviously, that makes you homophobic.
Is there a gluten-free special?
There's a bunch.
GOT A MARCIE WITH EXTRA CHEESE FOR MAXINE!

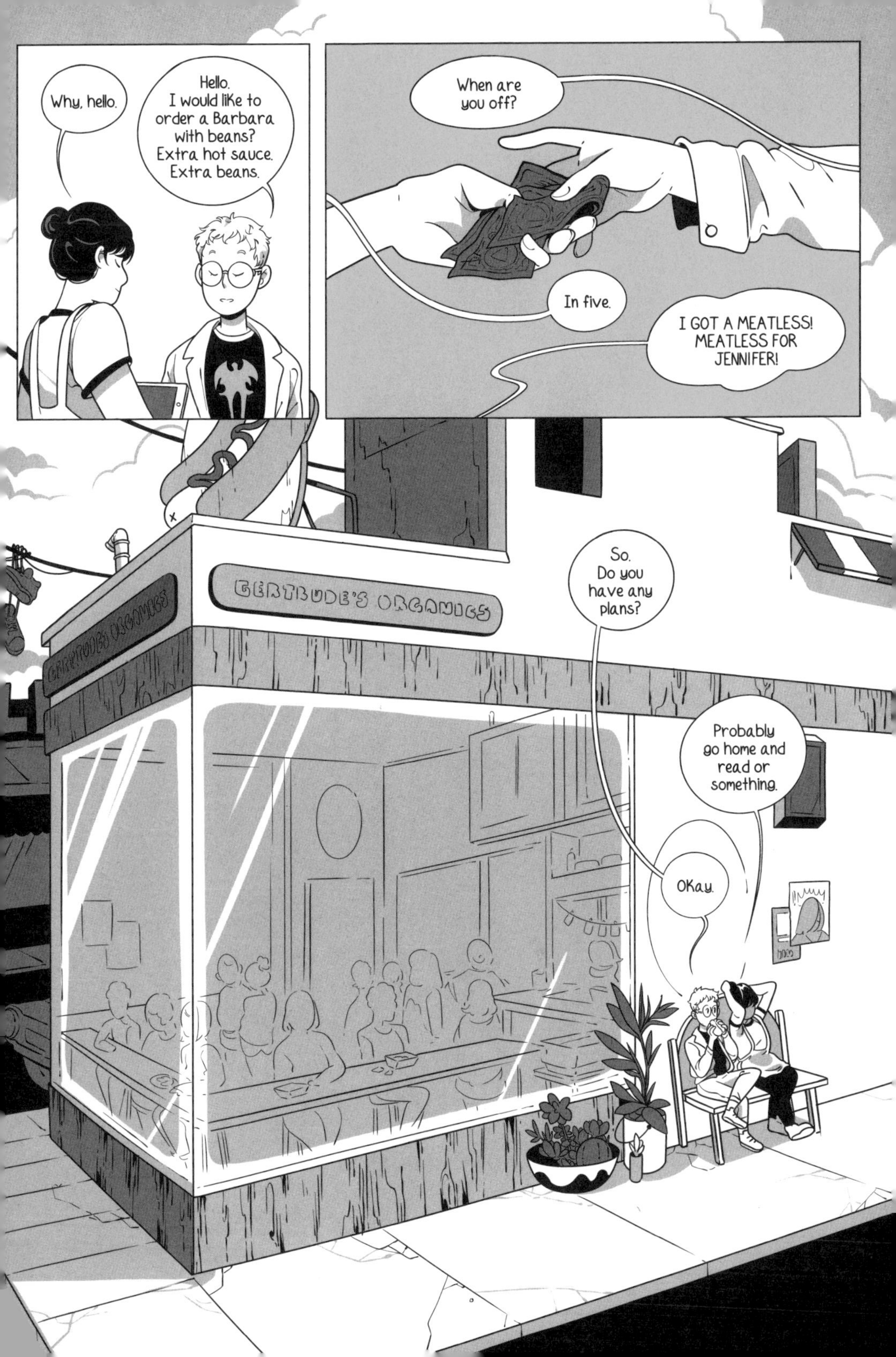
Why, hello.
Hello. I would like to order a Barbara with beans? Extra hot sauce. Extra beans.
When are you off?
In five.
I GOT A MEATLESS! MEATLESS FOR JENNIFER!
GERTRUDE'S ORGANICS
So. Do you have any plans?
Probably go home and read or something.
Okay.

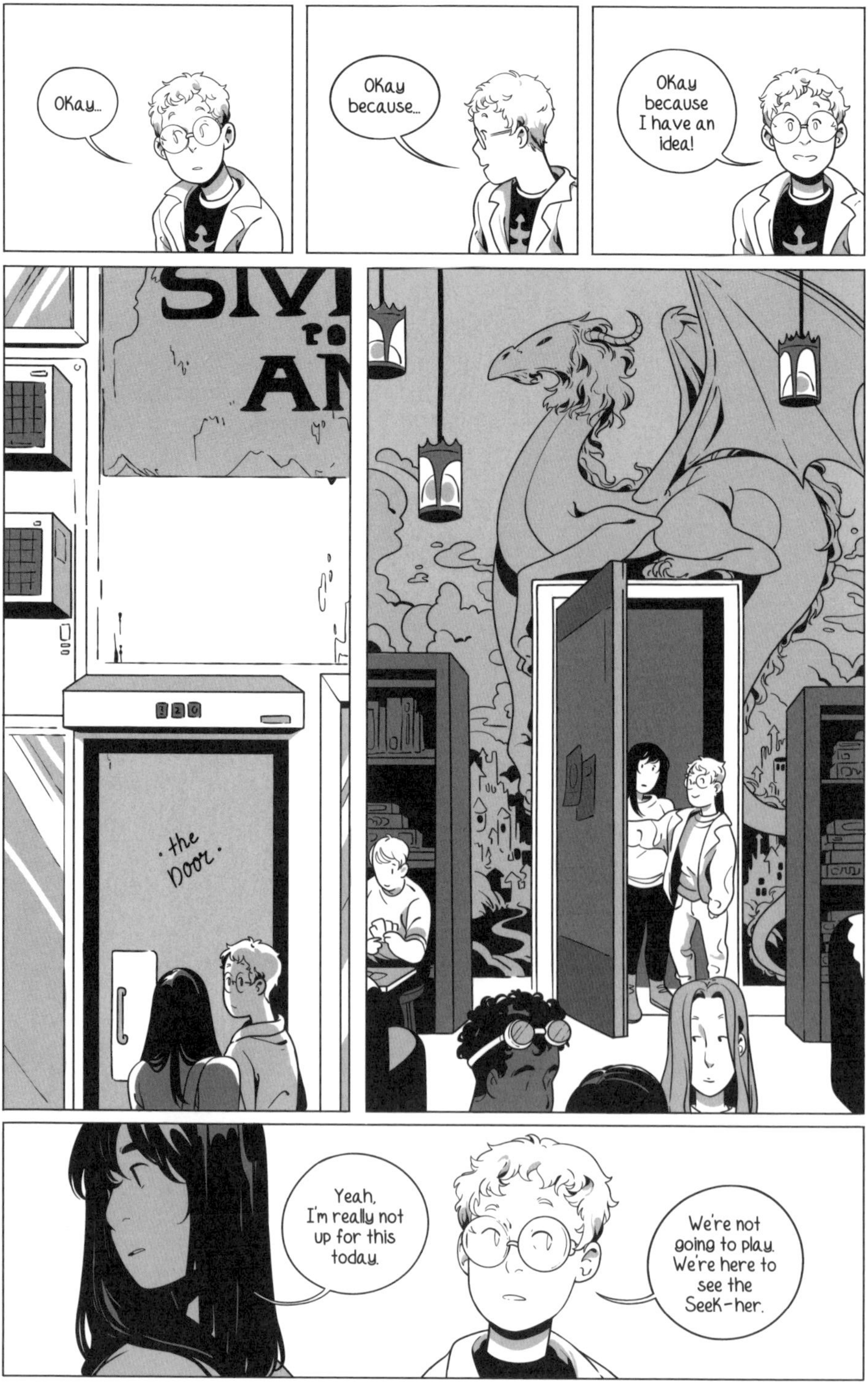
OKay...
OKay because...
OKay because I have an idea!
the Door
Yeah, I'm really not up for this today.
We're not going to play. We're here to see the SeeK-her.

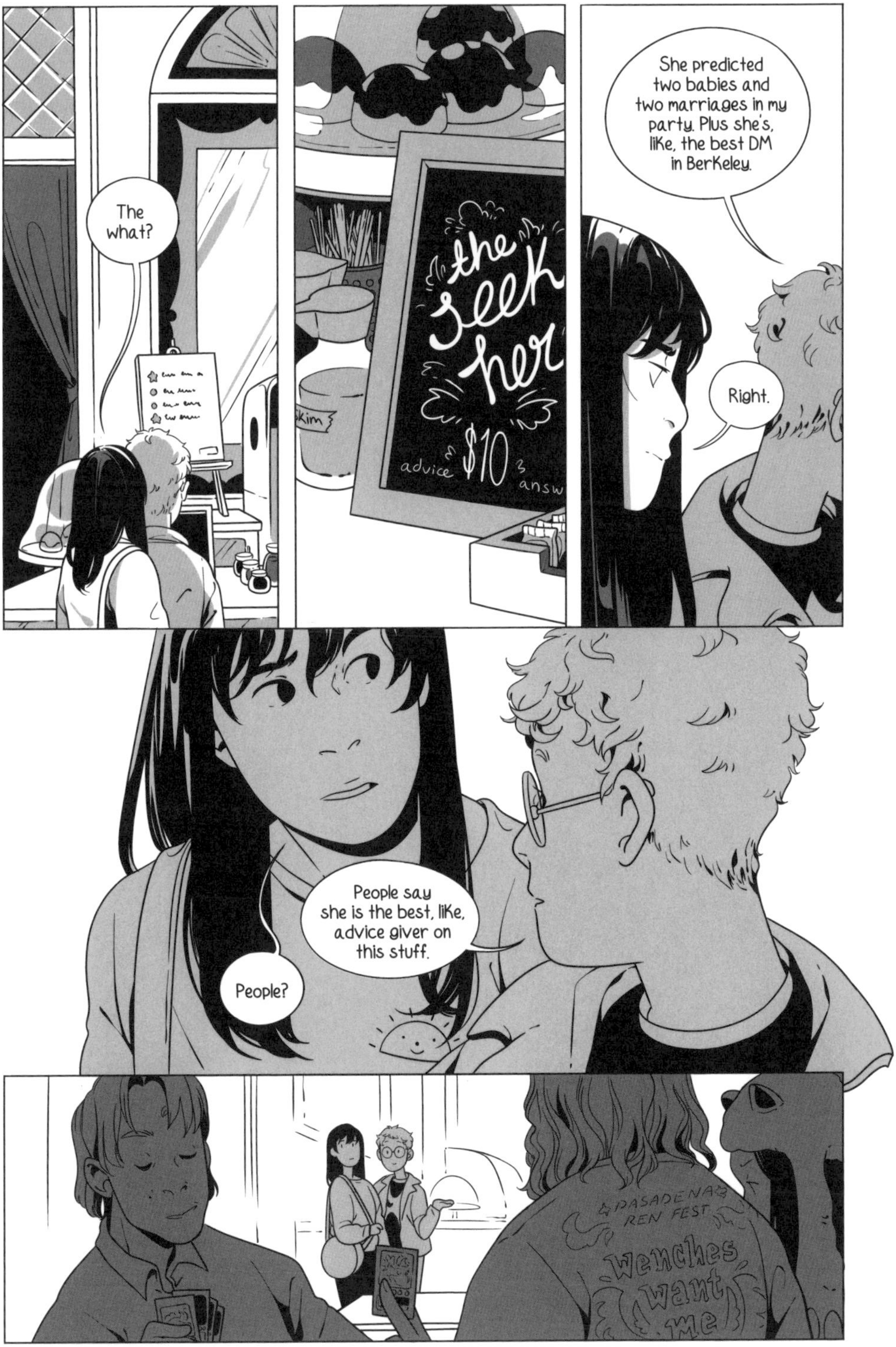
The what?
the seek her
advice
$10
She predicted two babies and two marriages in my party. Plus she's, like, the best DM in Berkeley.
Right.
People say she is the best, like, advice giver on this stuff.
People?
PASADENA
REN FEST
wenches want me

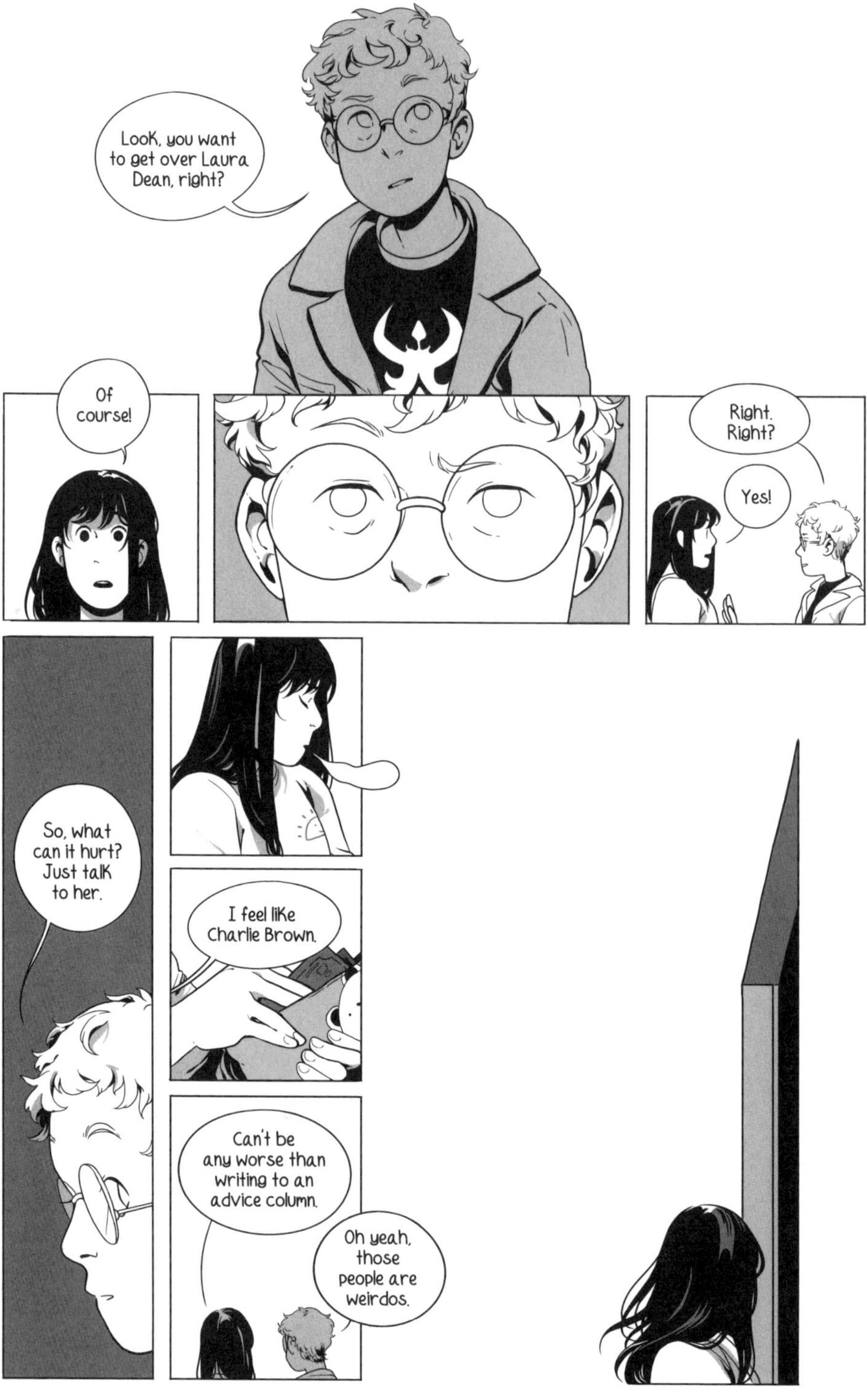
Look, you want to get over Laura Dean, right?
Of course!
Right. Right?
Yes!
So, what can it hurt? Just talk to her.
I feel like Charlie Brown.
Can't be any worse than writing to an advice column.
Oh yeah, those people are weirdos.

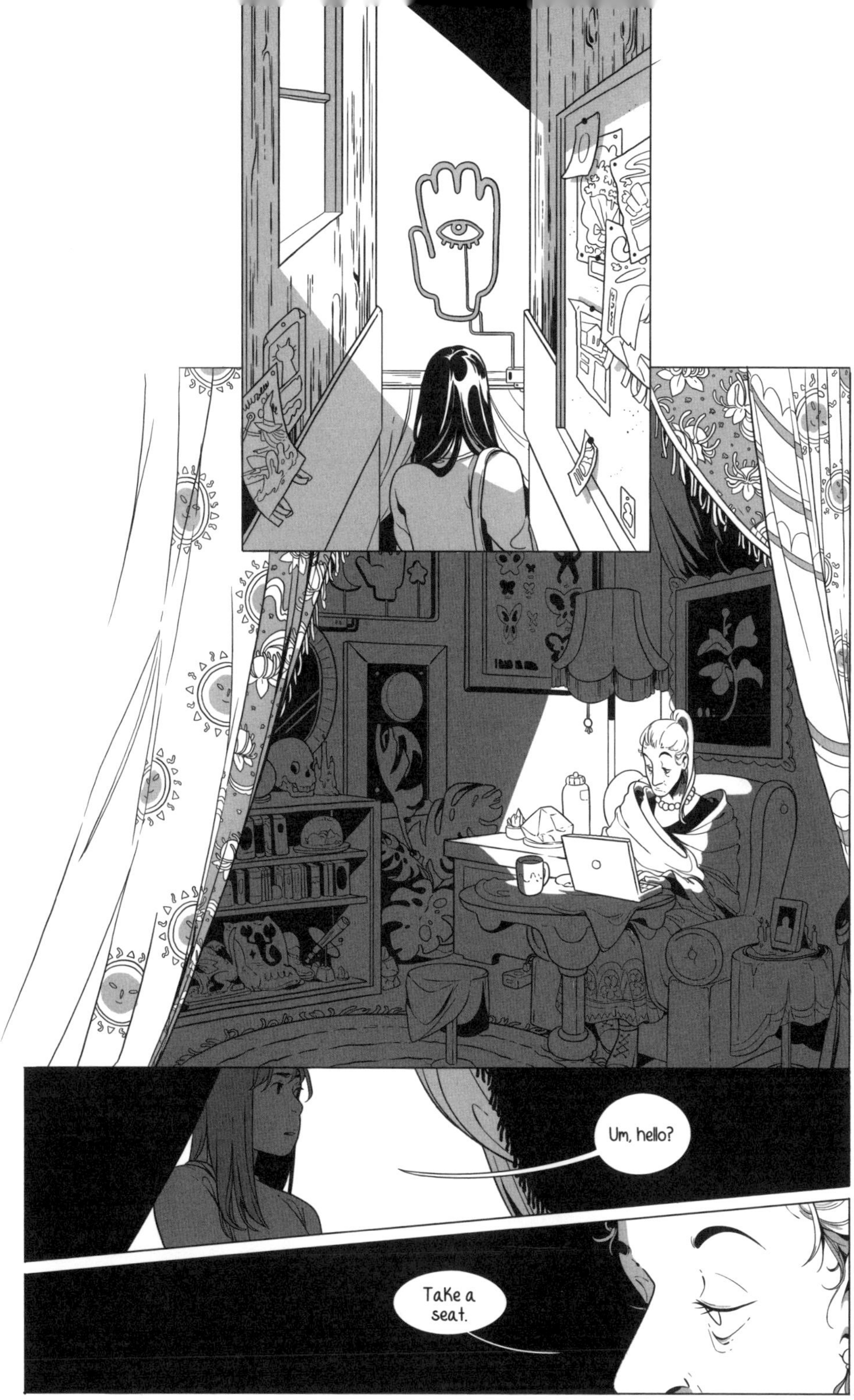
Um, hello?
Take a seat.

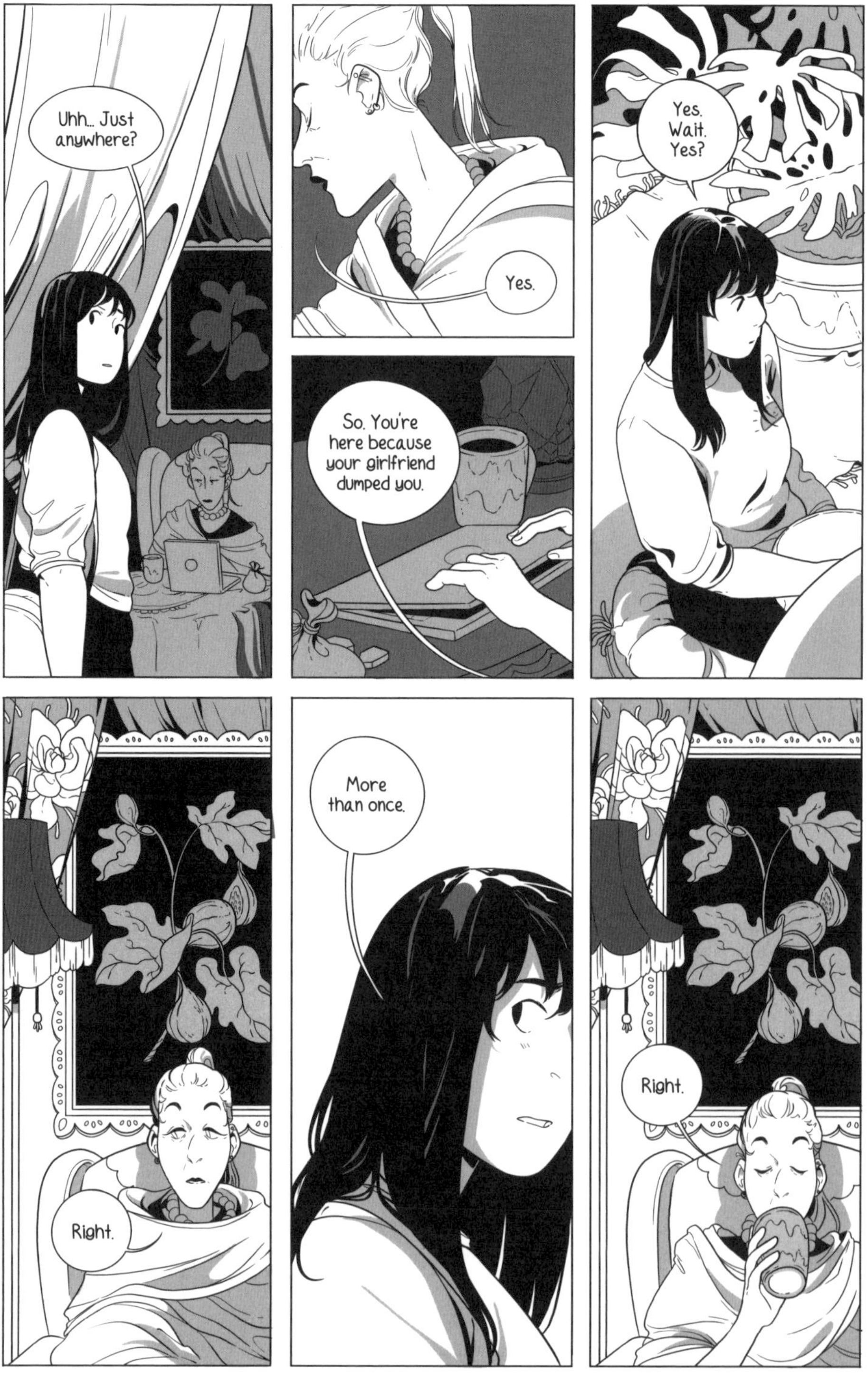
Uhh... Just anywhere?
Yes.
So. You're here because your girlfriend dumped you.
Yes. Wait. Yes?
Right.
More than once.
Right.

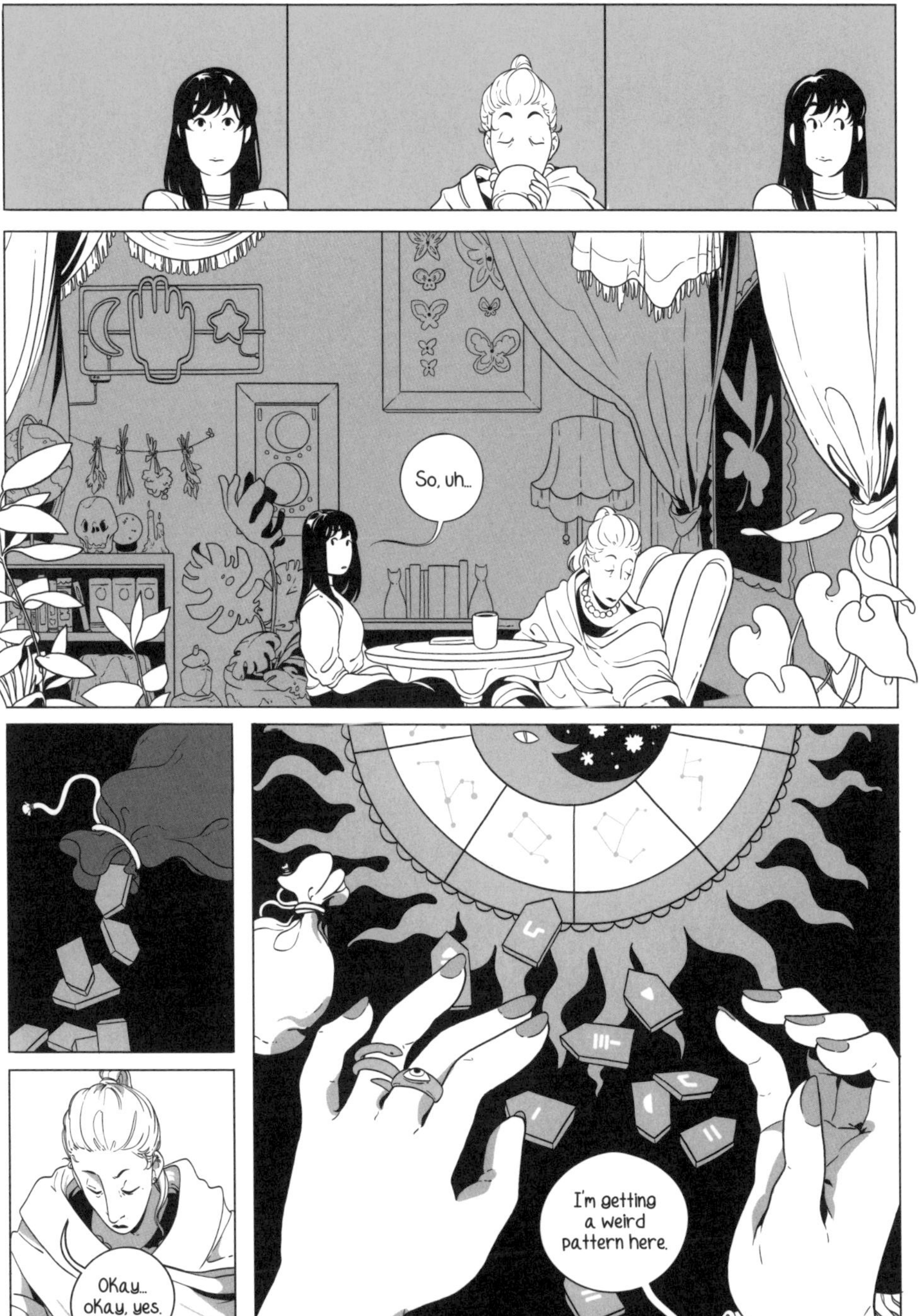
So, uh...
I'm getting
a weird
pattern here.
Okay...
okay, yes.

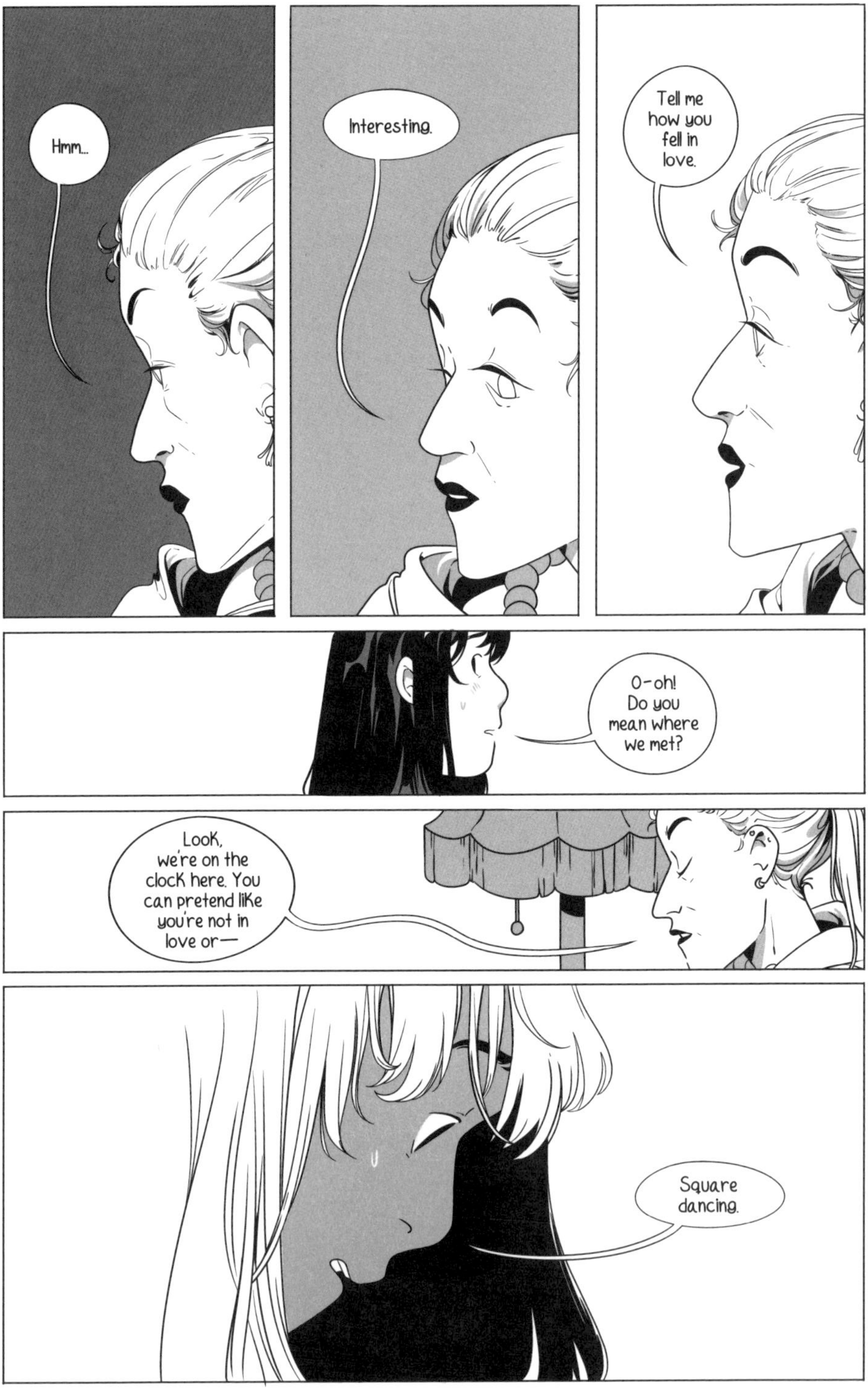
Hmm...
Interesting.
Tell me how you fell in love.
O-oh! Do you mean where we met?
Look, we're on the clock here. You can pretend like you're not in love or—
Square dancing.

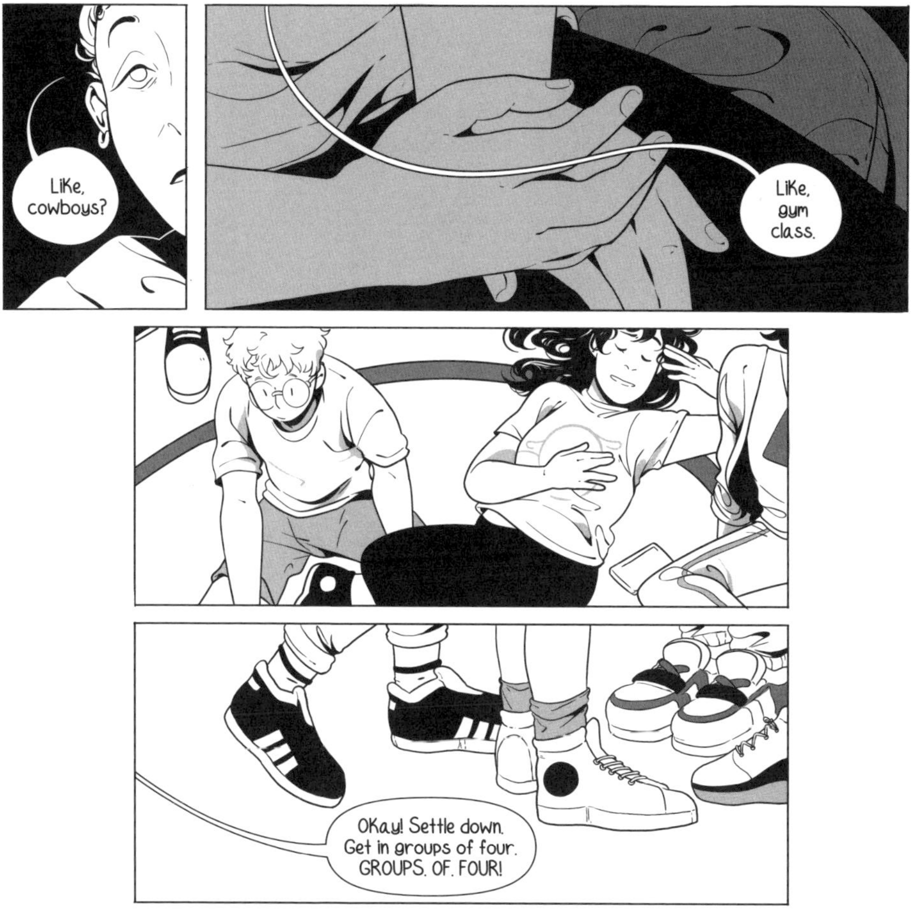
Like, cowboys?
Like, gym class.
Okay! Settle down. Get in groups of four. GROUPS. OF. FOUR!

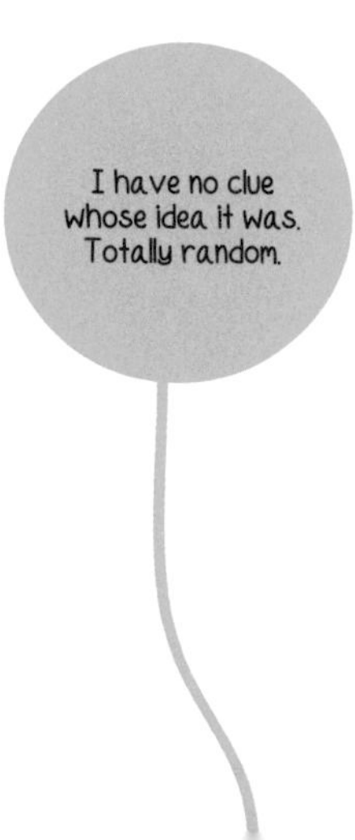
I have no clue whose idea it was. Totally random.

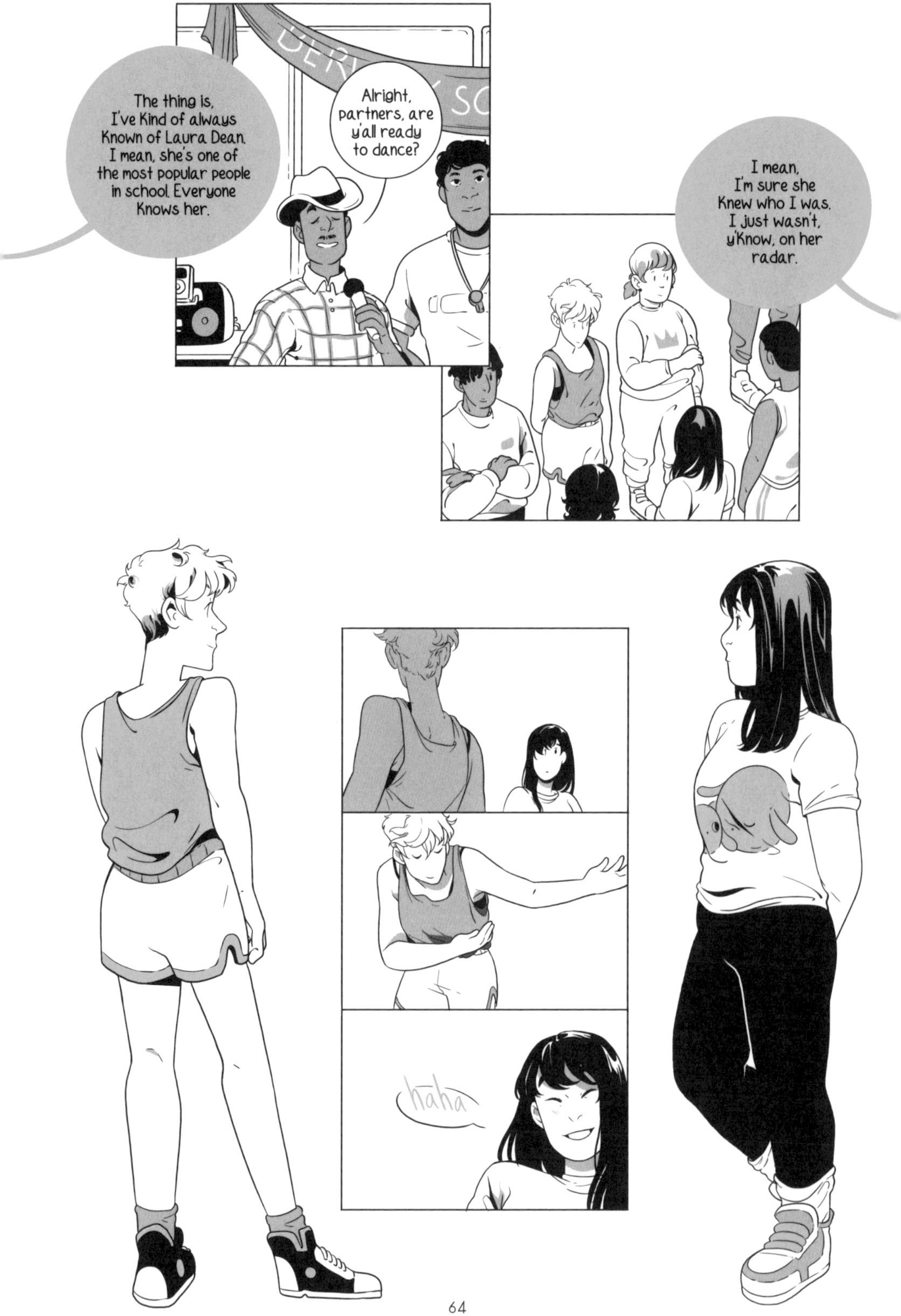
The thing is, I've Kind of always Known of Laura Dean. I mean, she's one of the most popular people in school. Everyone Knows her.
Alright, partners, are y'all ready to dance?
I mean, I'm sure she Knew who I was. I just wasn't, y'Know, on her radar.
haha

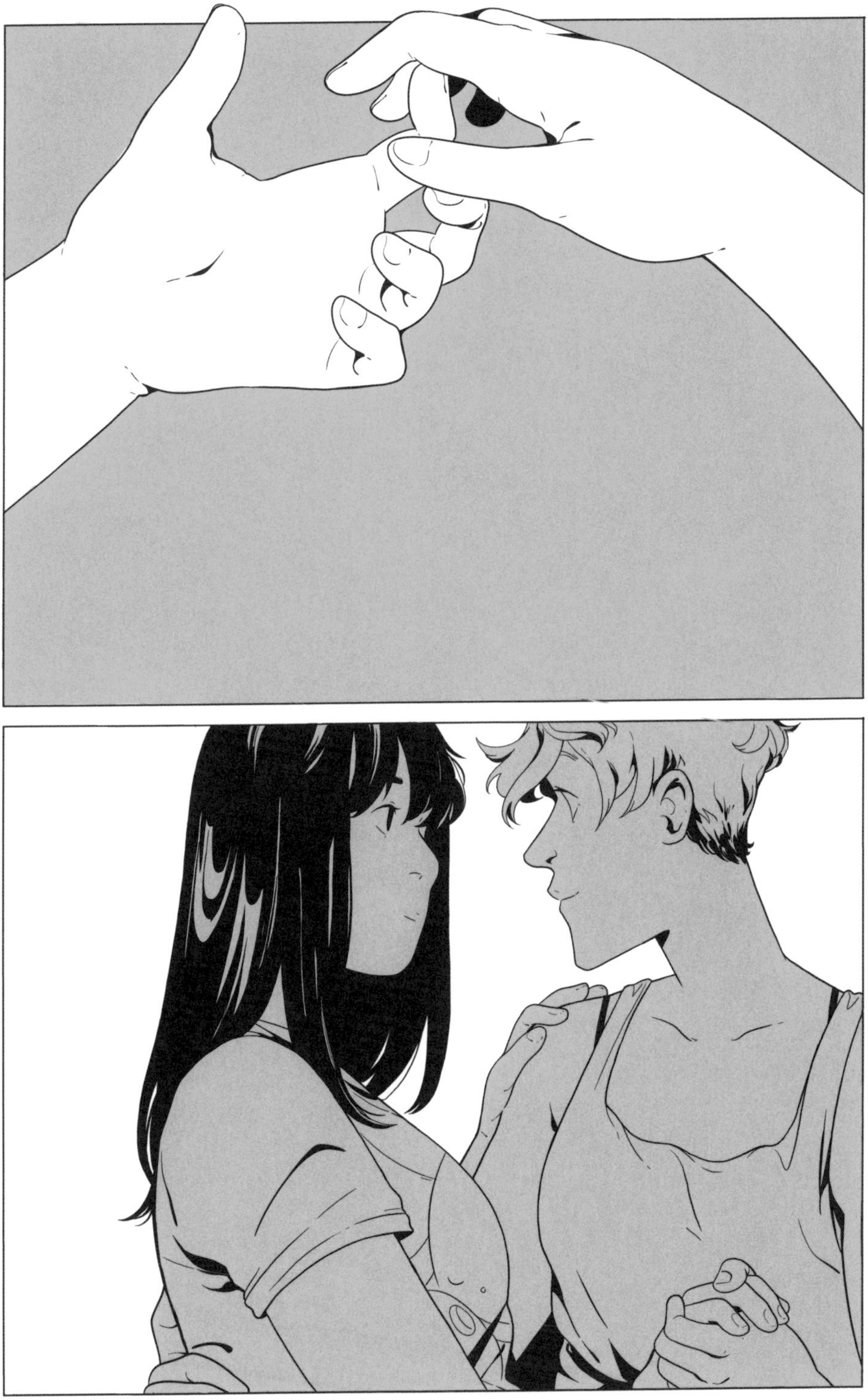

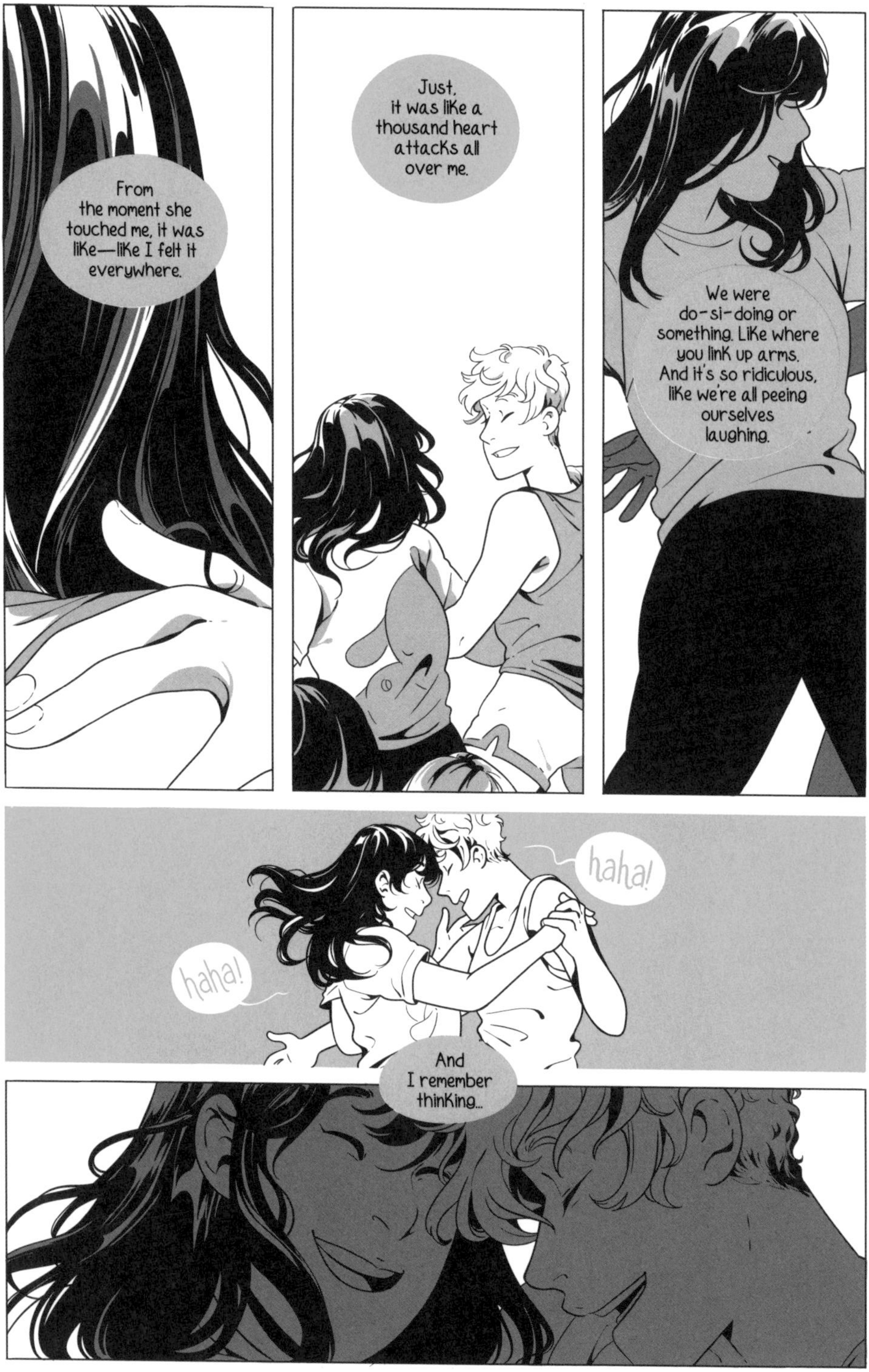
From the moment she touched me, it was like—like I felt it everywhere.
Just, it was like a thousand heart attacks all over me.
We were do-si-doing or something. Like where you link up arms. And it's so ridiculous, like we're all peeing ourselves laughing.
haha!
haha!
And I remember thinking...

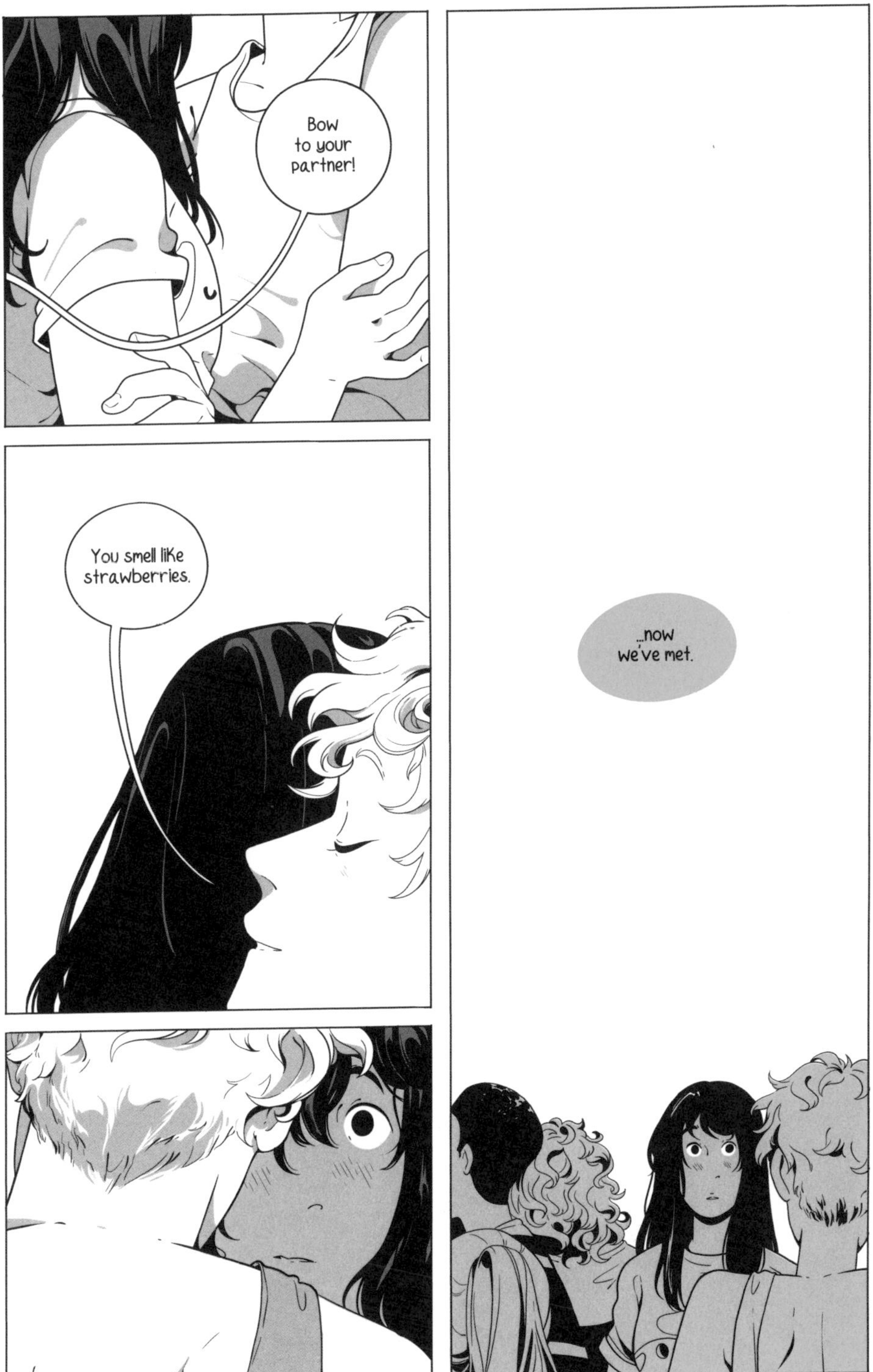
Bow to your partner!
You smell like strawberries.
...now we've met.

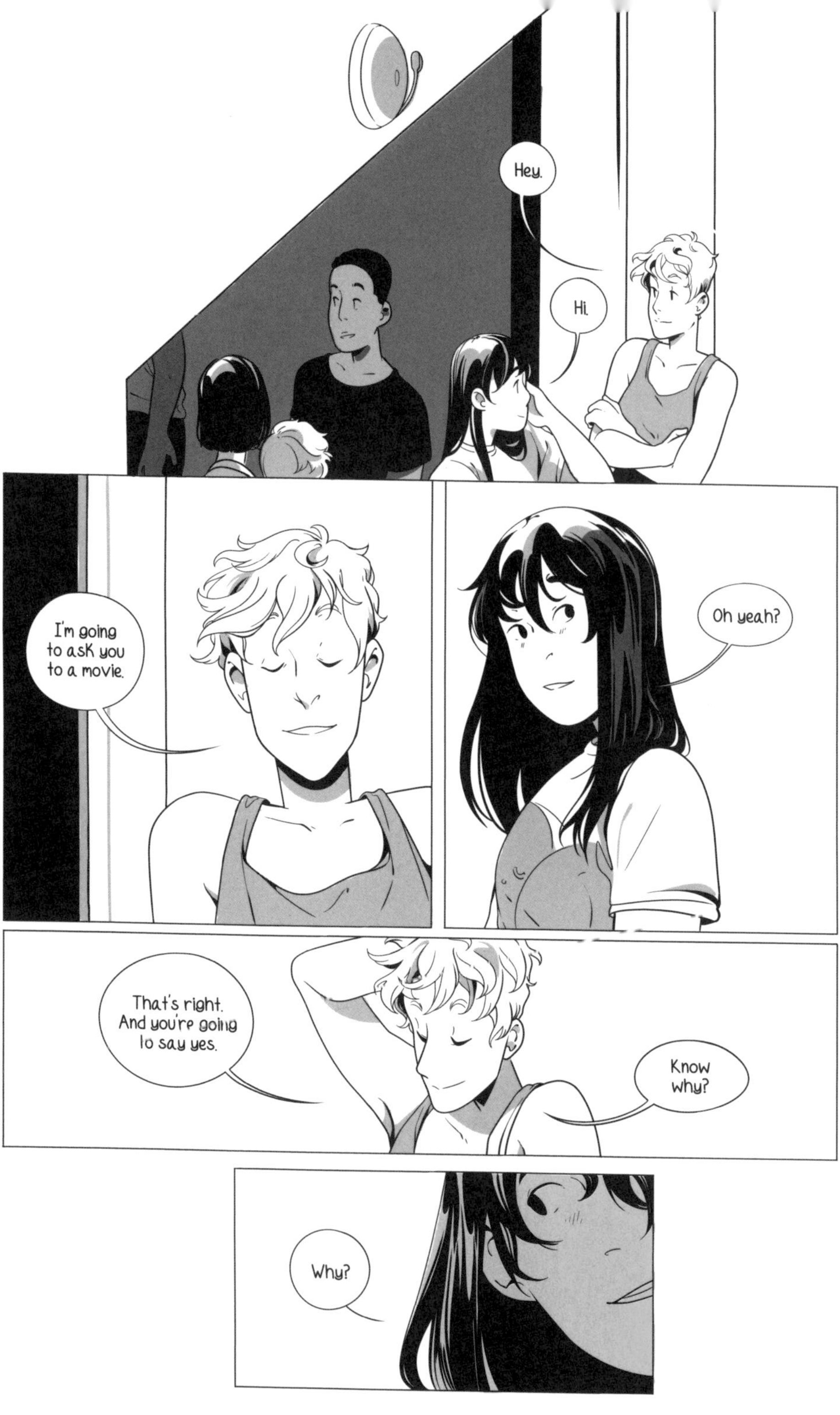
Hey.
Hi.
I'm going to ask you to a movie.
Oh yeah?
That's right. And you're going to say yes.
Know why?
Why?

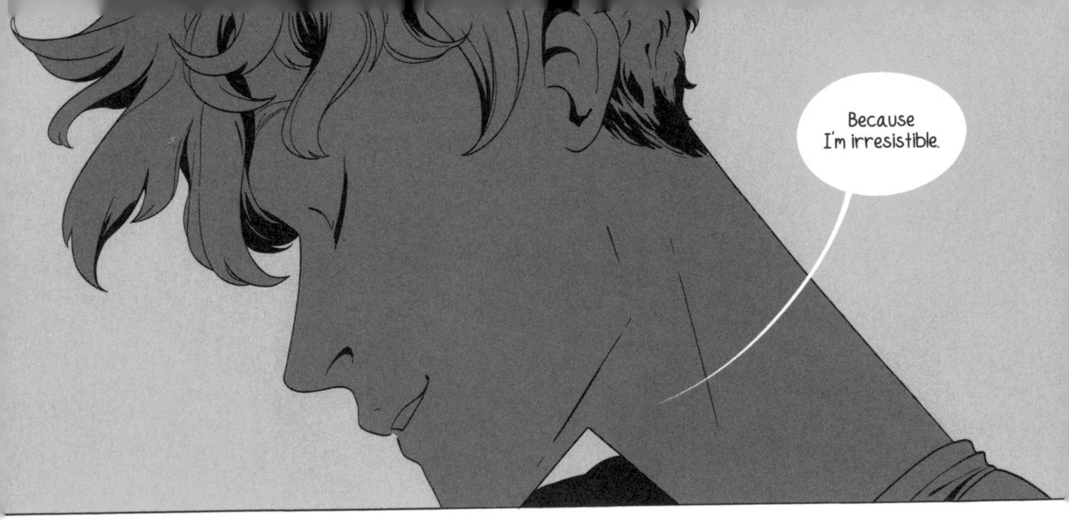
Because
I'm irresistible.

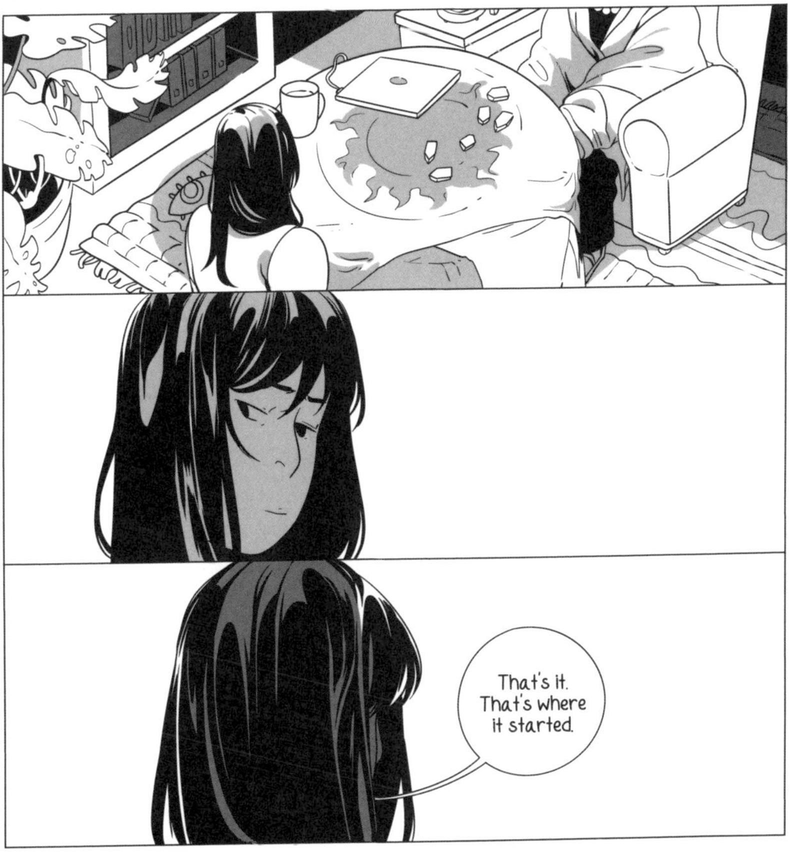
That's it.
That's where
it started.

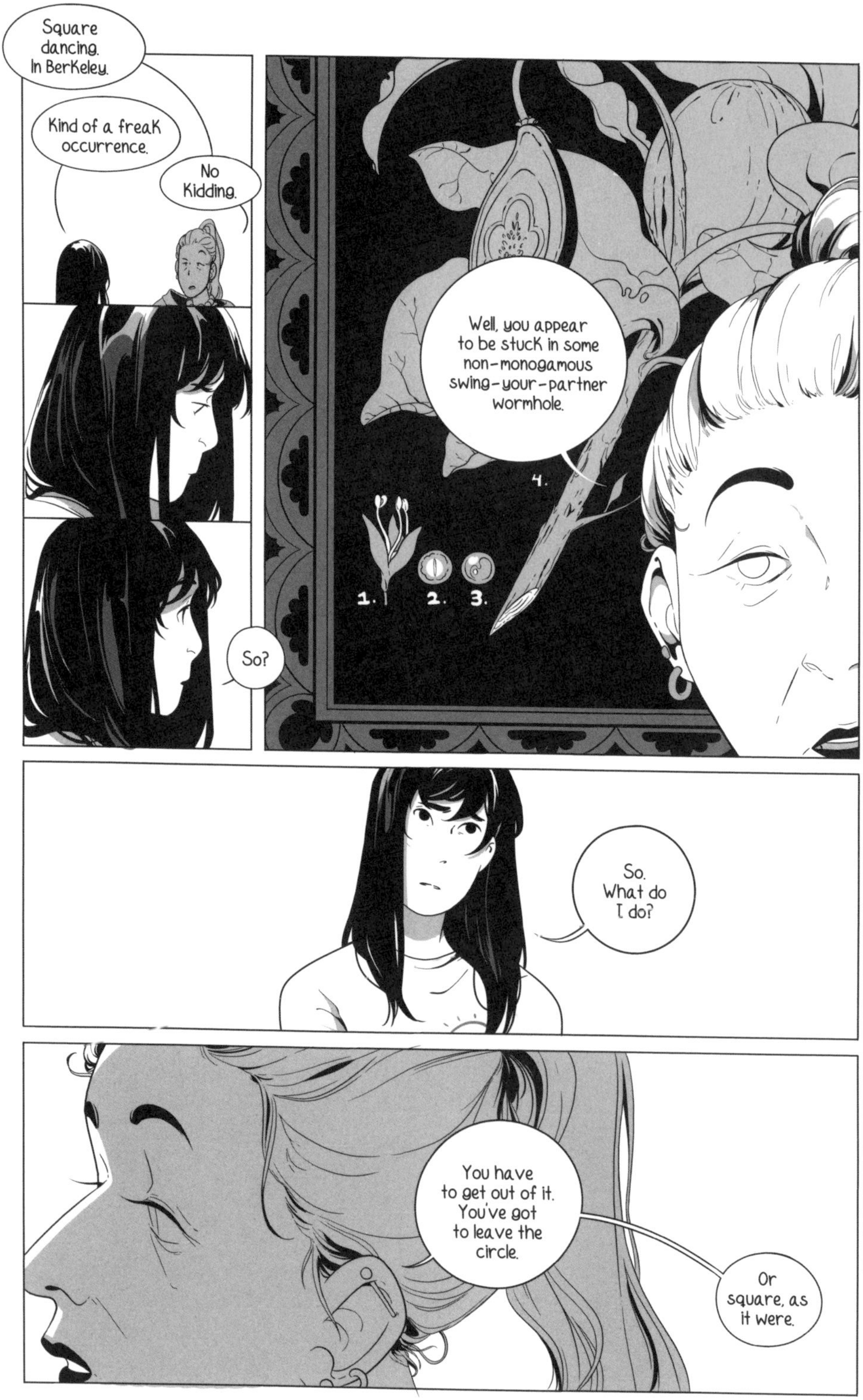
Square dancing. In BerKeley.
Kind of a freaK occurrence.
No Kidding.
Well, you appear to be stucK in some non-monogamous swing-your-partner wormhole.
1.
2.
3.
4.
So?
So. What do I do?
You have to get out of it. You've got to leave the circle.
Or square, as it were.

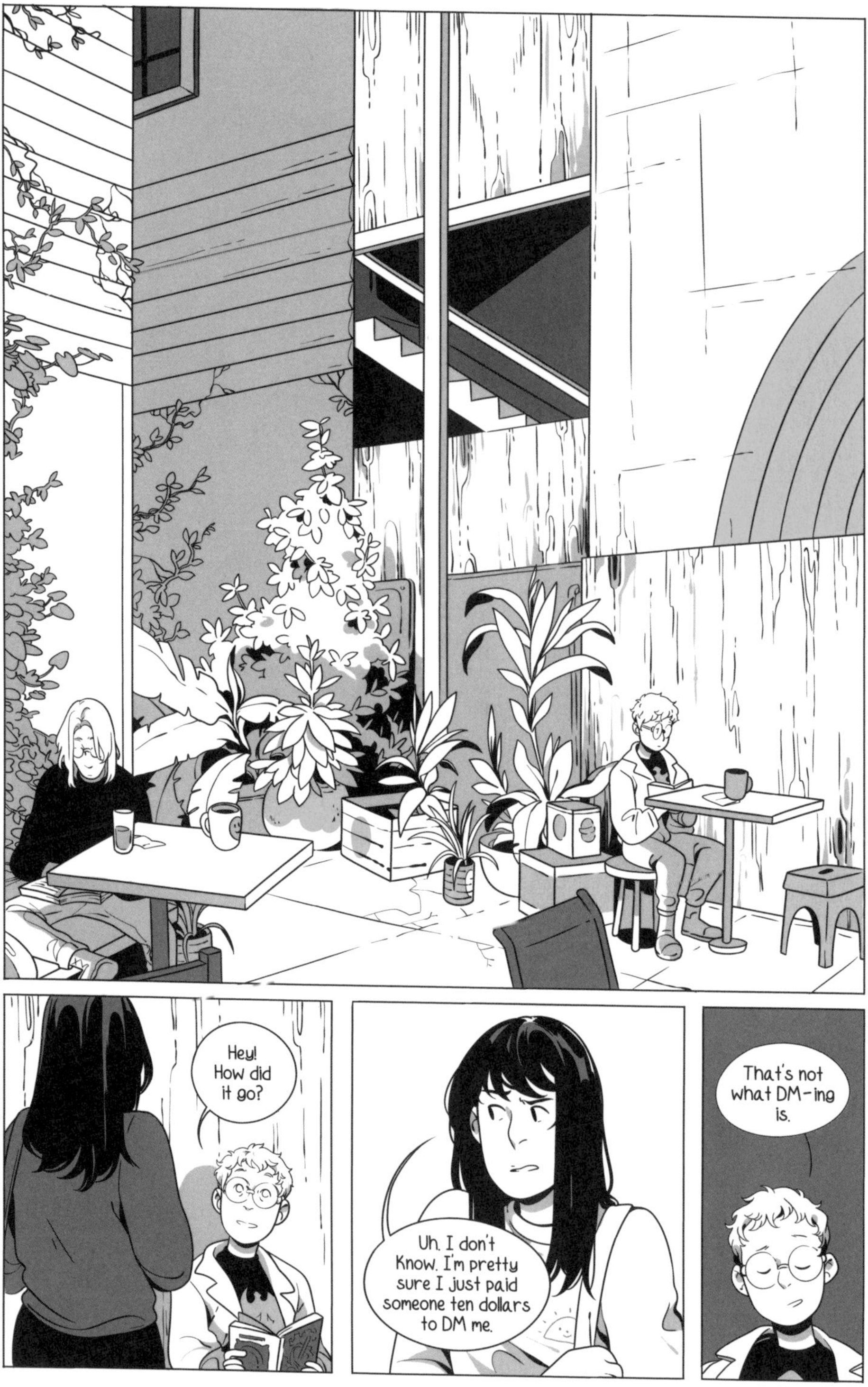
Hey! How did it go?
Uh. I don't Know. I'm pretty sure I just paid someone ten dollars to DM me.
That's not what DM-ing is.

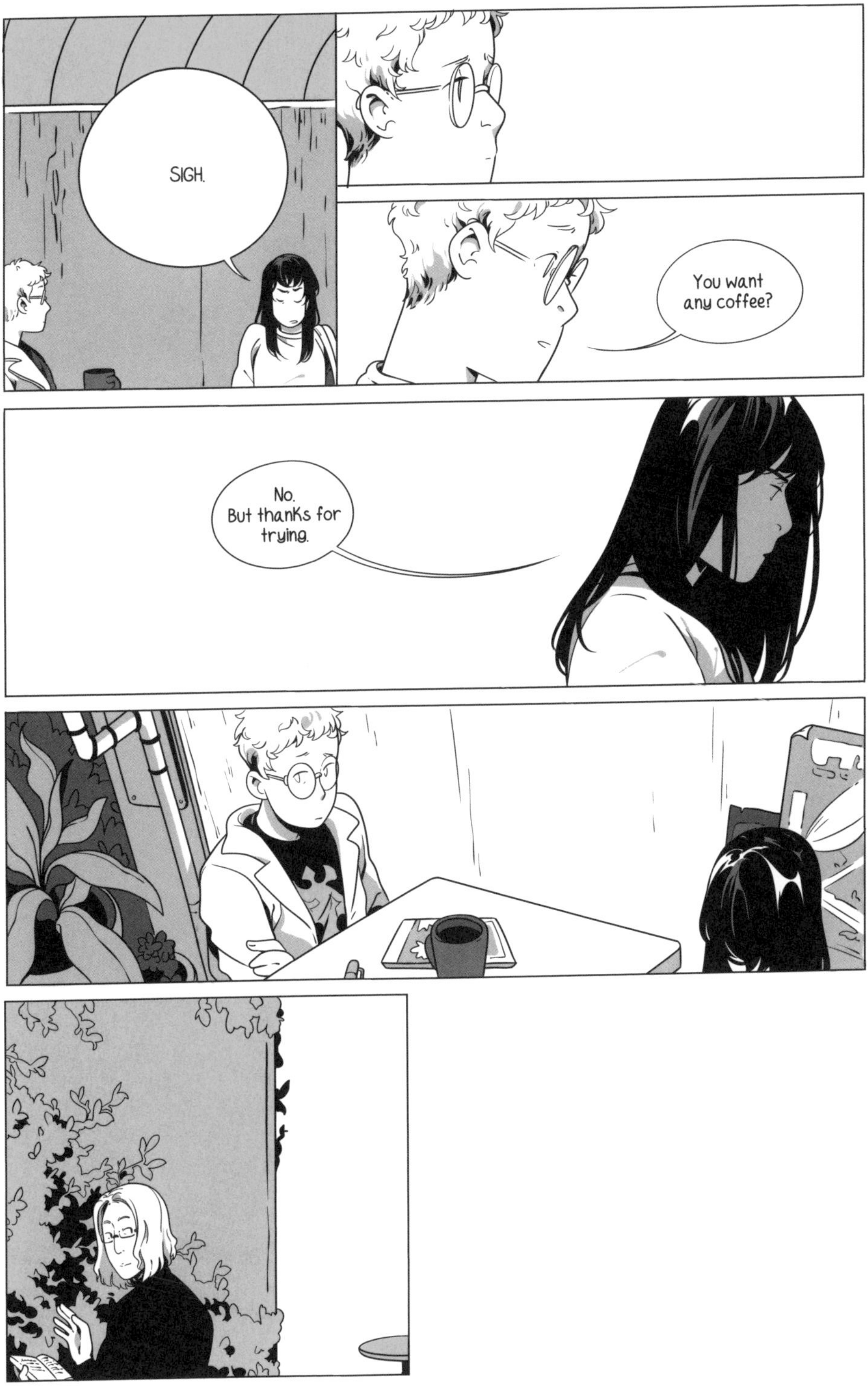
SIGH.
You want any coffee?
No. But thanks for trying.

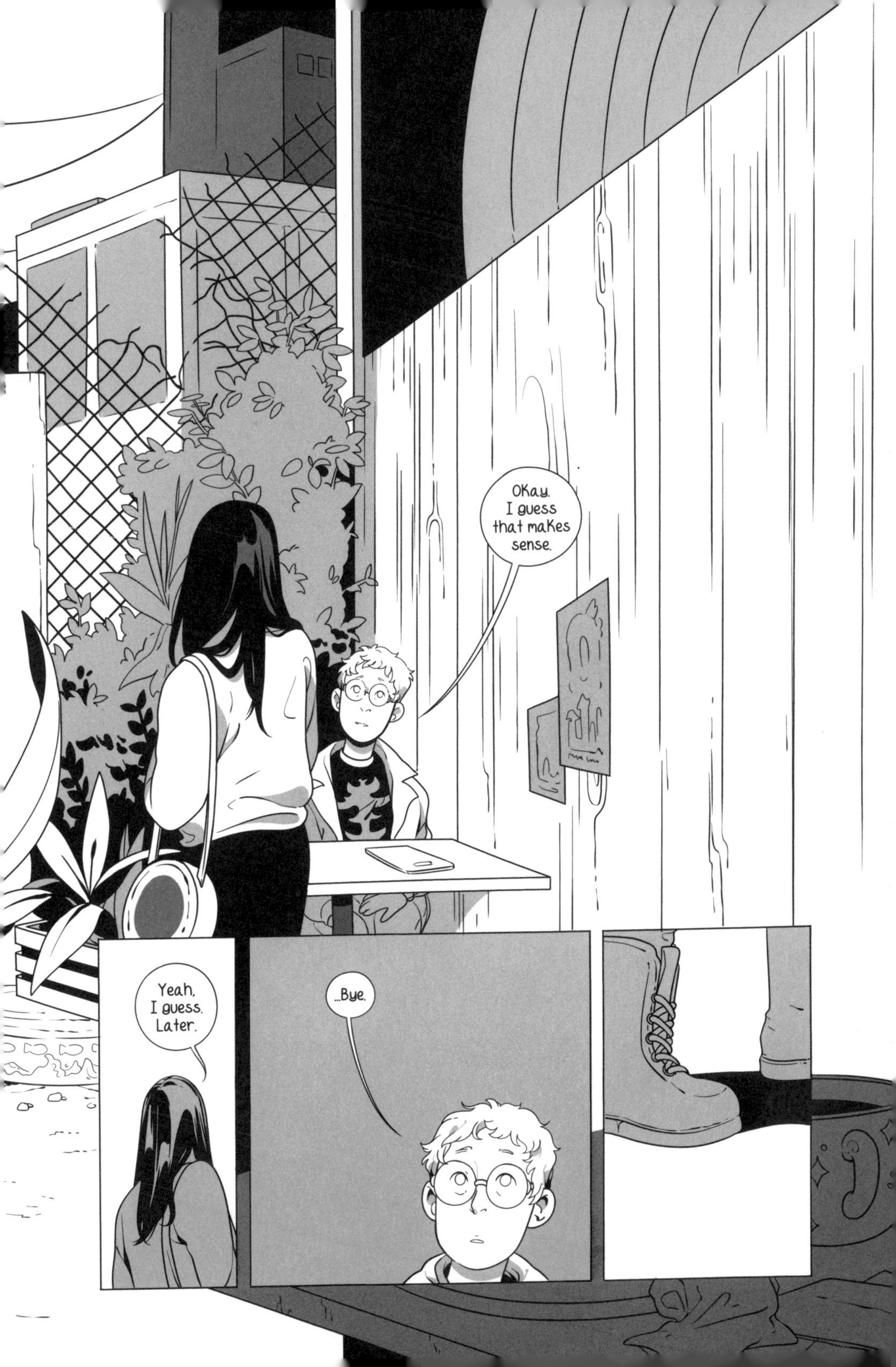
OKay. I guess that maKes sense.
Yeah, I guess. Later.
...Bye.

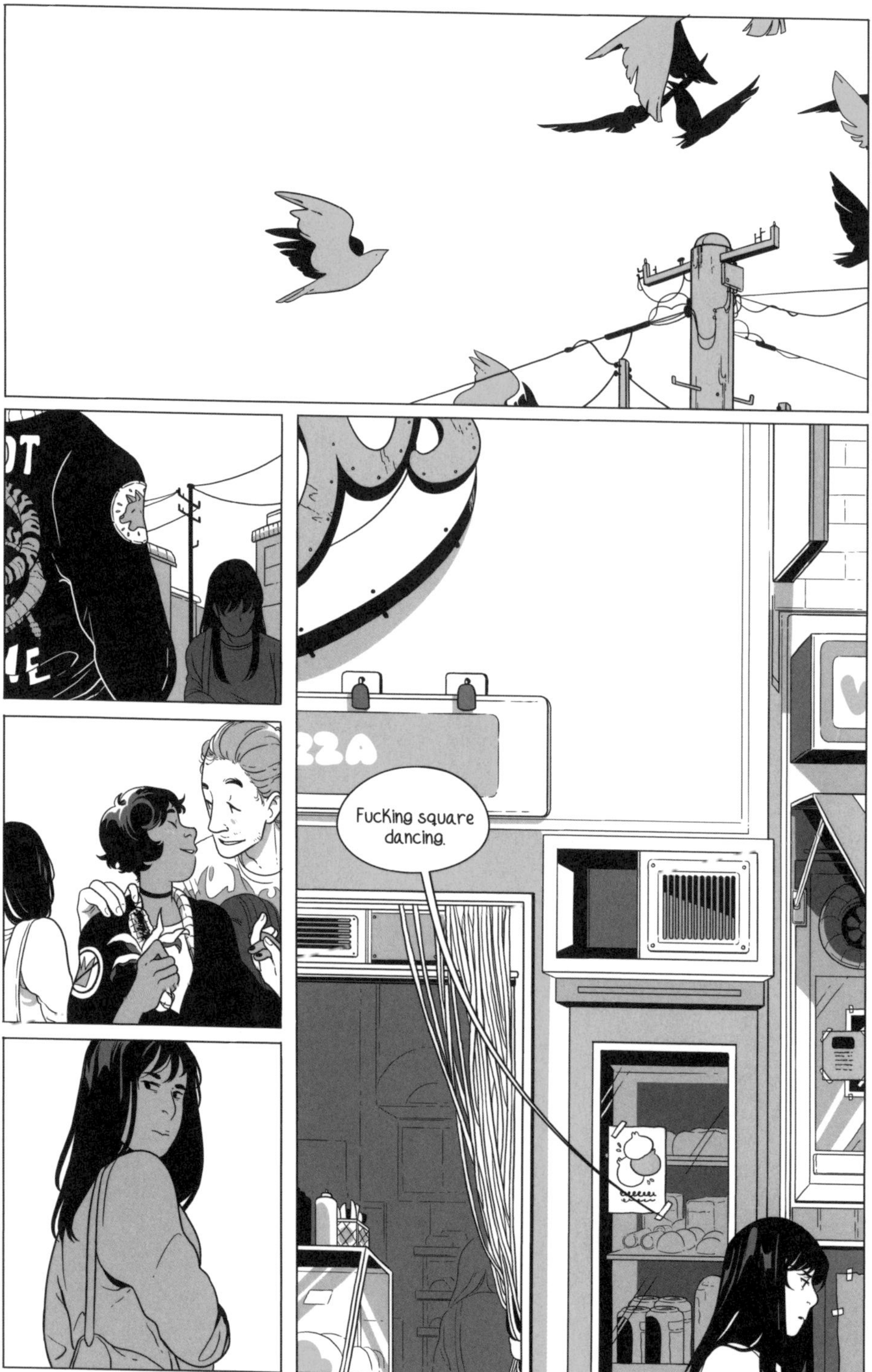
Fucking square dancing.

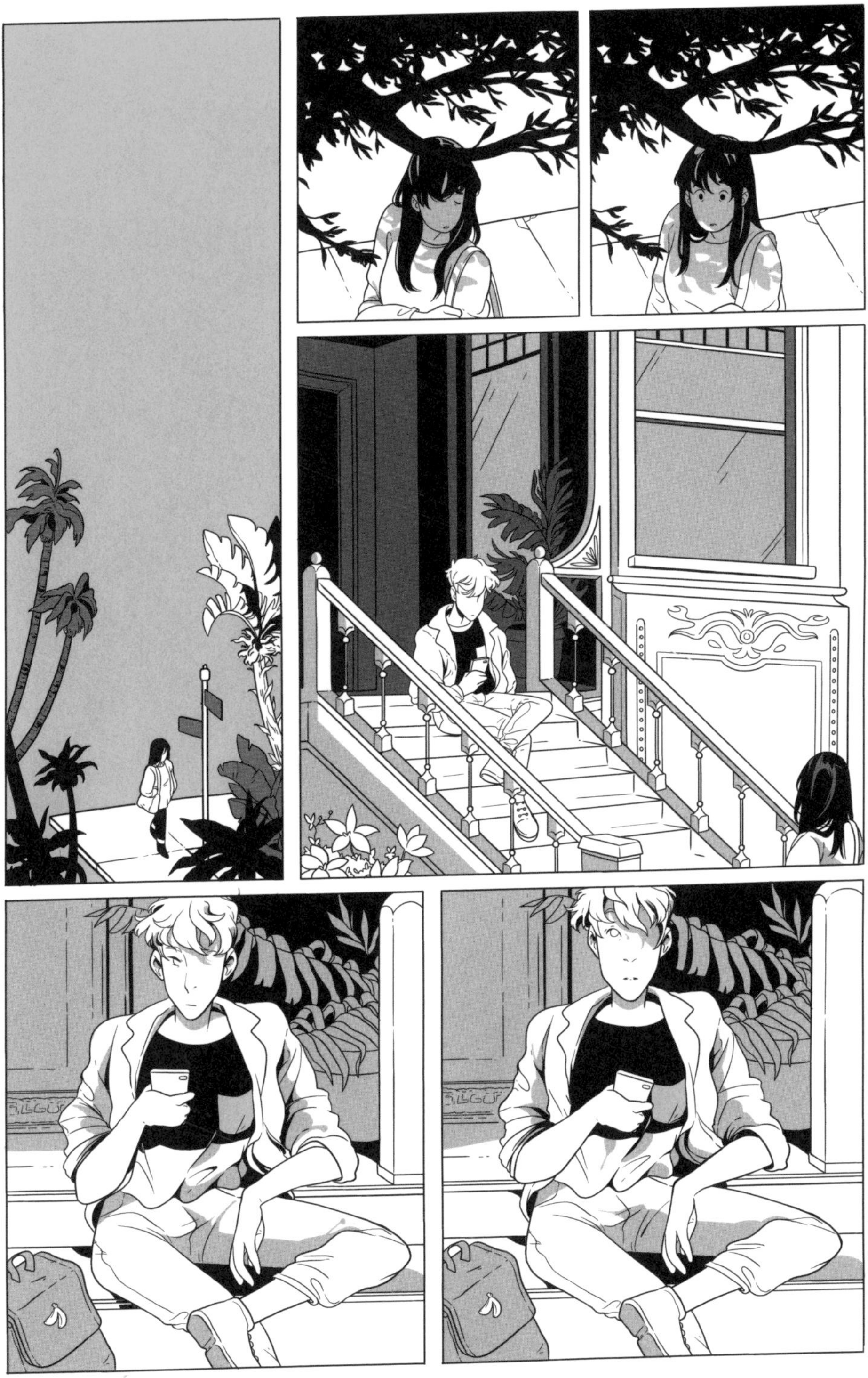

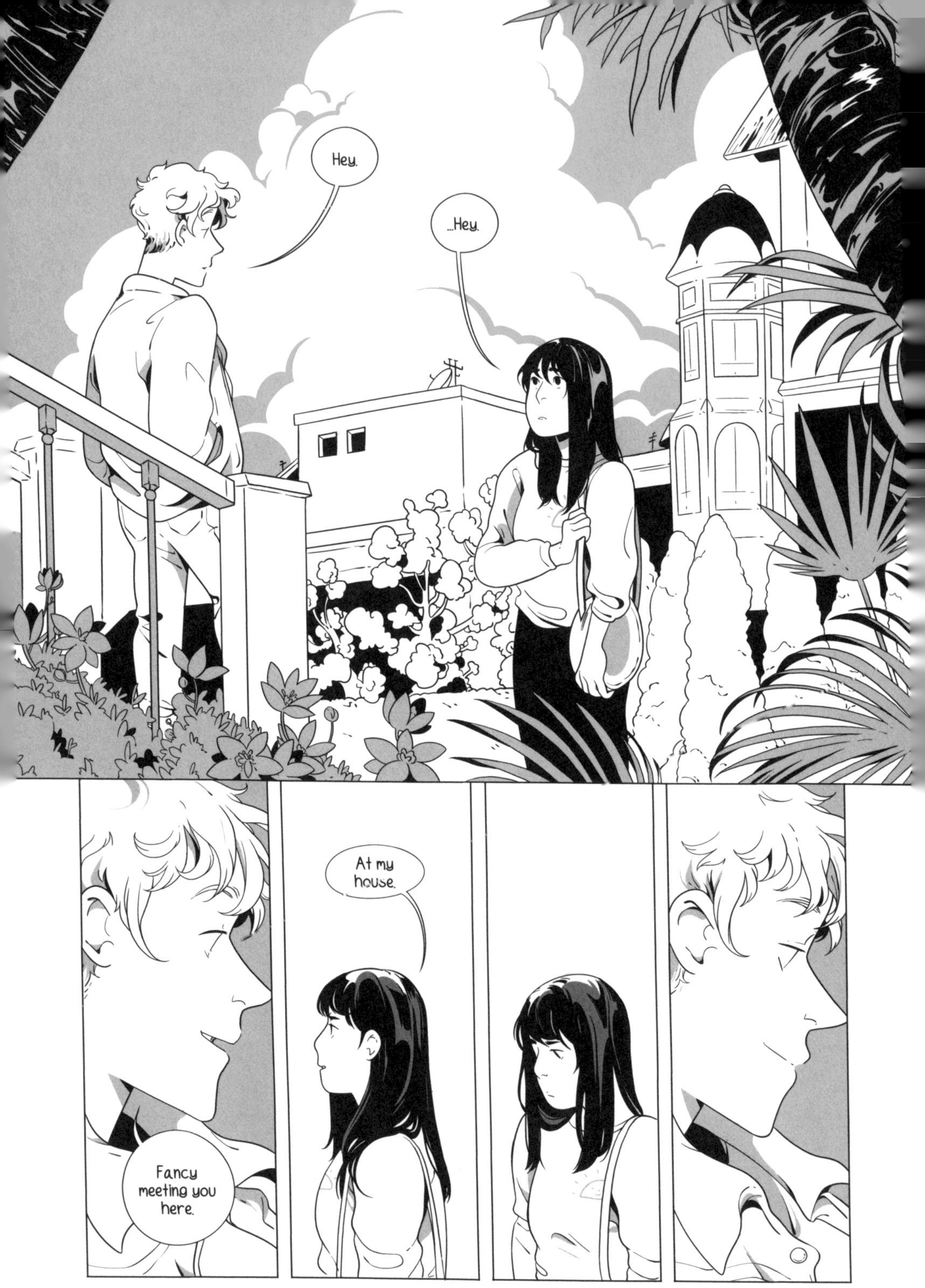
Hey.
...Hey.
Fancy meeting you here.
At my house.

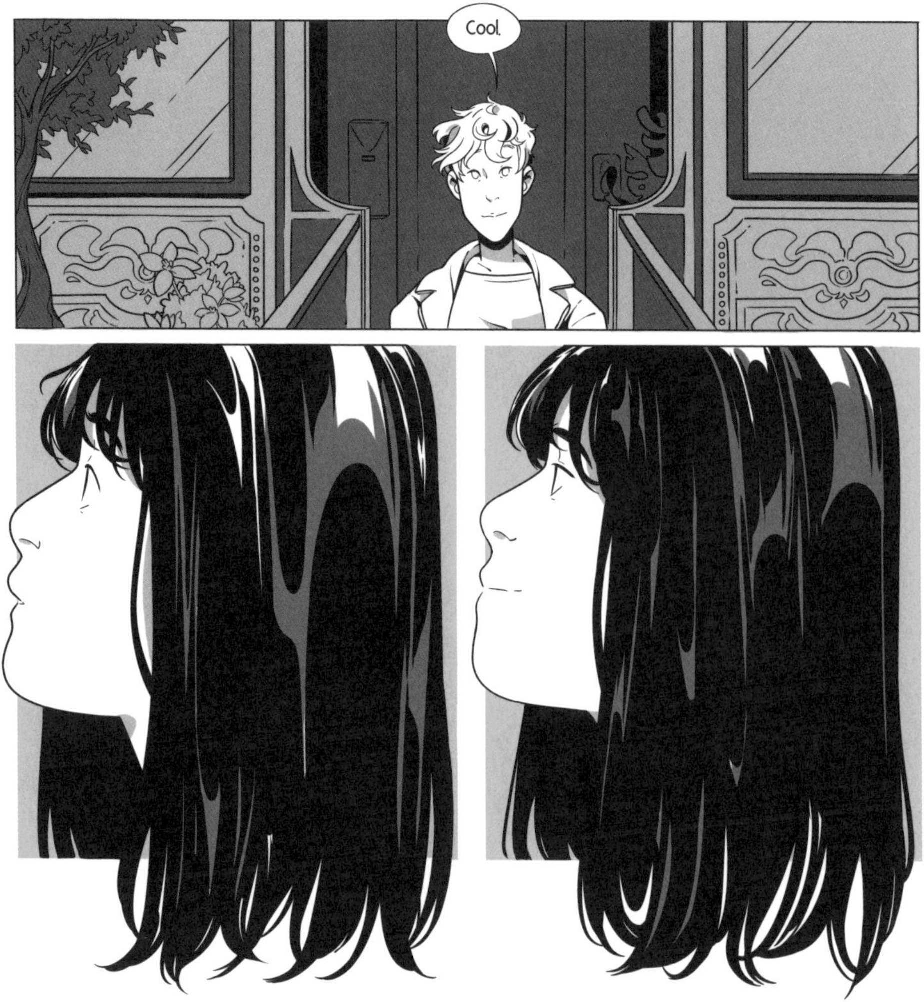
Cool.

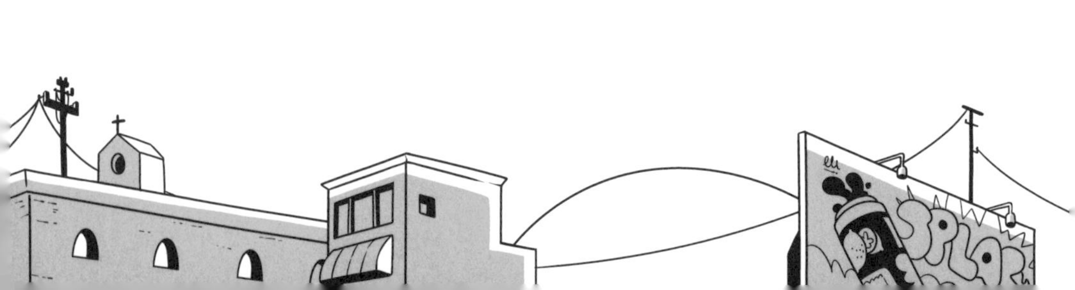

Dear Anna Vice,
Me again.
So. Update.

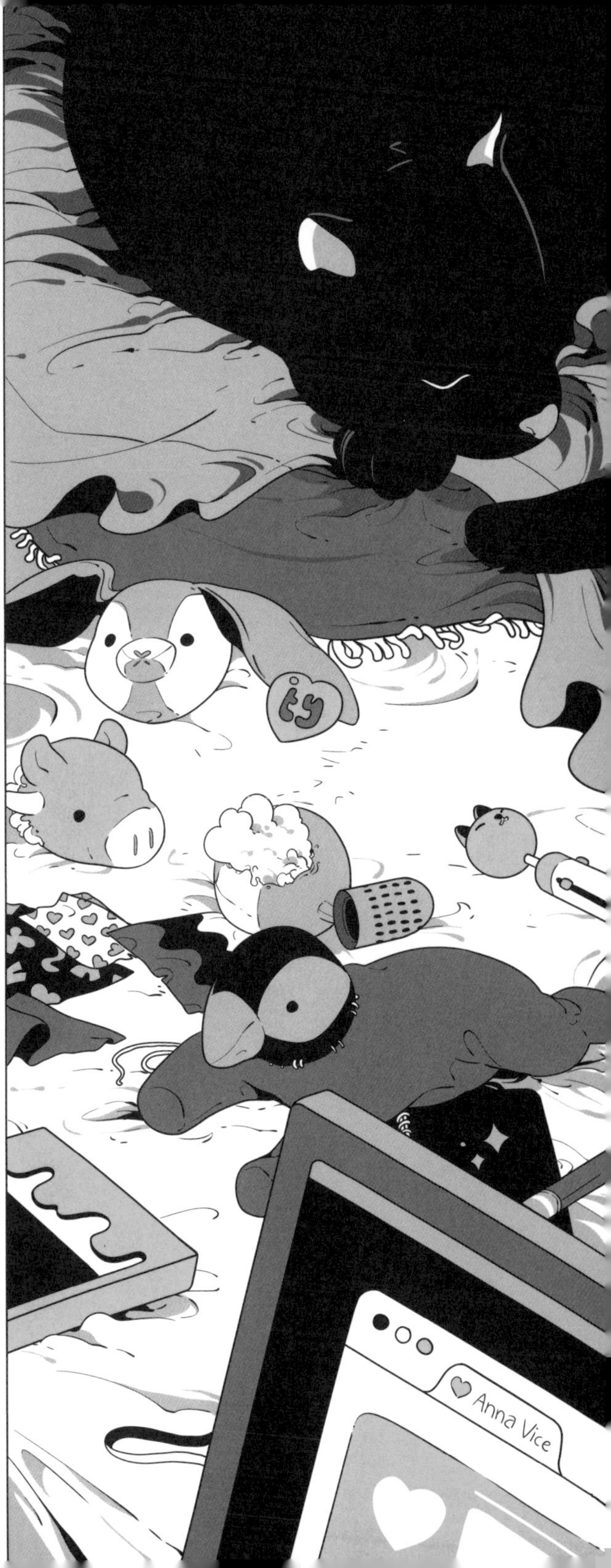
ty
Anna Vice

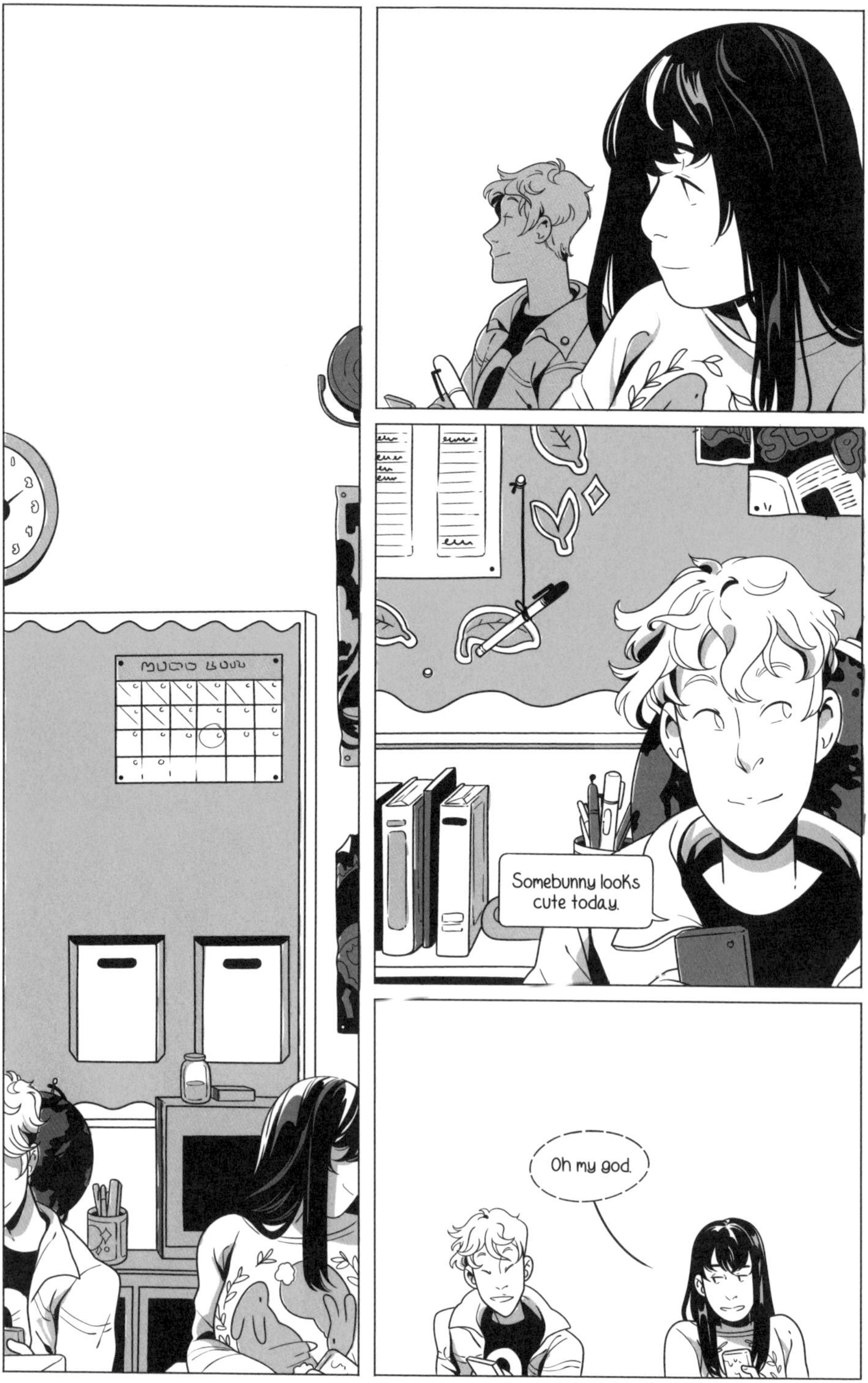
Somebunny looks cute today.
Oh my god.

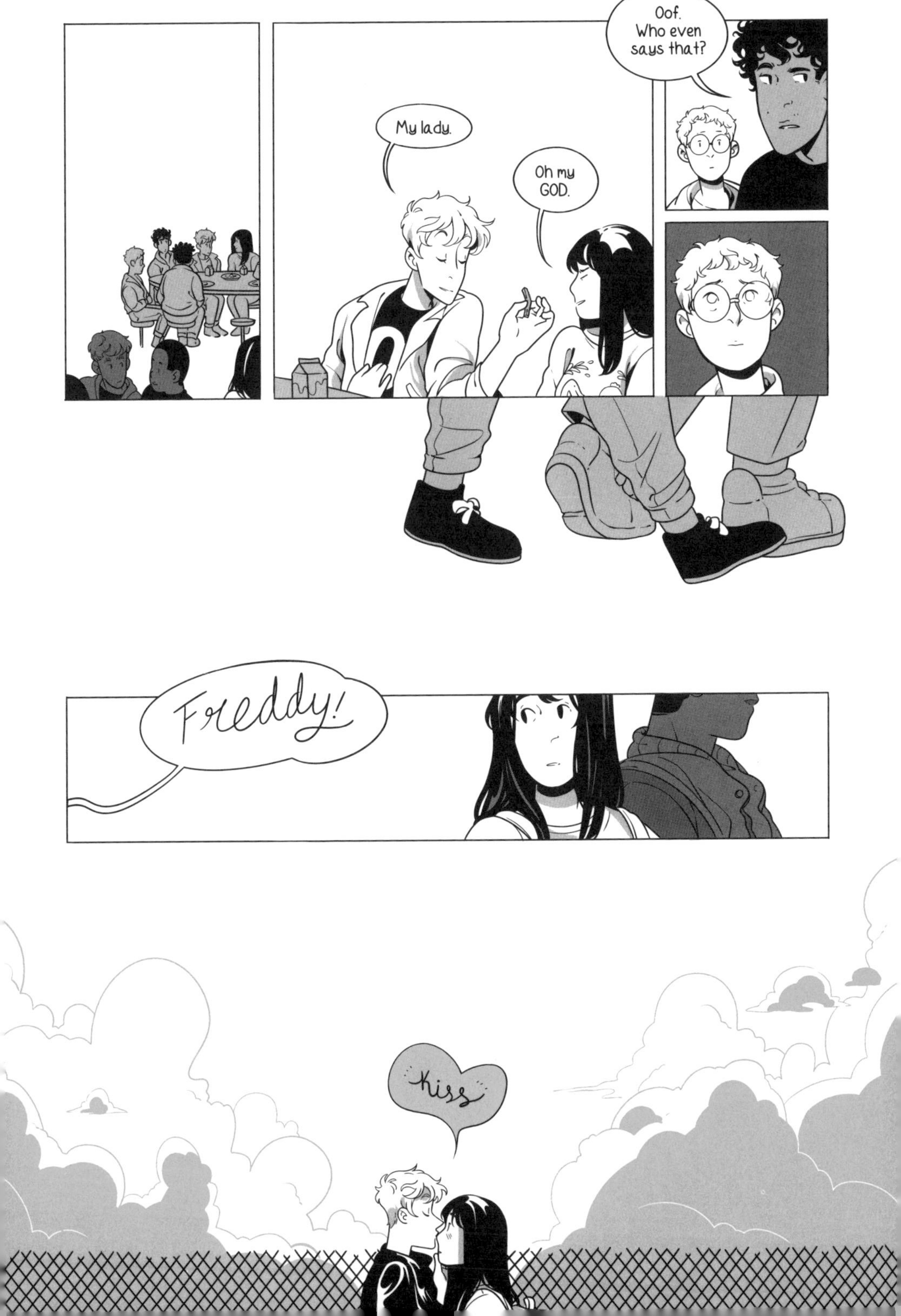
My lady.
Oh my GOD.
Oof. Who even says that?
Freddy!
Kiss

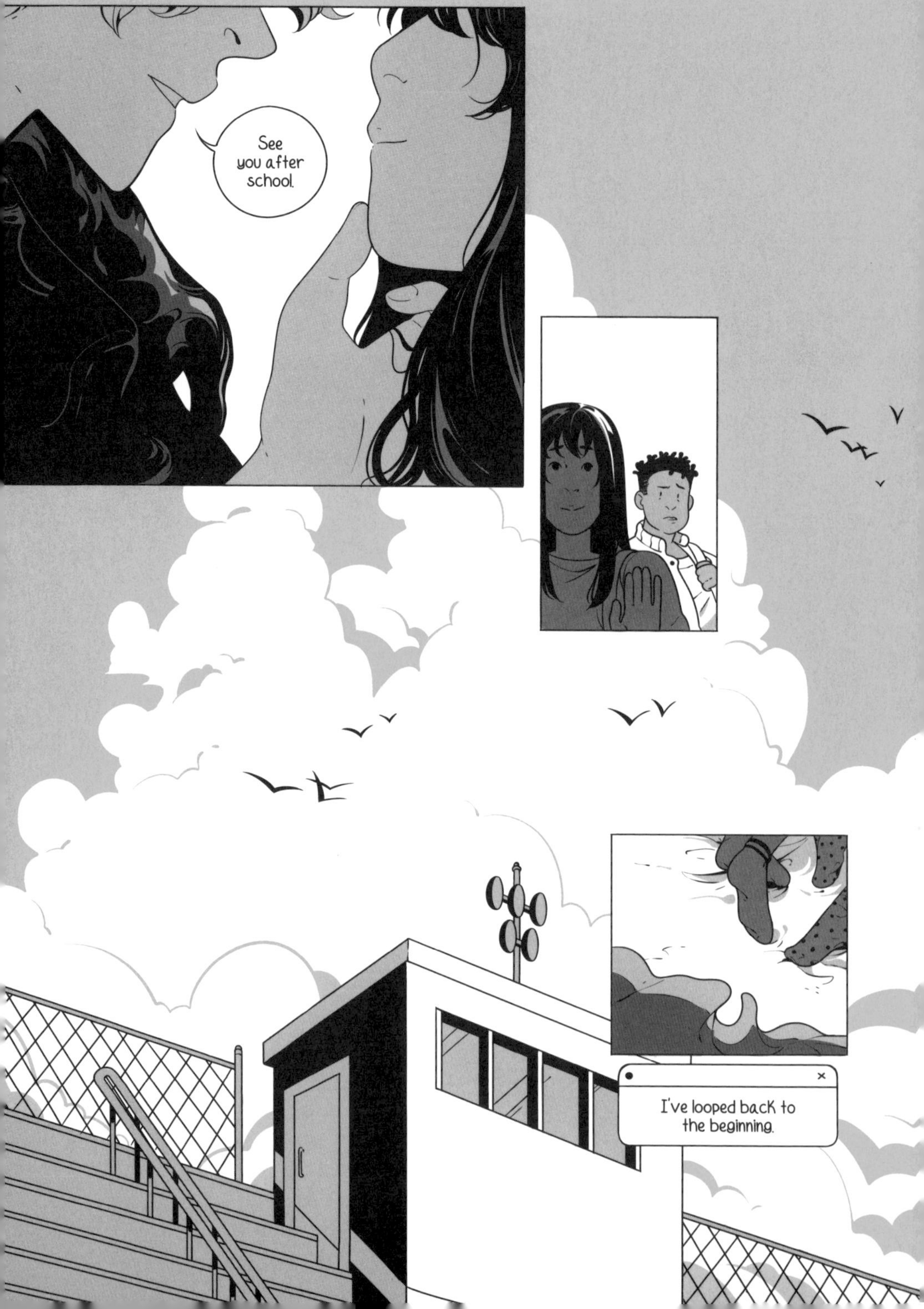

See you after school.
I've looped back to the beginning.

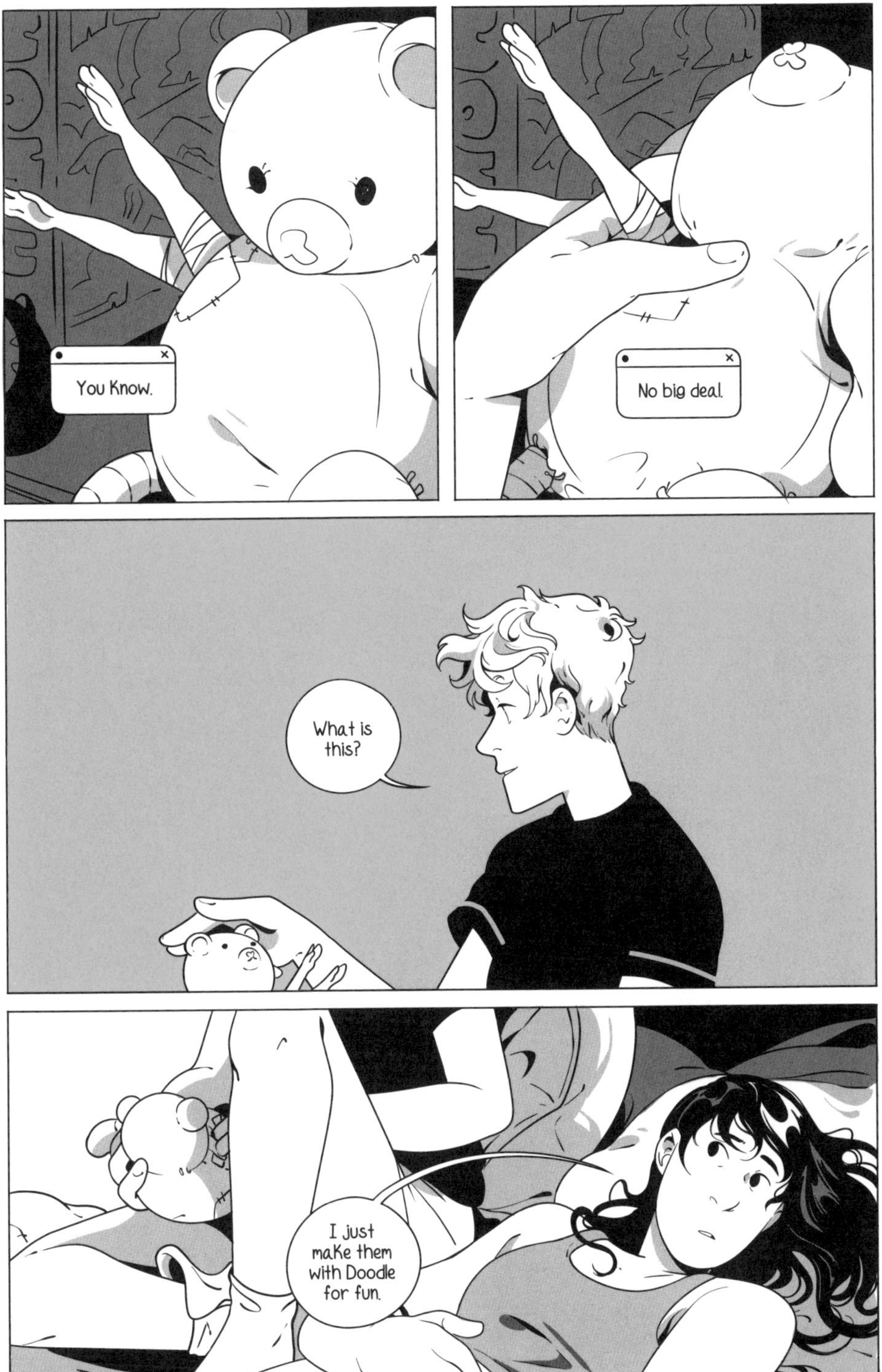
You Know.
No big deal.
What is this?
I just make them with Doodle for fun.

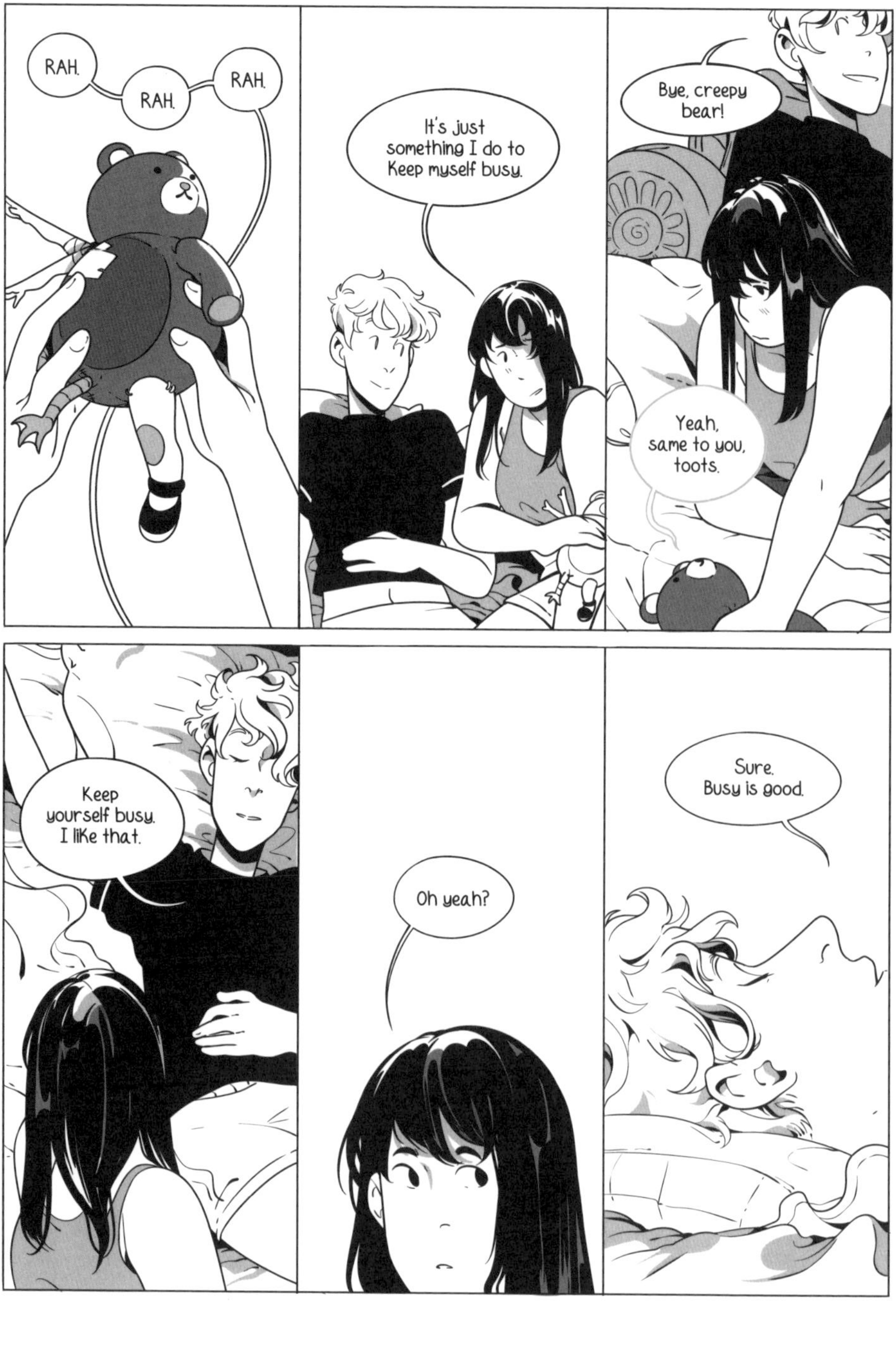
RAH.
RAH.
RAH.
It's just something I do to Keep myself busy.
Bye, creepy bear!
Yeah, same to you, toots.
Keep yourself busy. I like that.
Oh yeah?
Sure. Busy is good.

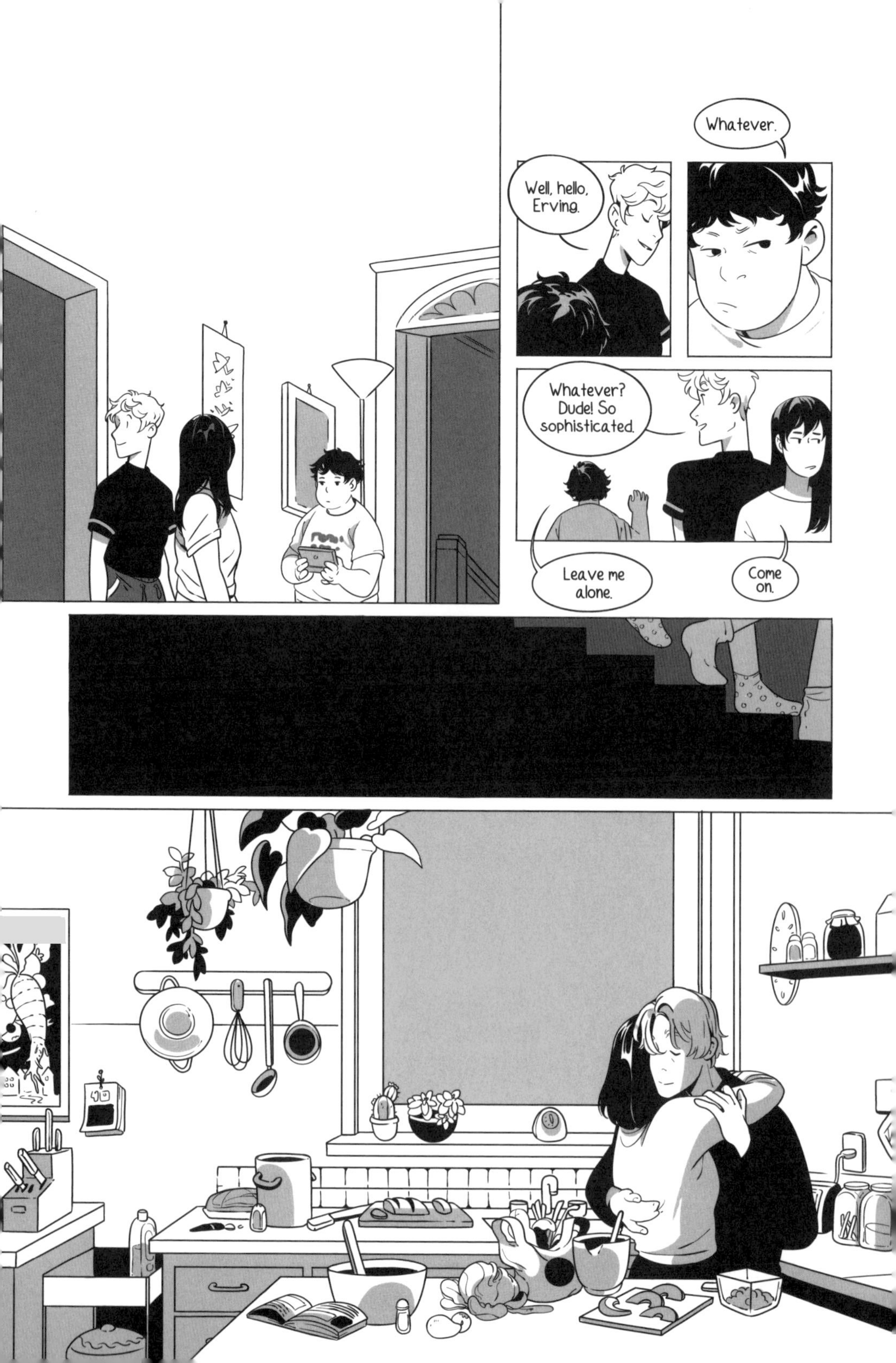
Well, hello, Erving.
Whatever.
Whatever? Dude! So sophisticated.
Leave me alone.
Come on.

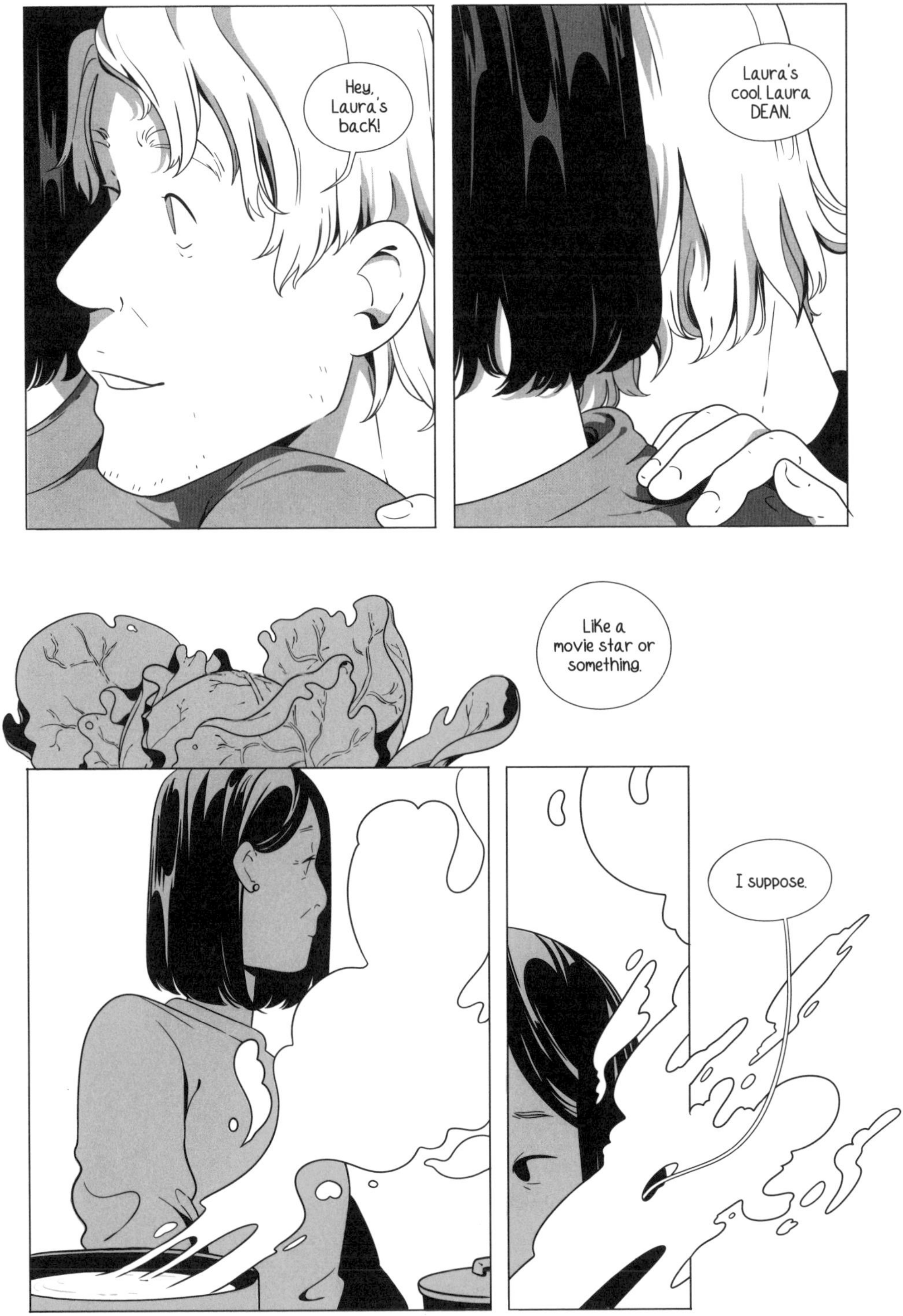
Hey, Laura's back!
Laura's cool. Laura DEAN.
Like a movie star or something.
I suppose.

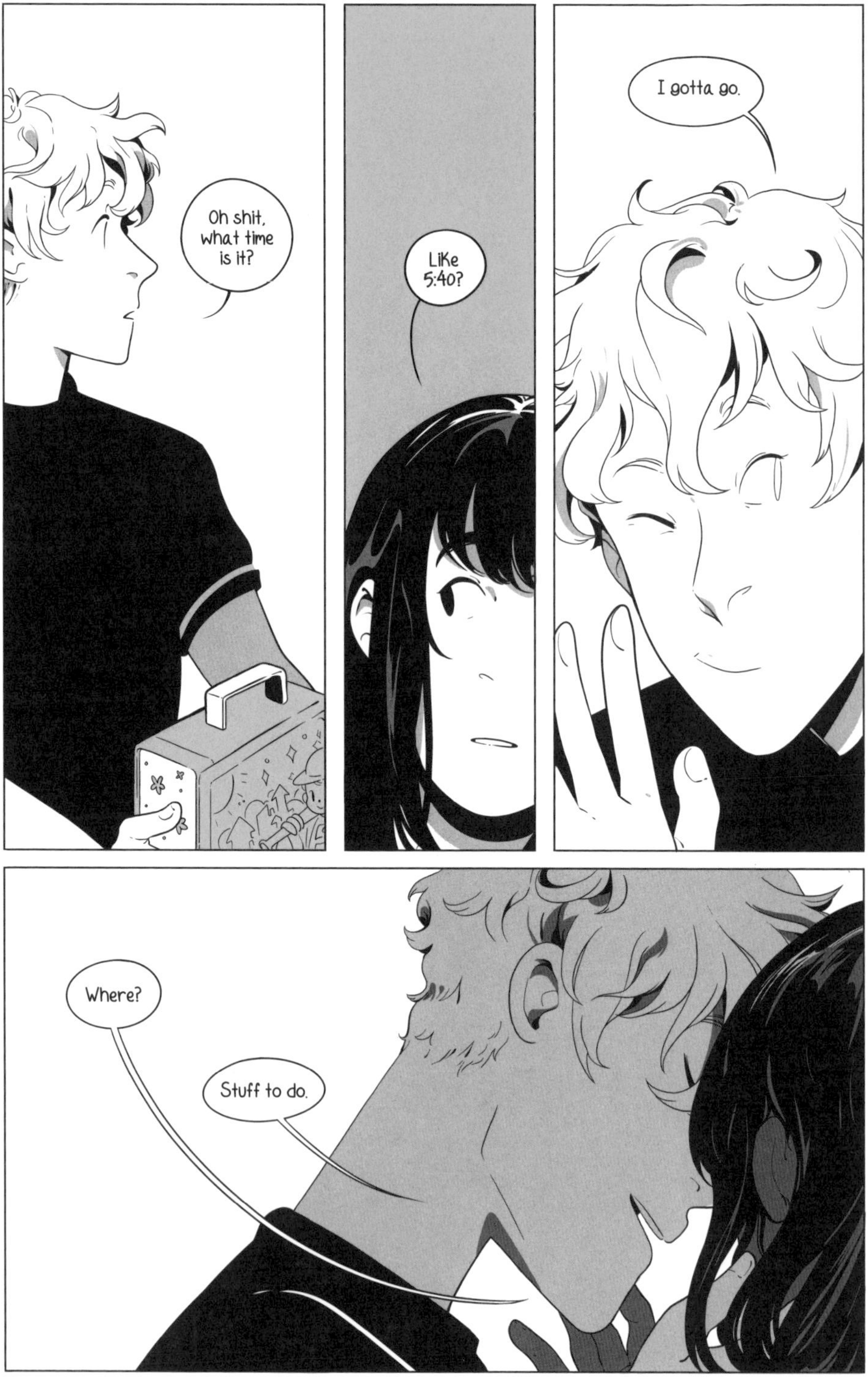
Oh shit, what time is it?
Like 5:40?
I gotta go.
Where?
Stuff to do.

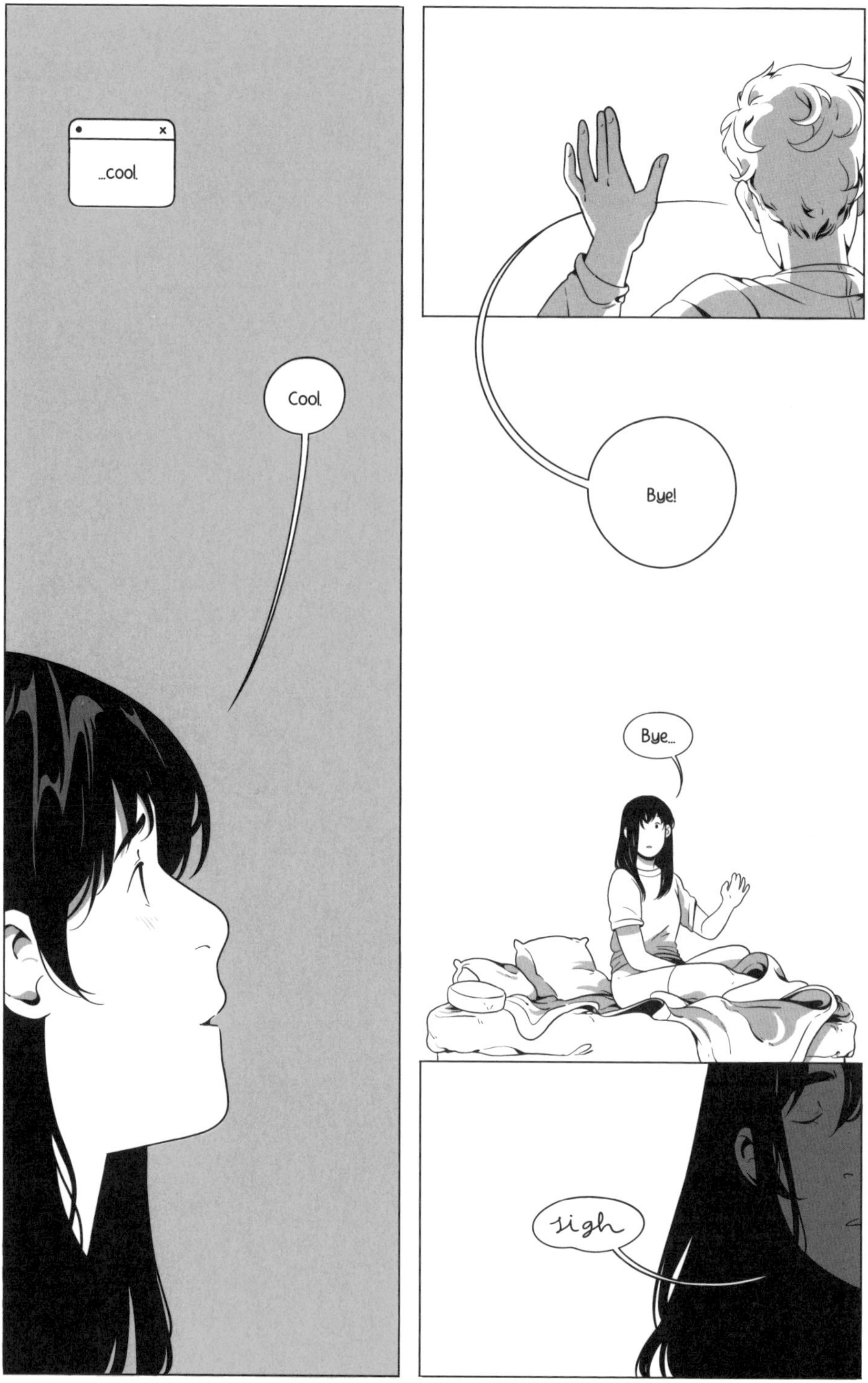
...cool.
Cool.
Bye!
Bye...
sigh

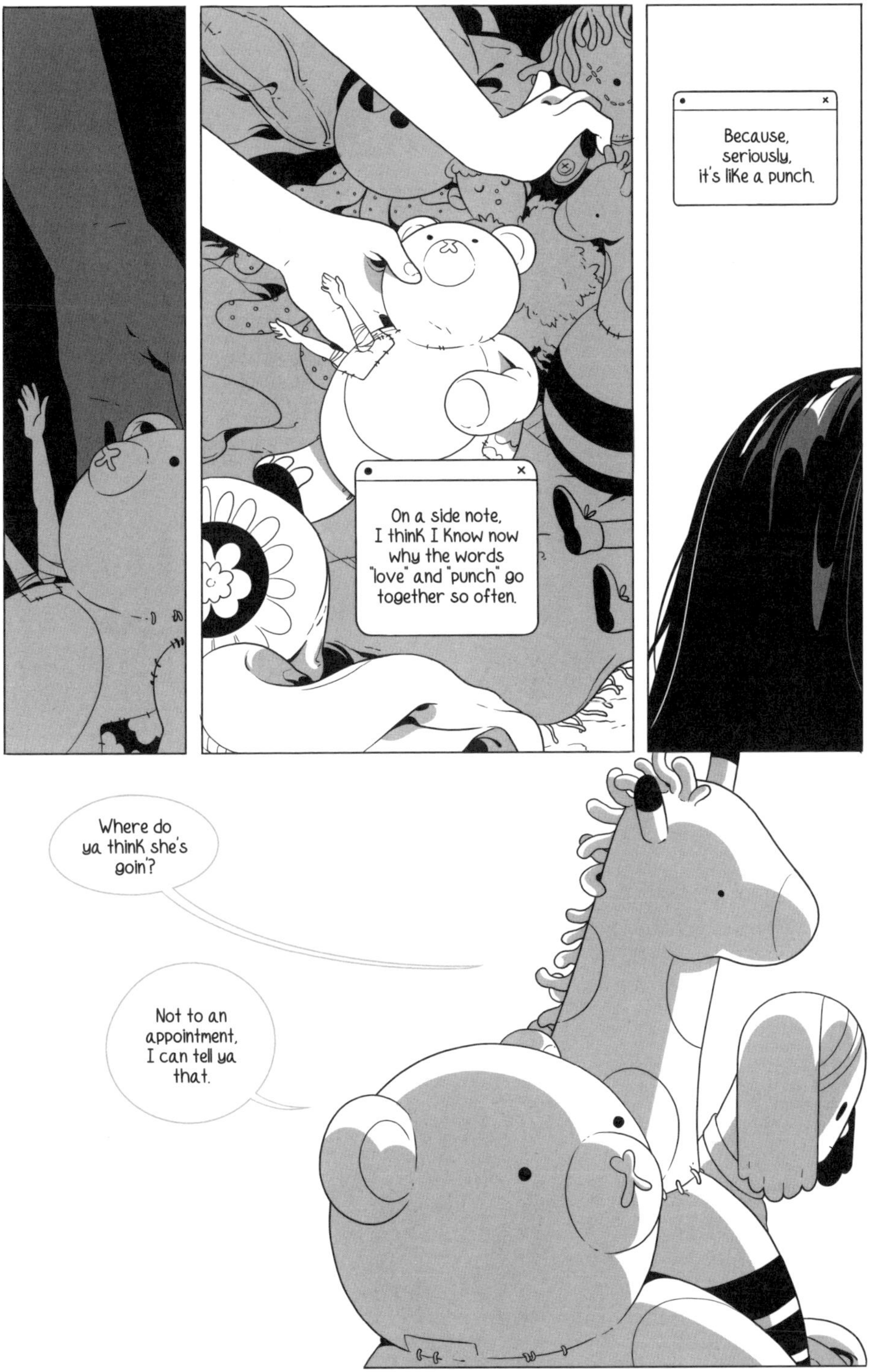
On a side note, I think I Know now why the words "love" and "punch" go together so often.
Because, seriously, it's like a punch.
Where do ya think she's goin'?
Not to an appointment, I can tell ya that.

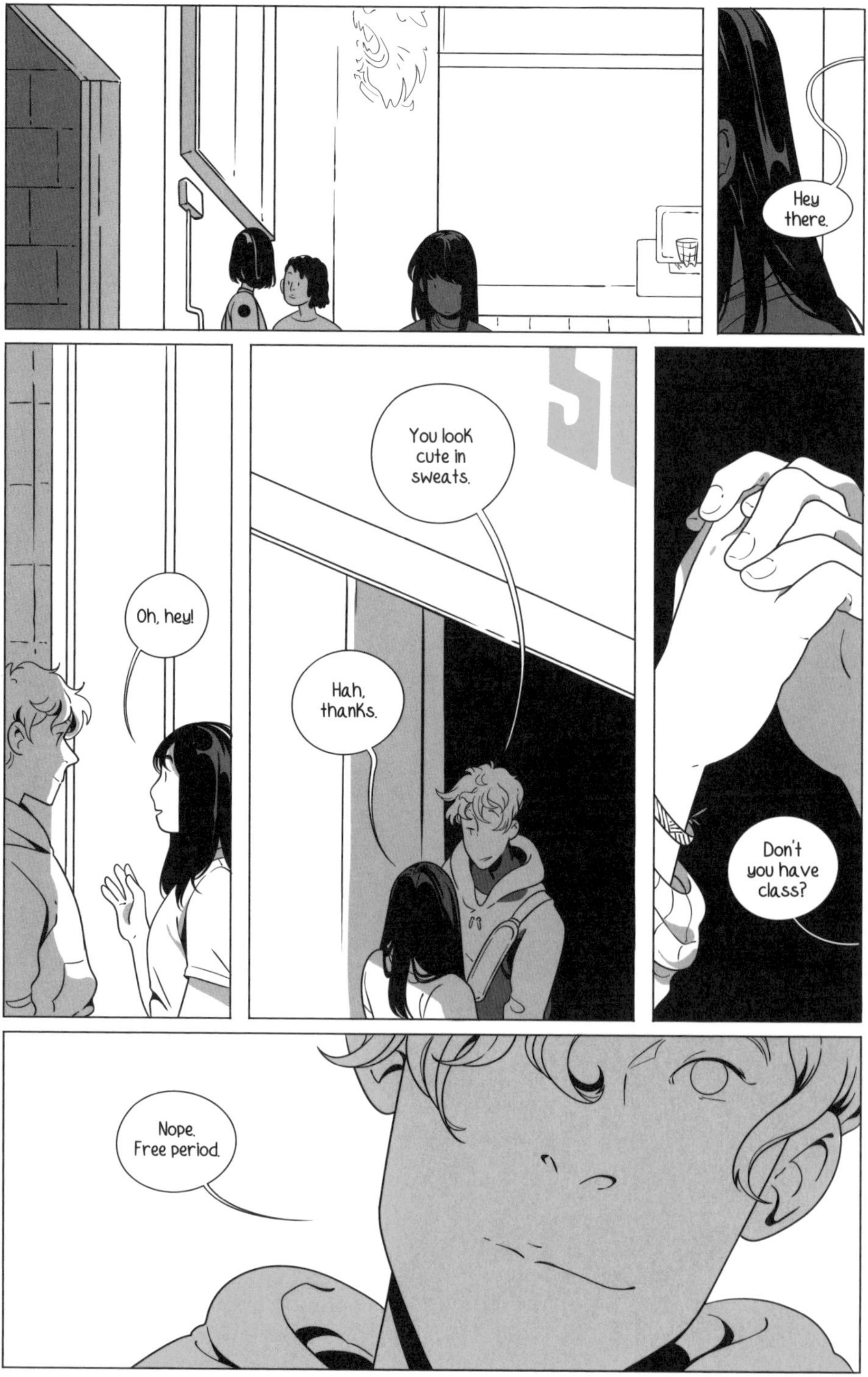
Hey there.
Oh, hey!
You look cute in sweats.
Hah, thanks.
Don't you have class?
Nope. Free period.

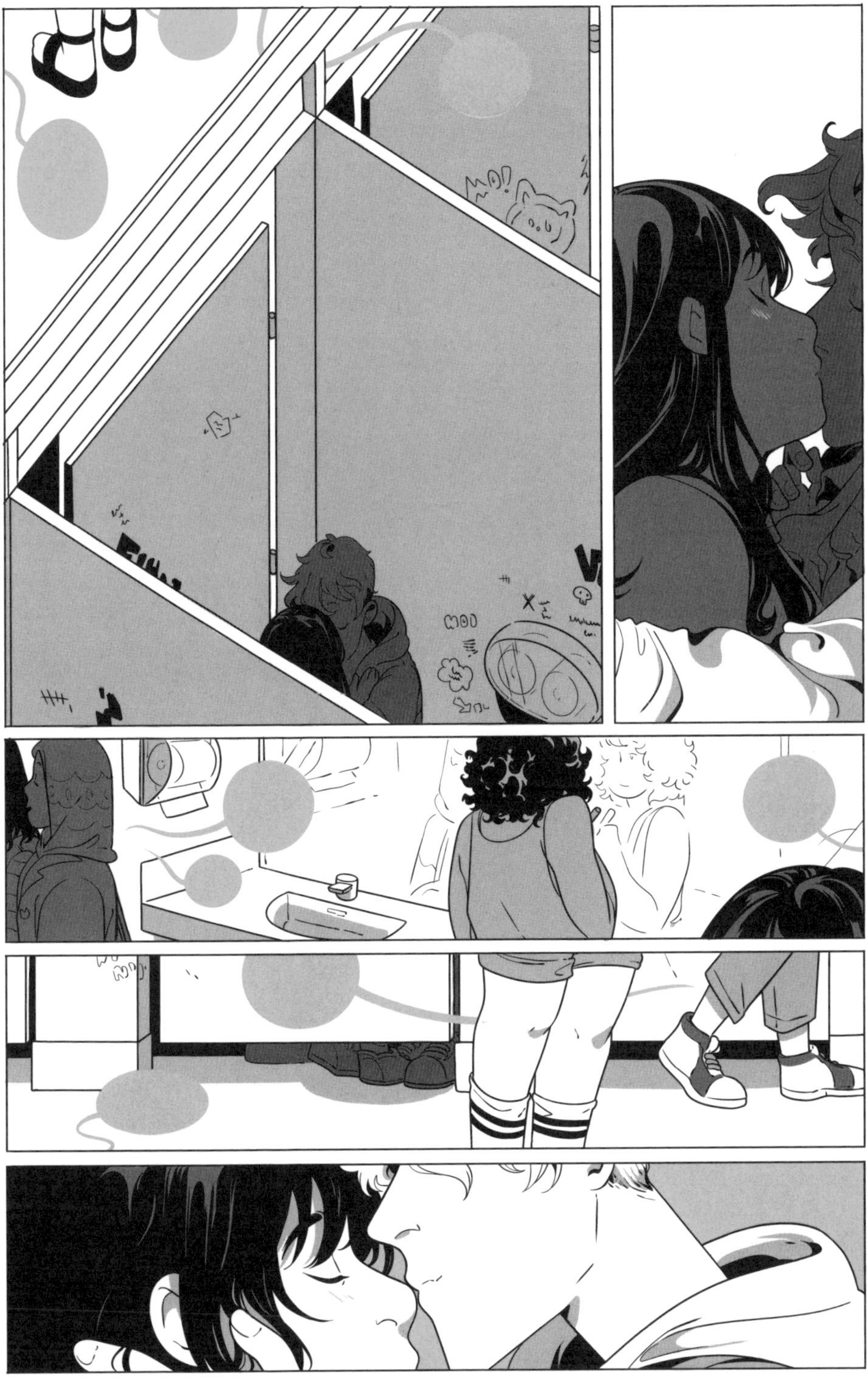

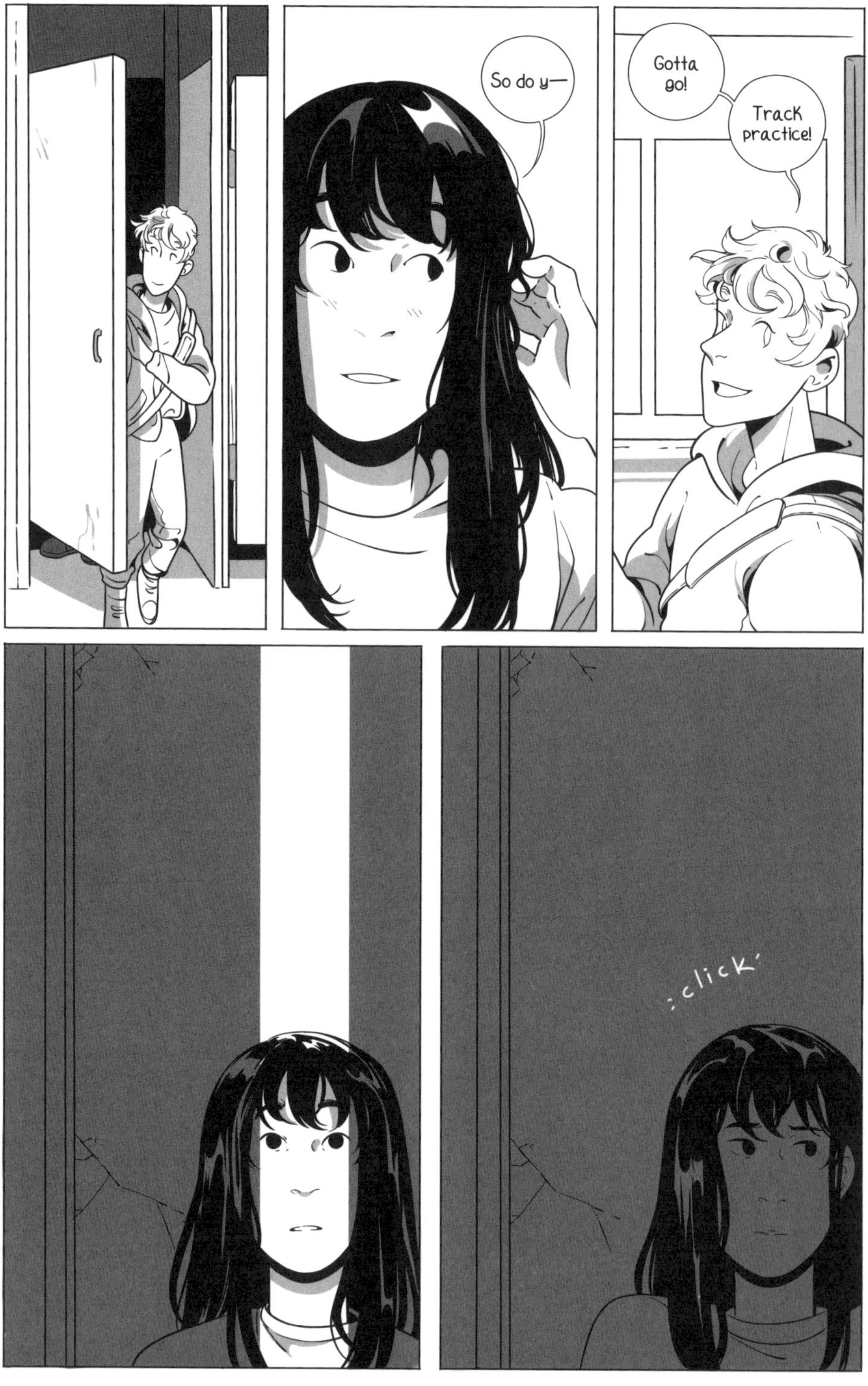
So do y—
Gotta go!
Track practice!
click

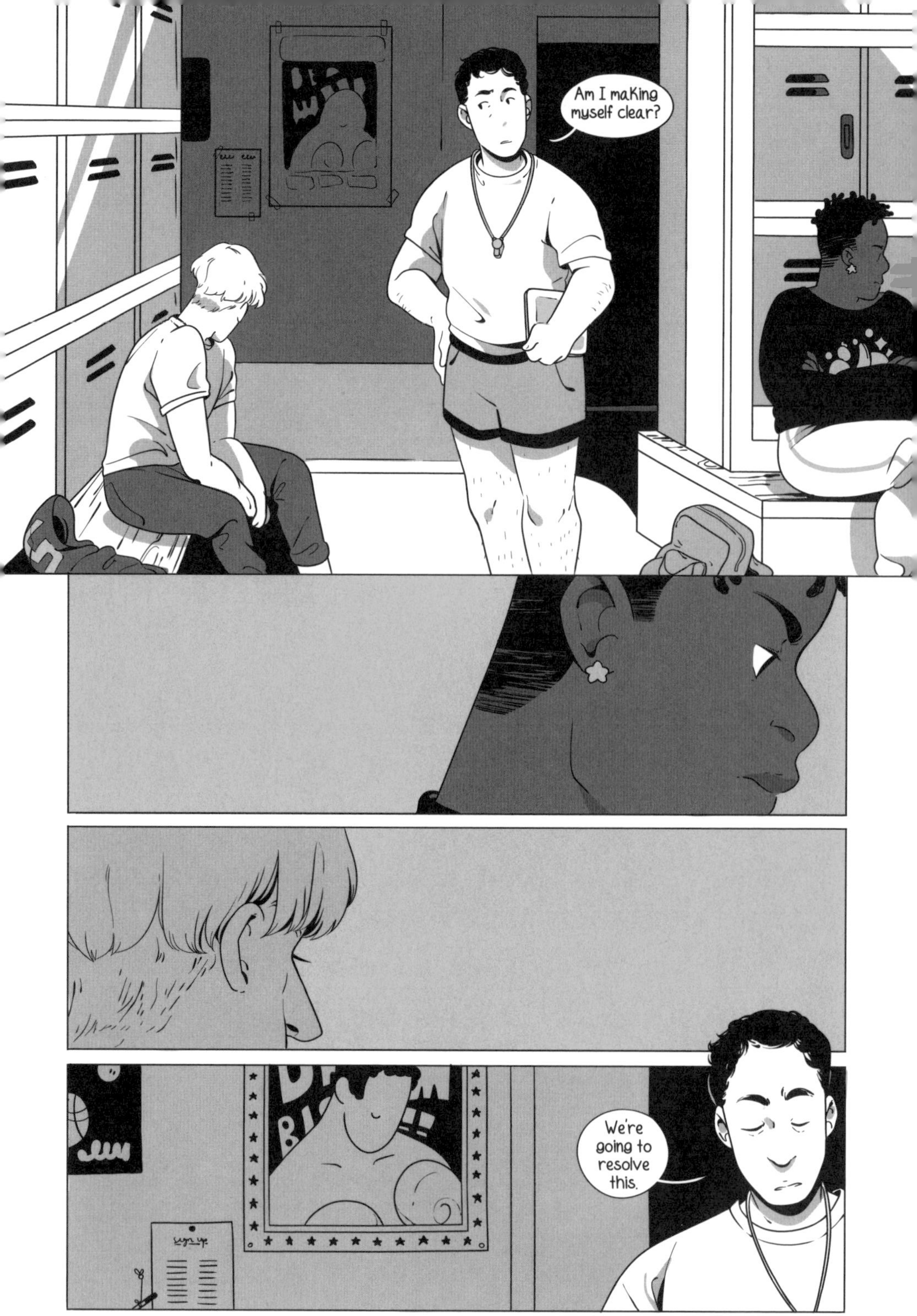
Am I making myself clear?
We're going to resolve this.

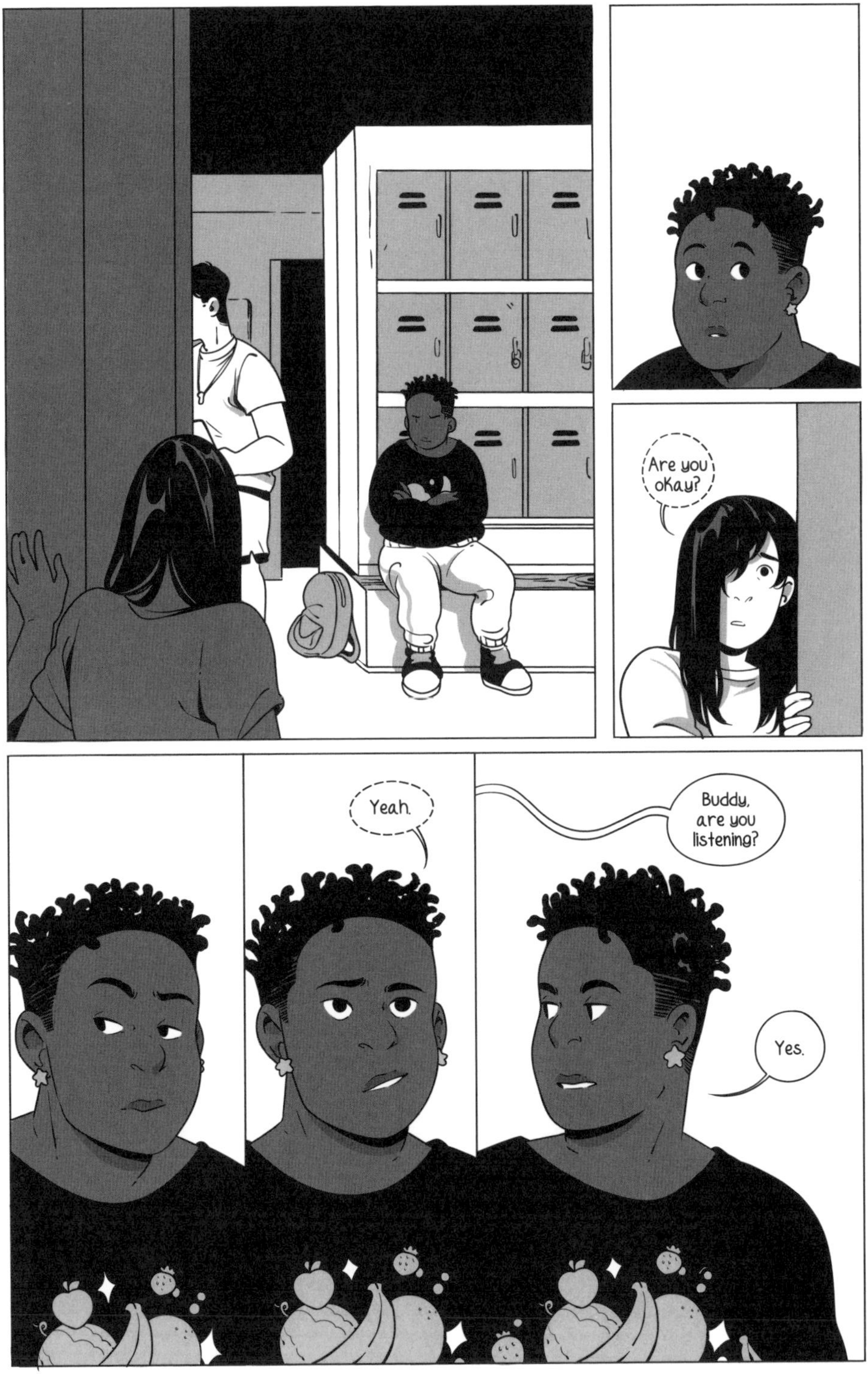
Are you oKay?
Yeah.
Buddy, are you listening?
Yes.

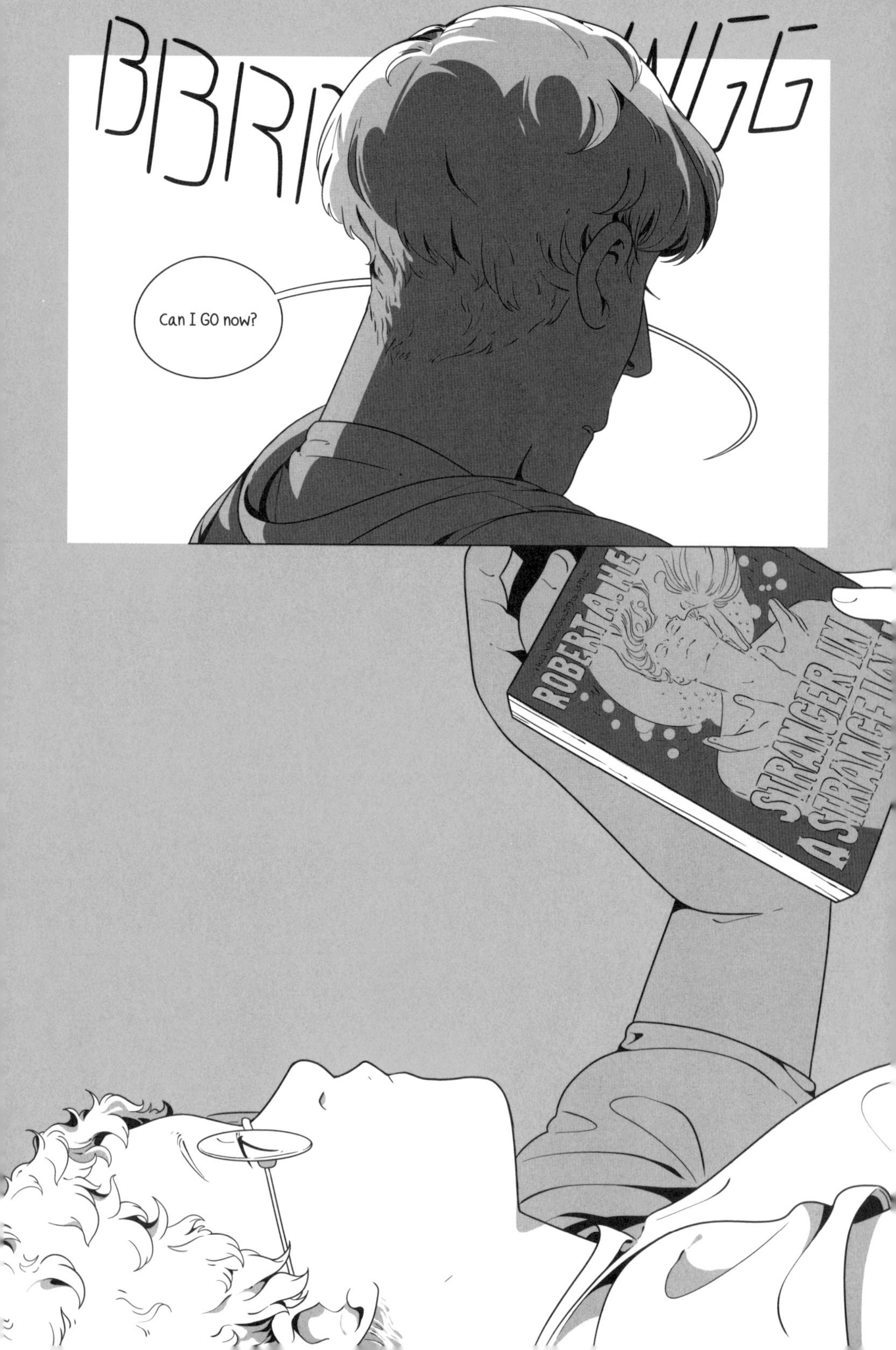
Can I GO now?
ROBERT A. HE
STRANGER IN A STRANGE LA

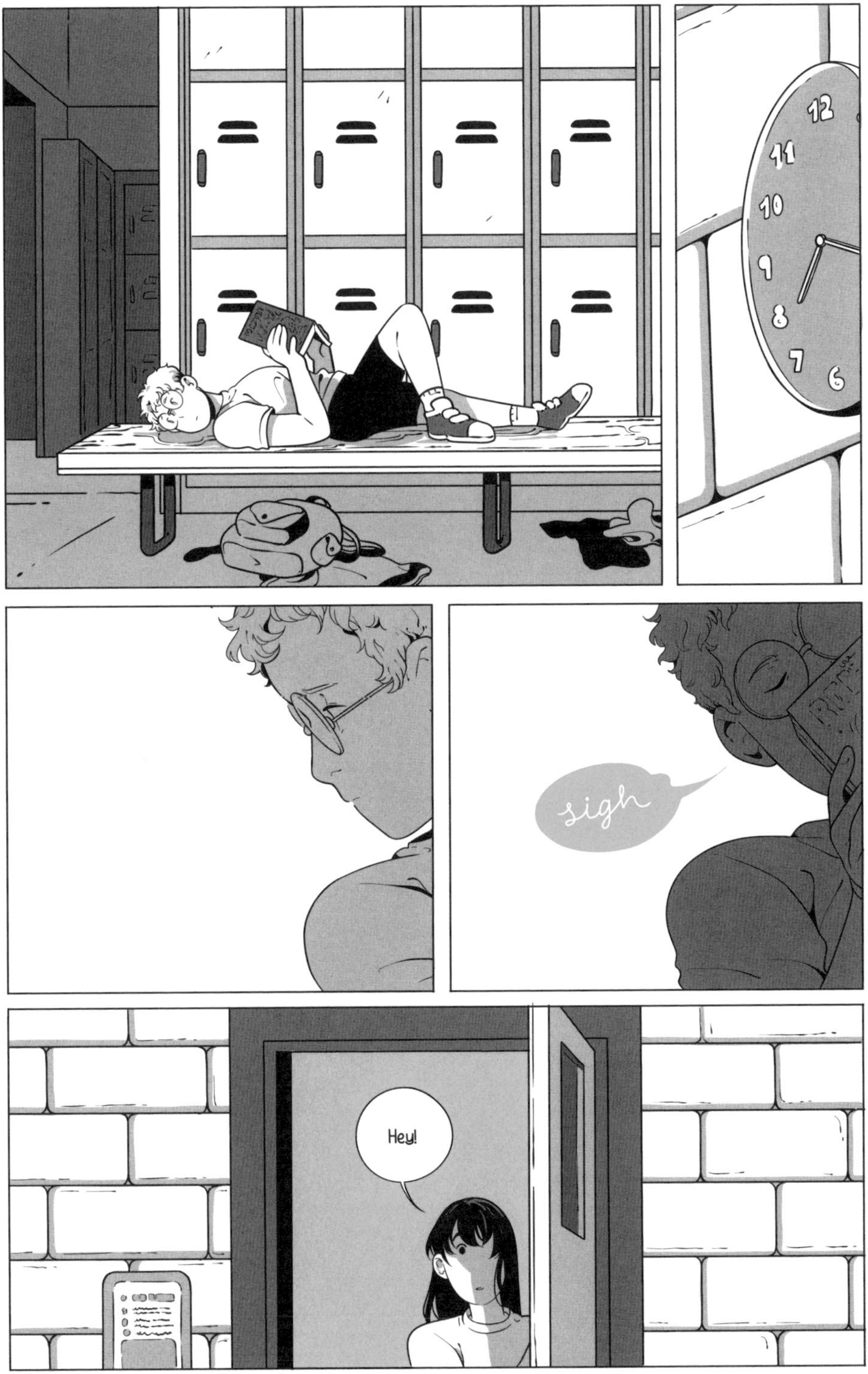
sigh
Hey!

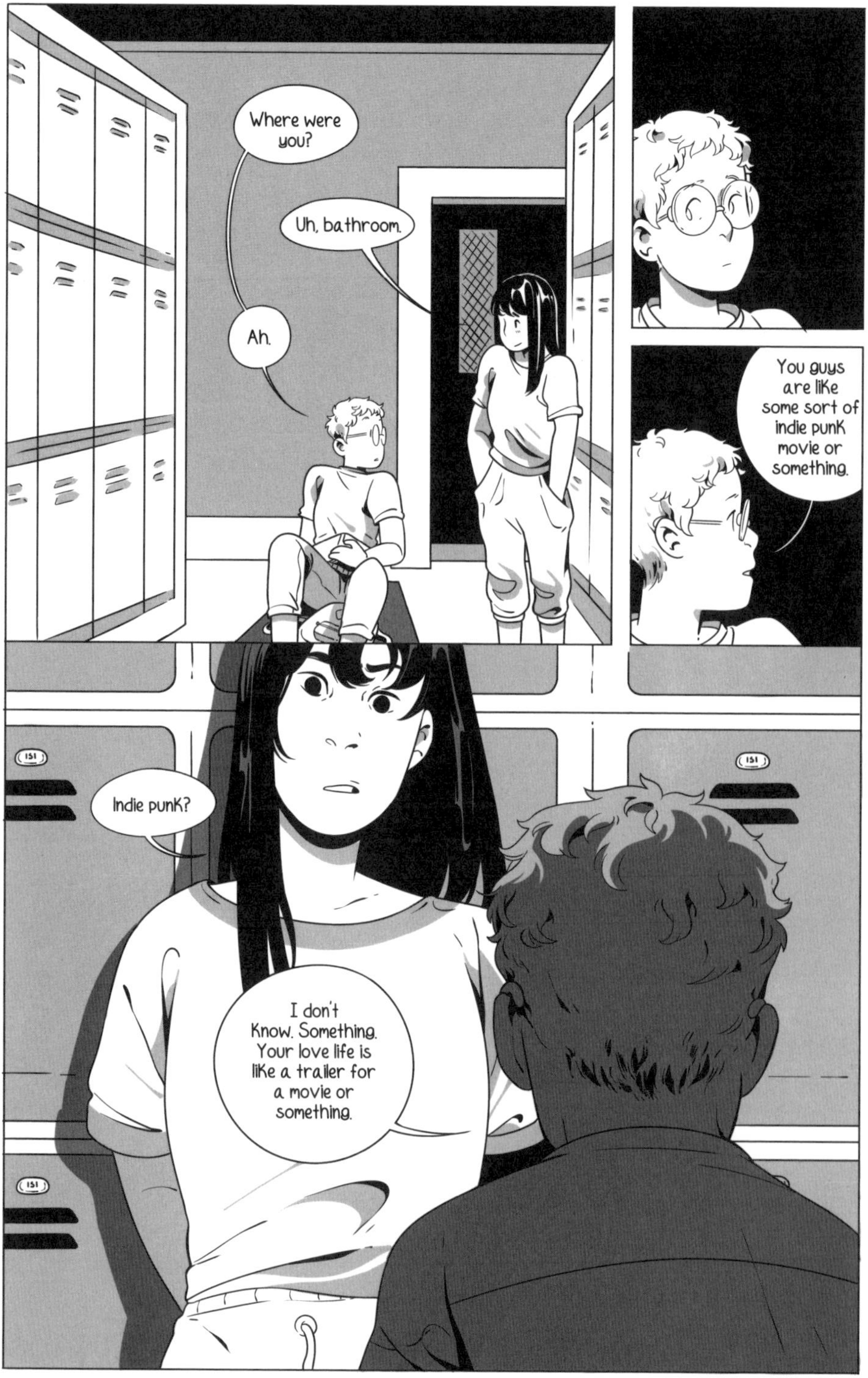
Where were you?
Uh, bathroom.
Ah.
You guys are like some sort of indie punk movie or something.
Indie punk?
I don't know. Something. Your love life is like a trailer for a movie or something.

What Kind
of movie?

I don't Know.
Forget I said
anything.

I just saw
Buddy. I think
something
happened
in the gym.

A fight or
something.

A fight?

✨ Buddy ✨

Are you alright??
Marcus is an ASSHOLE
BB

Not like a
fist-fight.

When?

Just now.
I passed him in the
hallway. He said he
was okay.

It was
probably just
that asshole
Marcus. Talking
shit. Again.

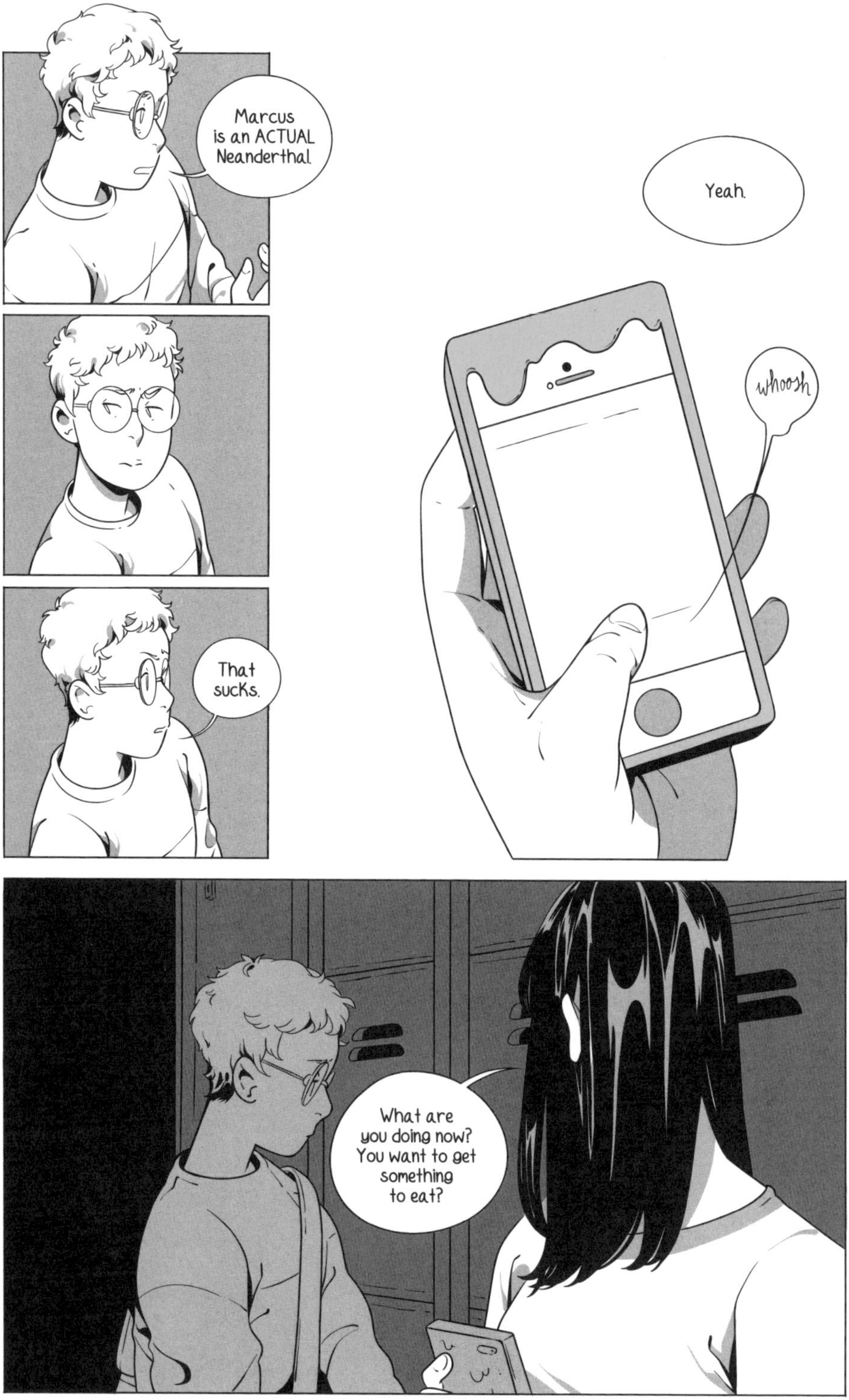
Marcus is an ACTUAL Neanderthal.
That sucks.
Yeah.
whoosh
What are you doing now? You want to get something to eat?

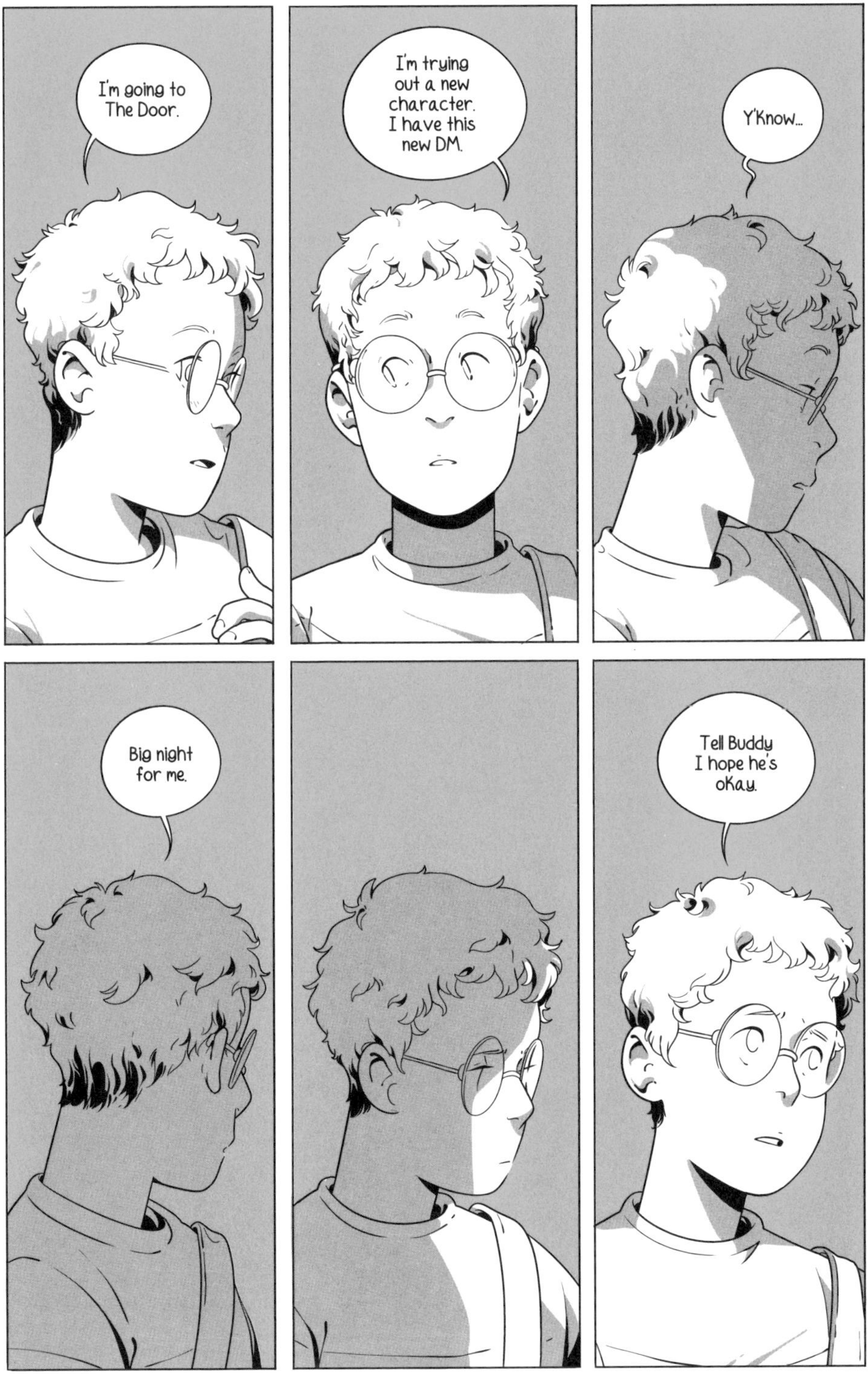
I'm going to The Door.
I'm trying out a new character. I have this new DM.
Y'Know...
Big night for me.
Tell Buddy I hope he's oKay.

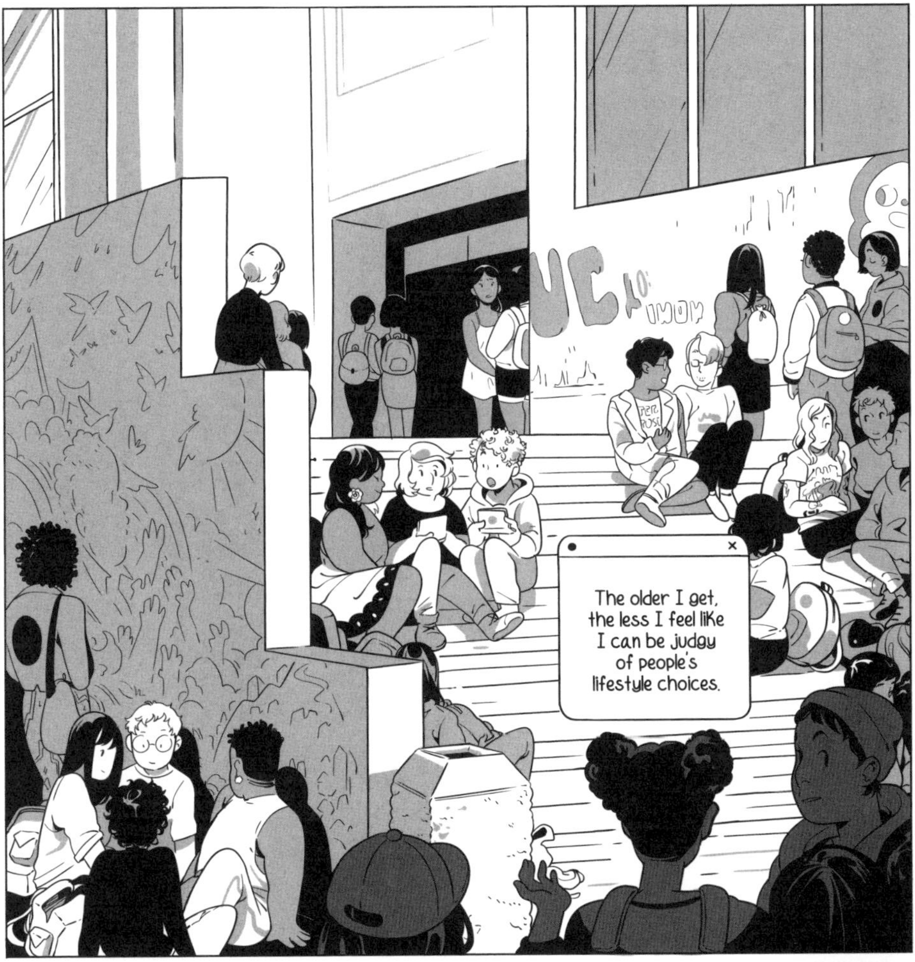
The older I get, the less I feel like I can be judgy of people's lifestyle choices.

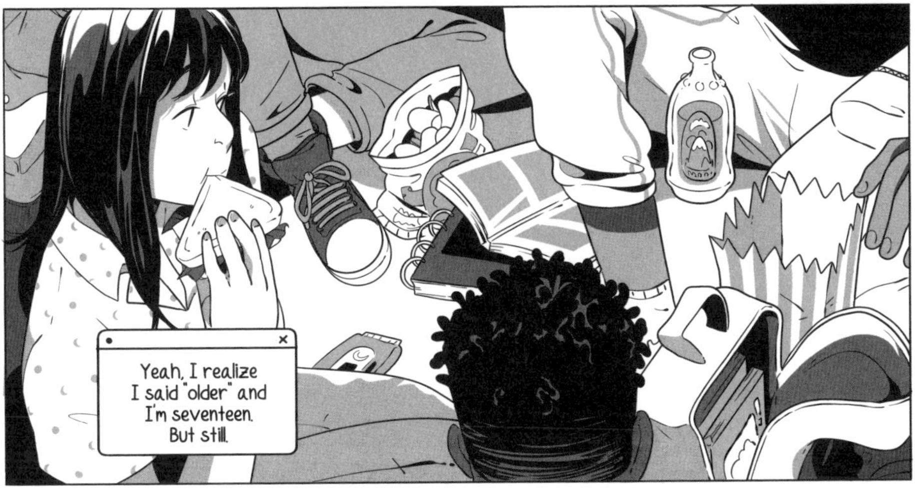
Yeah, I realize I said "older" and I'm seventeen. But still.

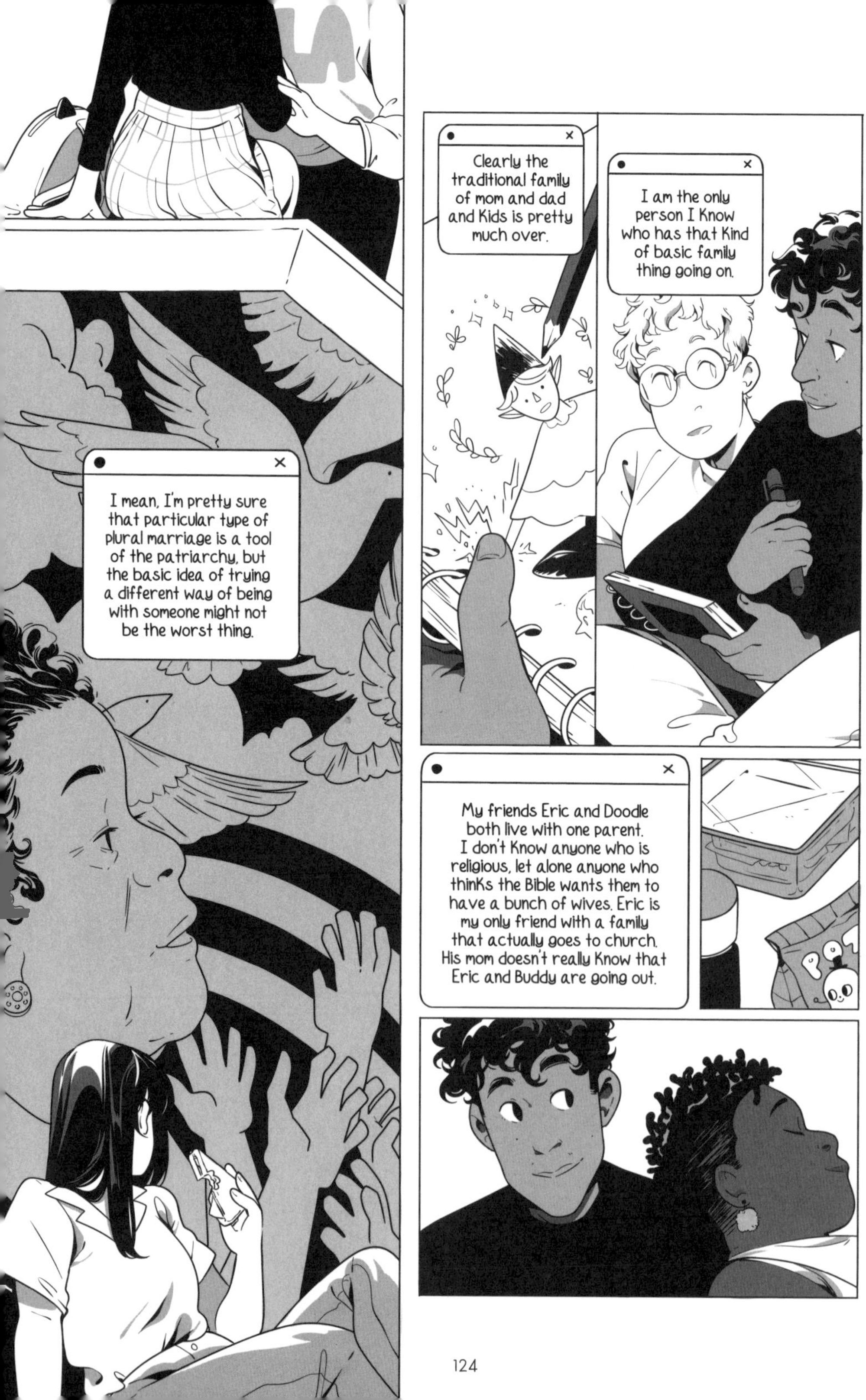
I mean, I'm pretty sure that particular type of plural marriage is a tool of the patriarchy, but the basic idea of trying a different way of being with someone might not be the worst thing.
Clearly the traditional family of mom and dad and Kids is pretty much over.
I am the only person I Know who has that Kind of basic family thing going on.
My friends Eric and Doodle both live with one parent. I don't Know anyone who is religious, let alone anyone who thinks the Bible wants them to have a bunch of wives. Eric is my only friend with a family that actually goes to church. His mom doesn't really Know that Eric and Buddy are going out.

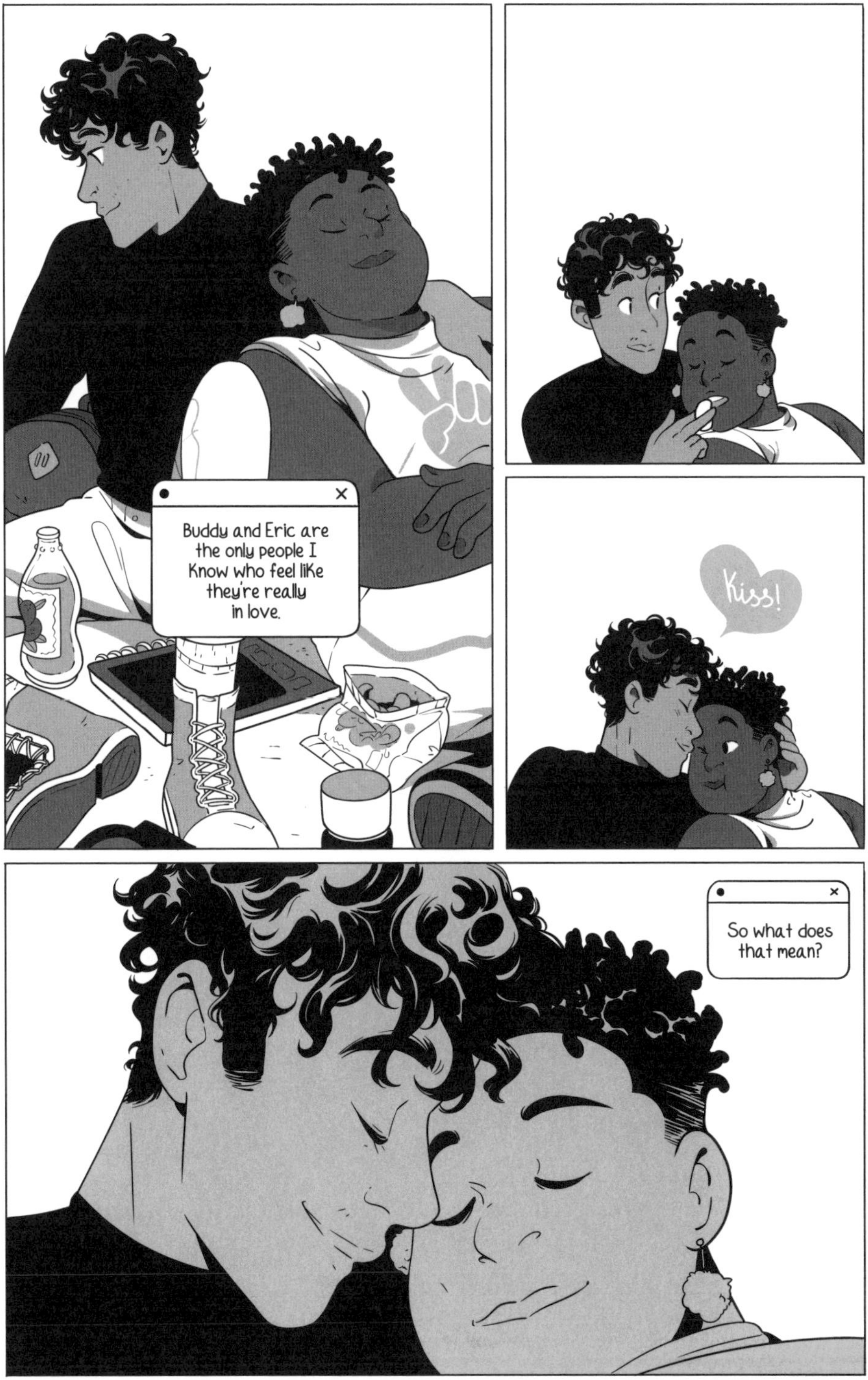
Buddy and Eric are the only people I know who feel like they're really in love.
Kiss!
So what does that mean?

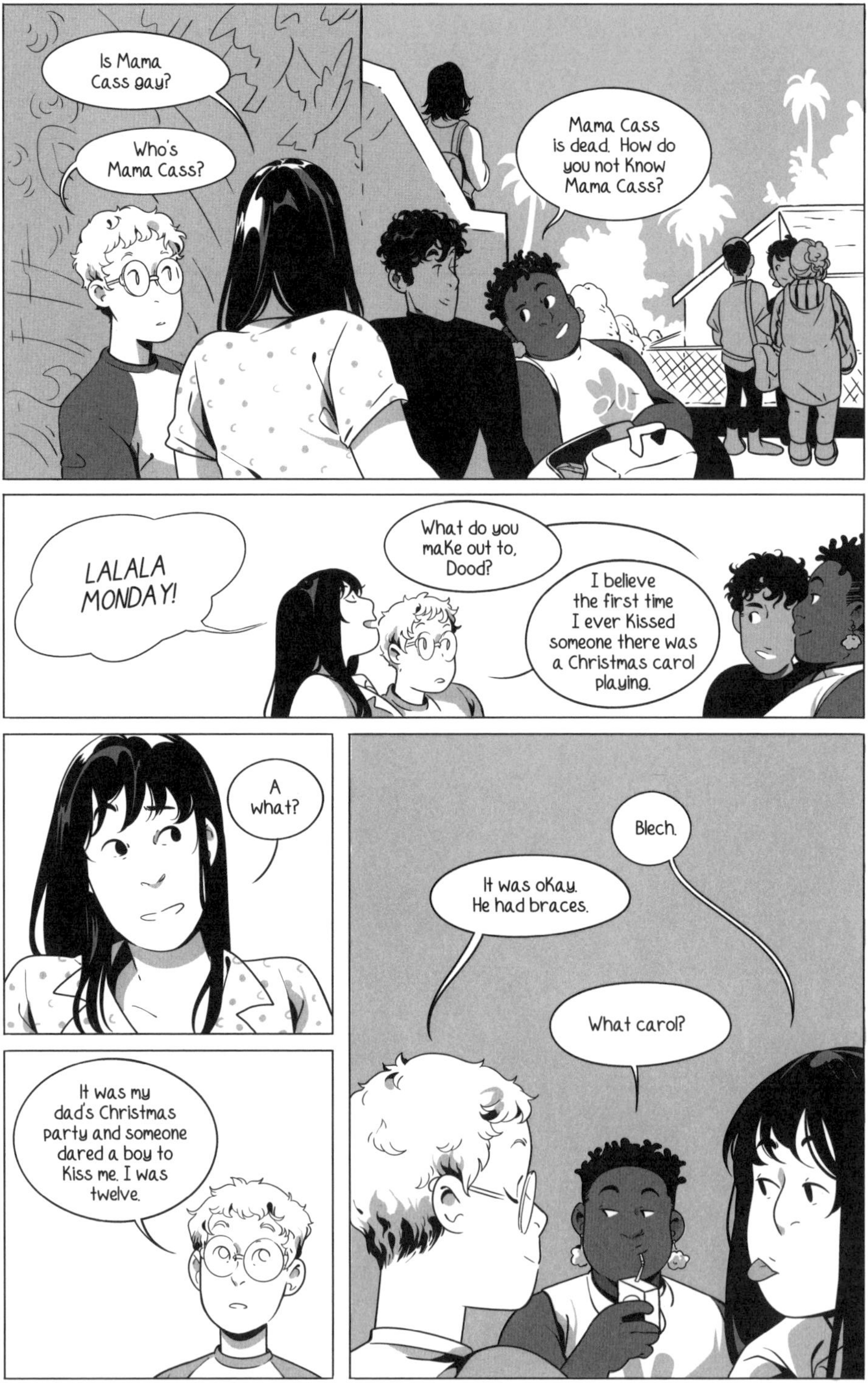
Is Mama Cass gay?
Who's Mama Cass?
Mama Cass is dead. How do you not Know Mama Cass?
LALALA MONDAY!
What do you maKe out to, Dood?
I believe the first time I ever Kissed someone there was a Christmas carol playing.
A what?
It was my dad's Christmas party and someone dared a boy to Kiss me. I was twelve.
Blech.
It was oKay. He had braces.
What carol?

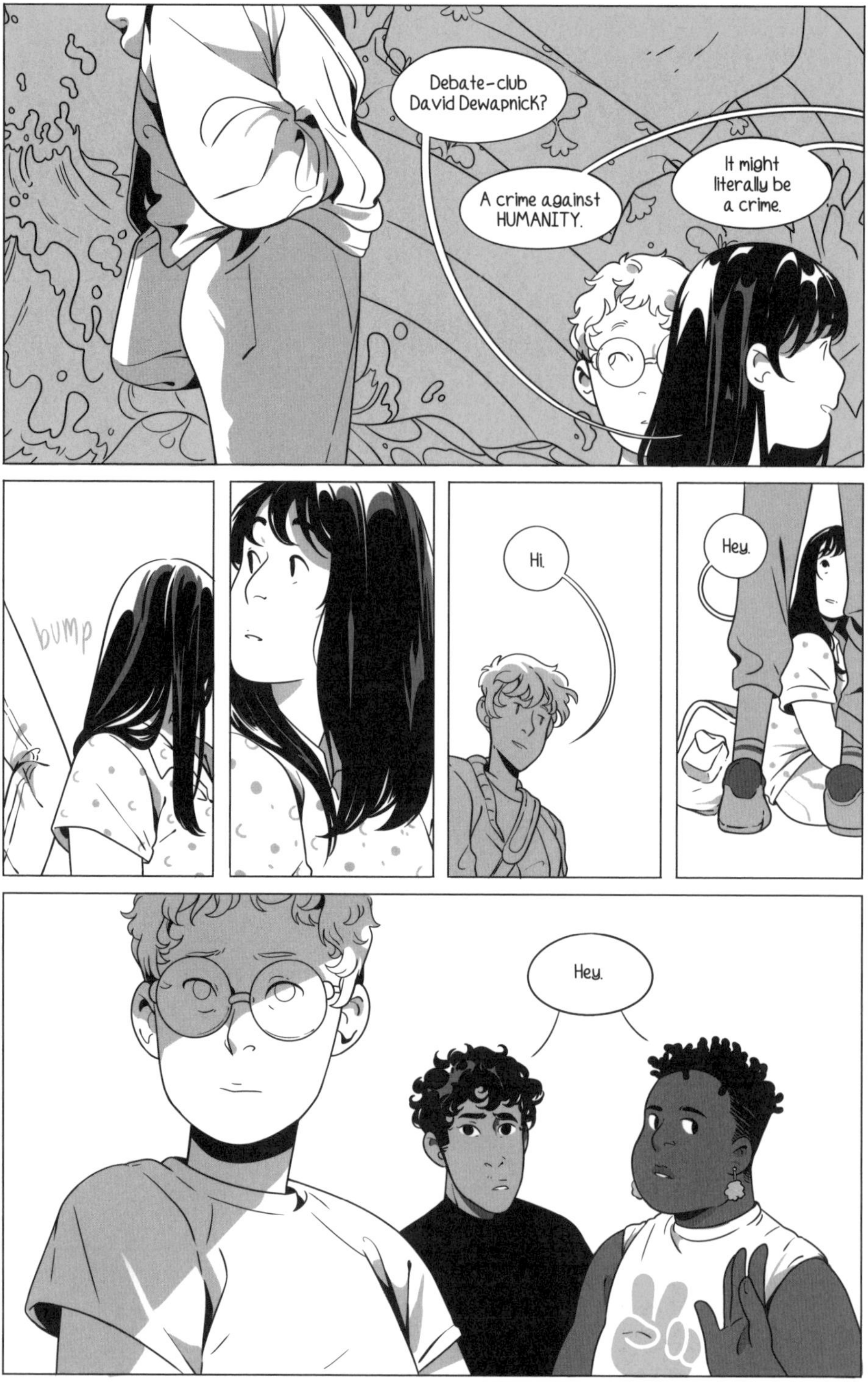
Debate-club
David Dewapnick?
A crime against
HUMANITY.
It might
literally be
a crime.
bump
Hi.
Hey.
Hey.

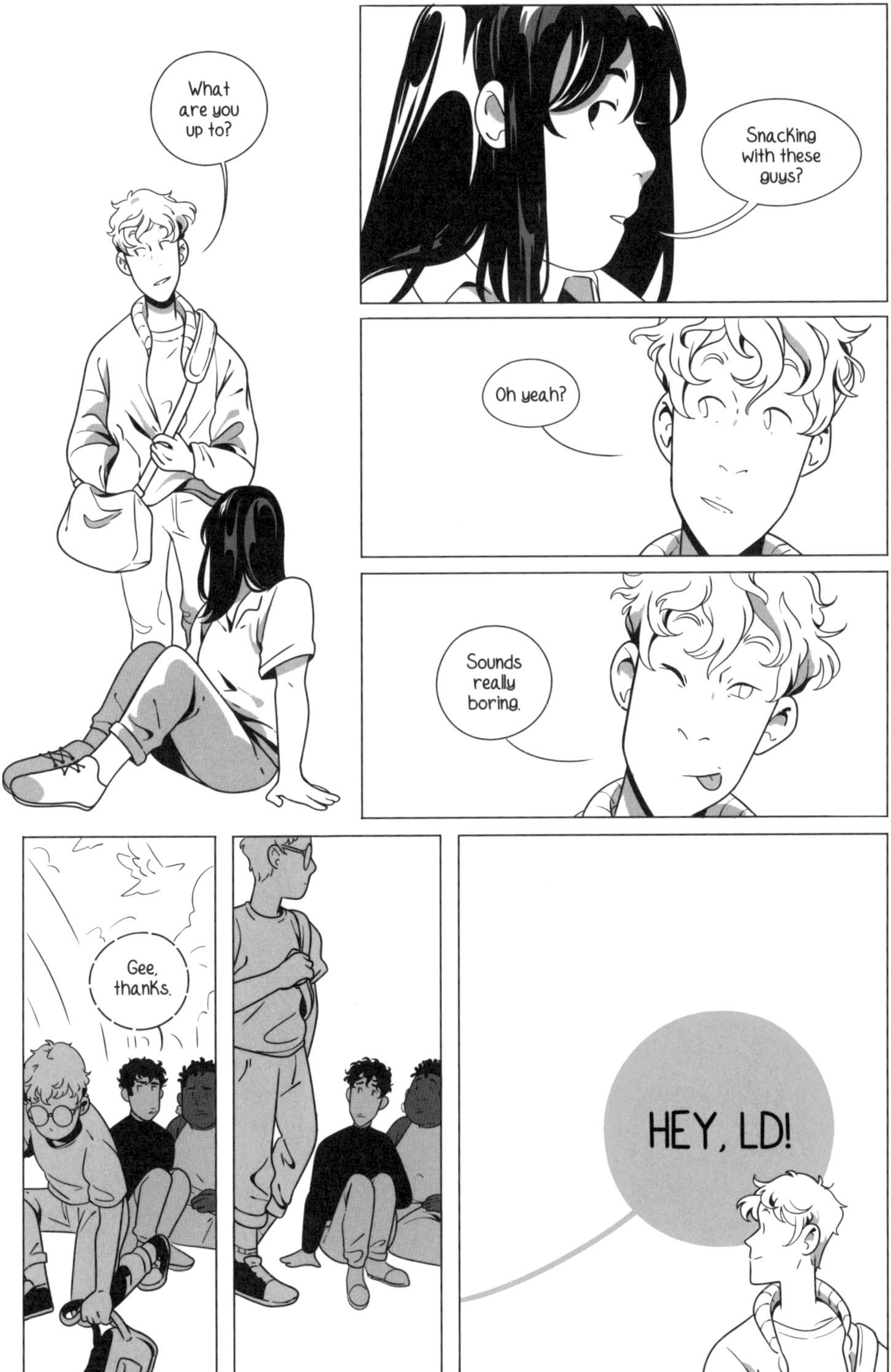
What are you up to?
Snacking with these guys?
Oh yeah?
Sounds really boring.
Gee, thanks.
HEY, LD!

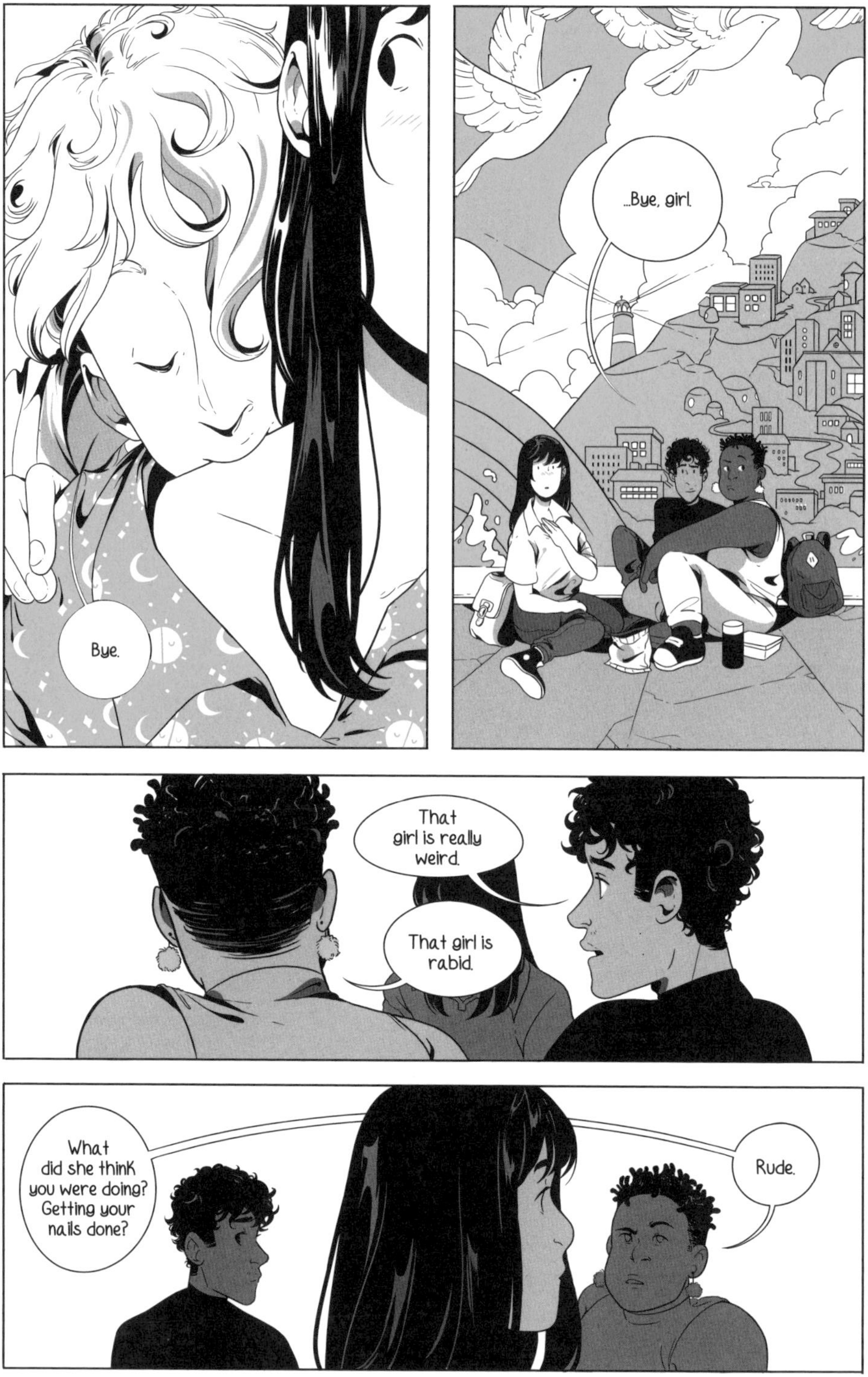
Bye.
...Bye, girl.
That girl is really weird.
That girl is rabid.
What did she think you were doing? Getting your nails done?
Rude.

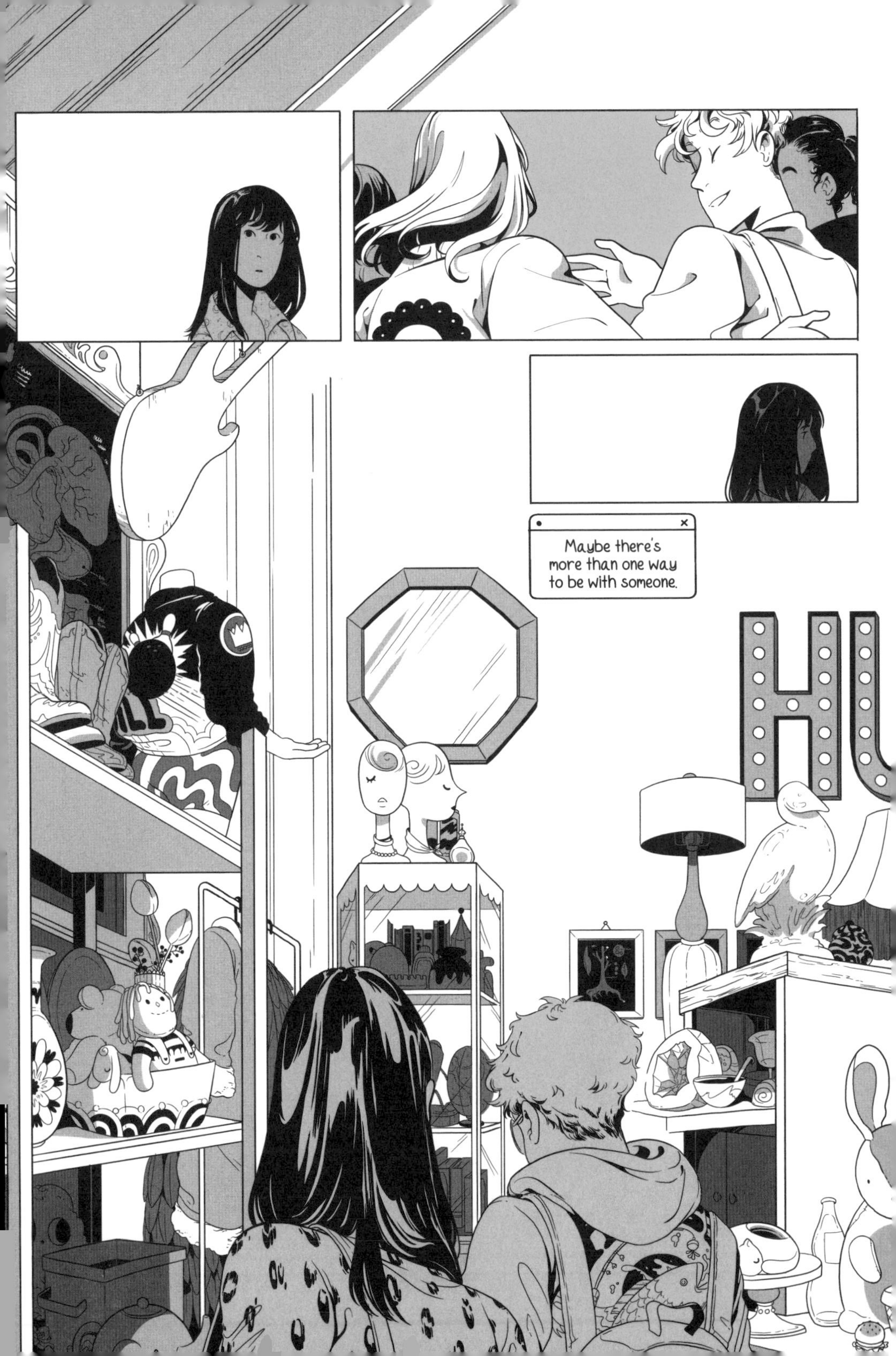
Maybe there's more than one way to be with someone.

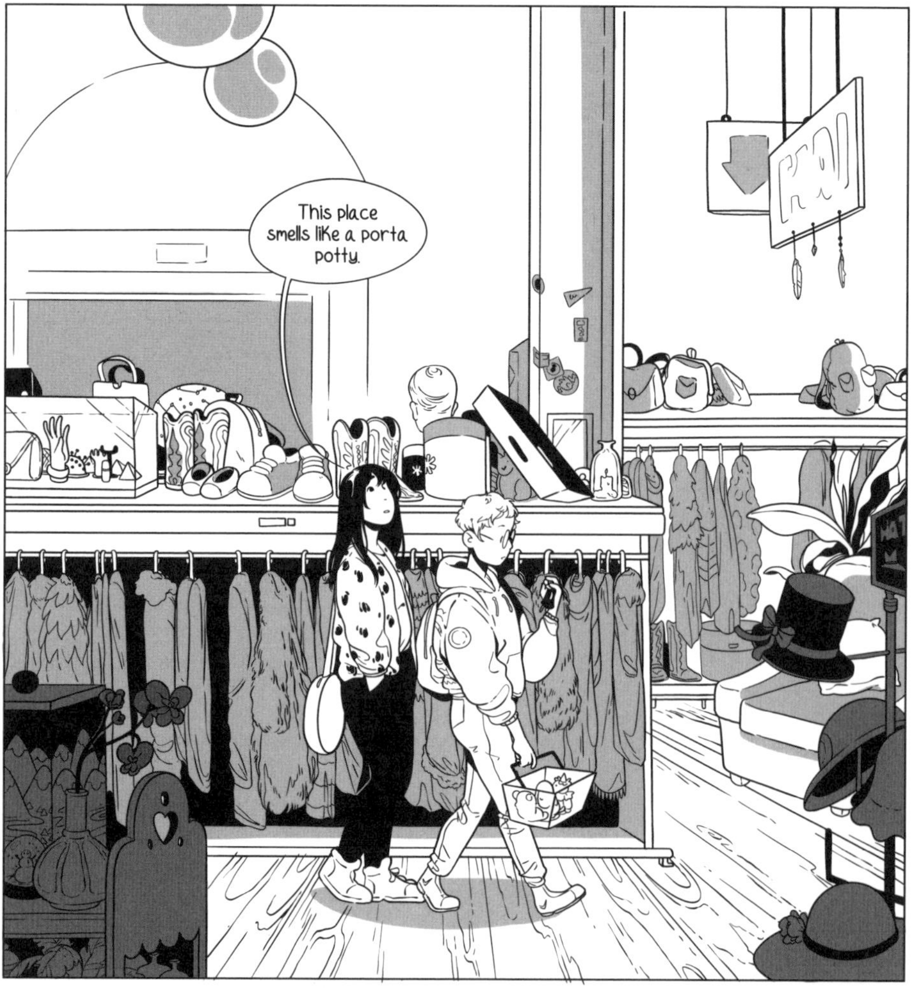
This place smells like a porta potty.

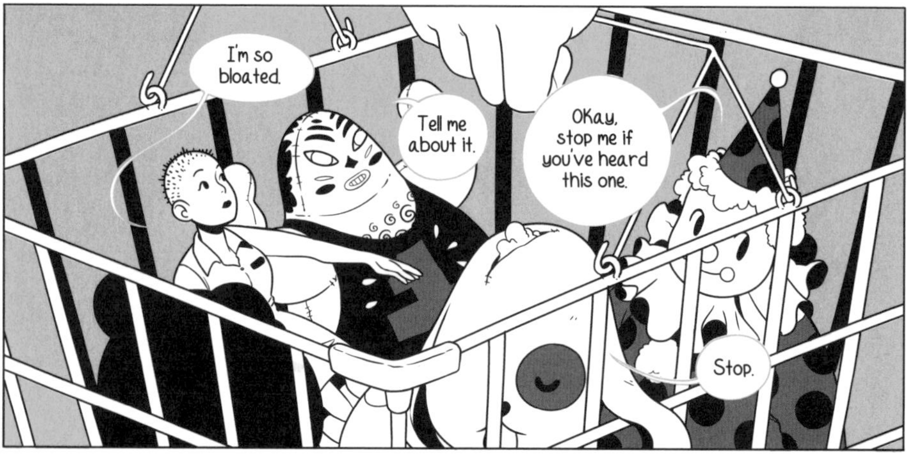
I'm so bloated.
Tell me about it.
OKay, stop me if you've heard this one.
Stop.

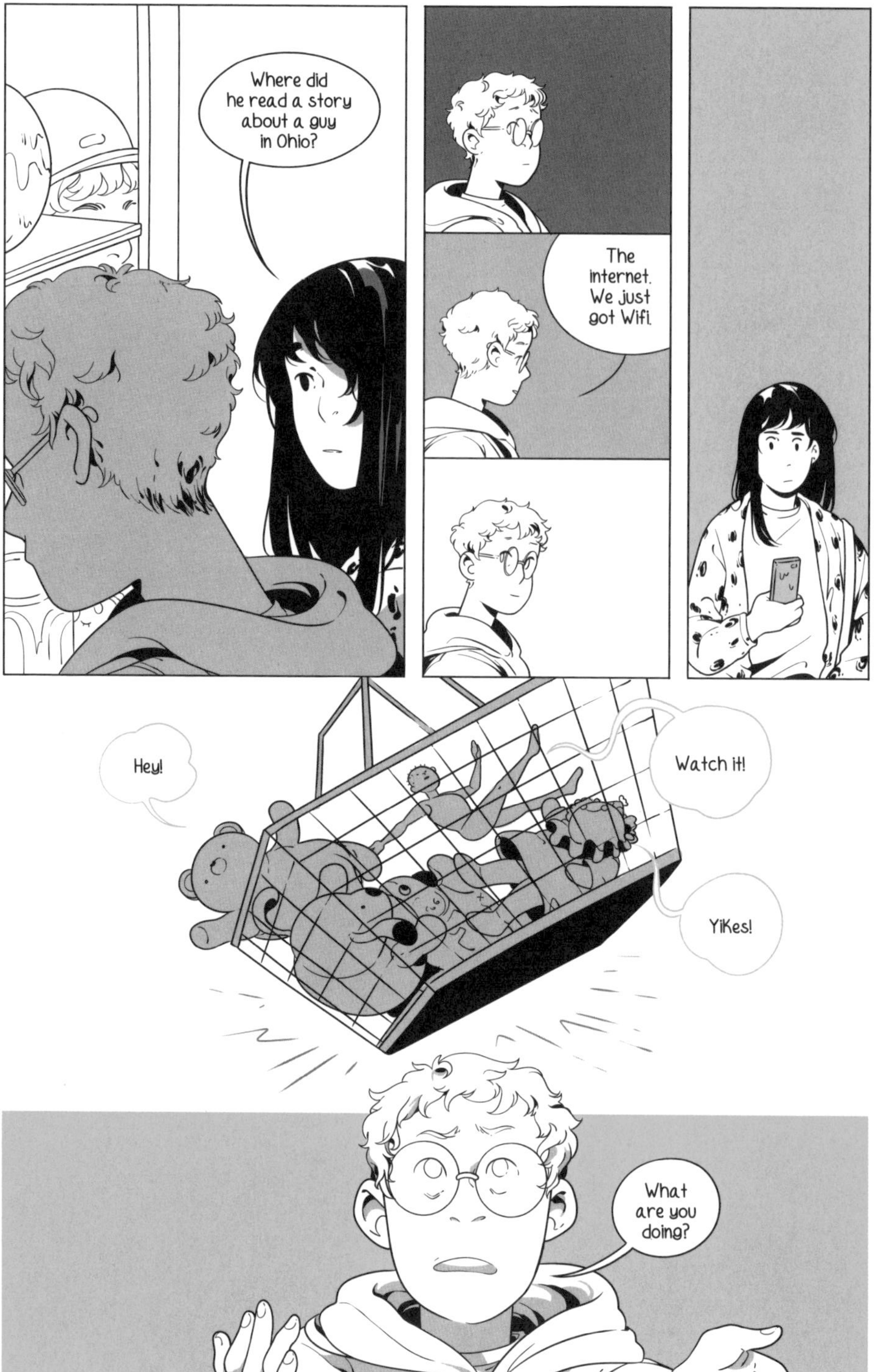
Where did he read a story about a guy in Ohio?
The internet. We just got Wifi.
Hey!
Watch it!
YiKes!
What are you doing?

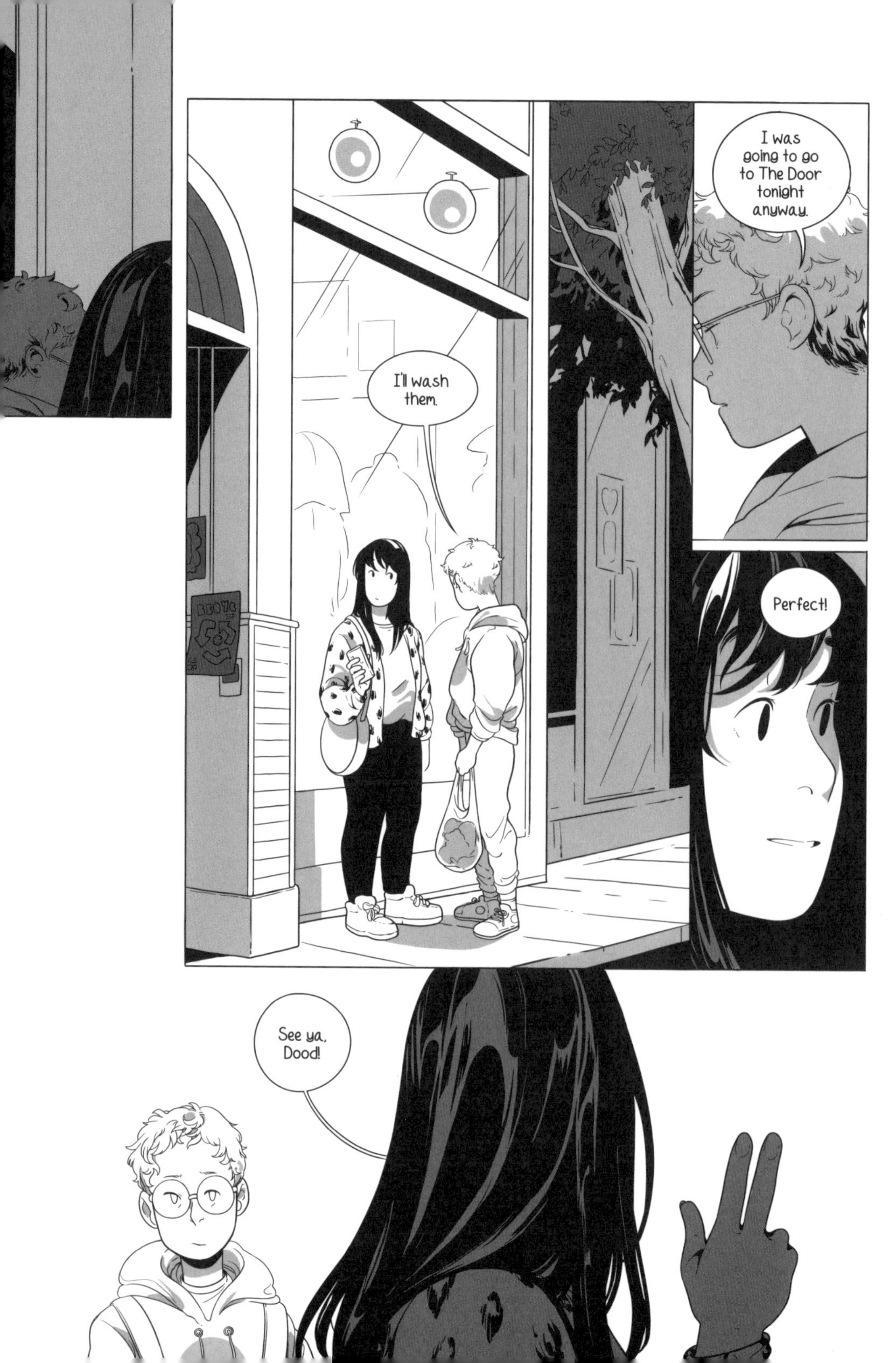
I'll wash them.
I was going to go to The Door tonight anyway.
Perfect!
See ya, Dood!

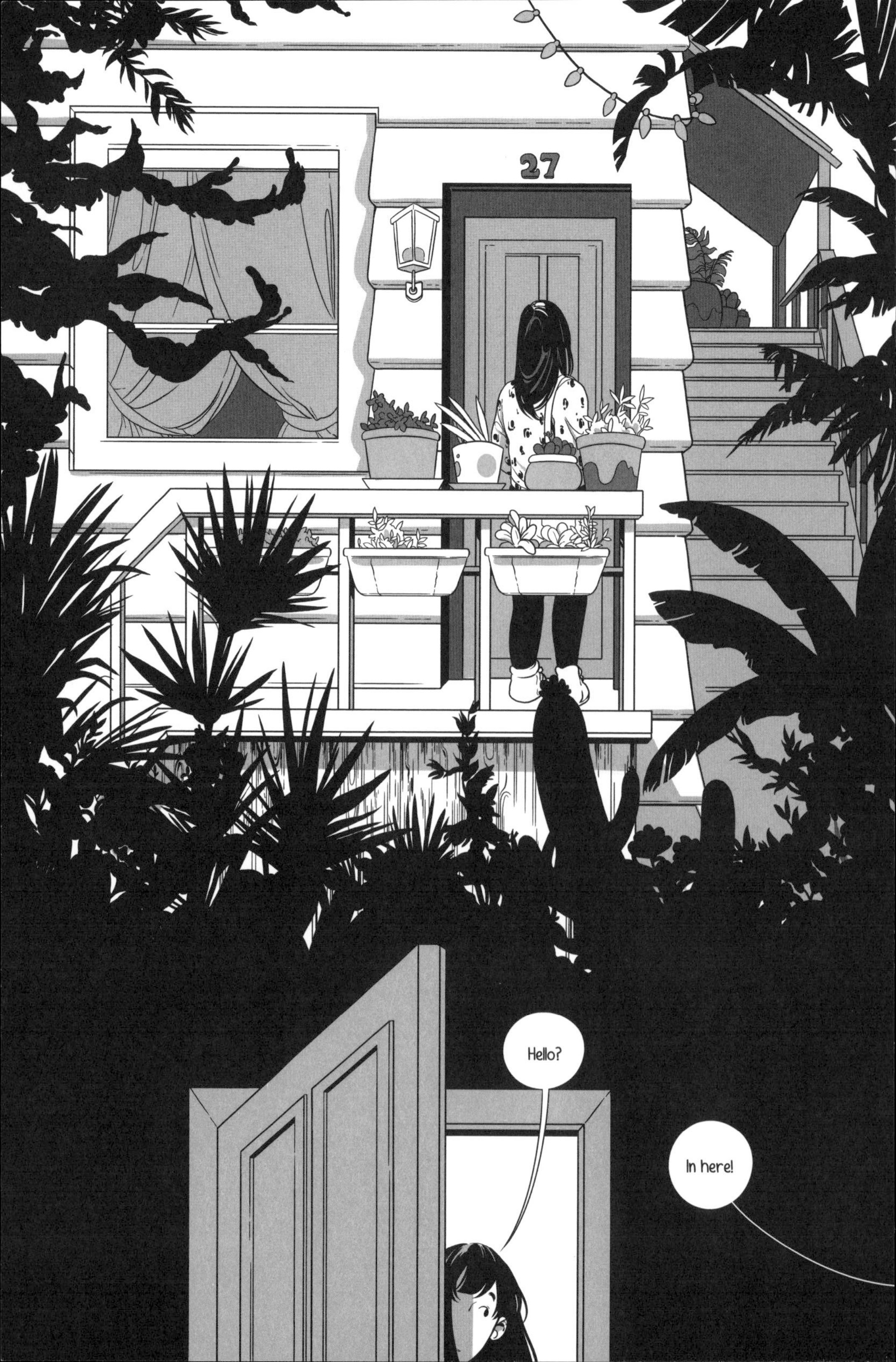
27
Hello?
In here!

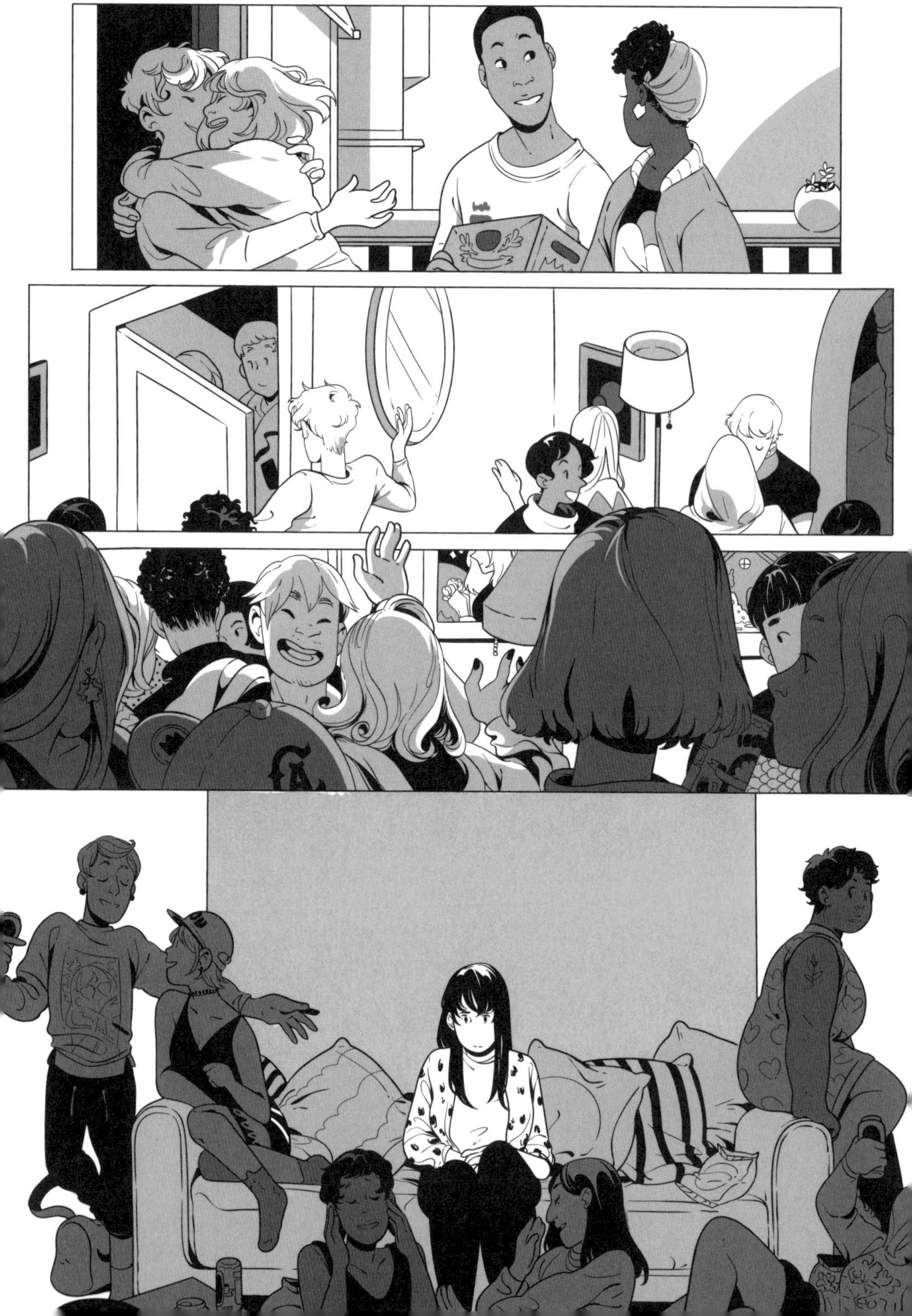

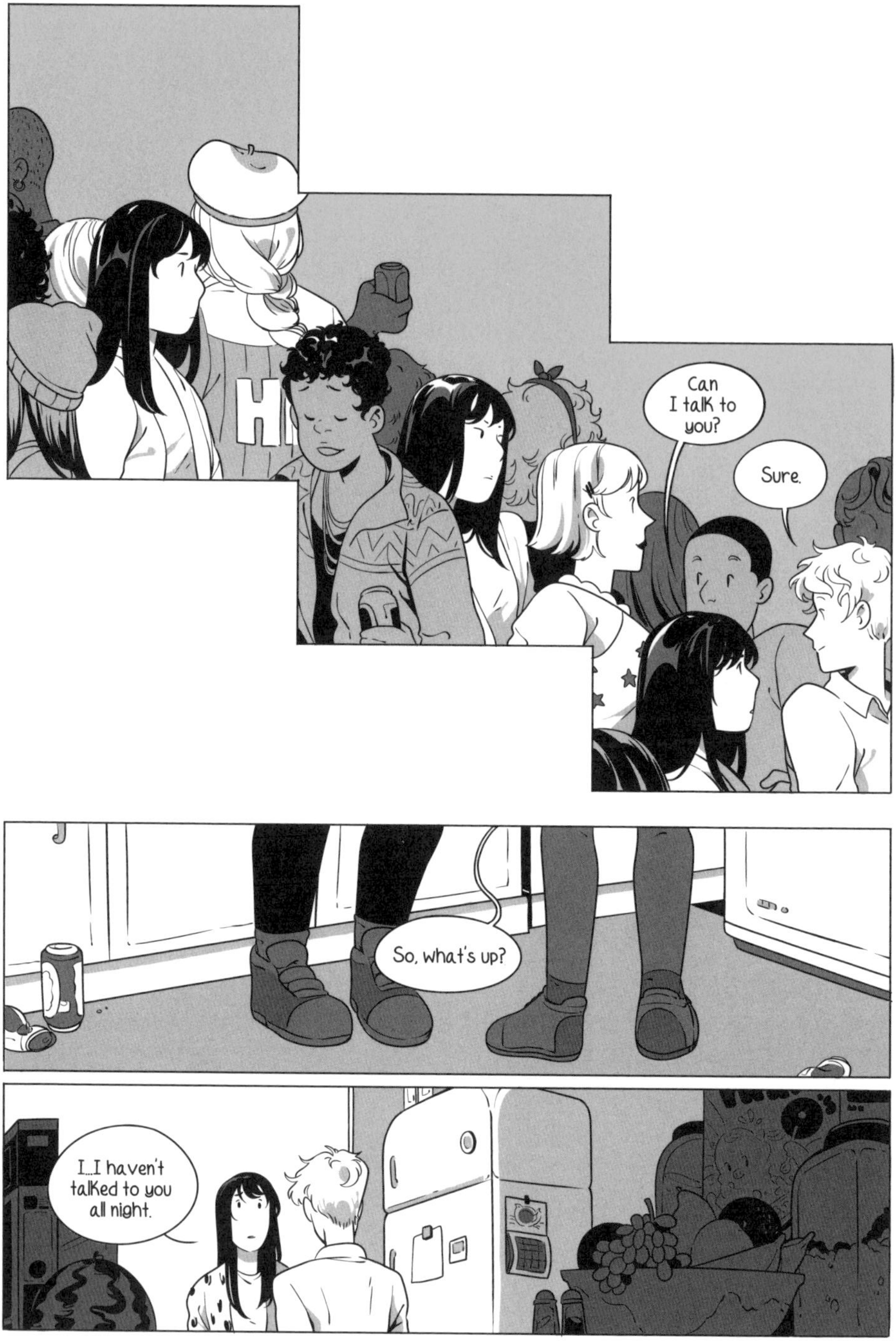
Can I talk to you?
Sure.
So, what's up?
I...I haven't talked to you all night.

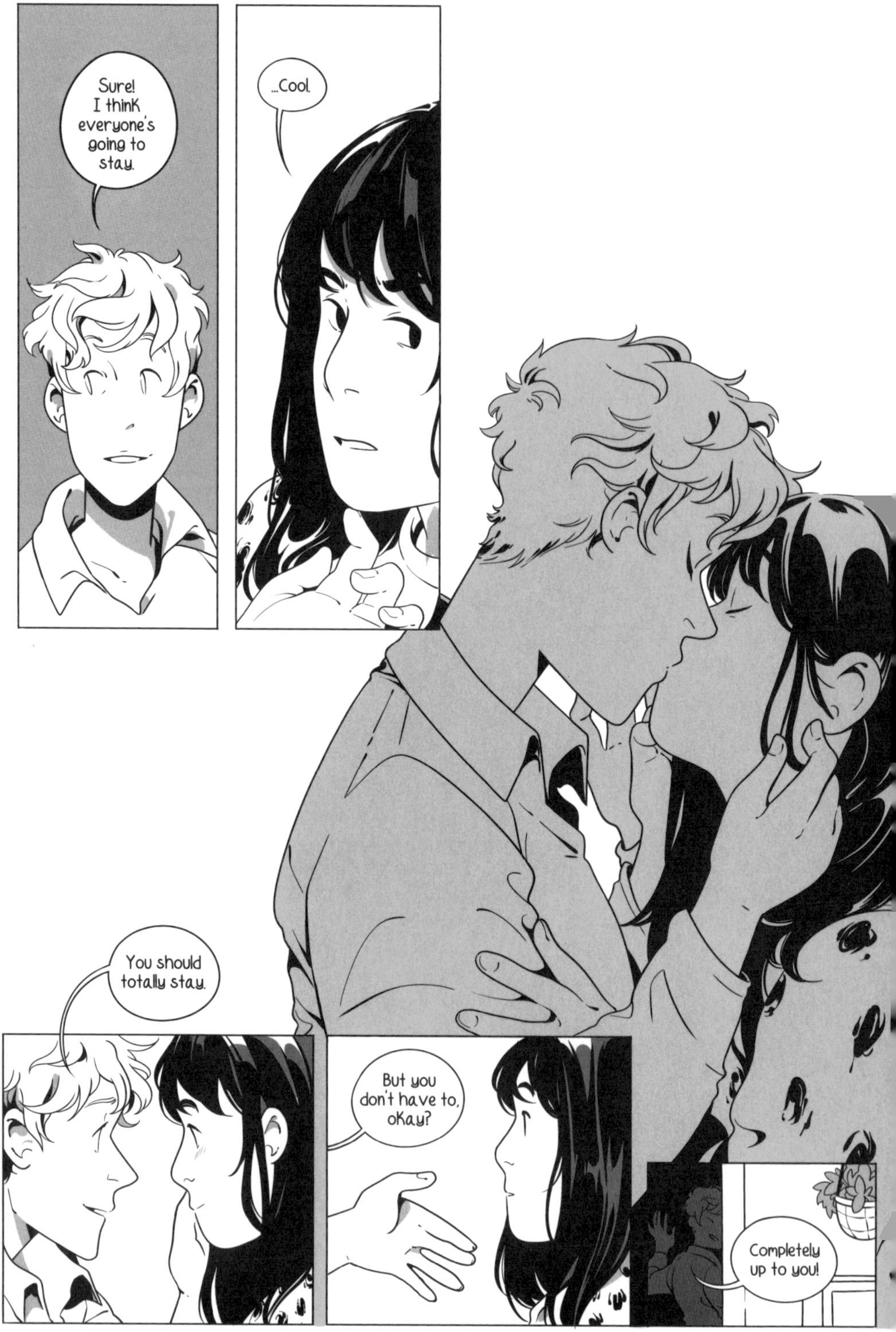
Sure! I think everyone's going to stay.
...Cool.
You should totally stay.
But you don't have to, okay?
Completely up to you!

149

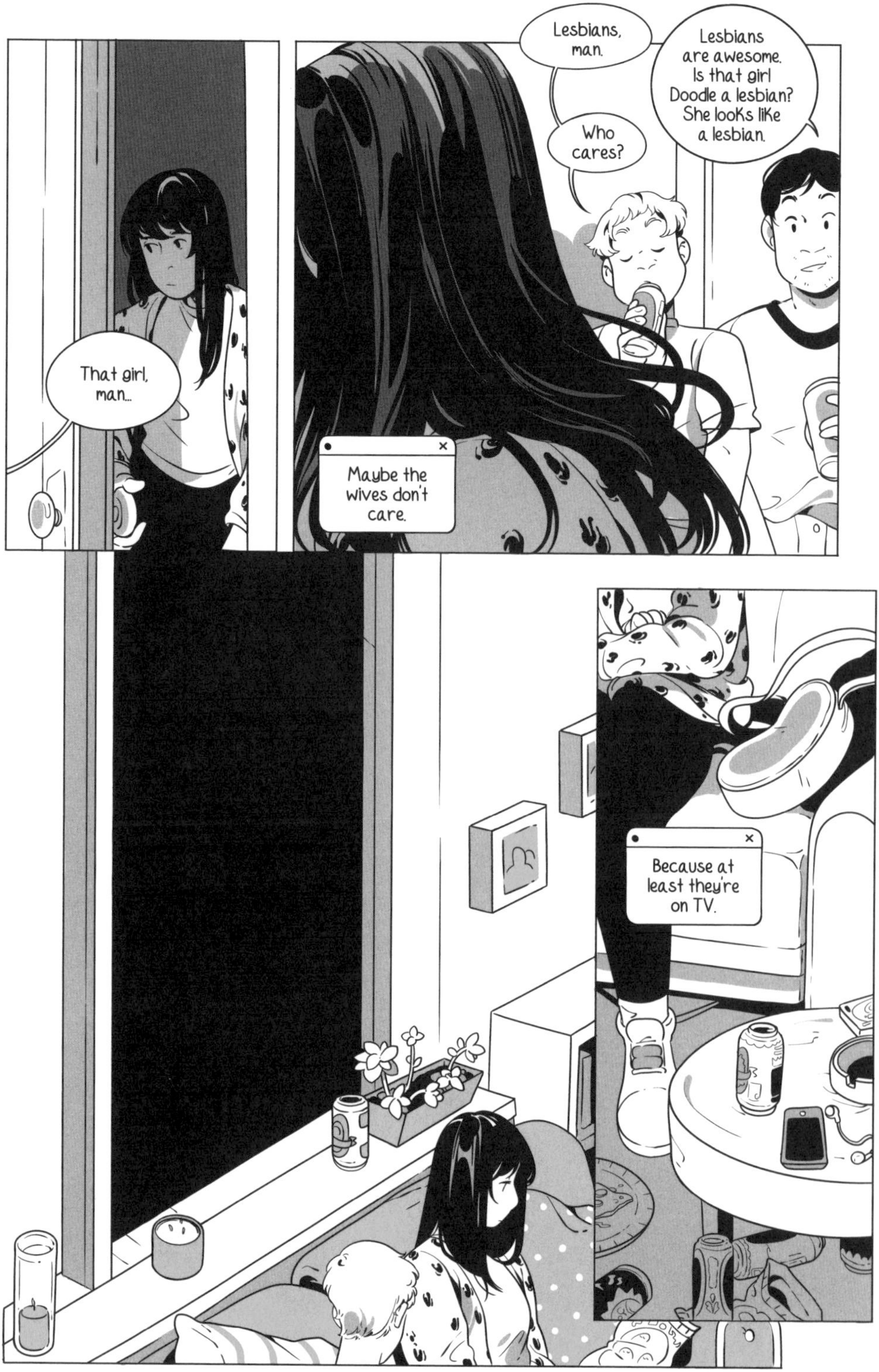
That girl, man...
Lesbians, man.
Who cares?
Lesbians are awesome. Is that girl Doodle a lesbian? She looks like a lesbian.
Maybe the wives don't care.
Because at least they're on TV.

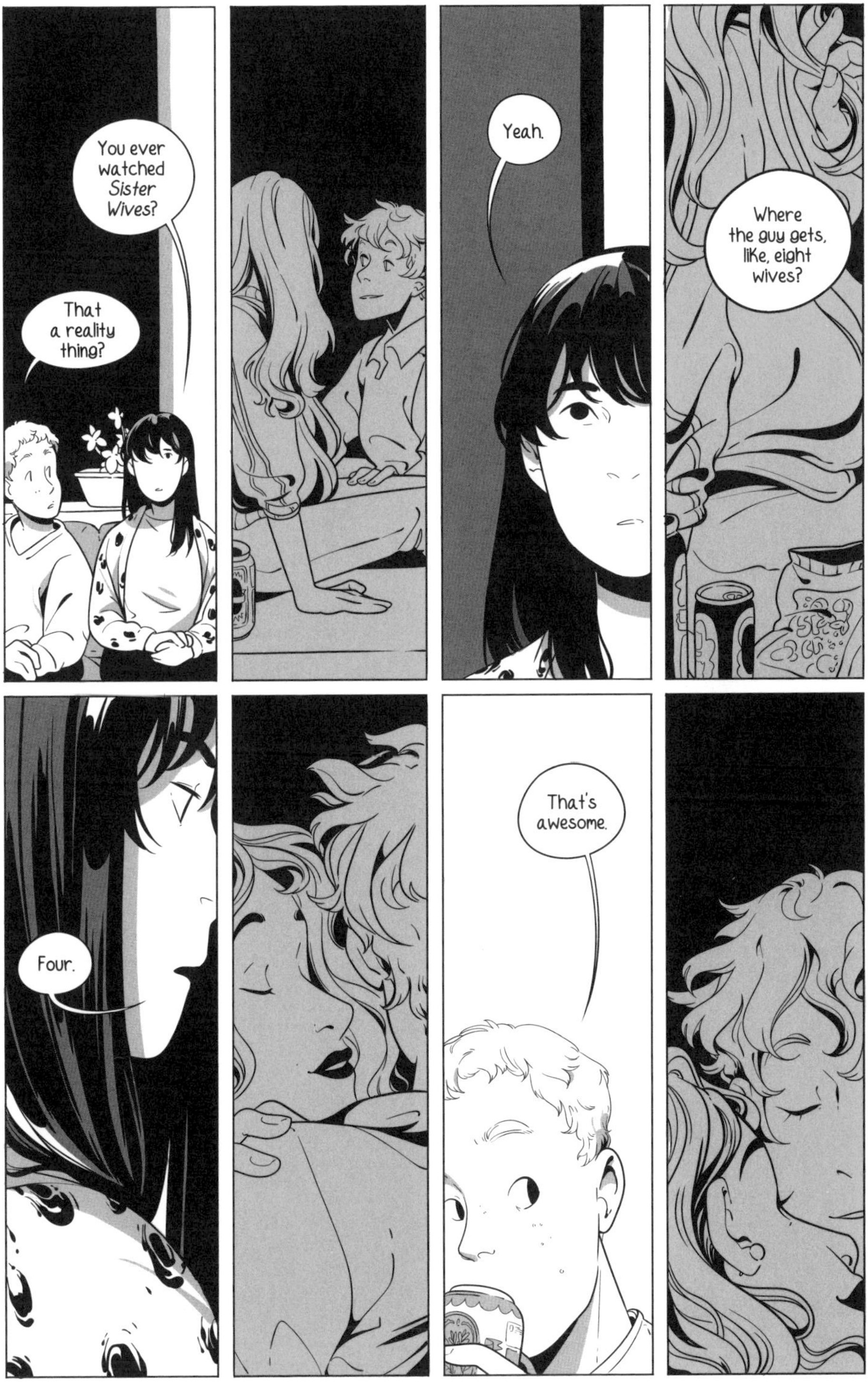
You ever watched Sister Wives?
That a reality thing?
Yeah.
Where the guy gets, like, eight wives?
Four.
That's awesome.

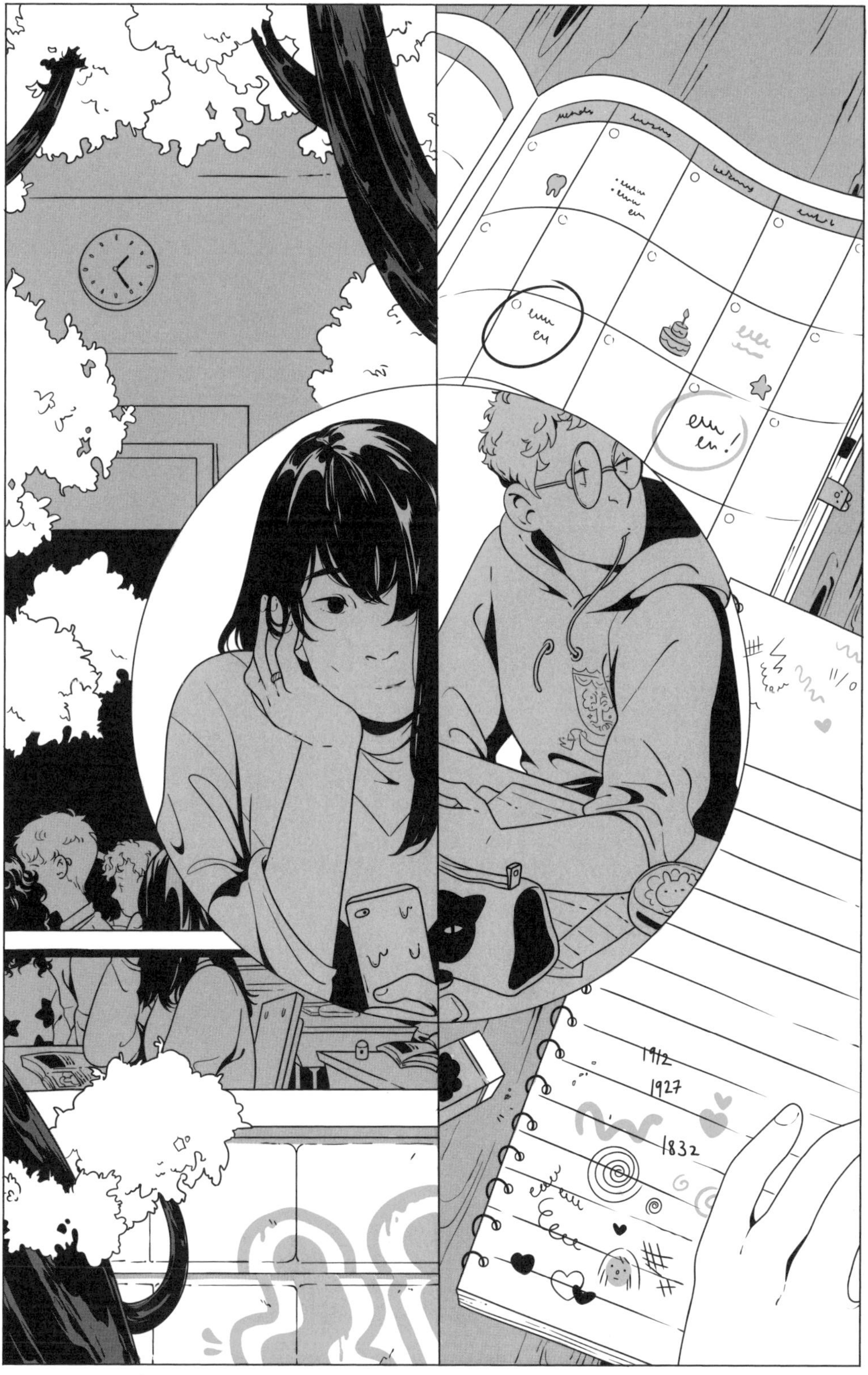
1912
1927
1832

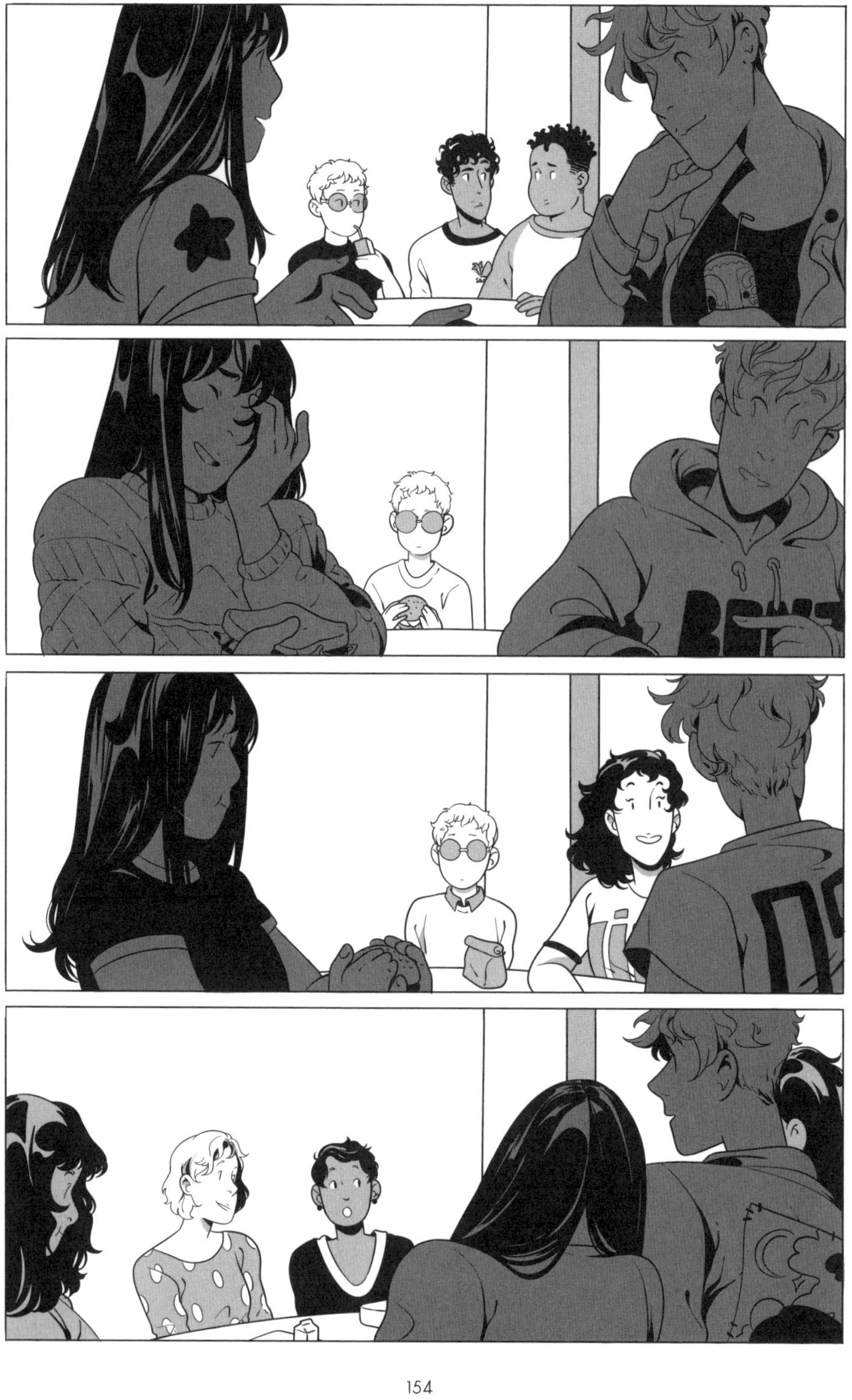

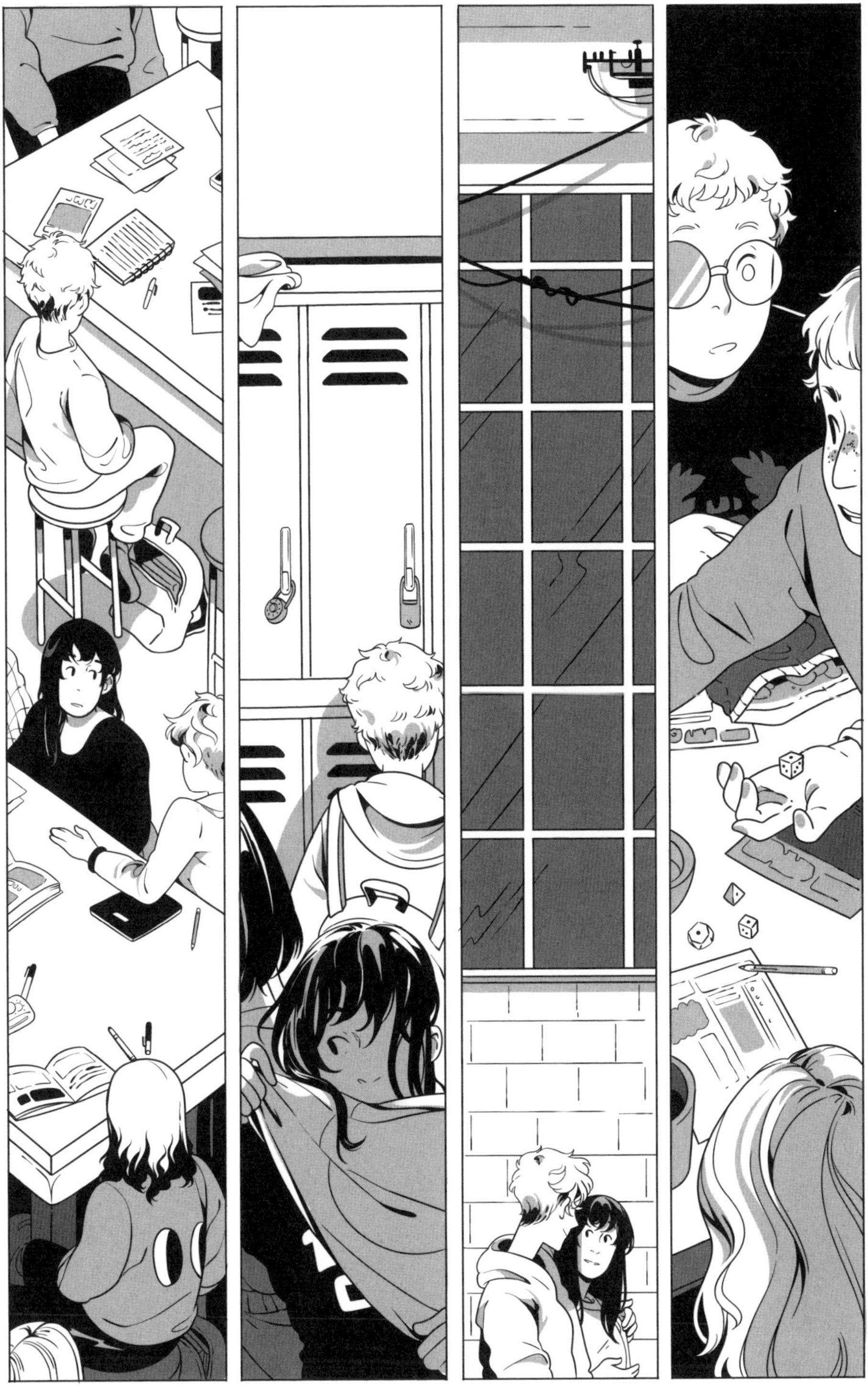

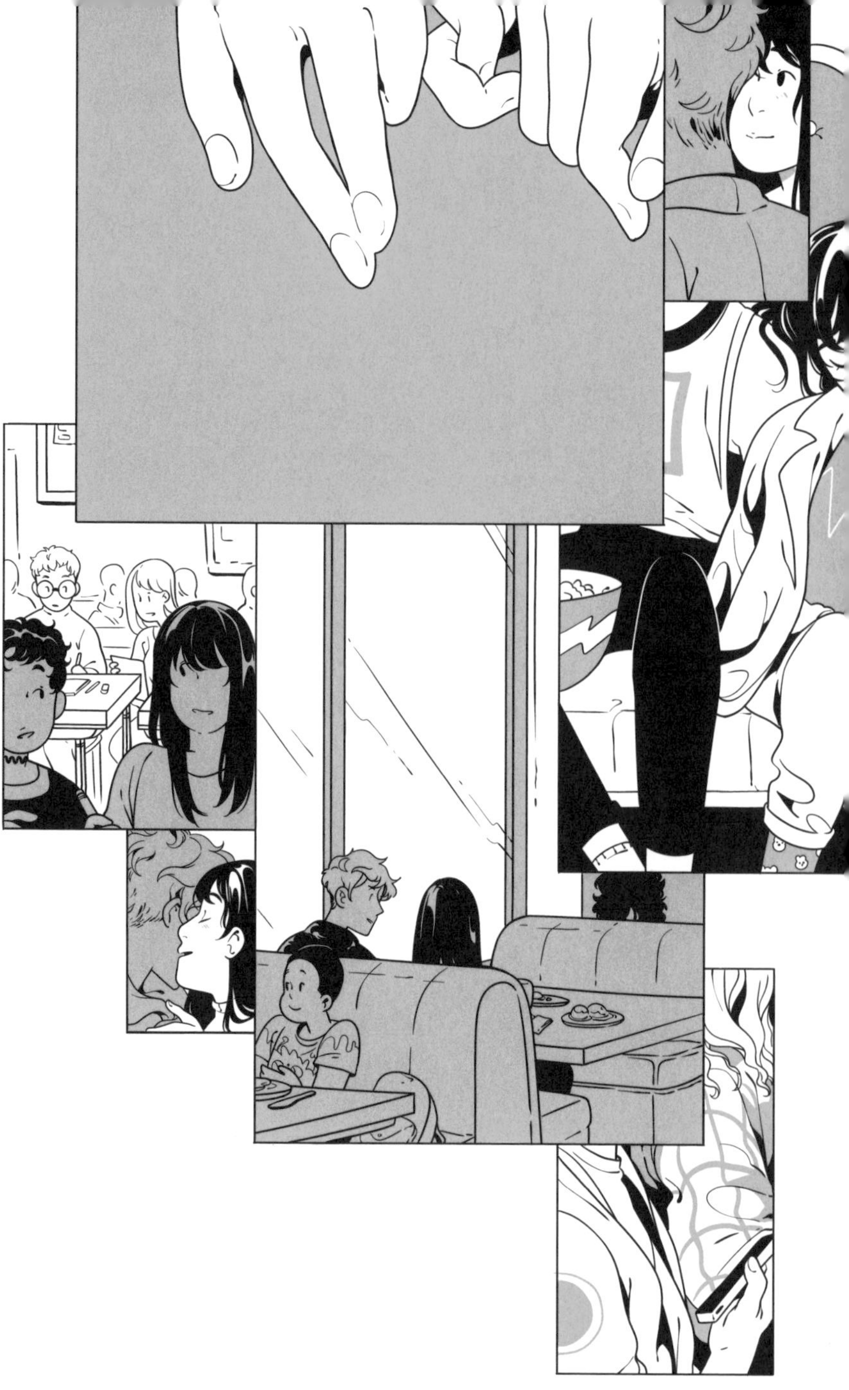

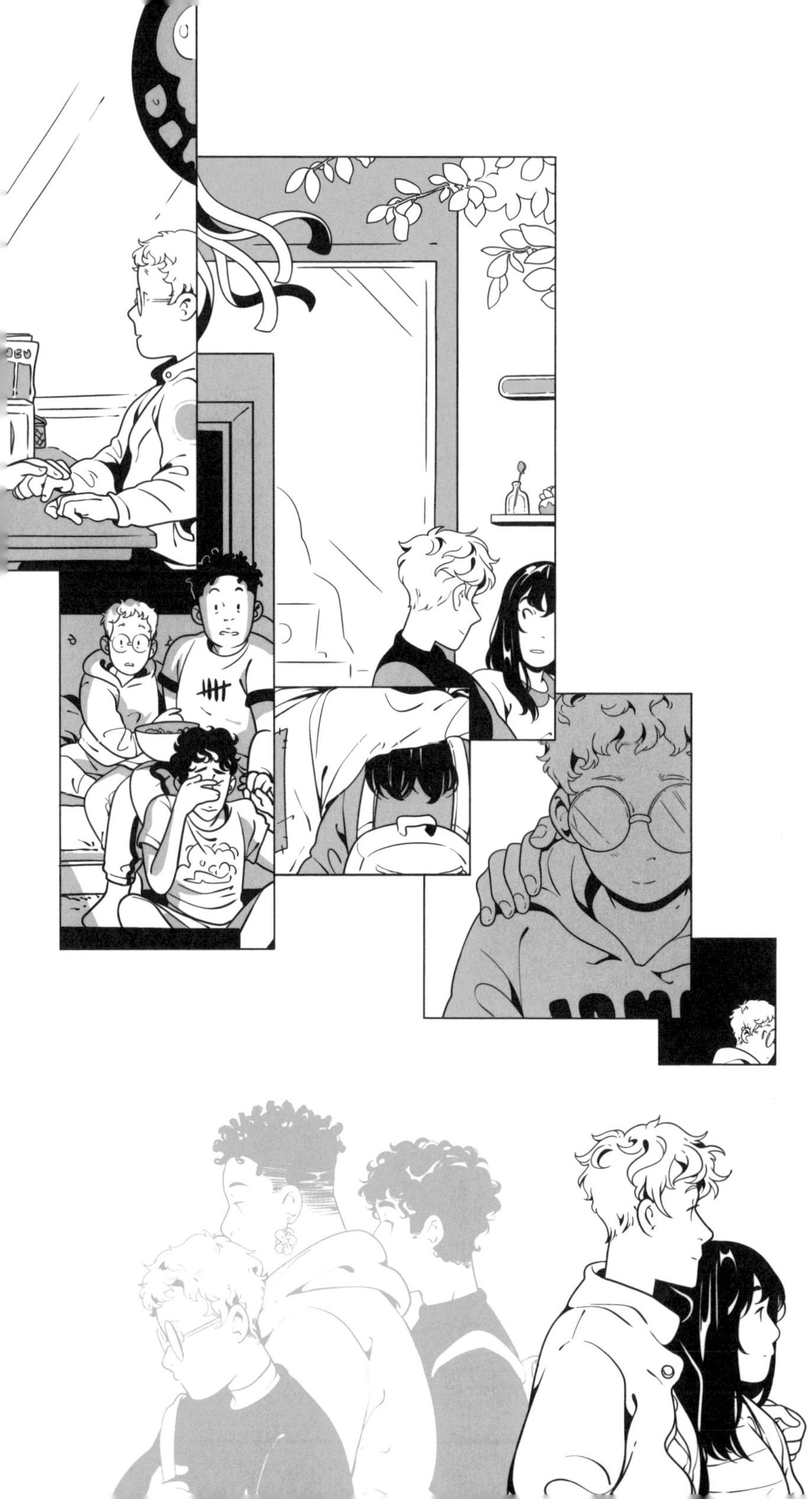

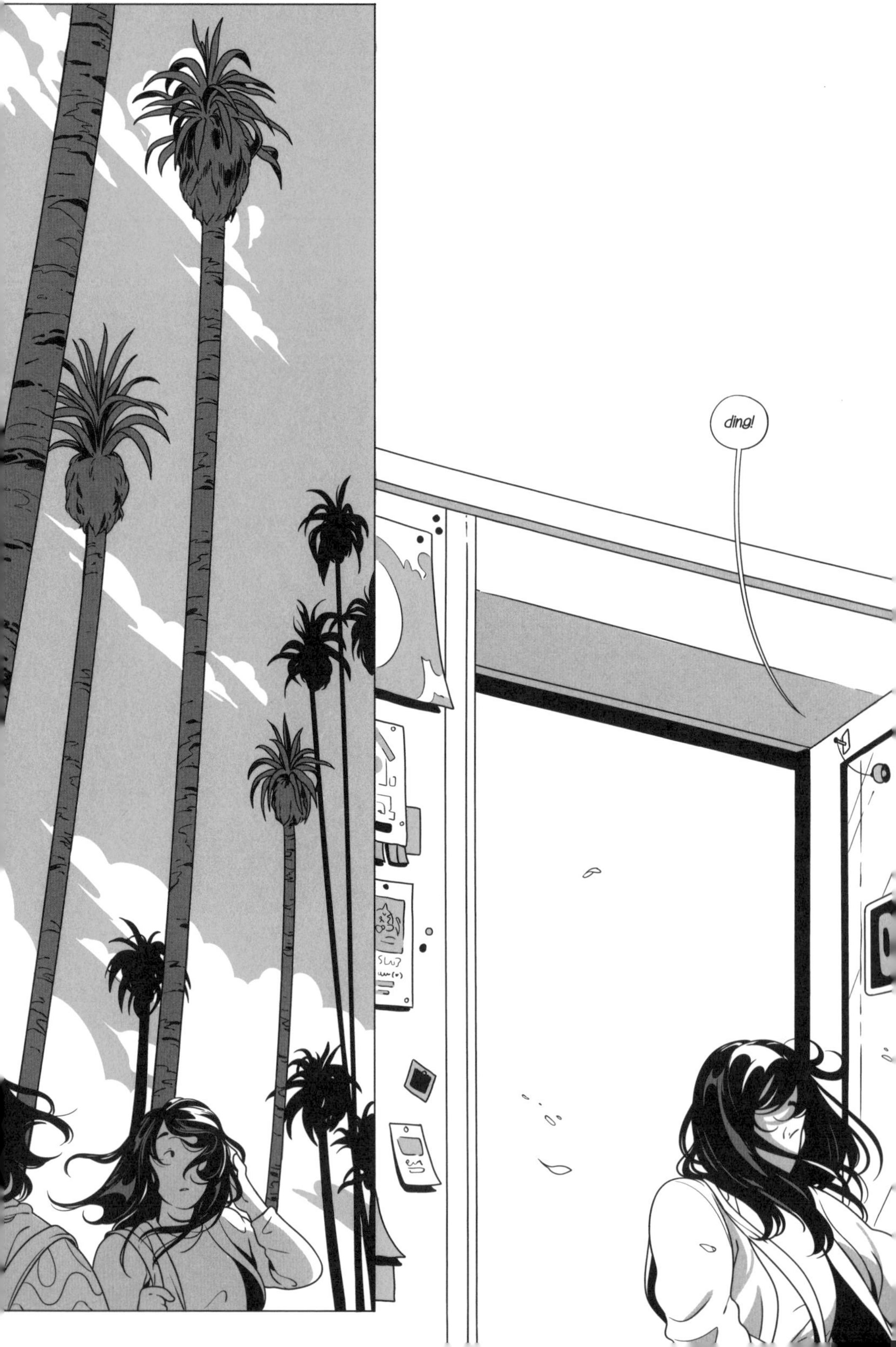
ding!

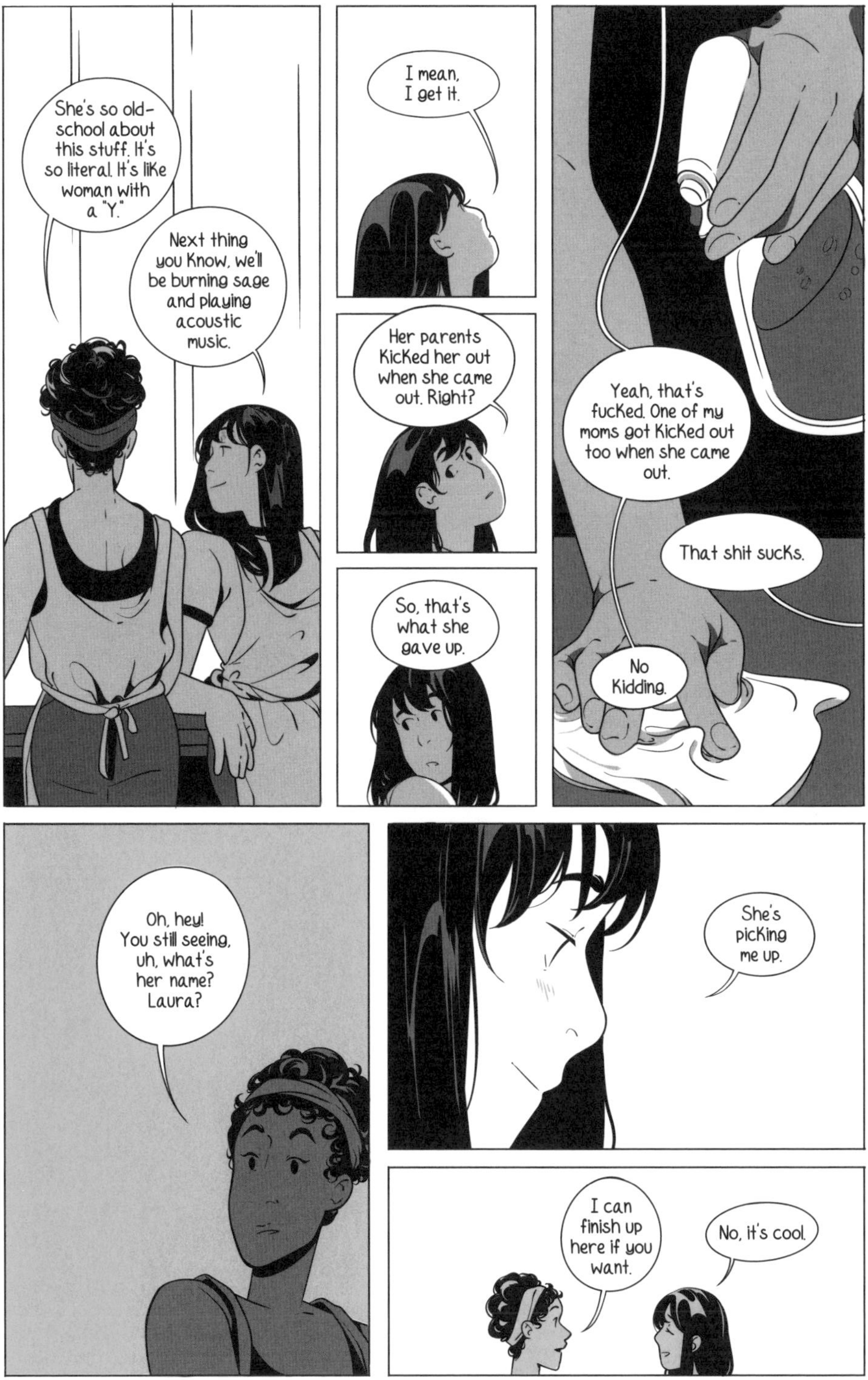
She's so old-school about this stuff. It's so literal. It's like woman with a "Y."
Next thing you know, we'll be burning sage and playing acoustic music.
I mean, I get it.
Her parents kicked her out when she came out. Right?
So, that's what she gave up.
Yeah, that's fucked. One of my moms got kicked out too when she came out.
That shit sucks.
No kidding.
Oh, hey! You still seeing, uh, what's her name? Laura?
She's picking me up.
I can finish up here if you want.
No, it's cool.

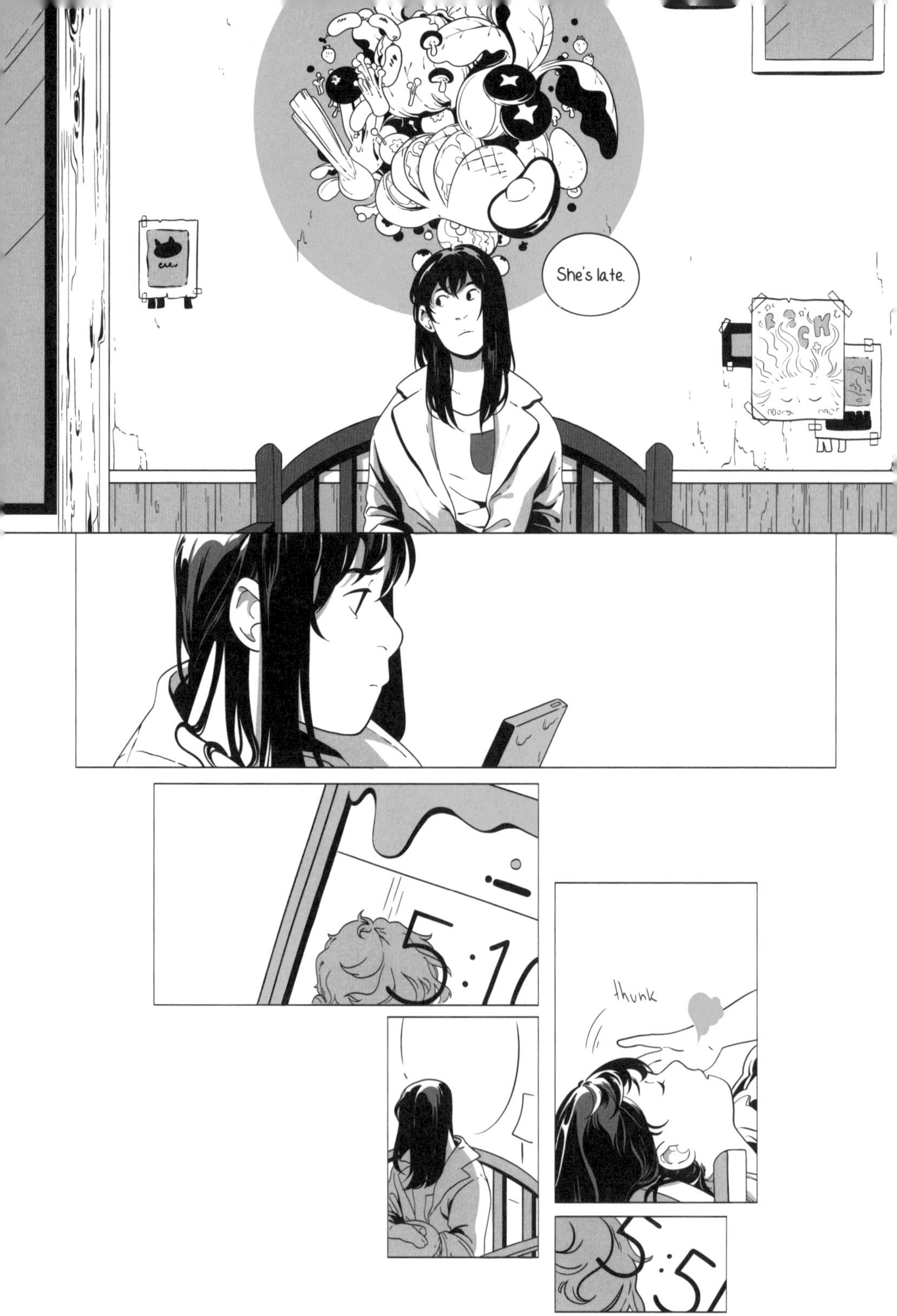
She's late.
thunk

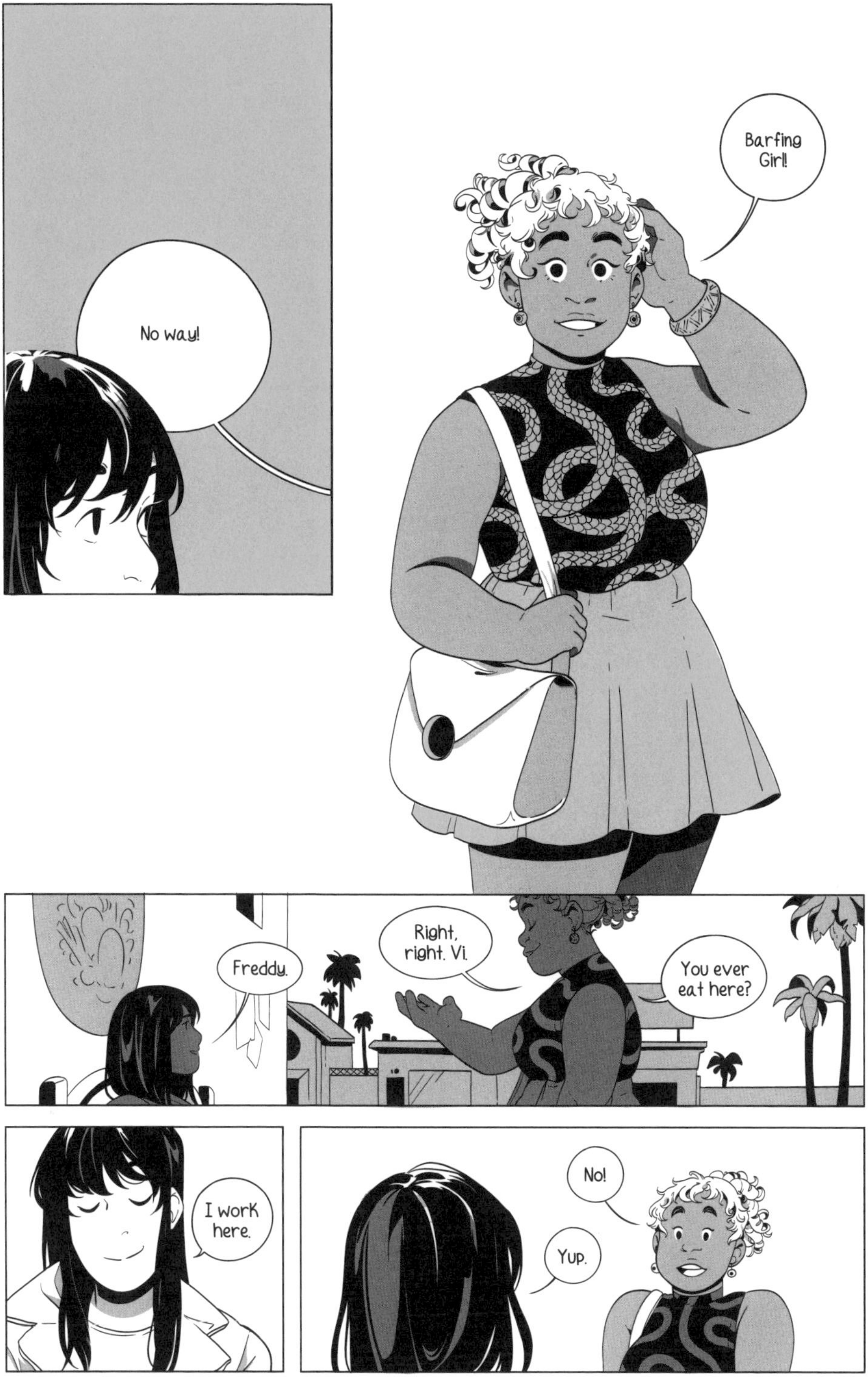
No way!
Barfing Girl!
Freddy.
Right, right. Vi.
You ever eat here?
I work here.
No!
Yup.

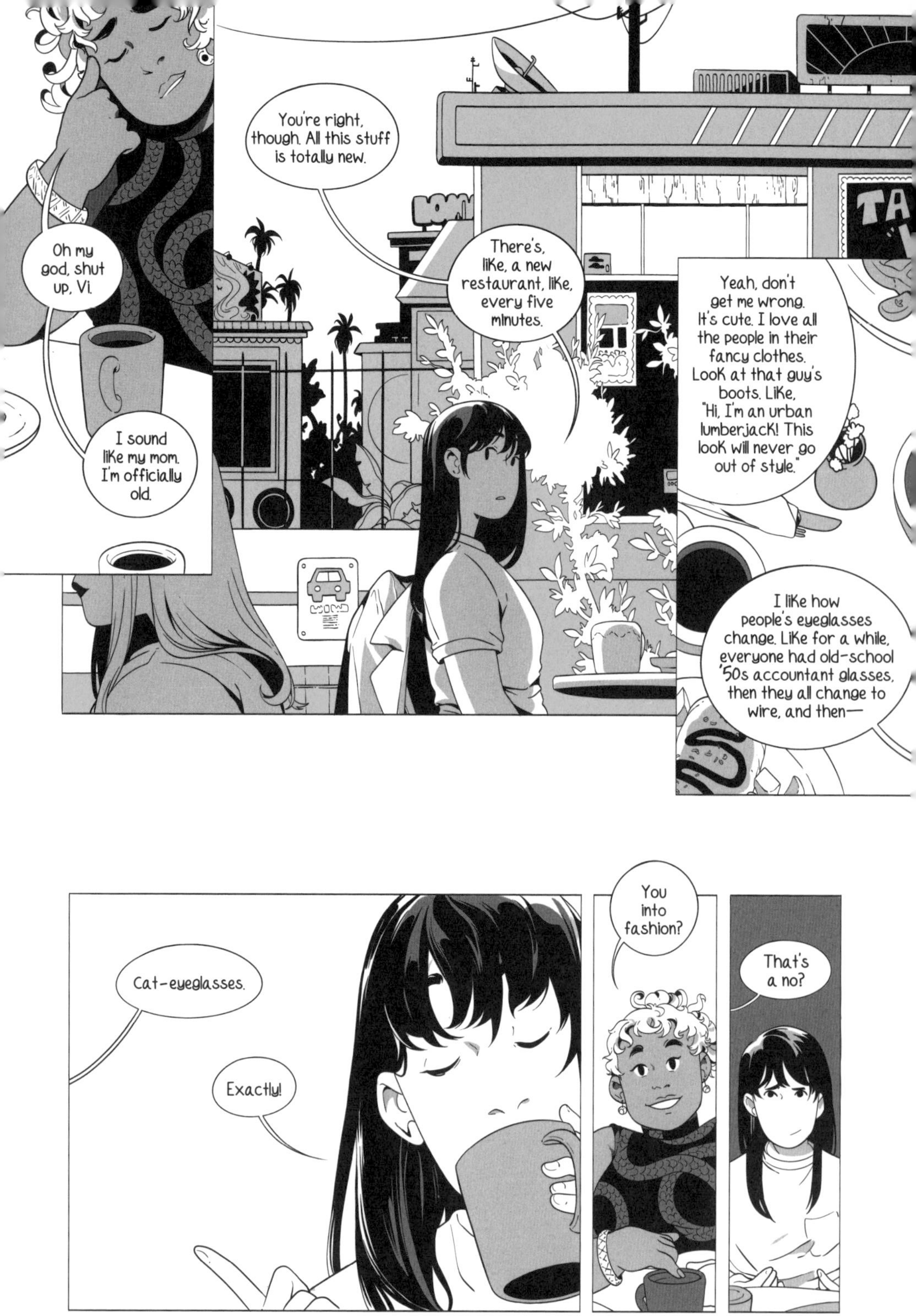
You're right, though. All this stuff is totally new.
Oh my god, shut up, Vi.
There's, like, a new restaurant, like, every five minutes.
I sound like my mom. I'm officially old.
Yeah, don't get me wrong. It's cute. I love all the people in their fancy clothes. Look at that guy's boots. Like, "Hi, I'm an urban lumberjack! This look will never go out of style."
I like how people's eyeglasses change. Like for a while, everyone had old-school '50s accountant glasses, then they all change to wire, and then—
Cat-eyeglasses.
Exactly!
You into fashion?
That's a no?

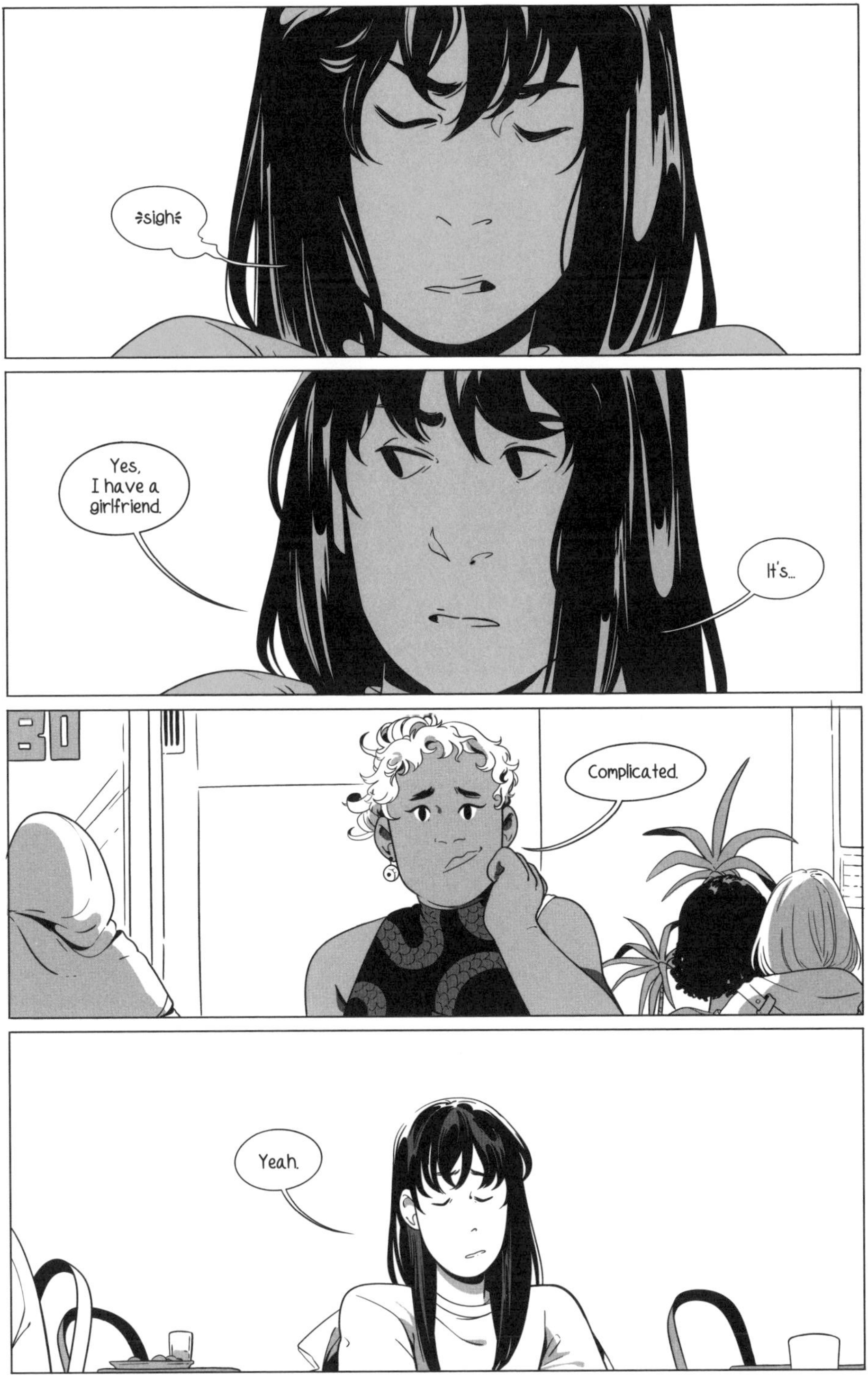
sigh
Yes, I have a girlfriend.
It's...
Complicated.
Yeah.

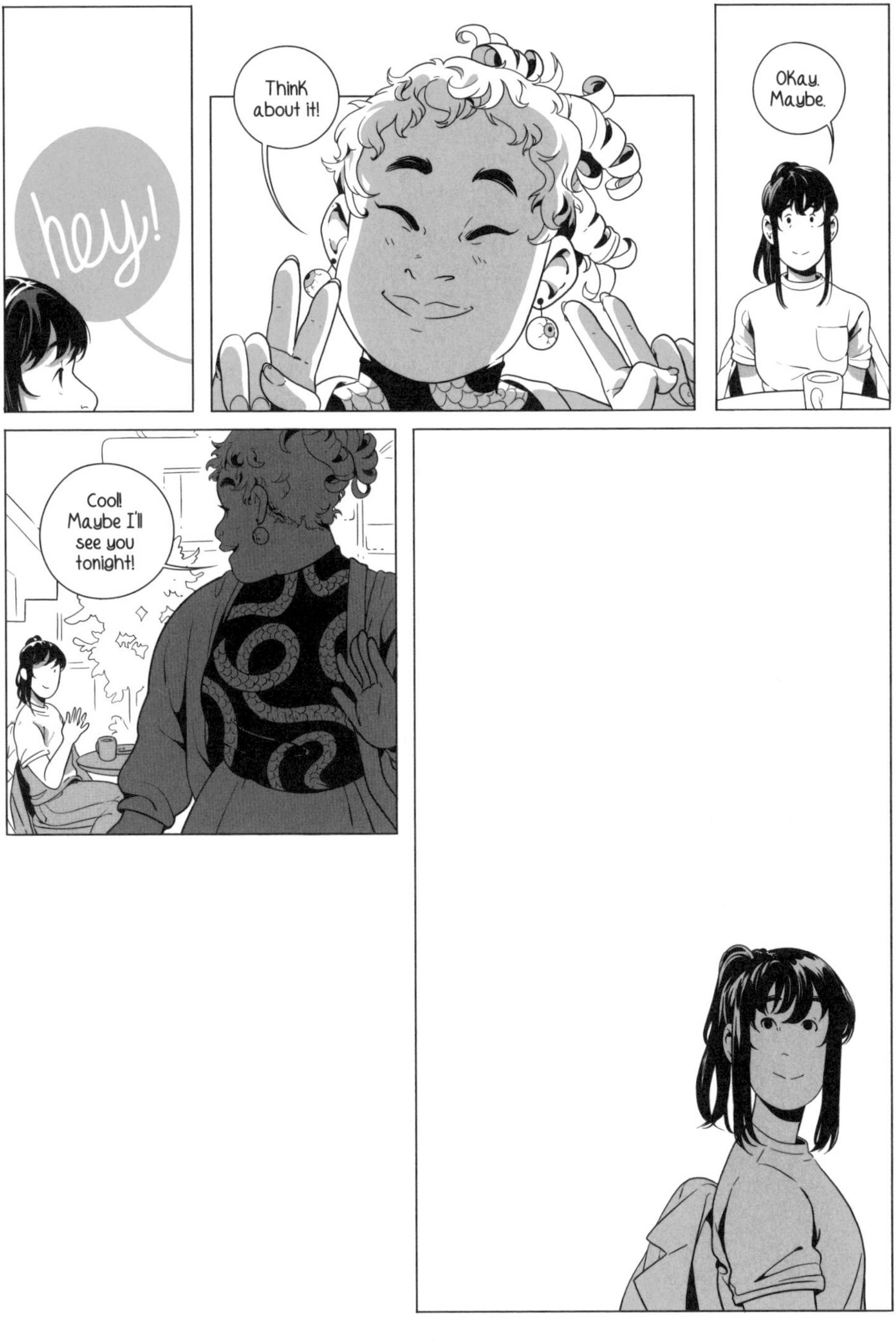
hey!
Think about it!
Okay. Maybe.
Cool! Maybe I'll see you tonight!

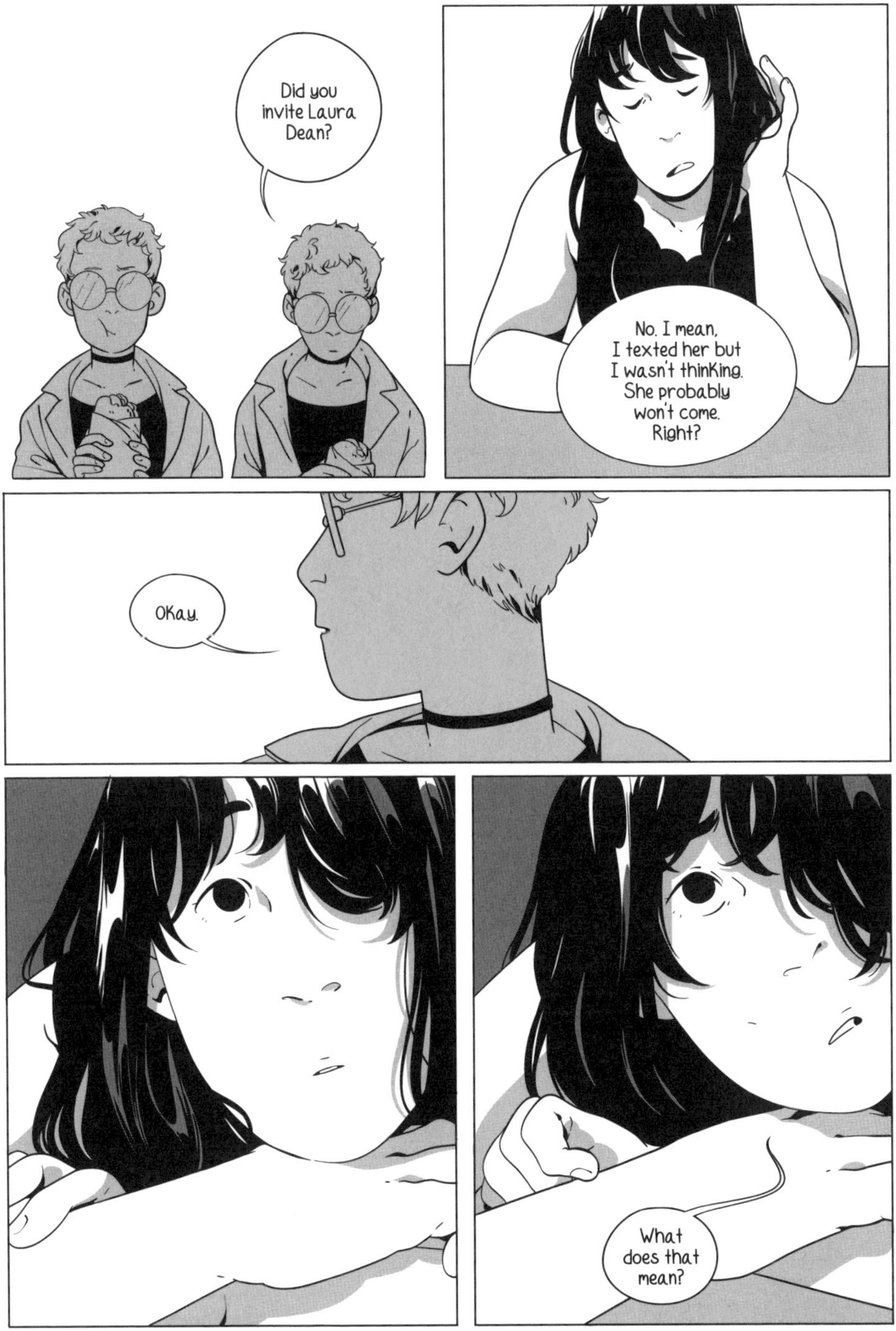
Did you invite Laura Dean?
No. I mean, I texted her but I wasn't thinking. She probably won't come. Right?
Okay.
What does that mean?

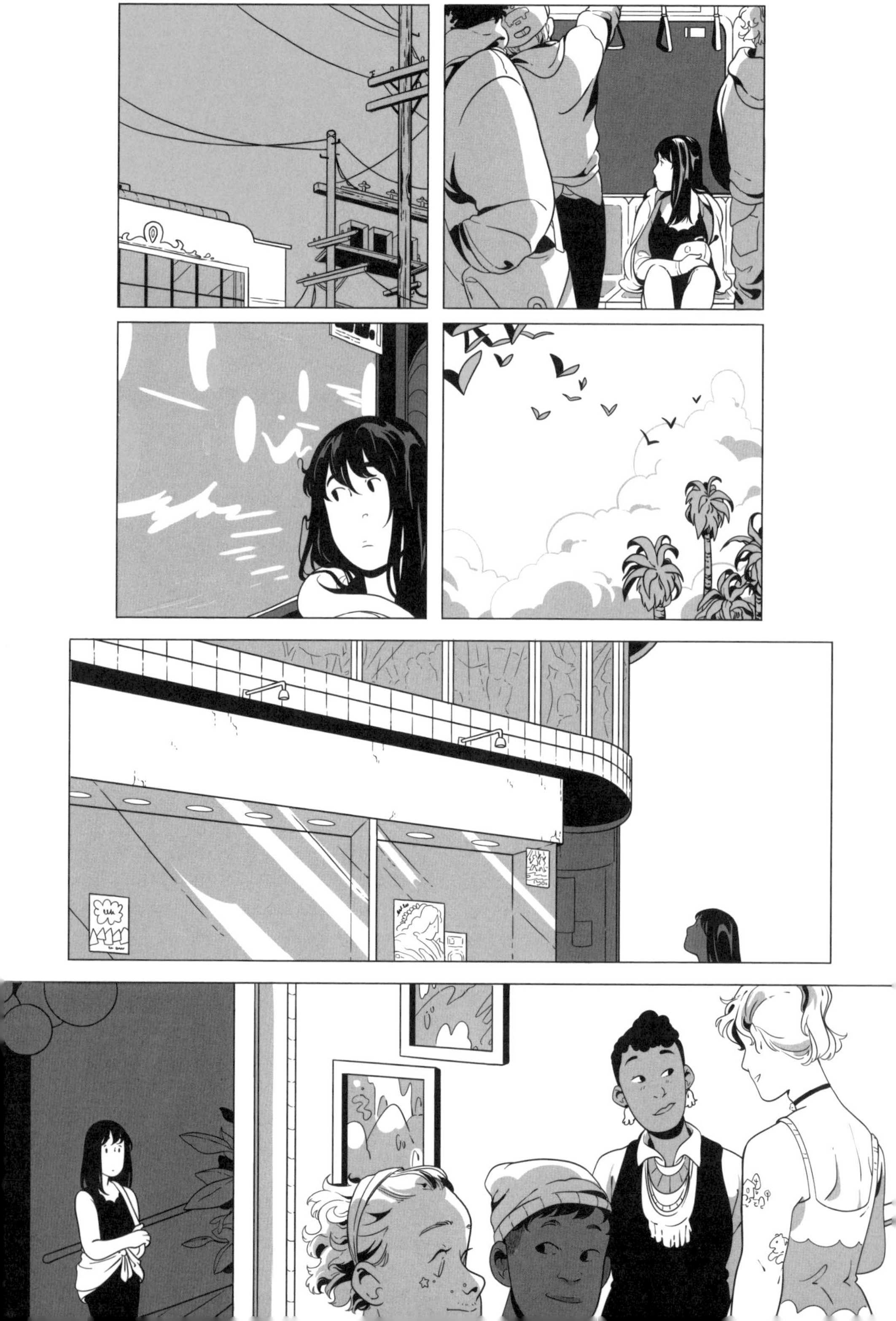

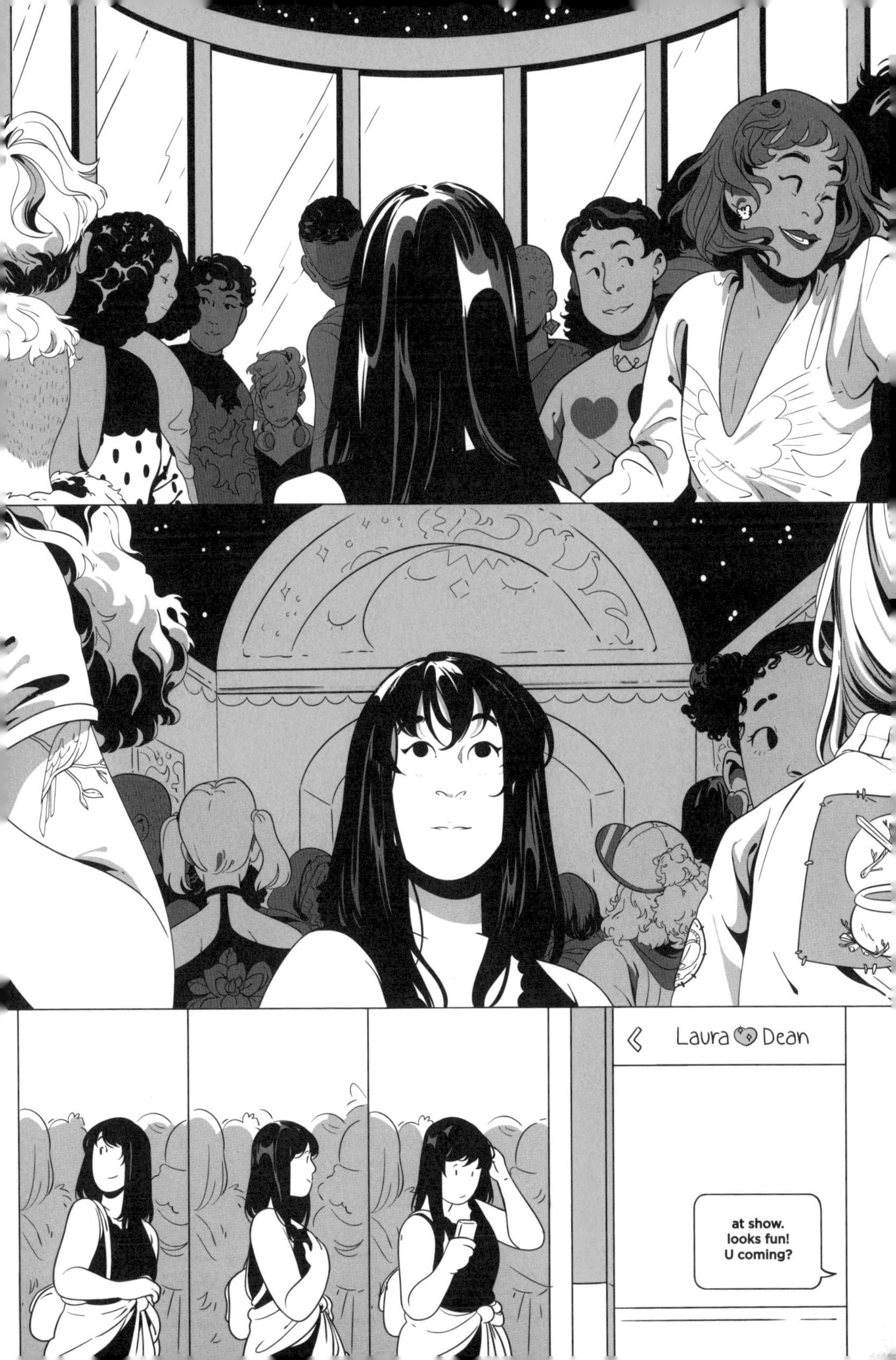
Laura Dean
at show.
looks fun!
U coming?

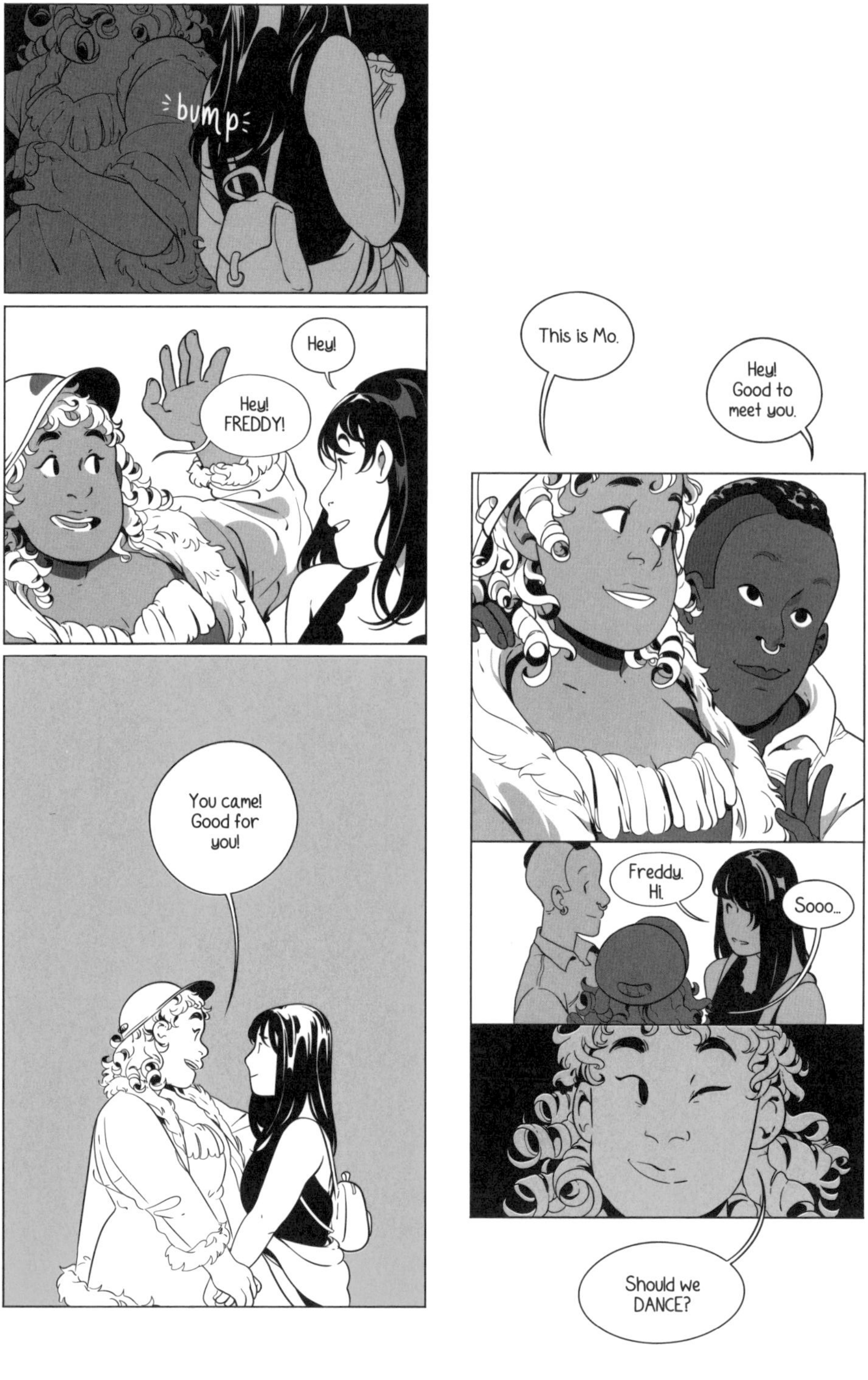
bump
Hey!
Hey!
FREDDY!
You came!
Good for
you!
This is Mo.
Hey!
Good to
meet you.
Freddy.
Hi.
Sooo...
Should we
DANCE?

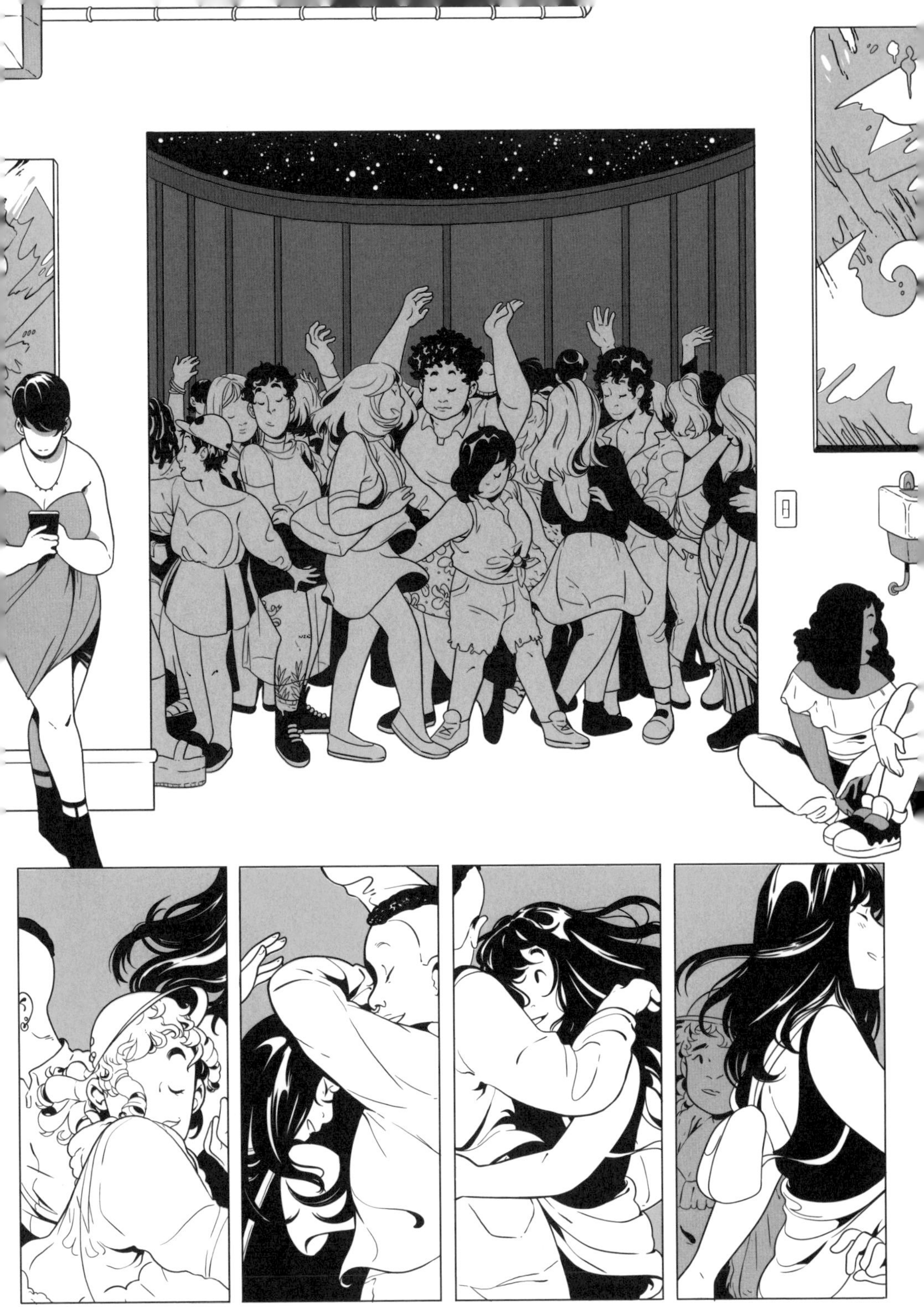

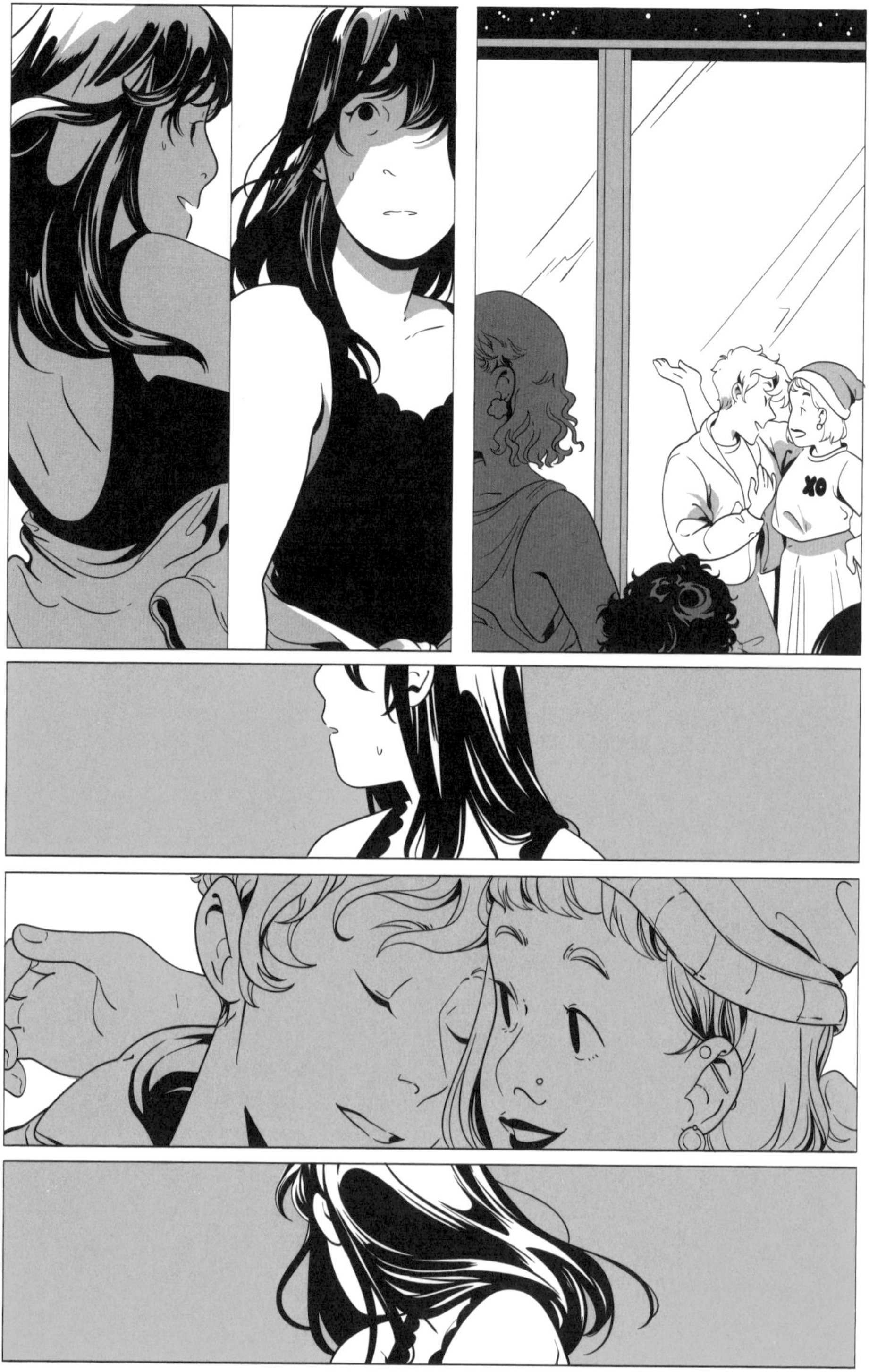
XO

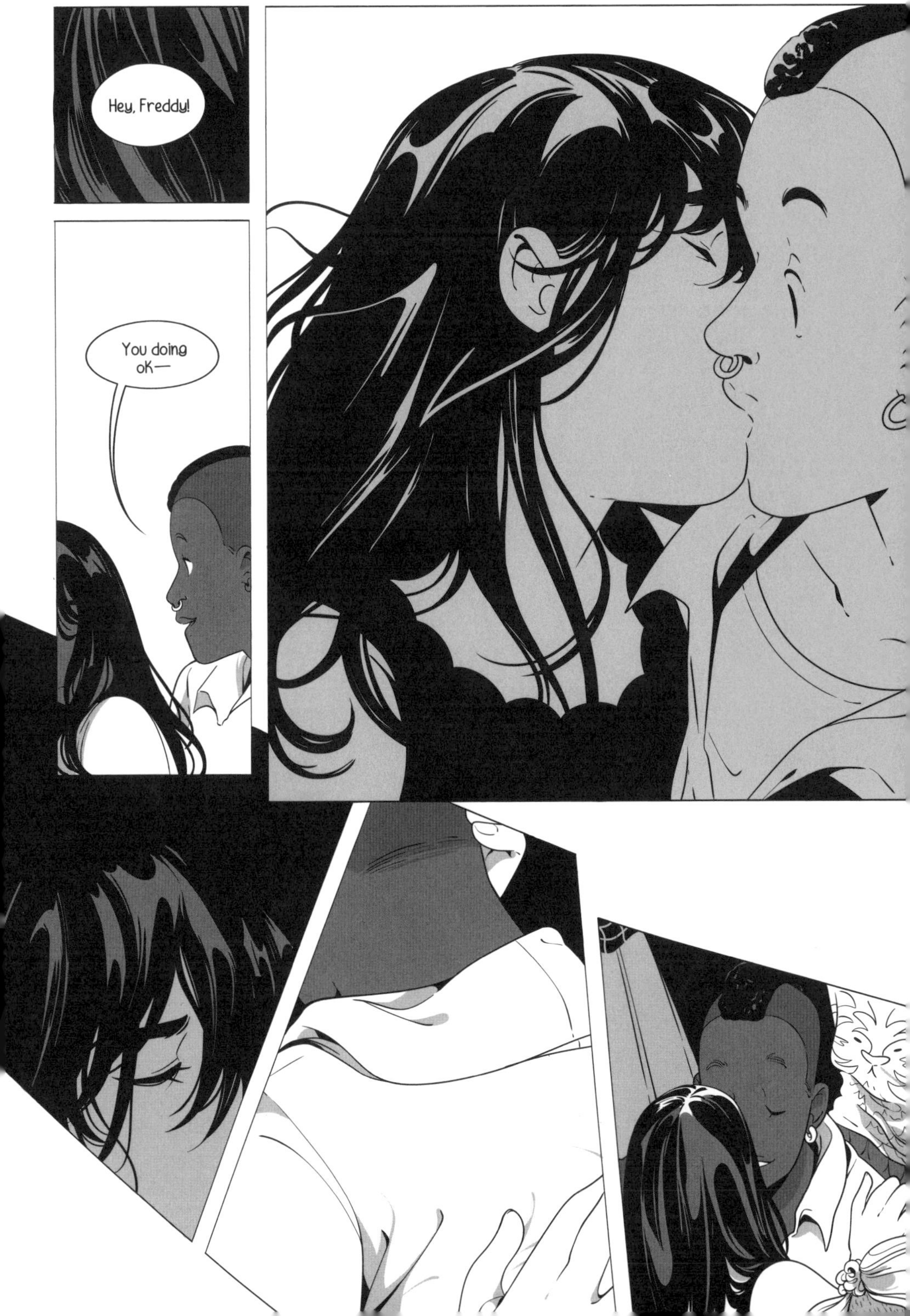
Hey, Freddy!
You doing ok—

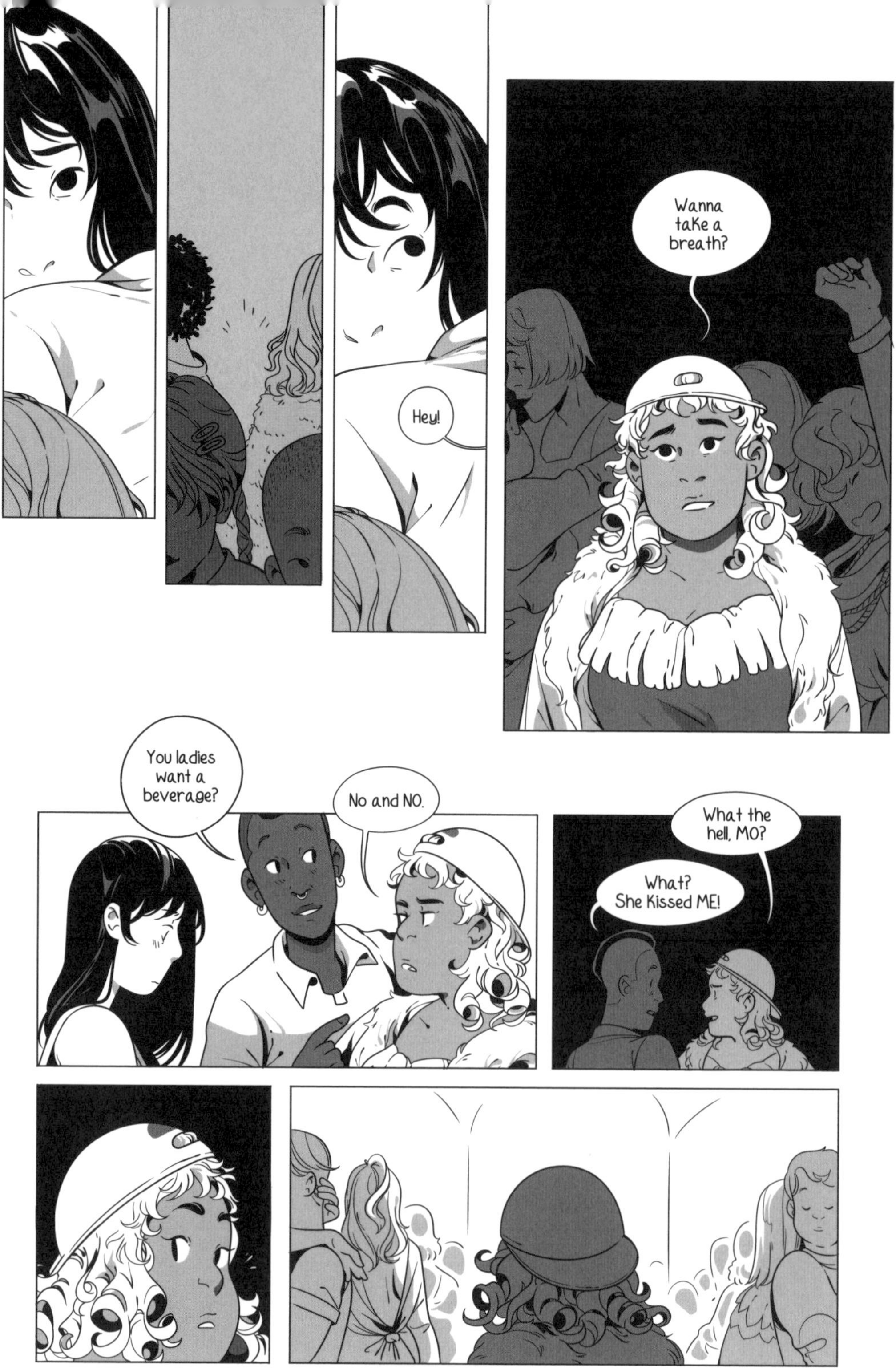
Hey!
Wanna take a breath?
You ladies want a beverage?
No and NO.
What the hell, MO?
What? She Kissed ME!

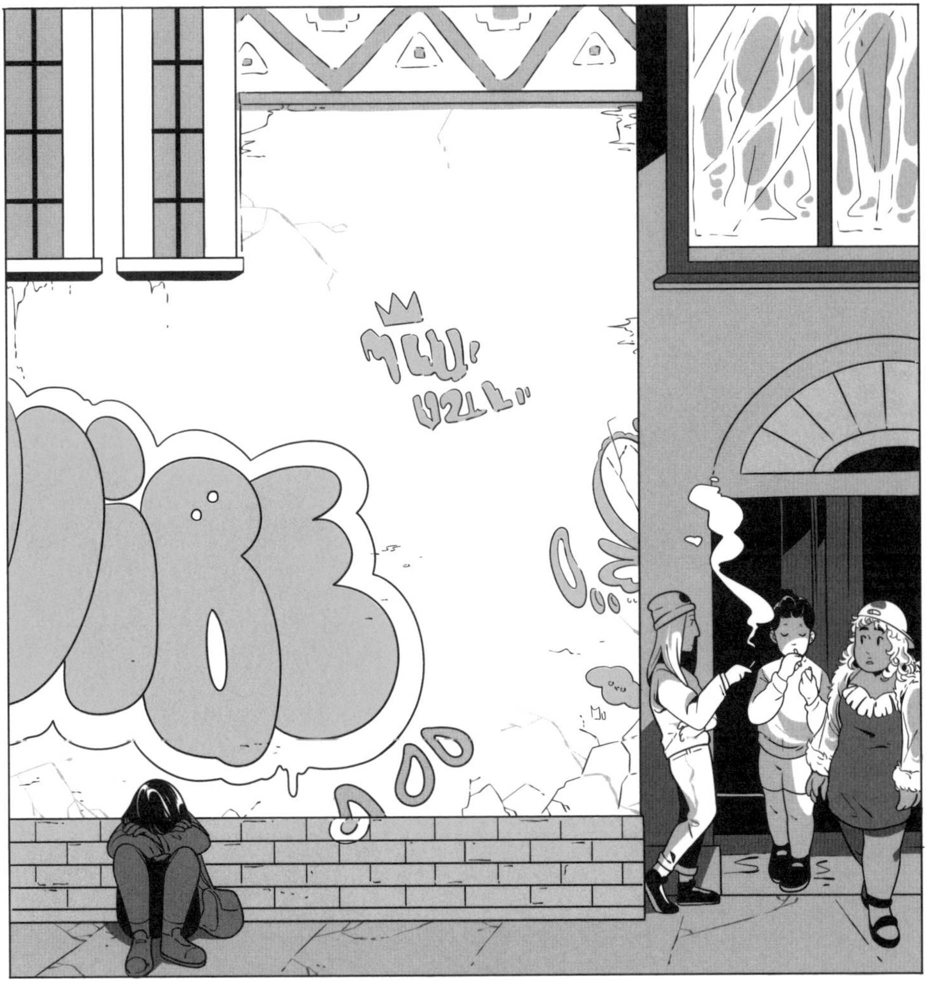

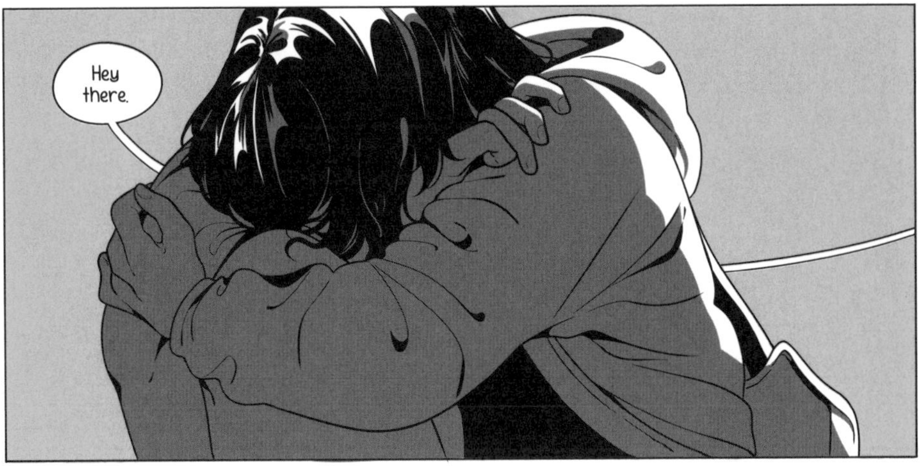
Hey there.

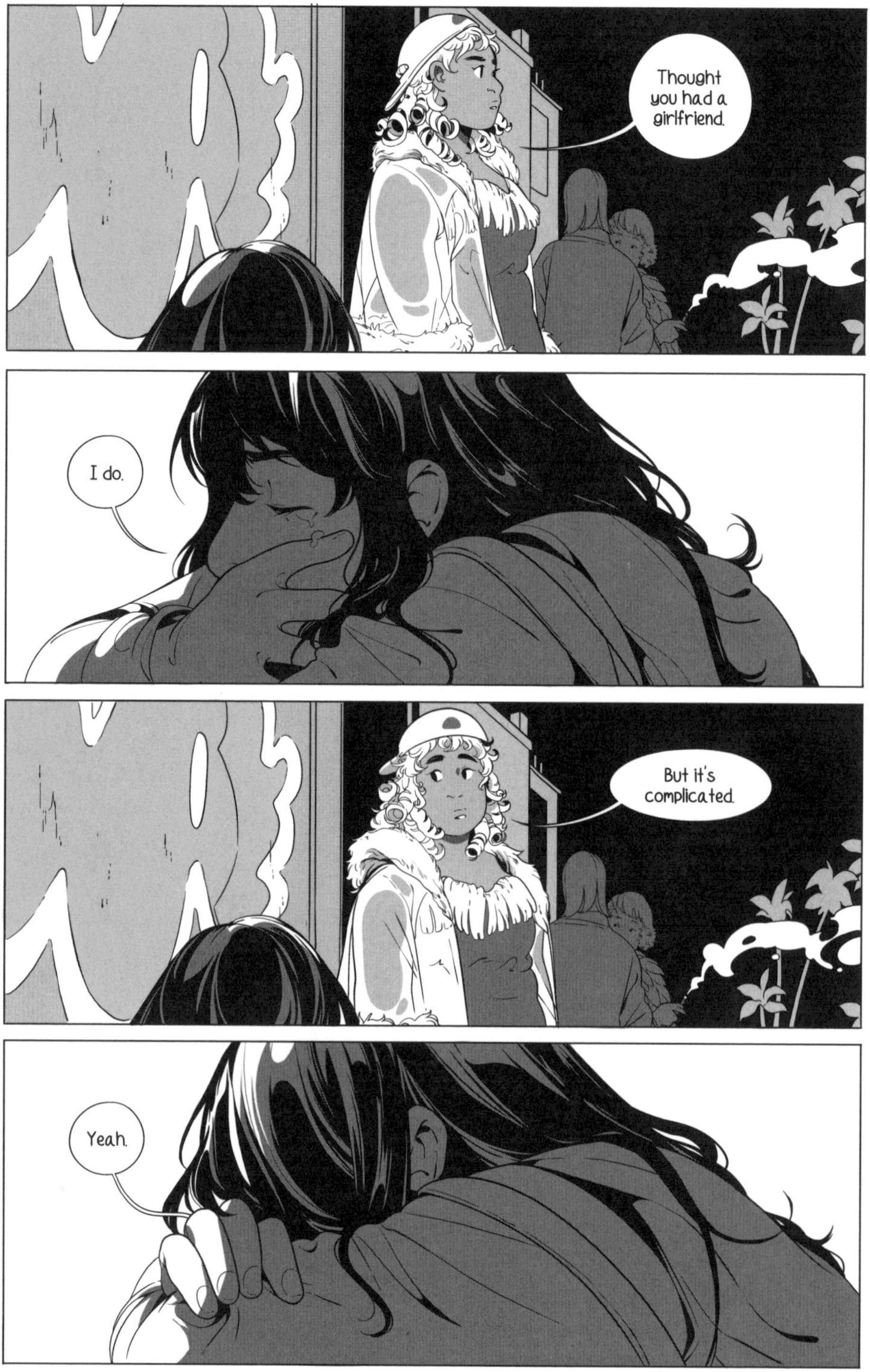
Thought you had a girlfriend.
I do.
But it's complicated.
Yeah.

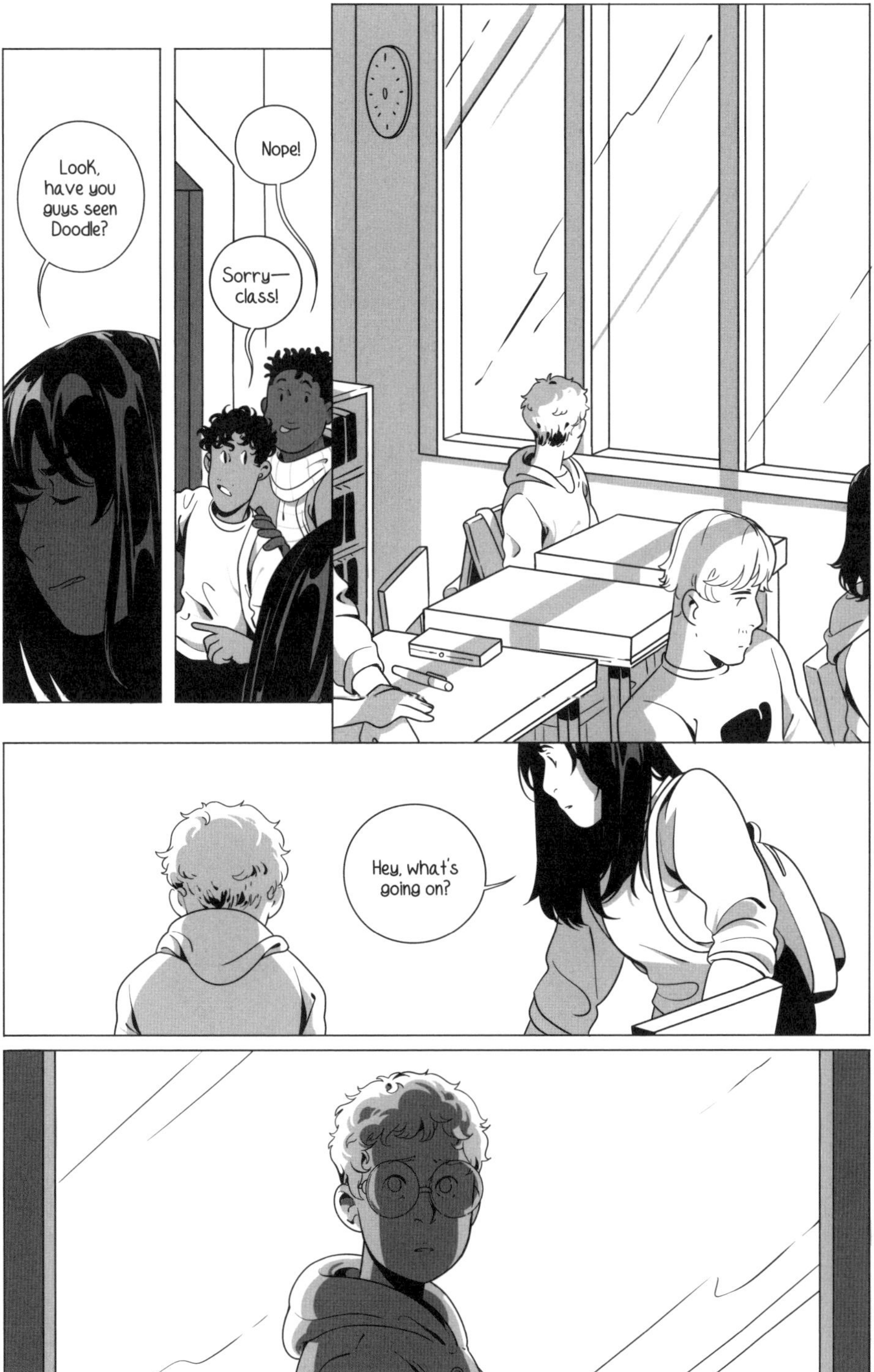
Look, have you guys seen Doodle?
Nope!
Sorry— class!
Hey, what's going on?

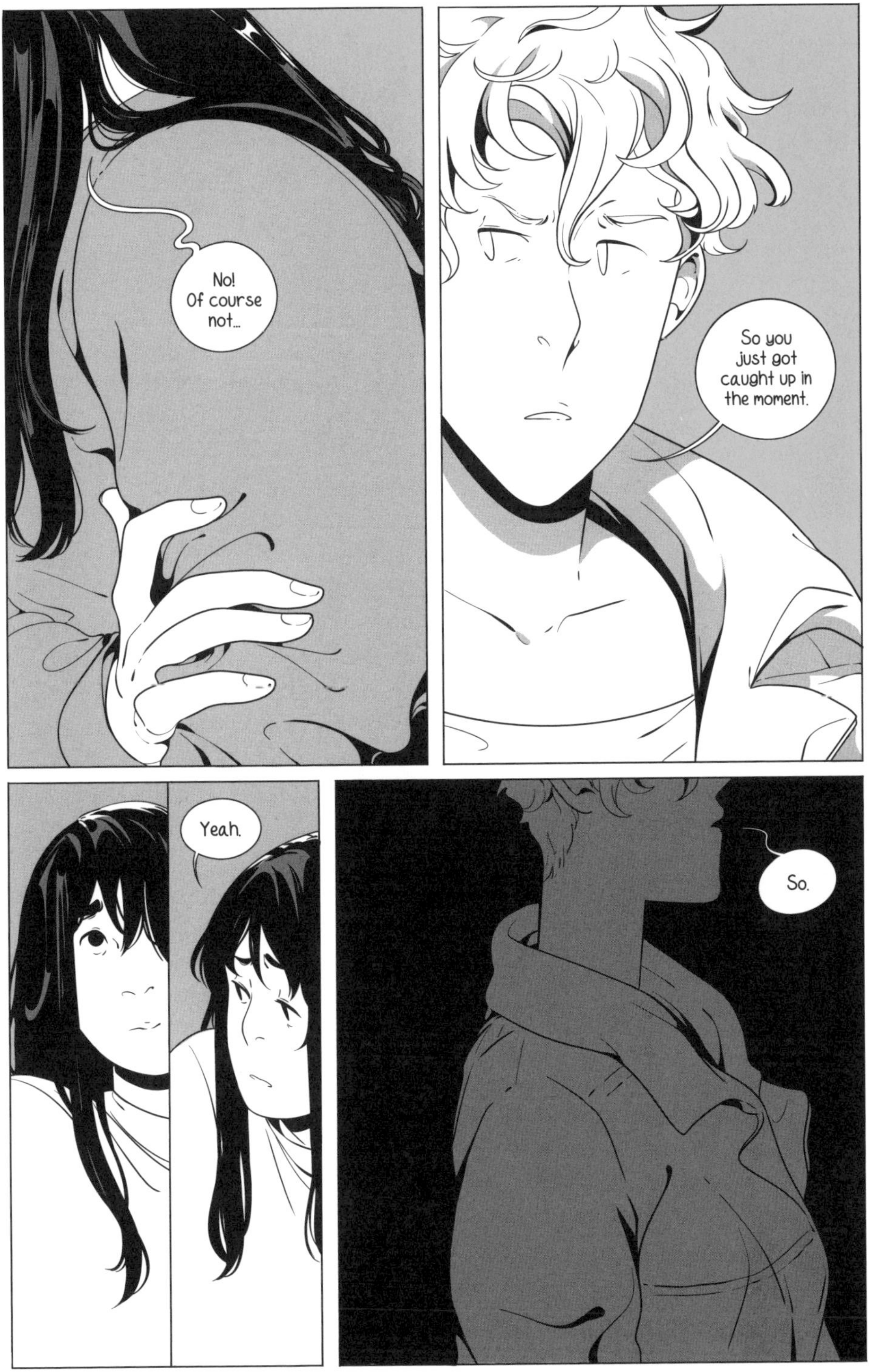
No! Of course not...
So you just got caught up in the moment.
Yeah.
So.

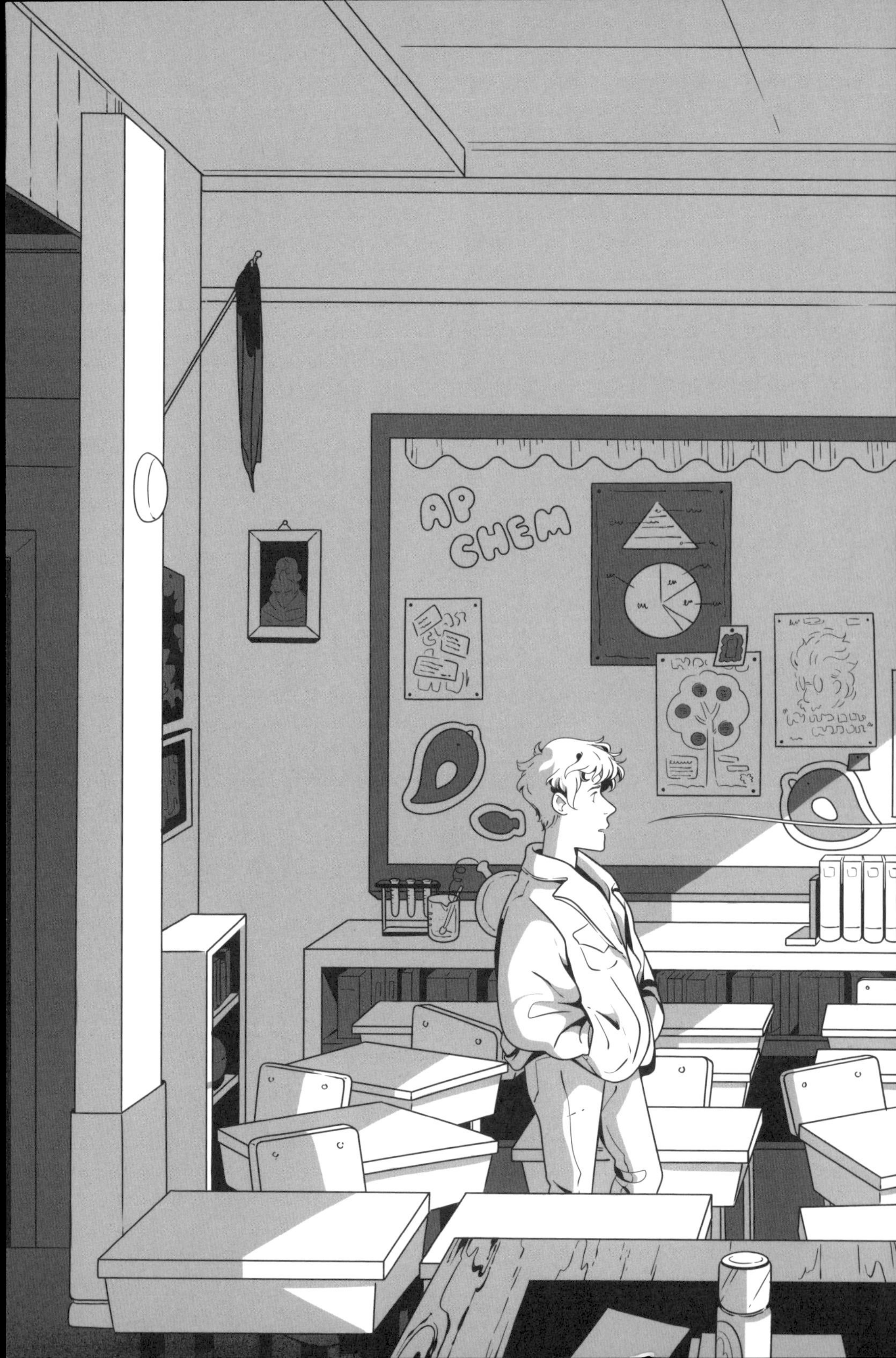
AP
CHEM

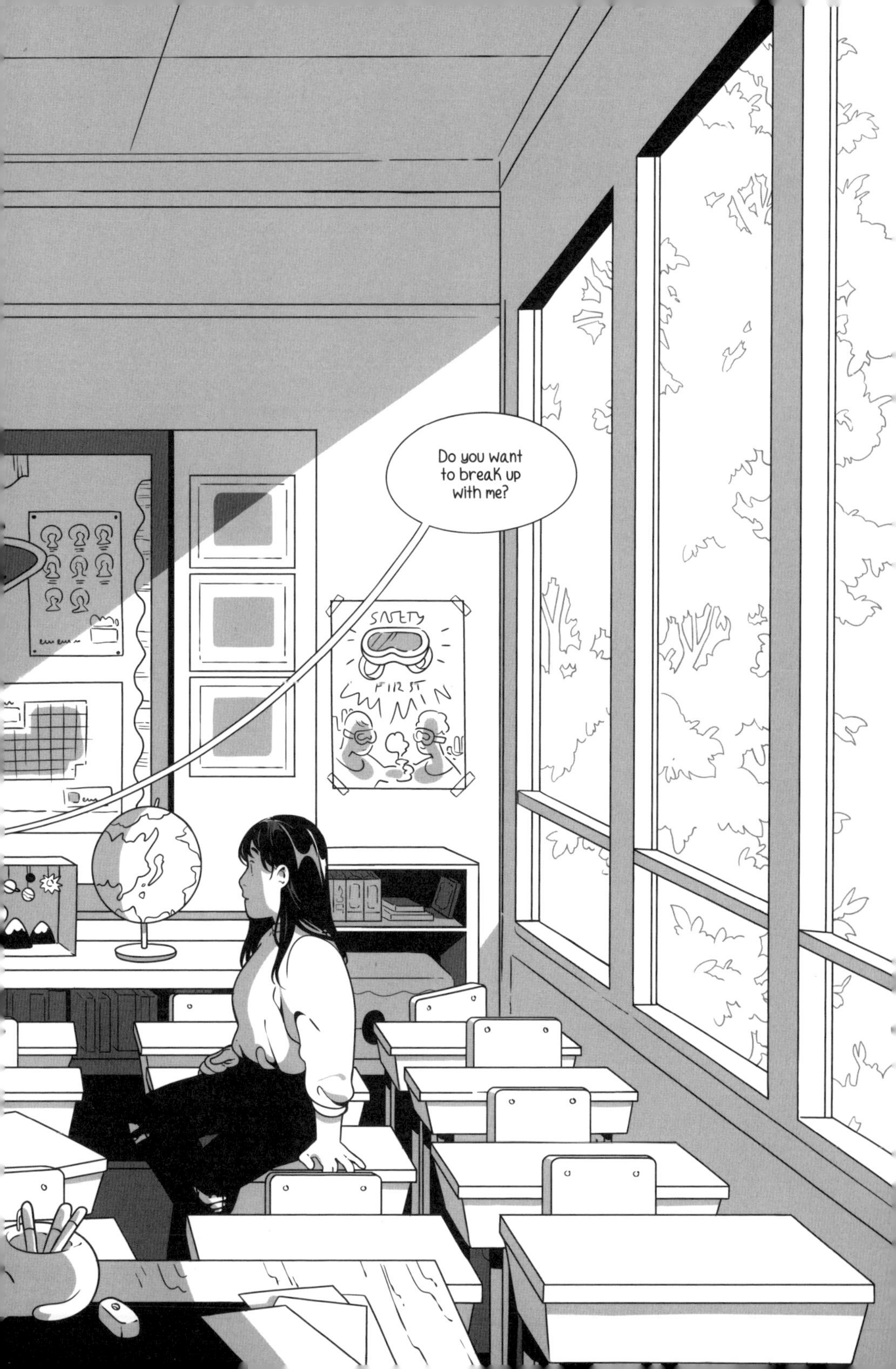
Do you want to breaK up with me?
SAFETY
FIRST

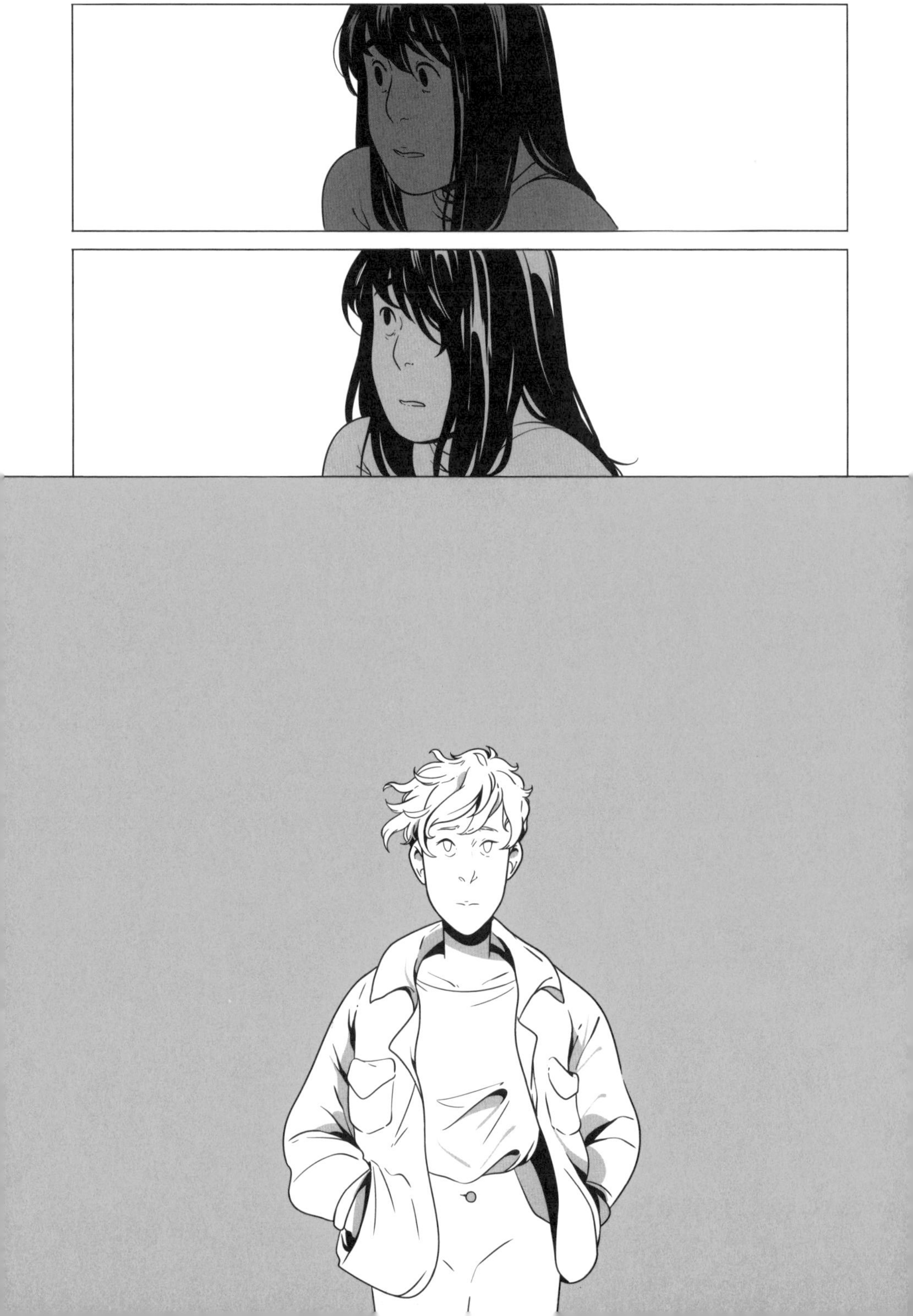

200

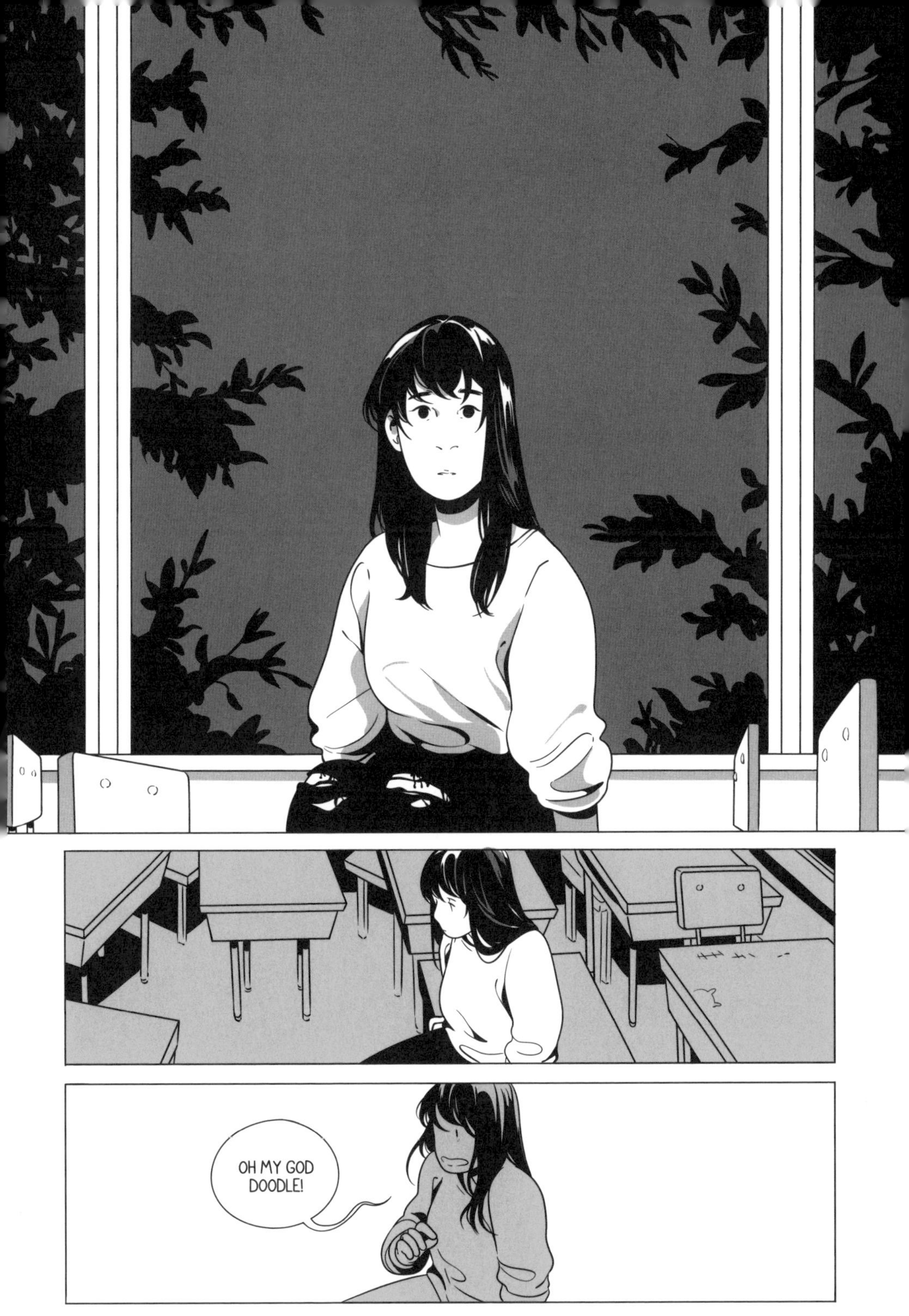
OH MY GOD DOODLE!

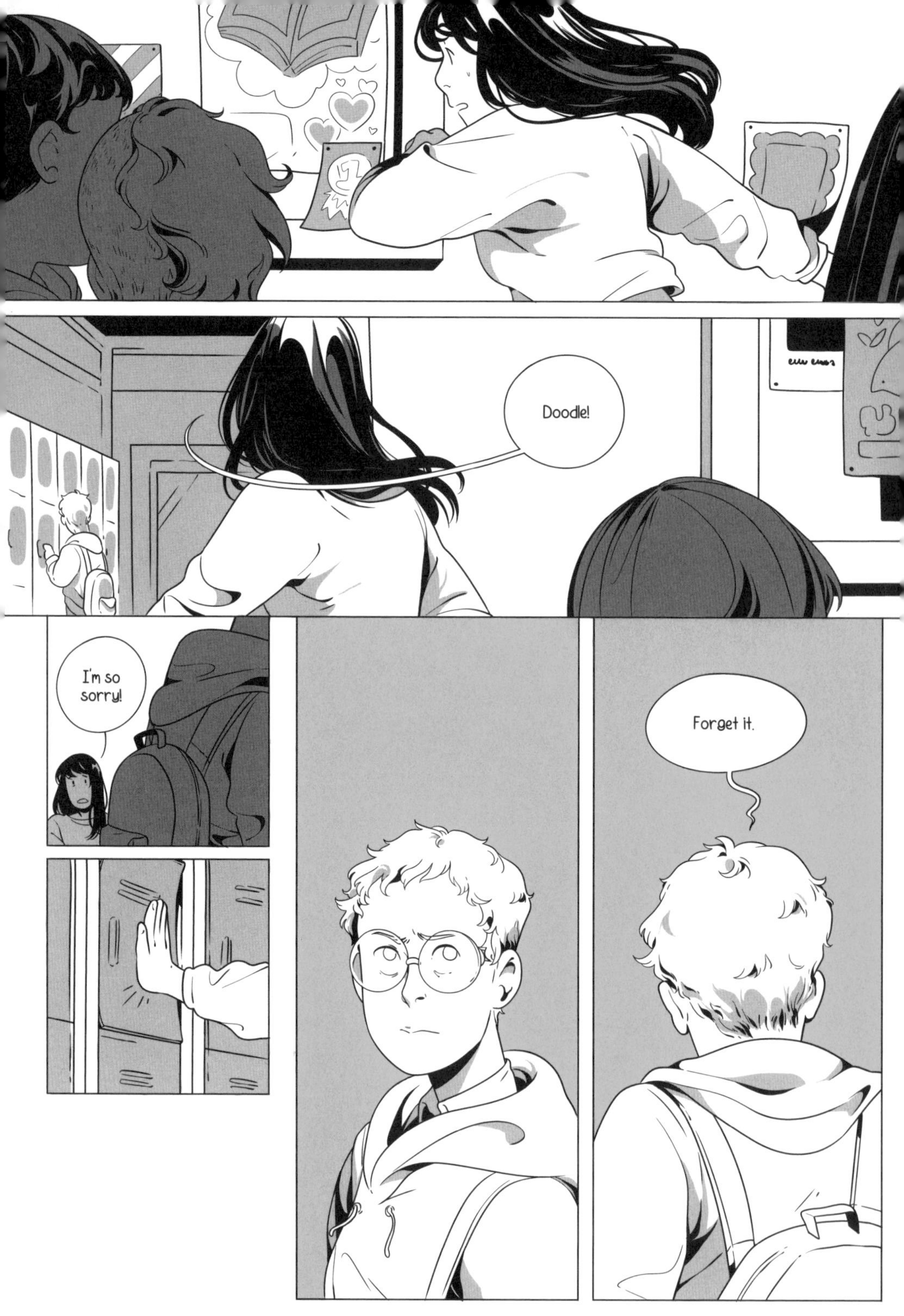

Doodle!
I'm so sorry!
Forget it.

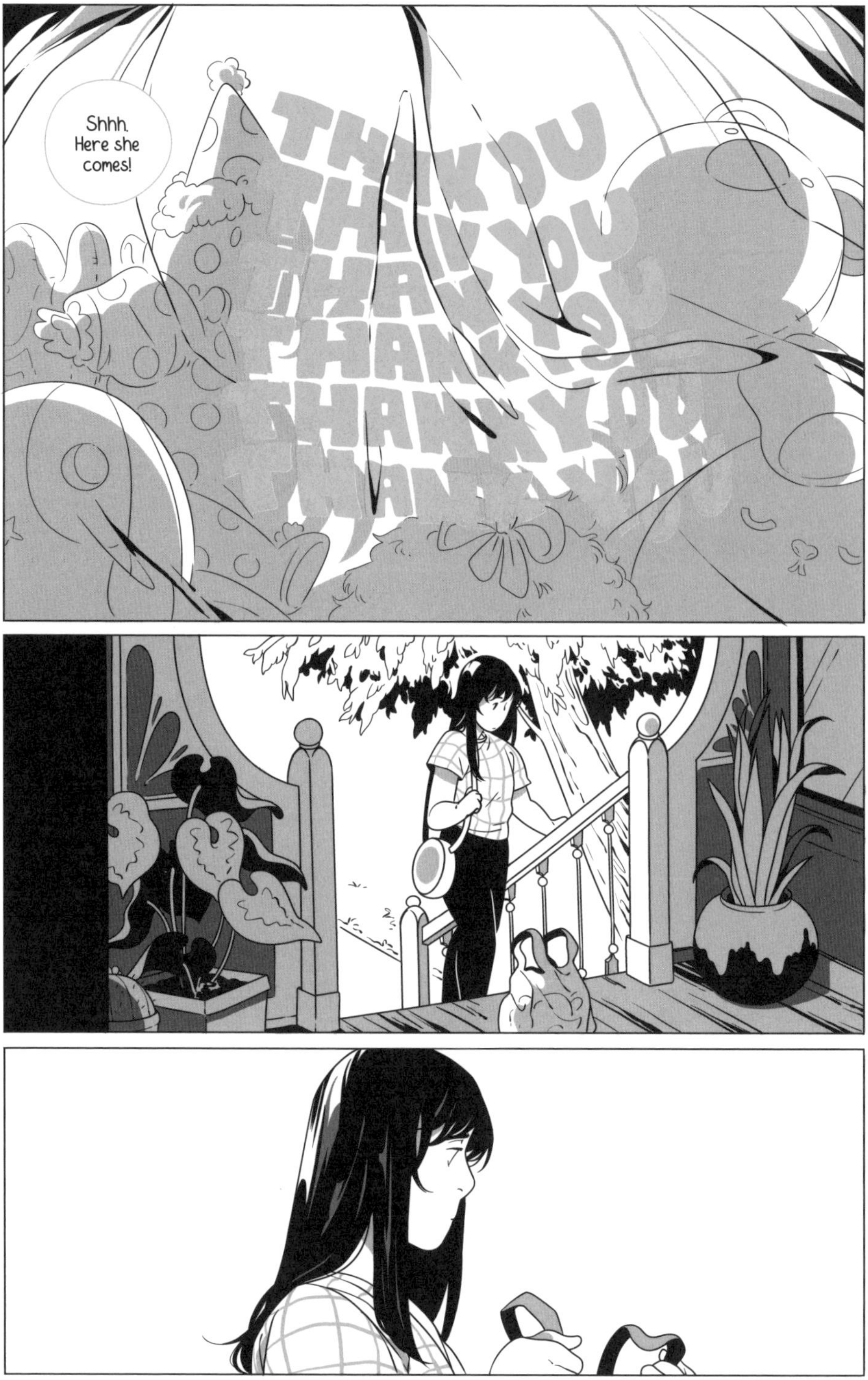
Shhh. Here she comes!

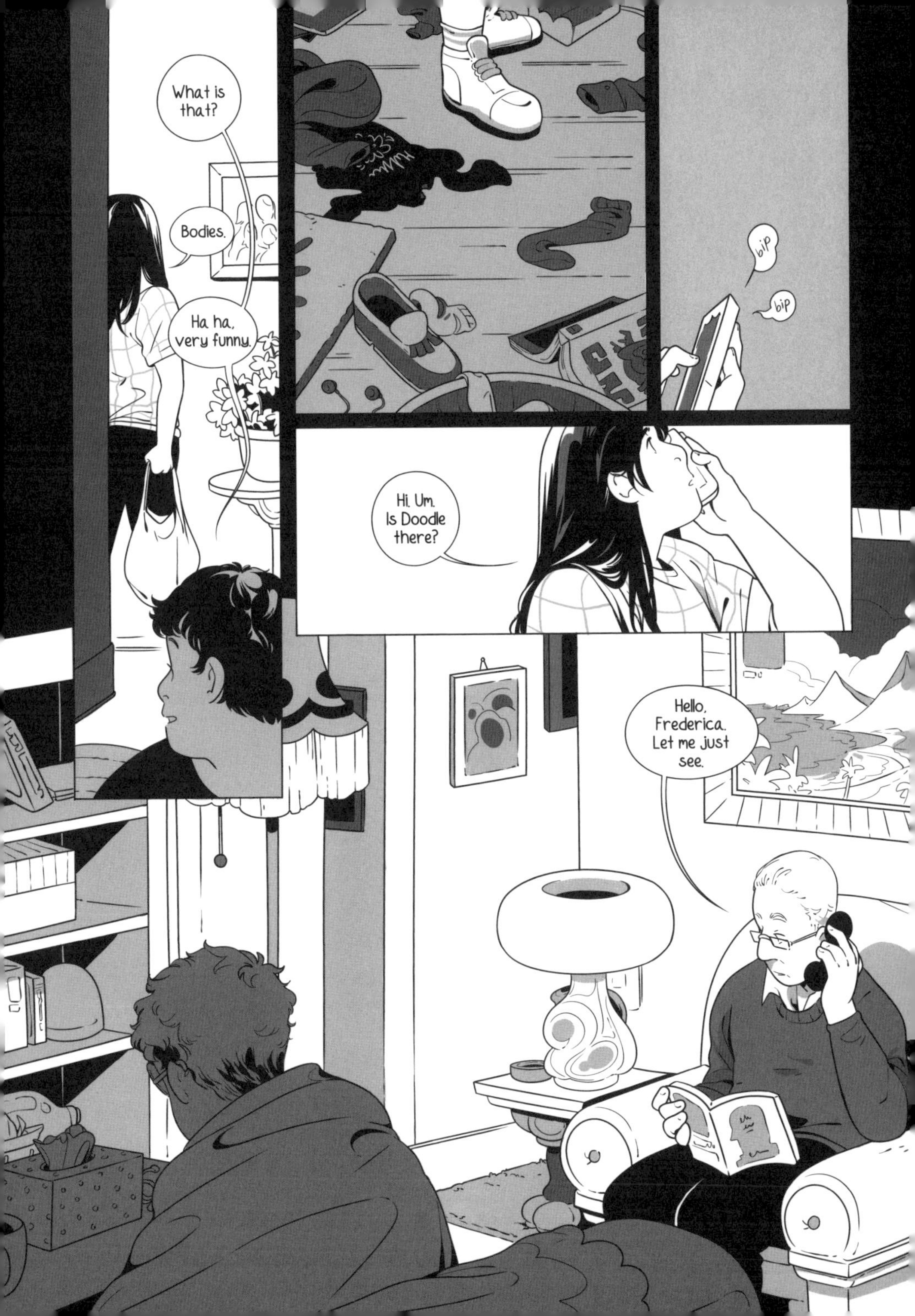
What is that?
Bodies.
Ha ha, very funny.
bip
bip
Hi. Um. Is Doodle there?
Hello, Frederica. Let me just see.

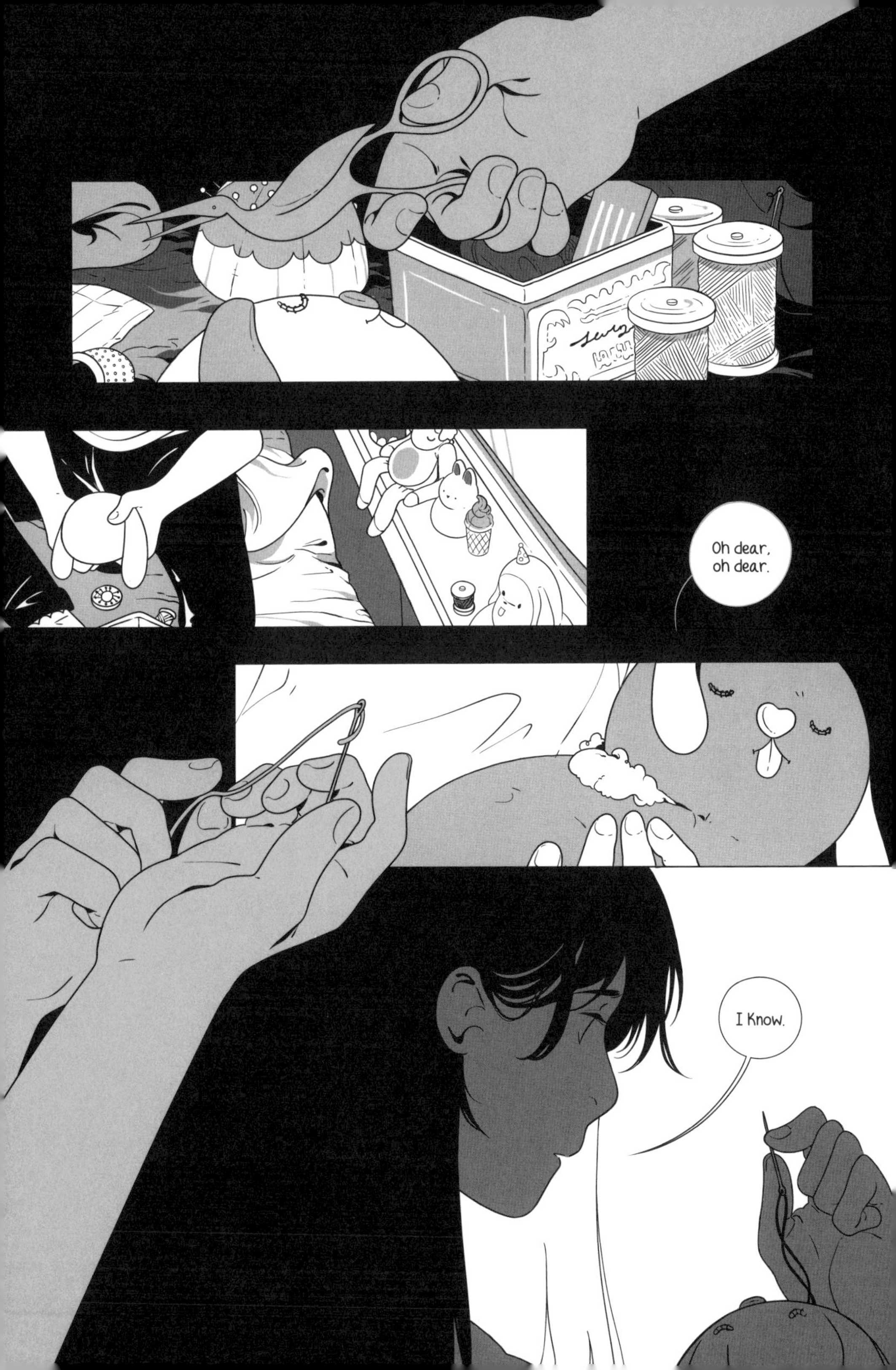
Oh dear, oh dear.
I Know.

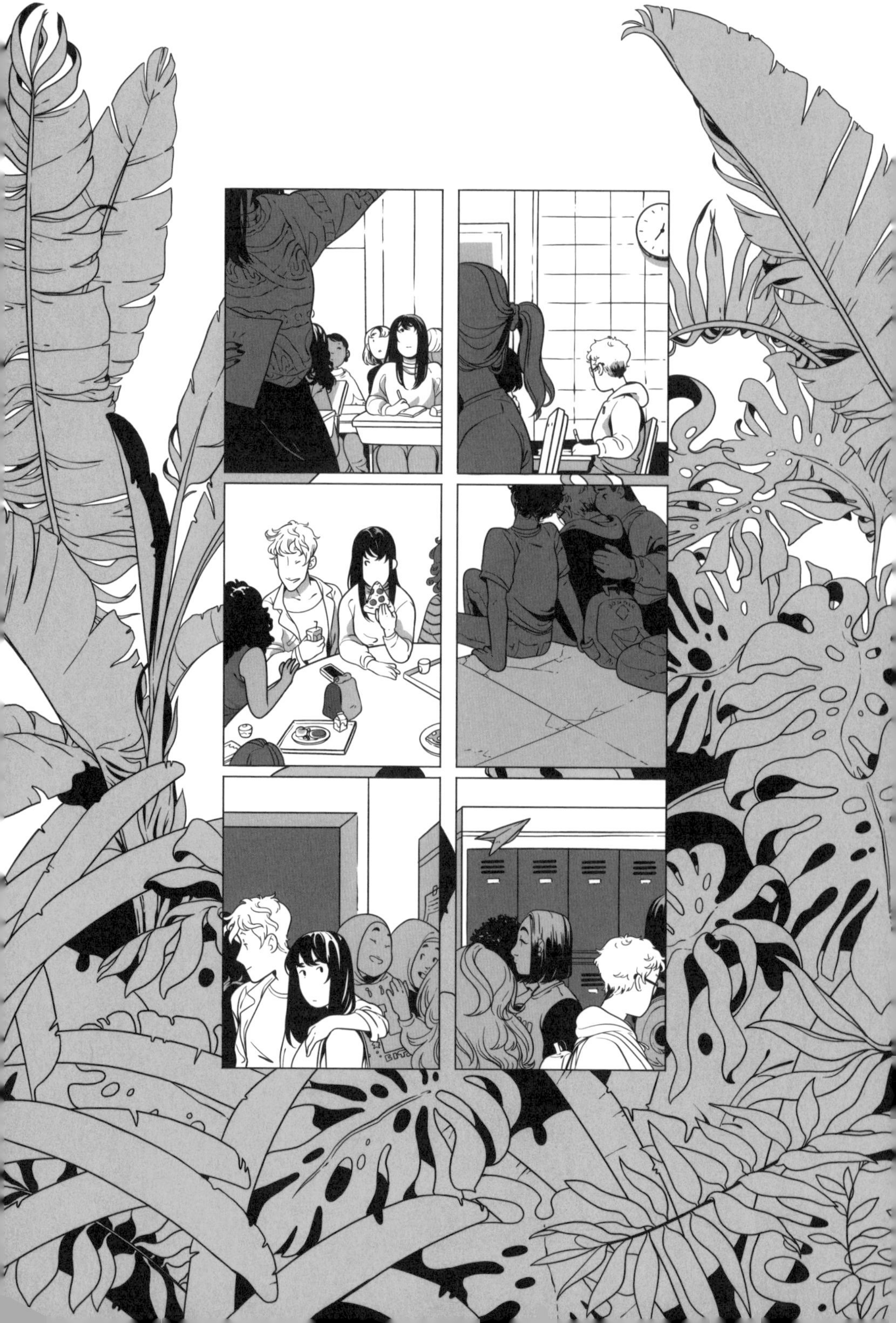

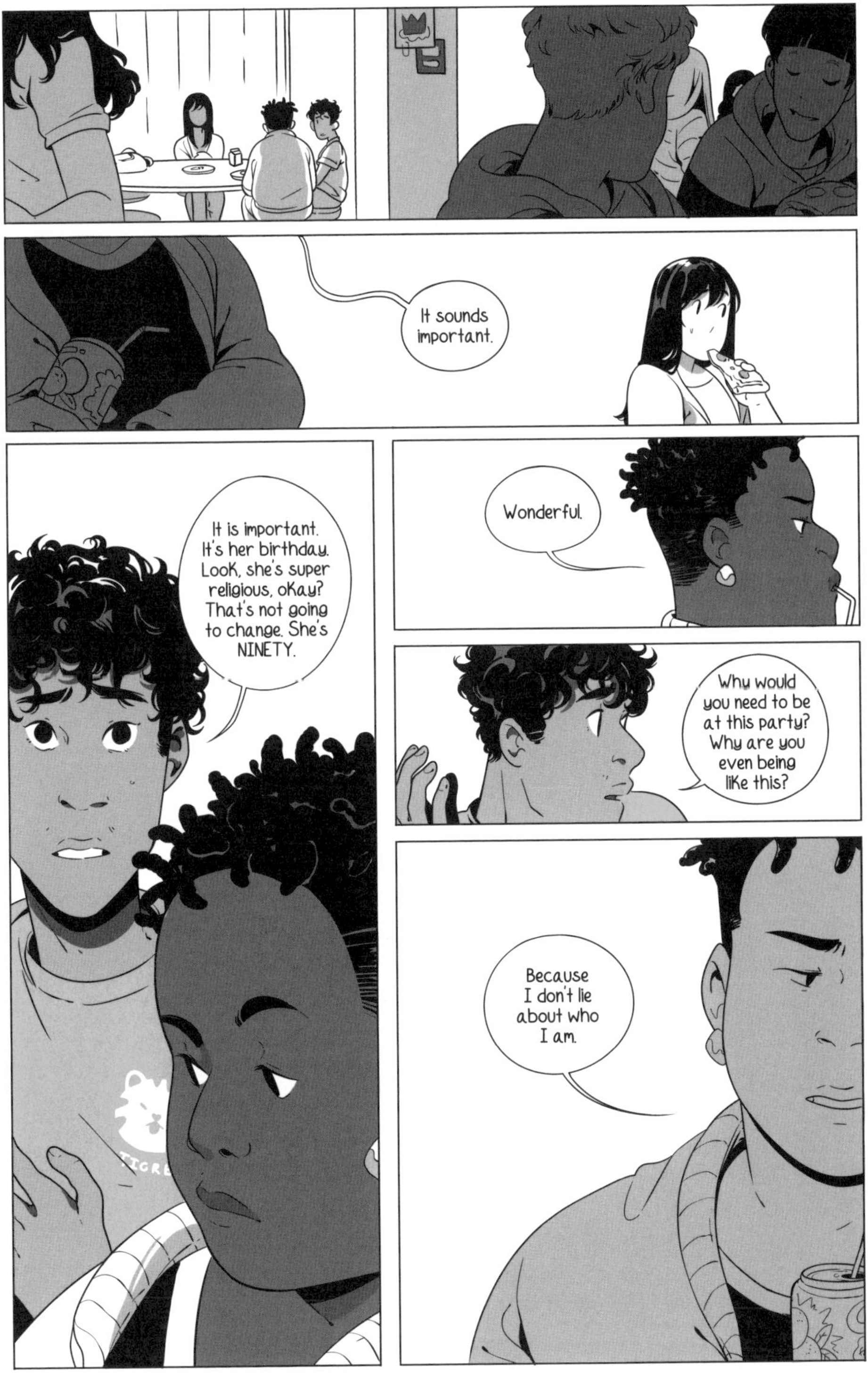
It sounds important.
It is important. It's her birthday. Look, she's super religious, okay? That's not going to change. She's NINETY.
Wonderful.
Why would you need to be at this party? Why are you even being like this?
Because I don't lie about who I am.

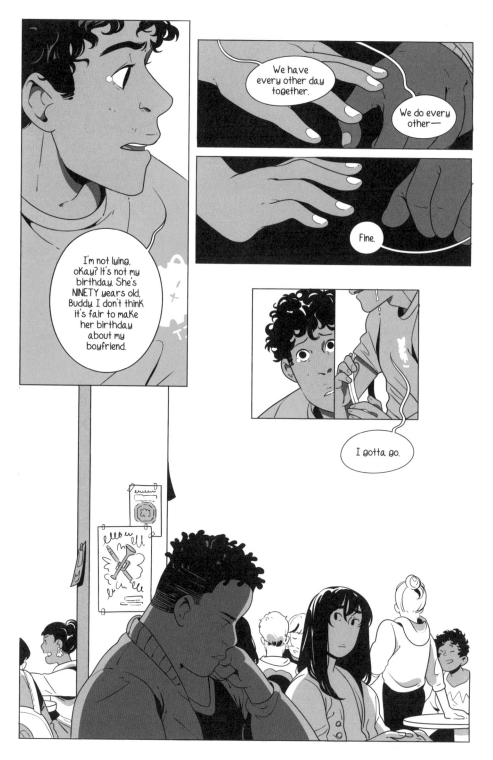

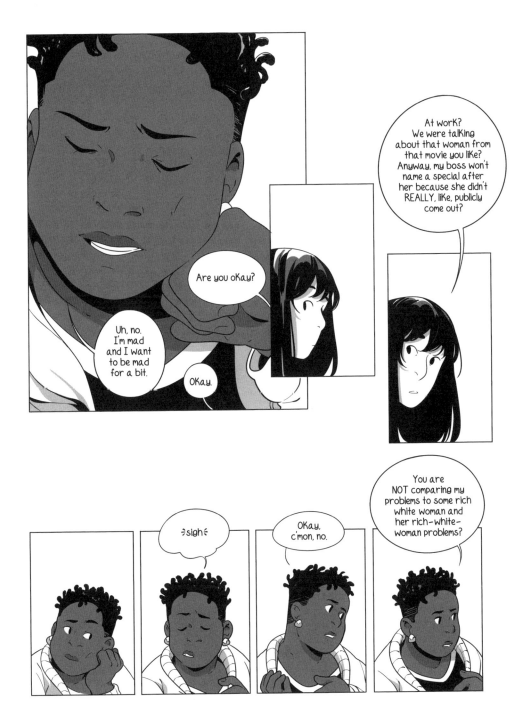

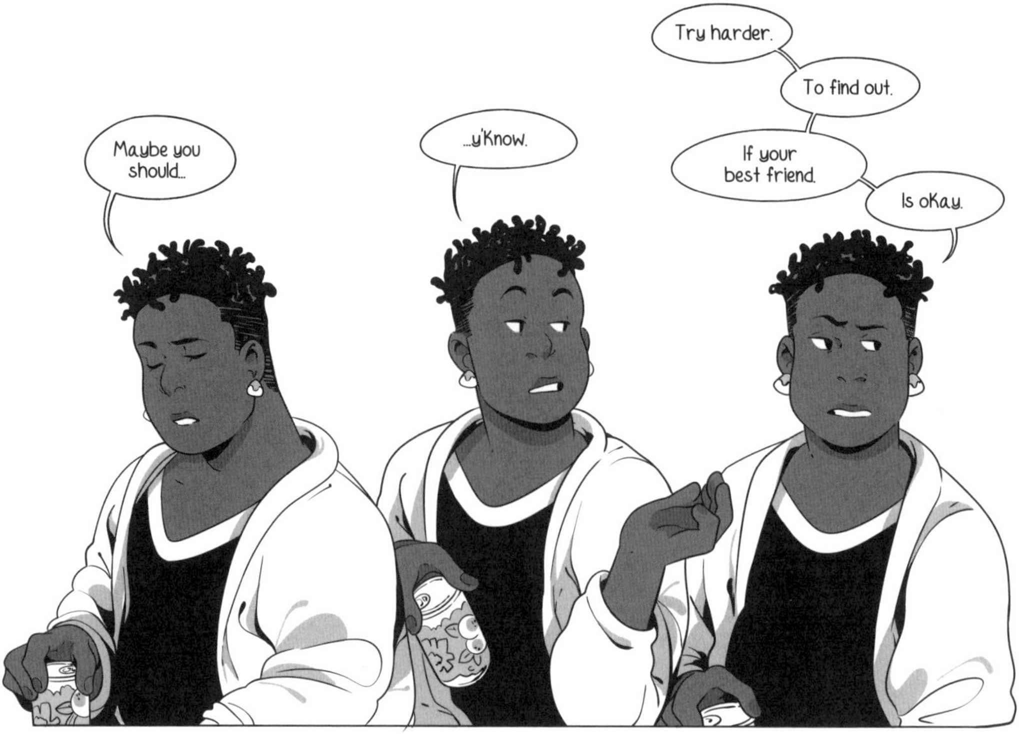
Maybe you should...
...y'know.
Try harder.
To find out.
If your best friend.
Is okay.

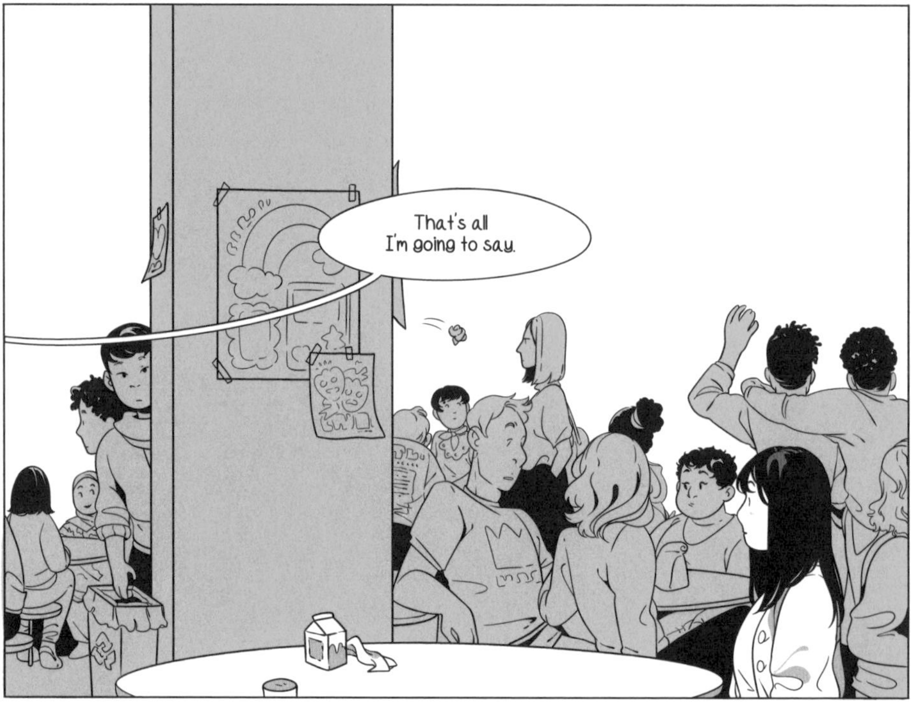
That's all I'm going to say.

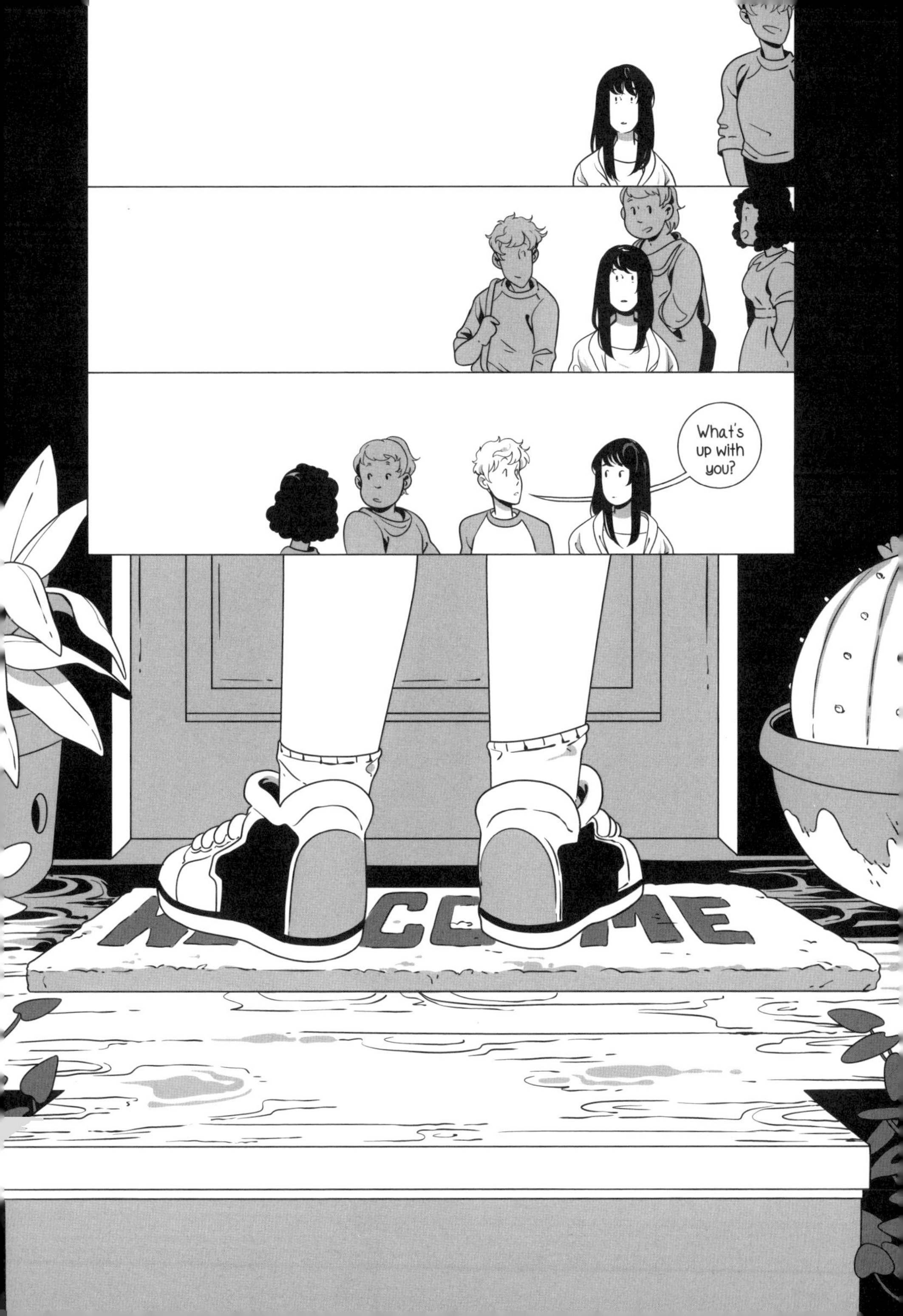
What's up with you?

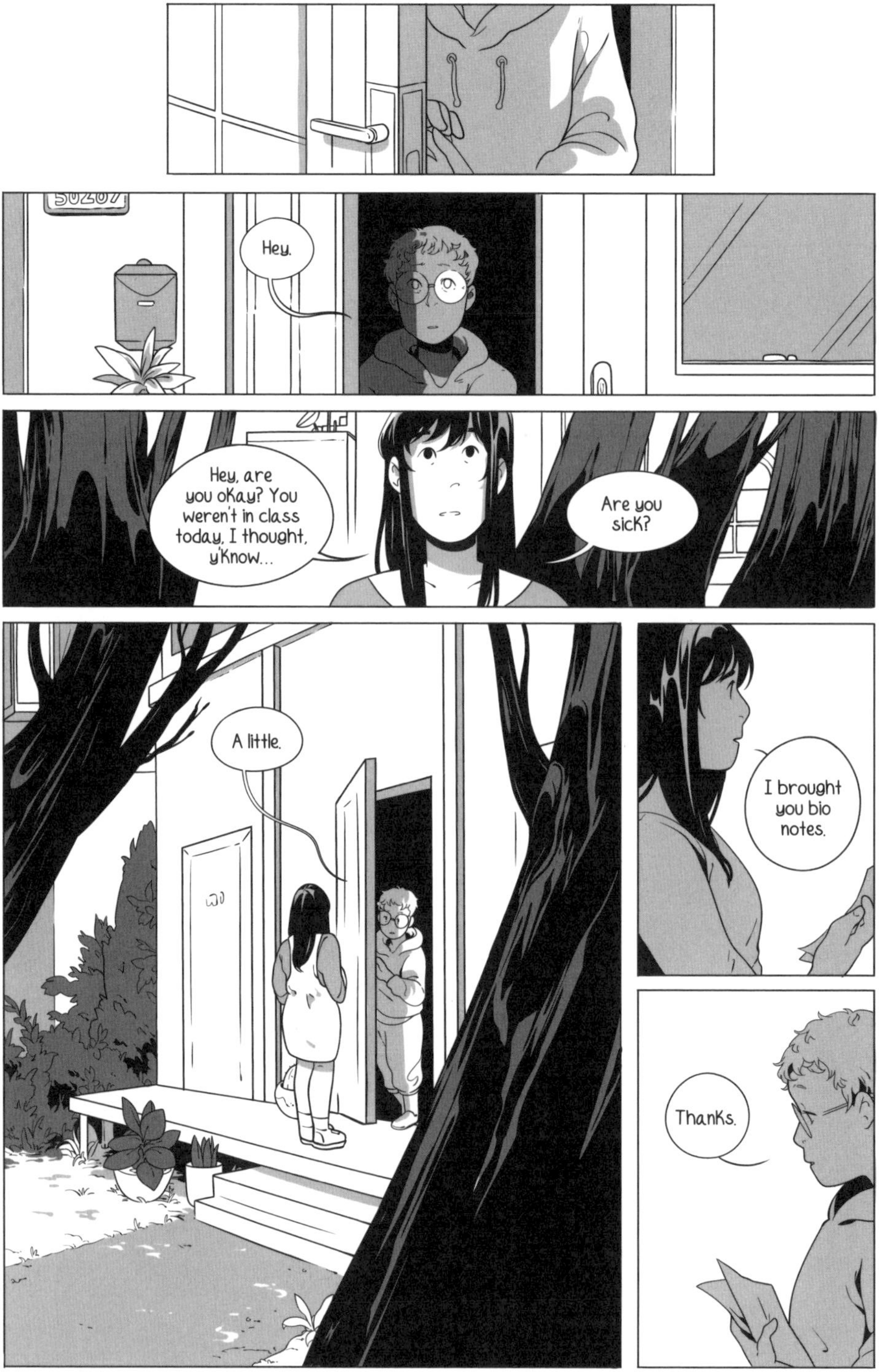
Hey.
Hey, are you okay? You weren't in class today, I thought, y'know...
Are you sick?
A little.
I brought you bio notes.
Thanks.

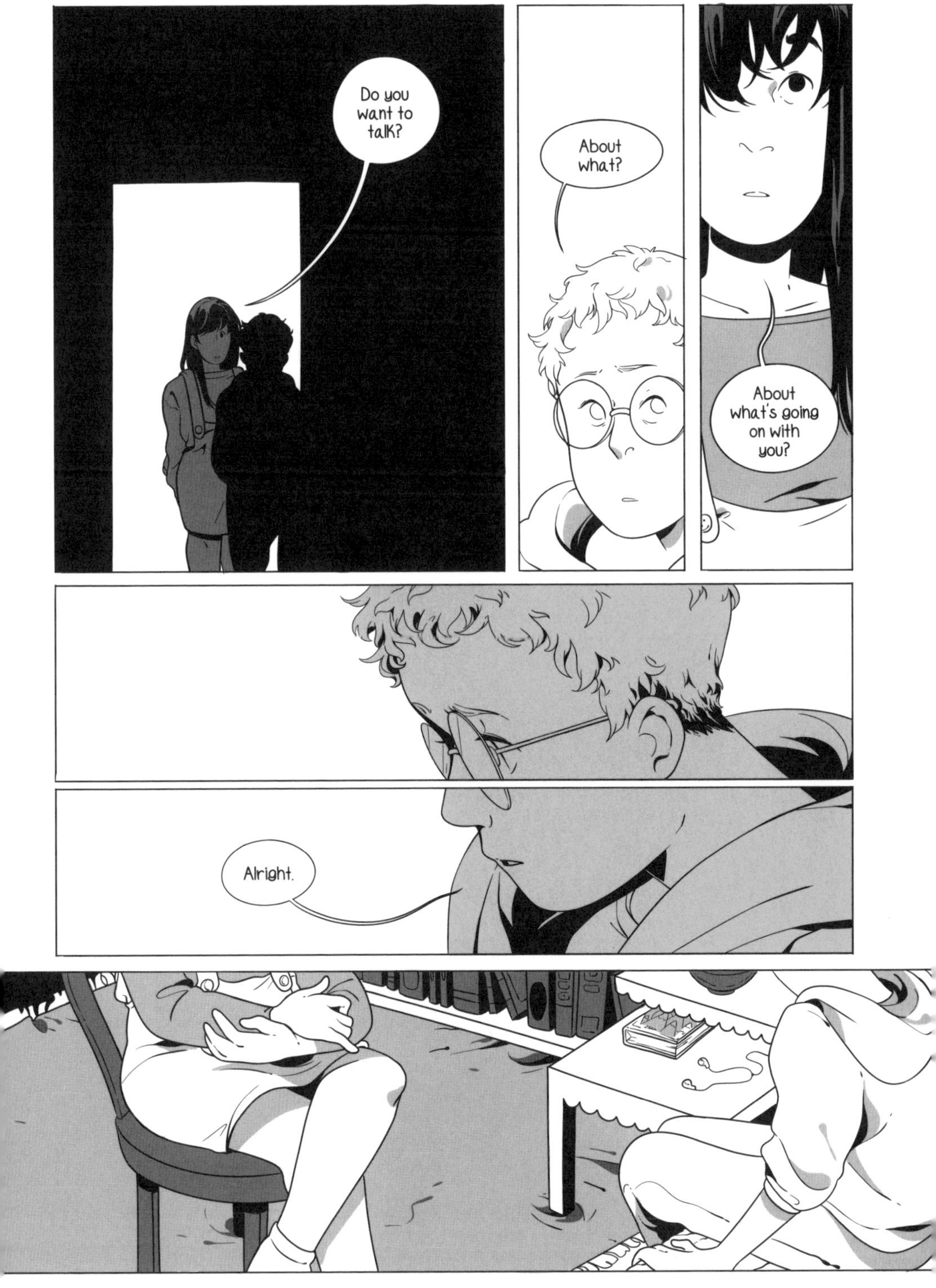

Do you want to talk?
About what?
About what's going on with you?
Alright.

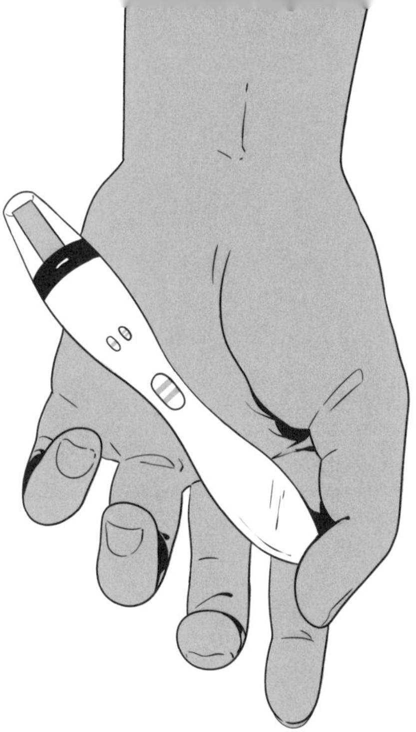

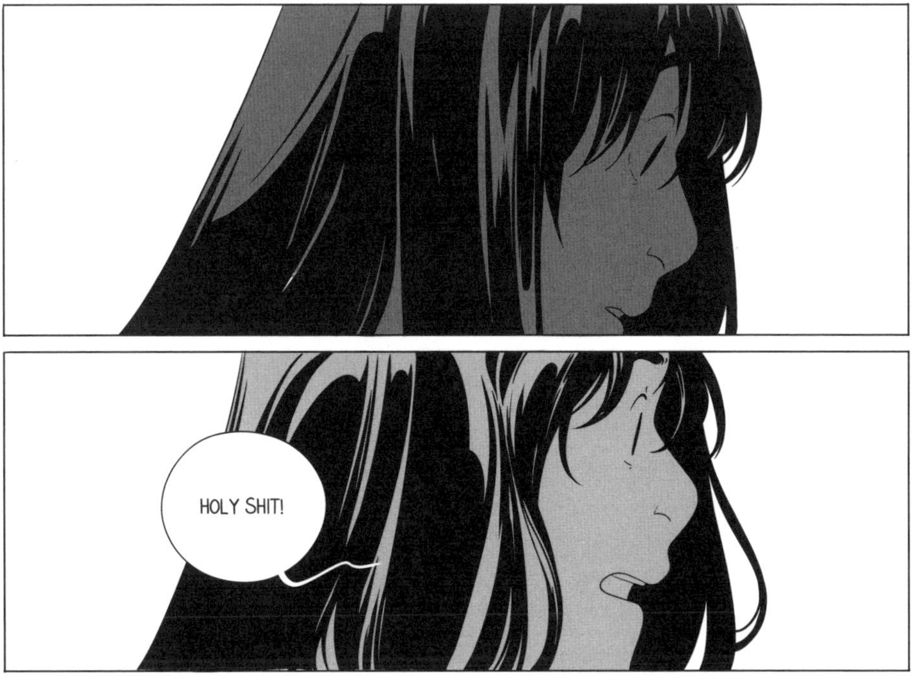
HOLY SHIT!

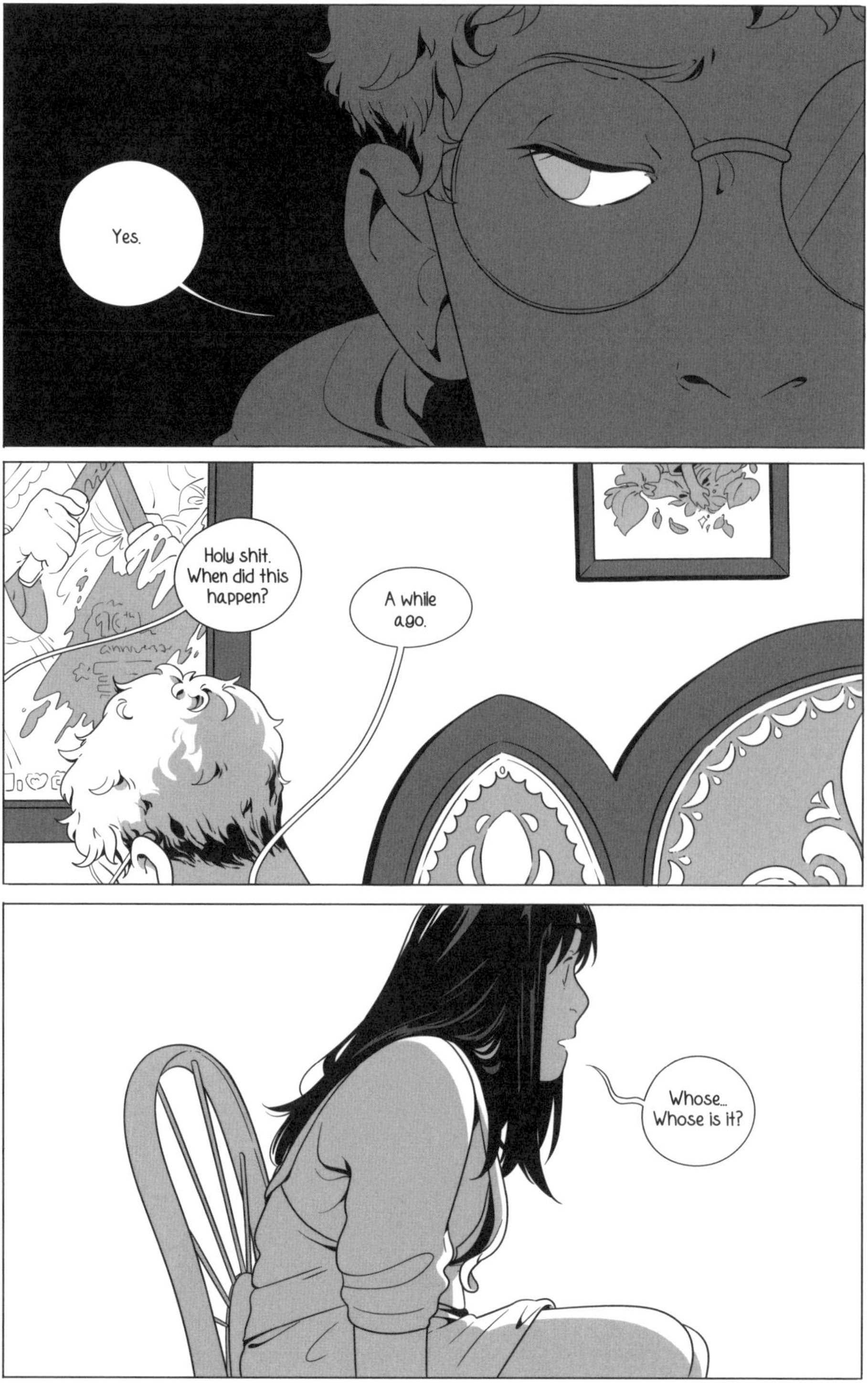
Yes.
Holy shit. When did this happen?
A while ago.
Whose... Whose is it?

Mine.

Who...

...Who did you sleep with?

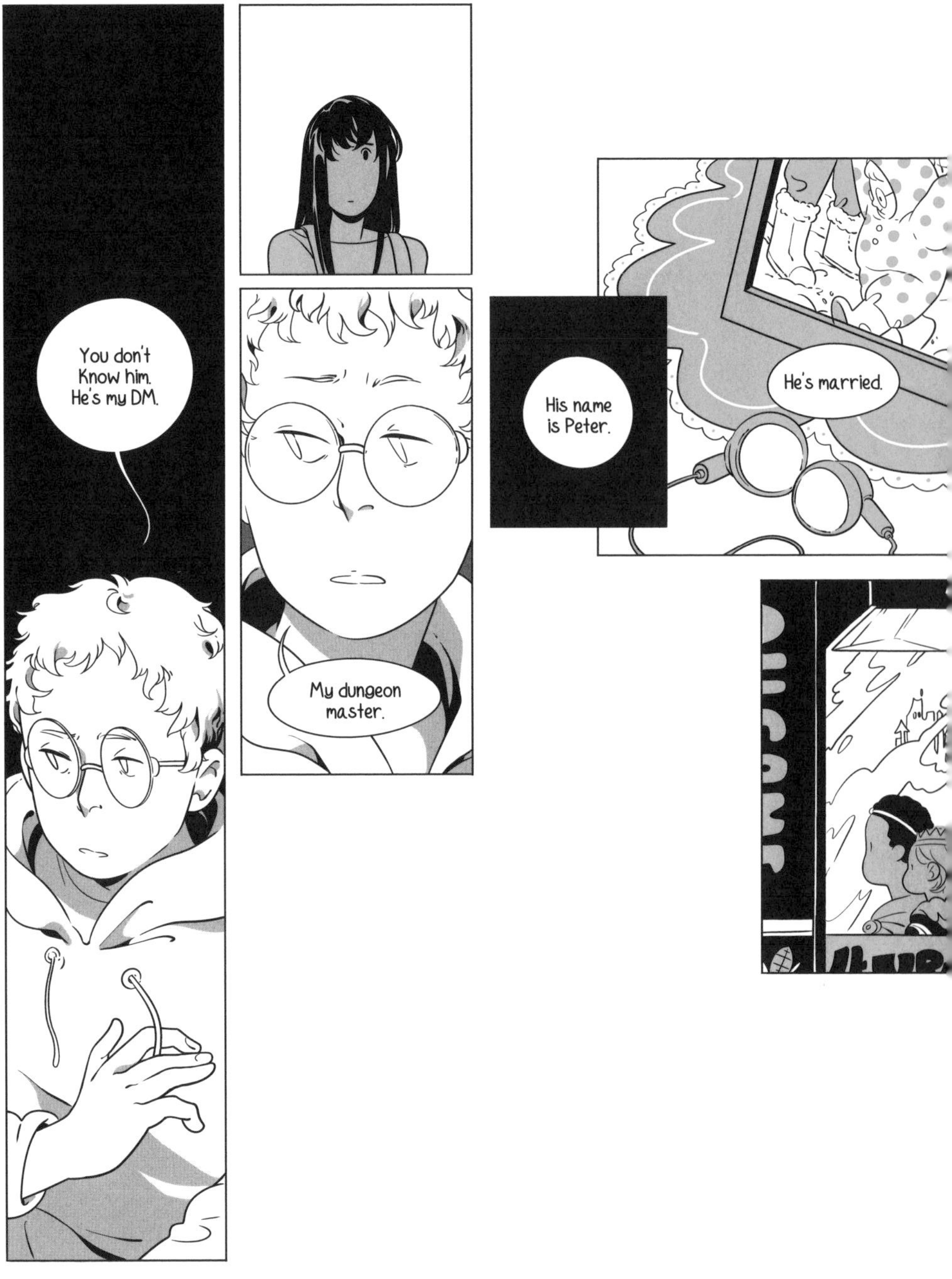
You don't Know him. He's my DM.
My dungeon master.
His name is Peter.
He's married.

We used a condom.

It broke.

I missed my period.

We bought a test.

...I bought a test.

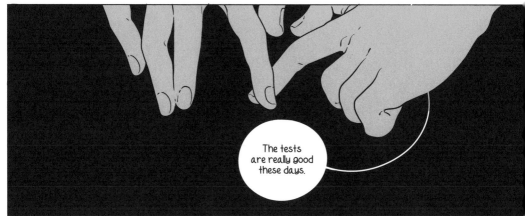

The tests are really good these days.

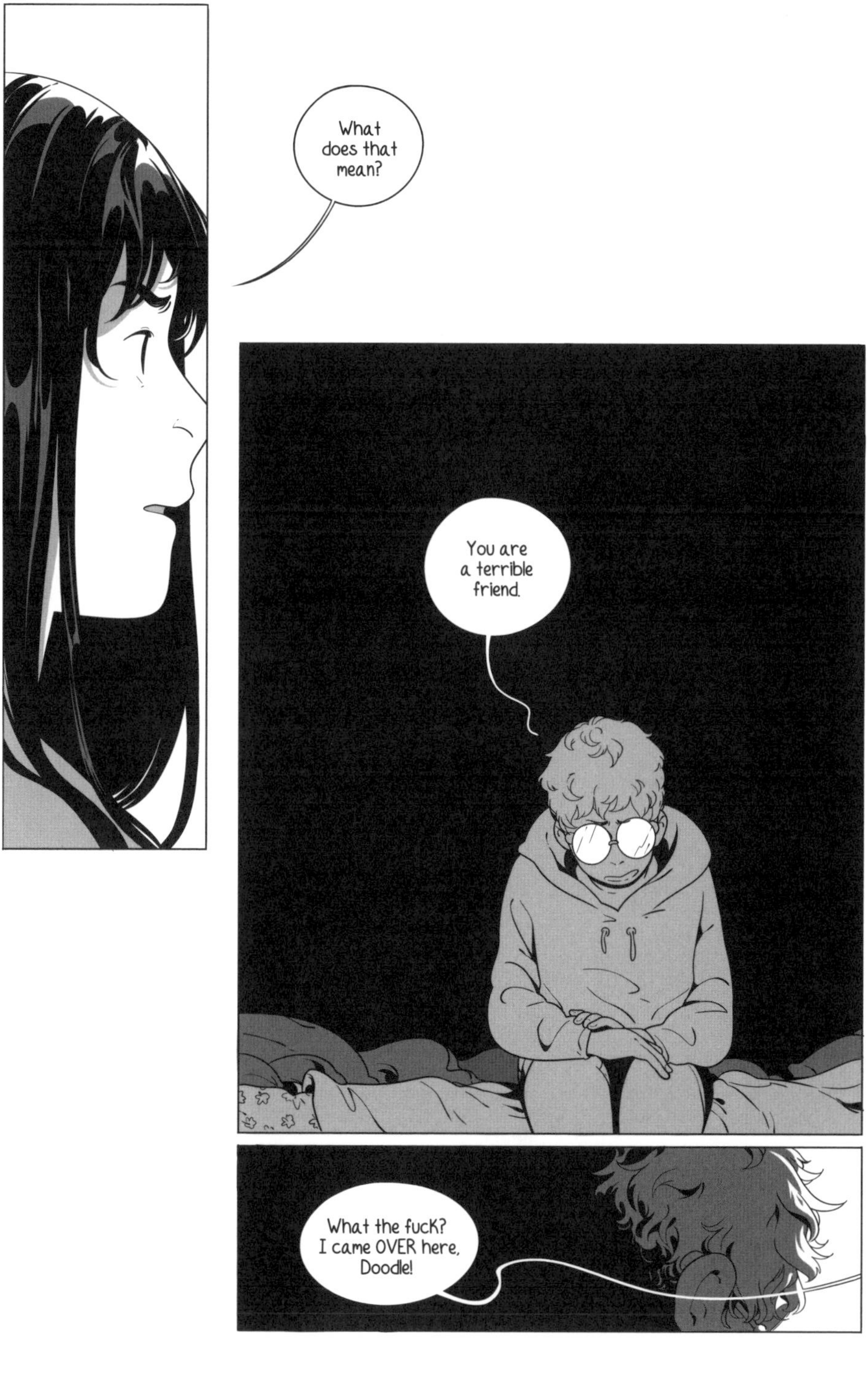
What does that mean?
You are a terrible friend.
What the fuck? I came OVER here, Doodle!

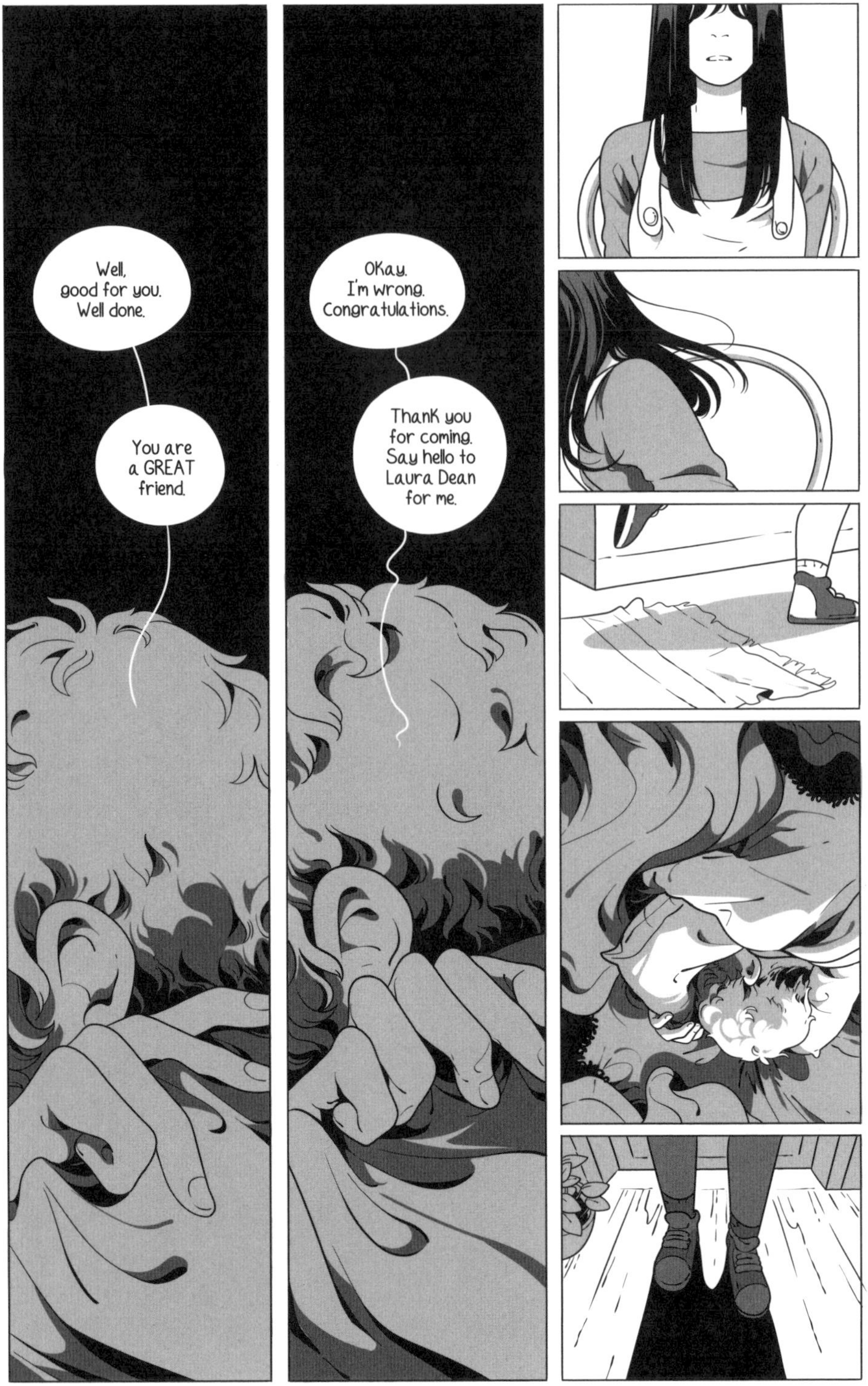
Well, good for you. Well done.
You are a GREAT friend.
OKay. I'm wrong. Congratulations.
Thank you for coming. Say hello to Laura Dean for me.

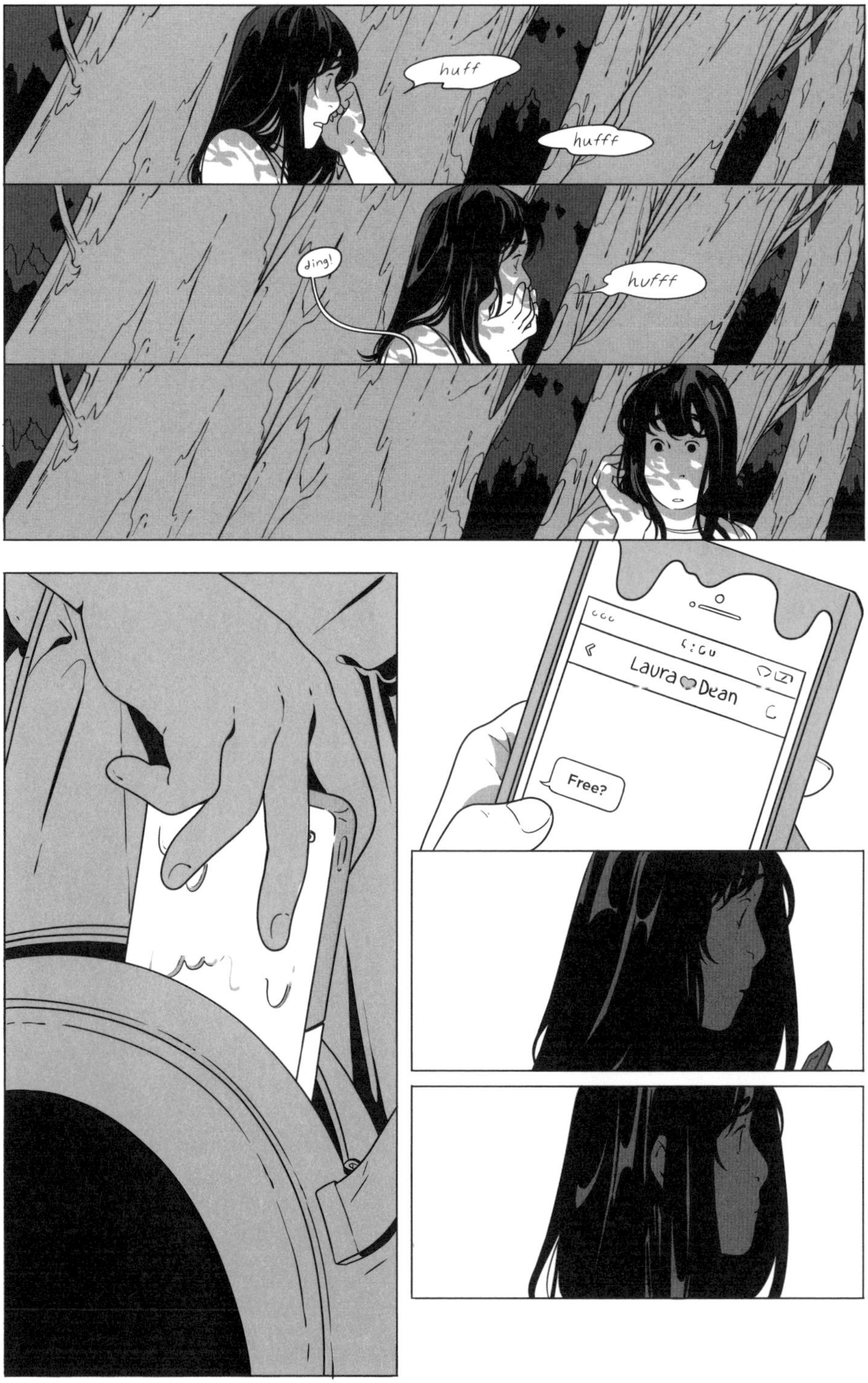
huff
hufff
ding!
hufff
Laura Dean
Free?

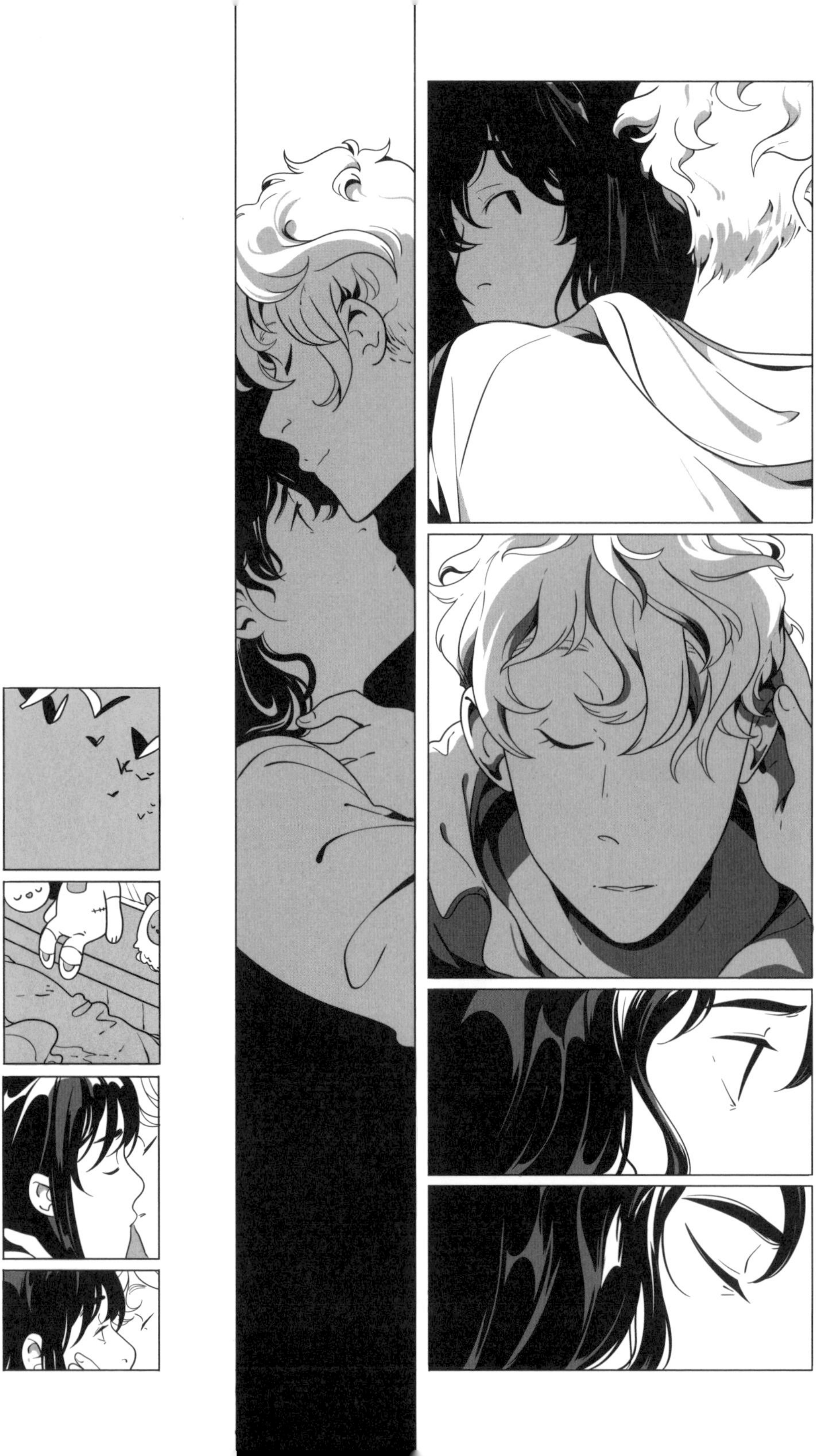

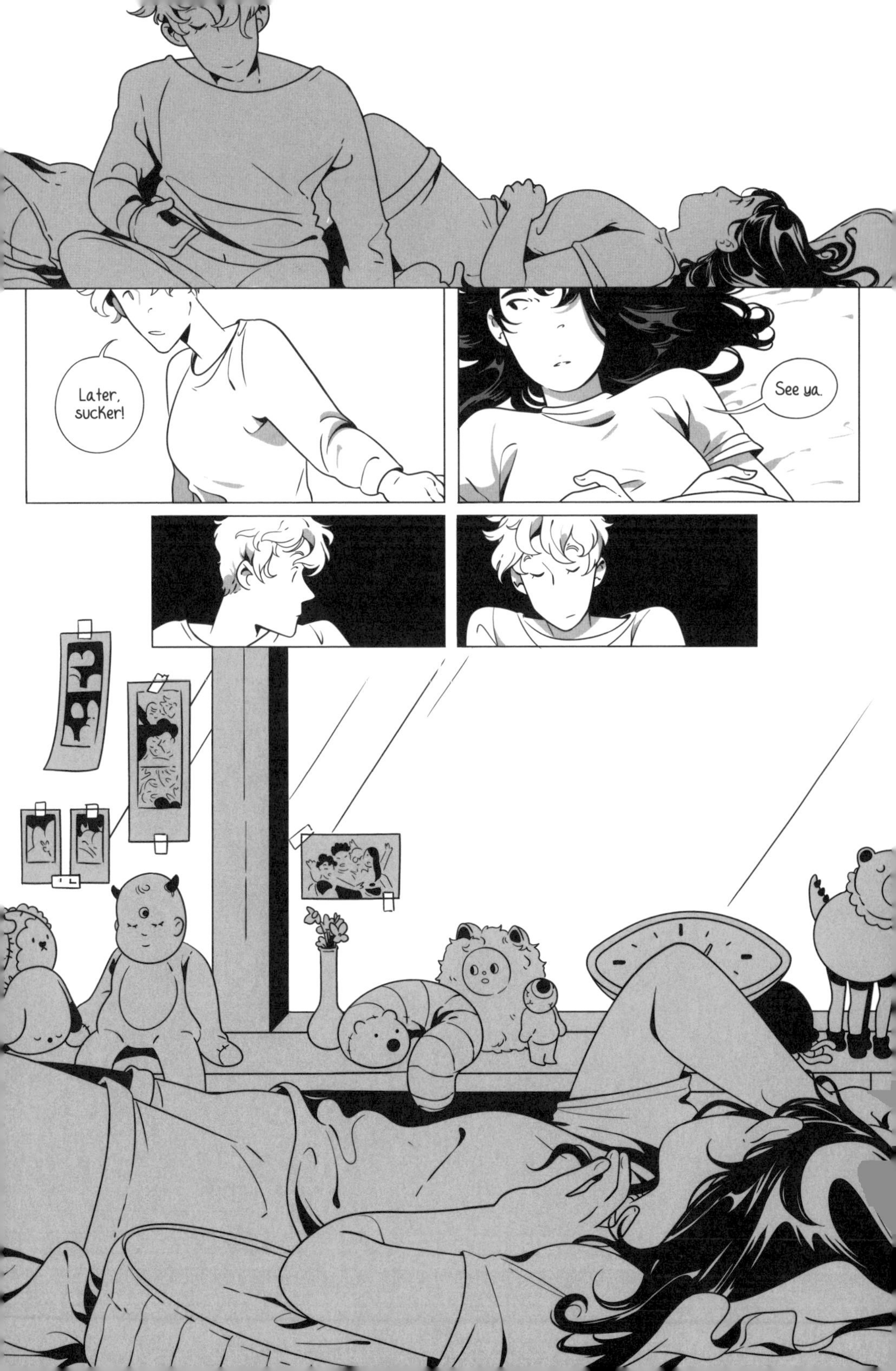
Later, sucker!
See ya.

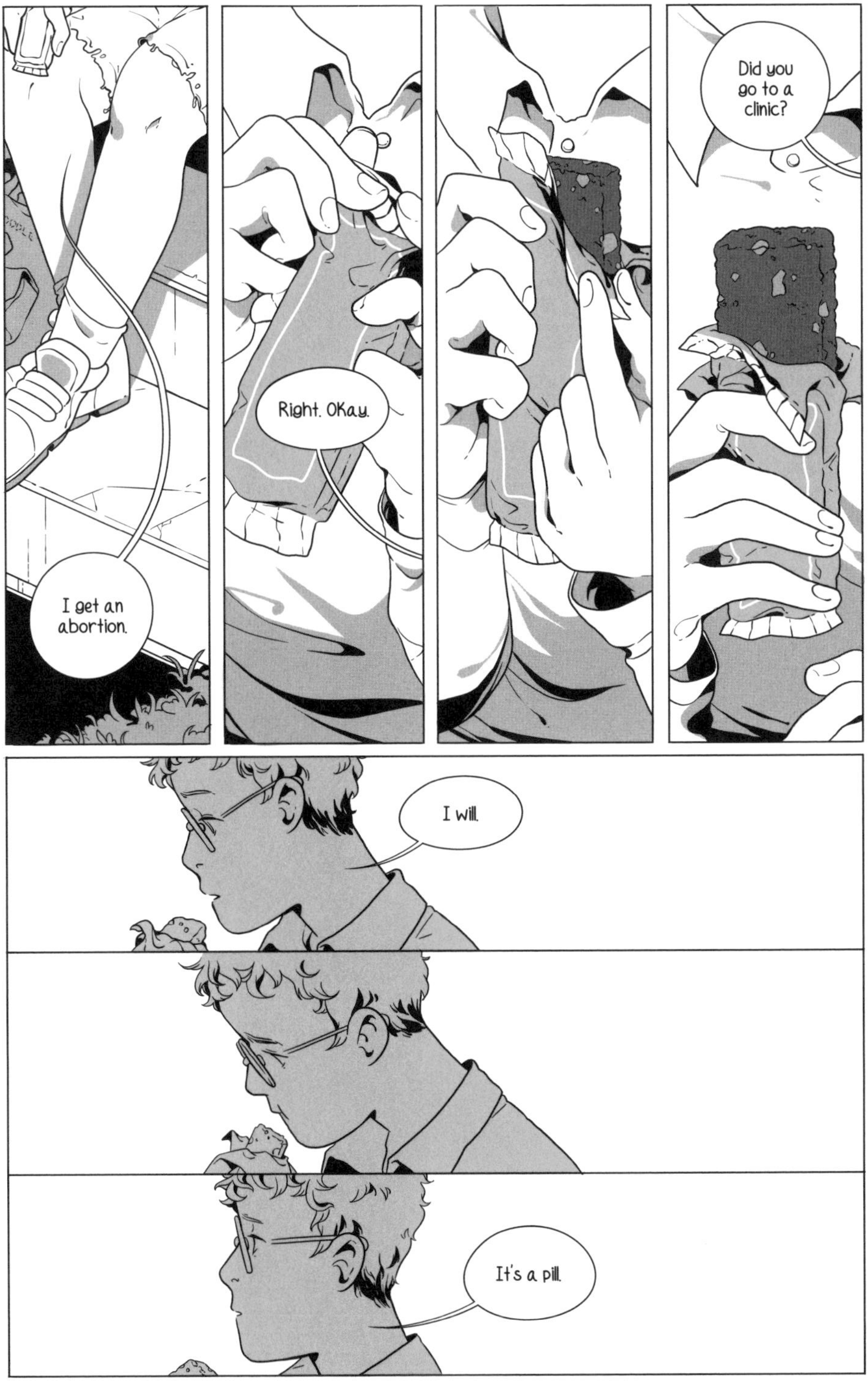
I get an abortion.
Right. OKay.
Did you go to a clinic?
I will.
It's a pill.

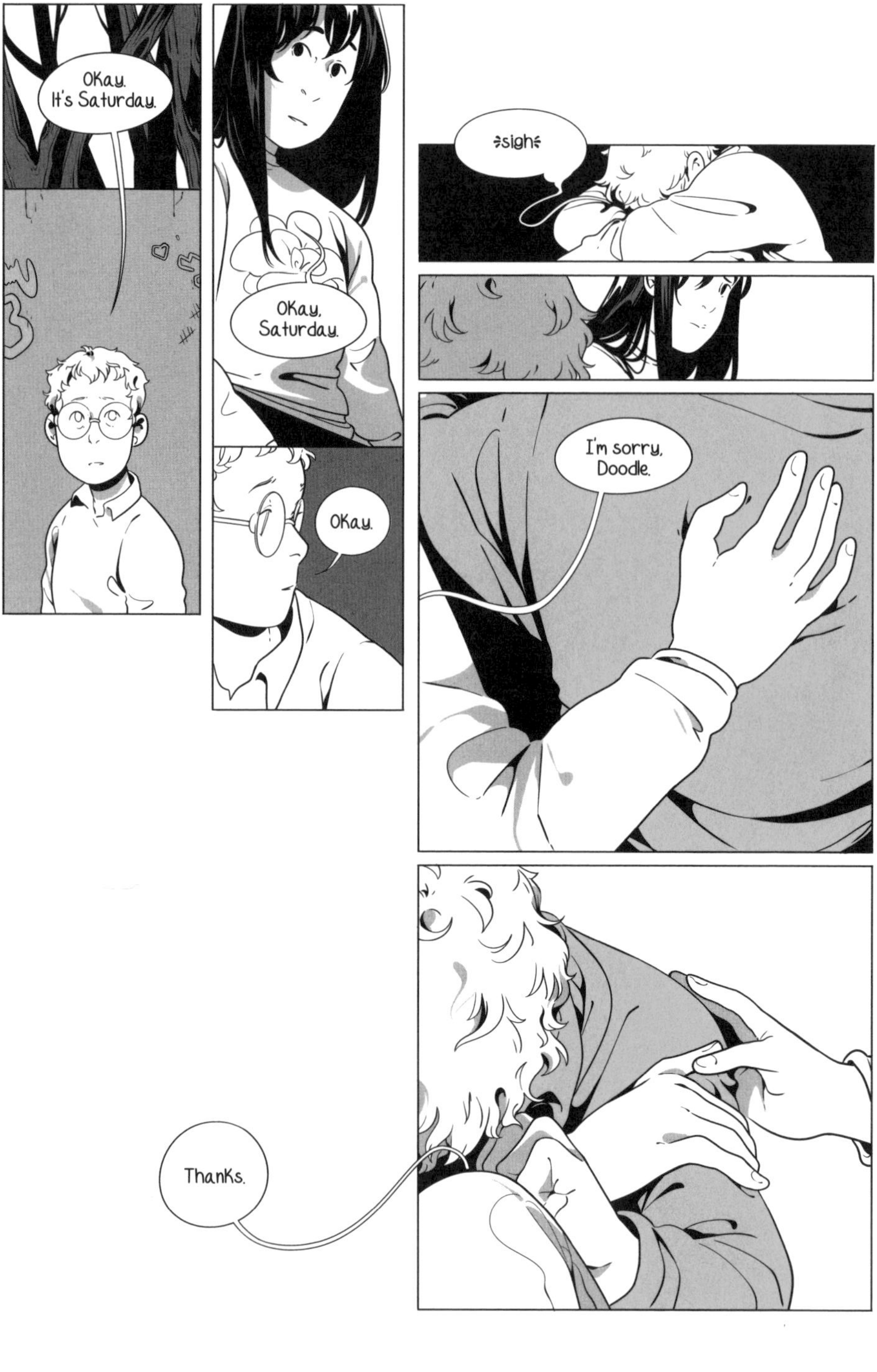
OKay. It's Saturday.
OKay, Saturday.
OKay.
sigh
I'm sorry, Doodle.
ThanKs.

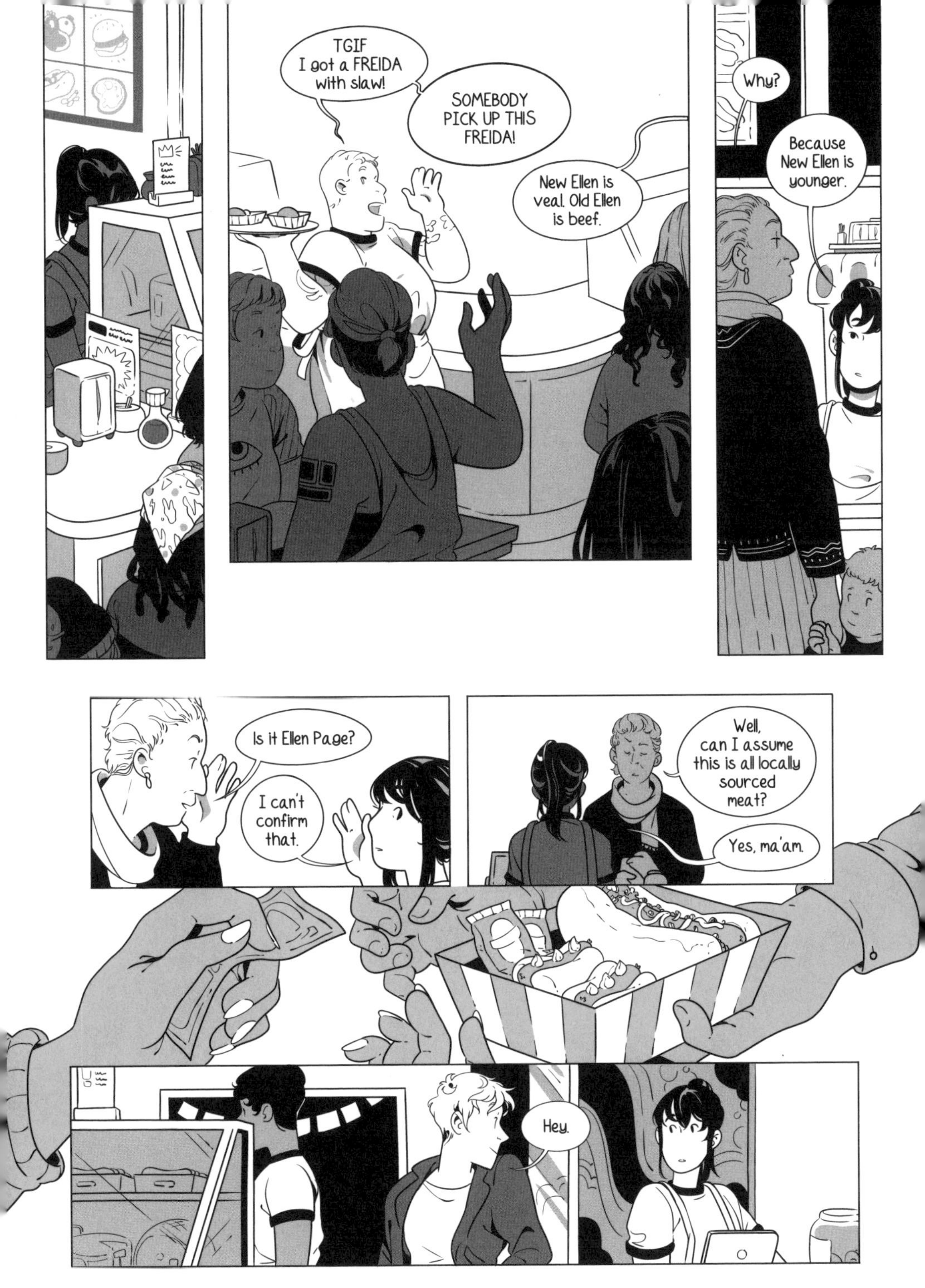
TGIF
I got a FREIDA
with slaw!
SOMEBODY
PICK UP THIS
FREIDA!
New Ellen is
veal. Old Ellen
is beef.
Why?
Because
New Ellen is
younger.
Is it Ellen Page?
I can't
confirm
that.
Well,
can I assume
this is all locally
sourced
meat?
Yes, ma'am.
Hey.

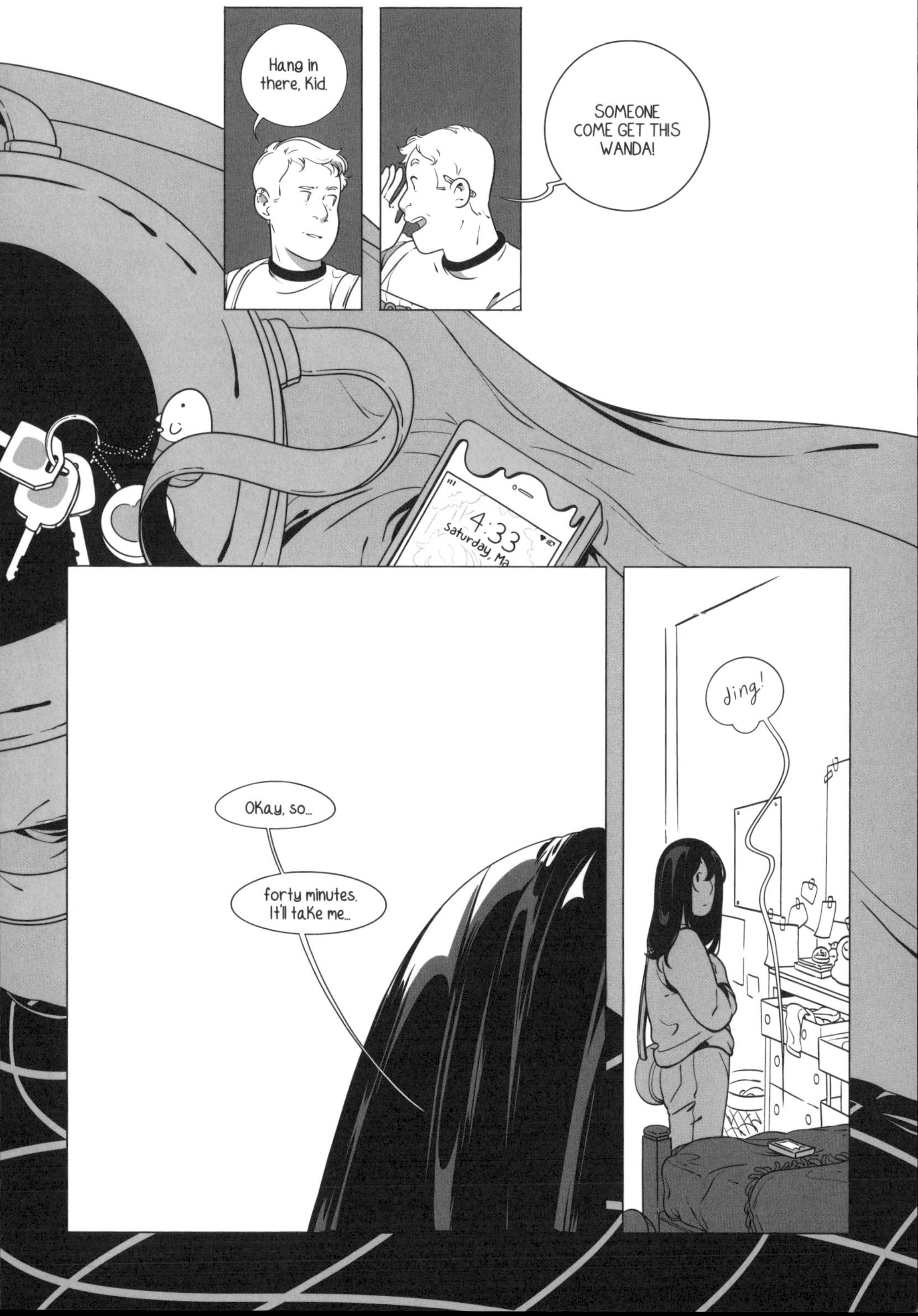
Hang in there, Kid.
SOMEONE COME GET THIS WANDA!
4:33
Saturday, Ma
OKay, so...
forty minutes. It'll taKe me...
ding!

243

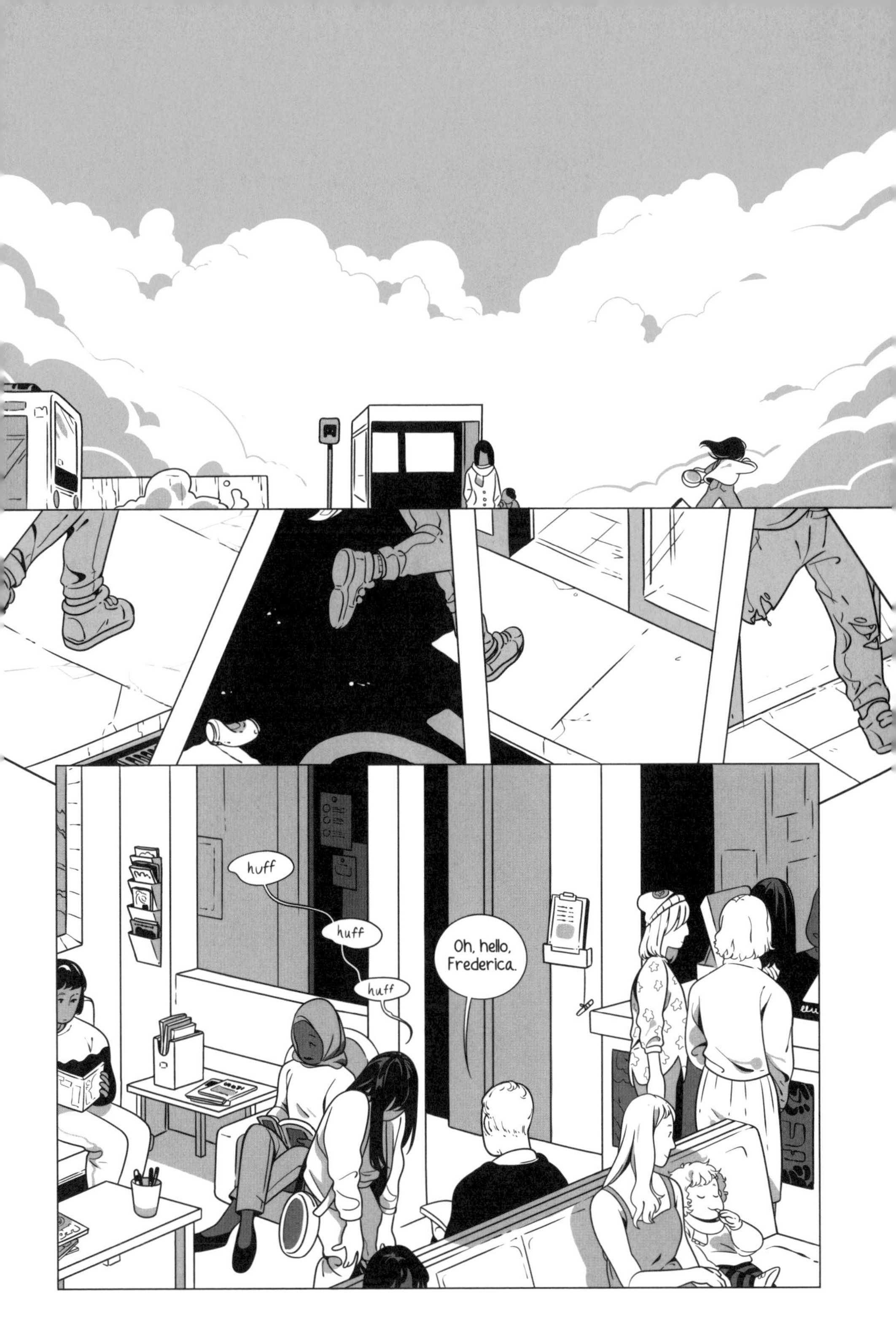
huff
huff
huff
Oh, hello, Frederica.

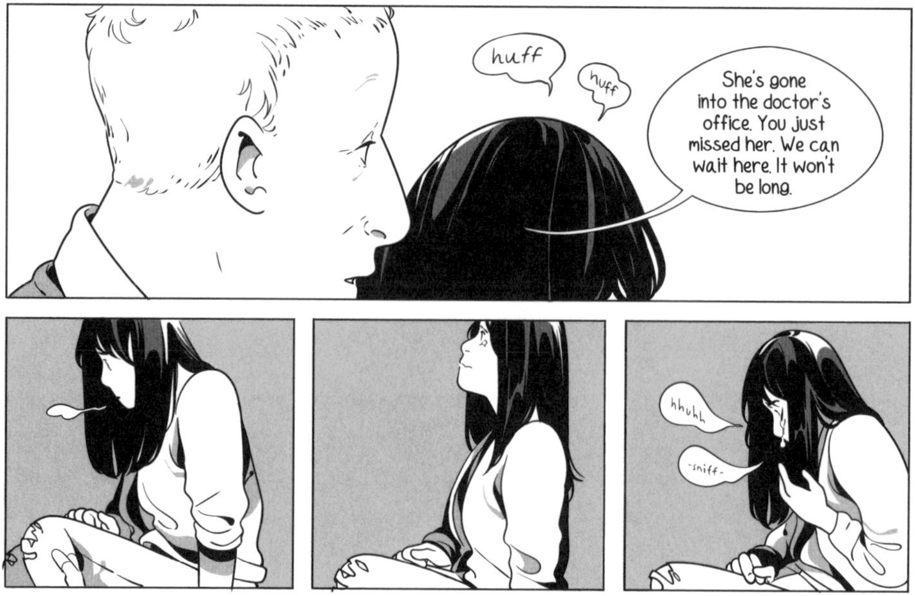
huff
huff
She's gone into the doctor's office. You just missed her. We can wait here. It won't be long.
hhuhh
-sniff-

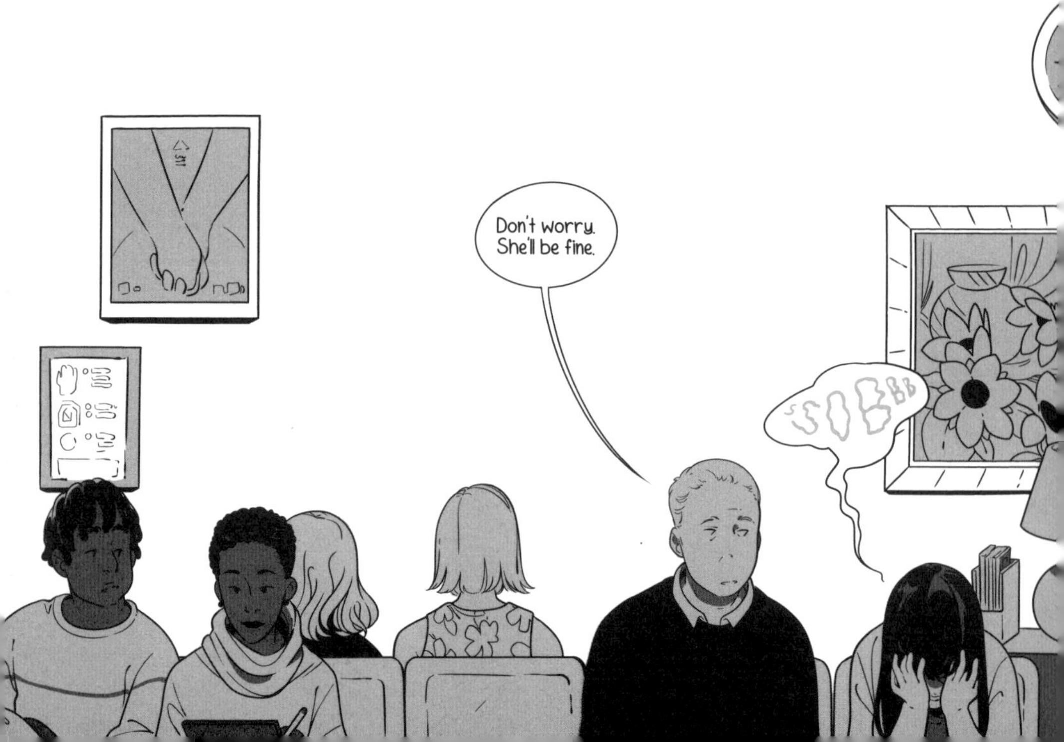
Don't worry. She'll be fine.
SOBBB

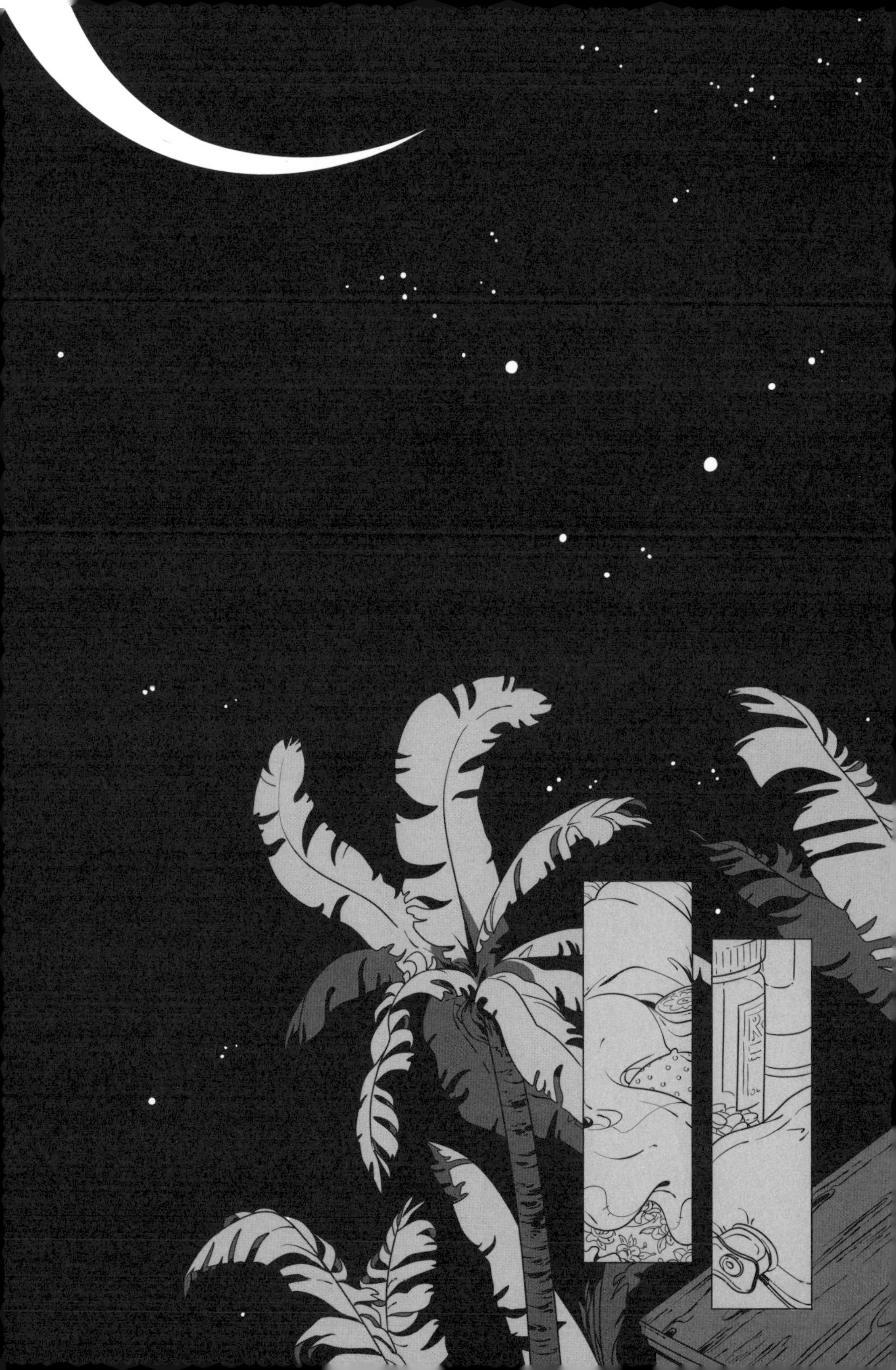

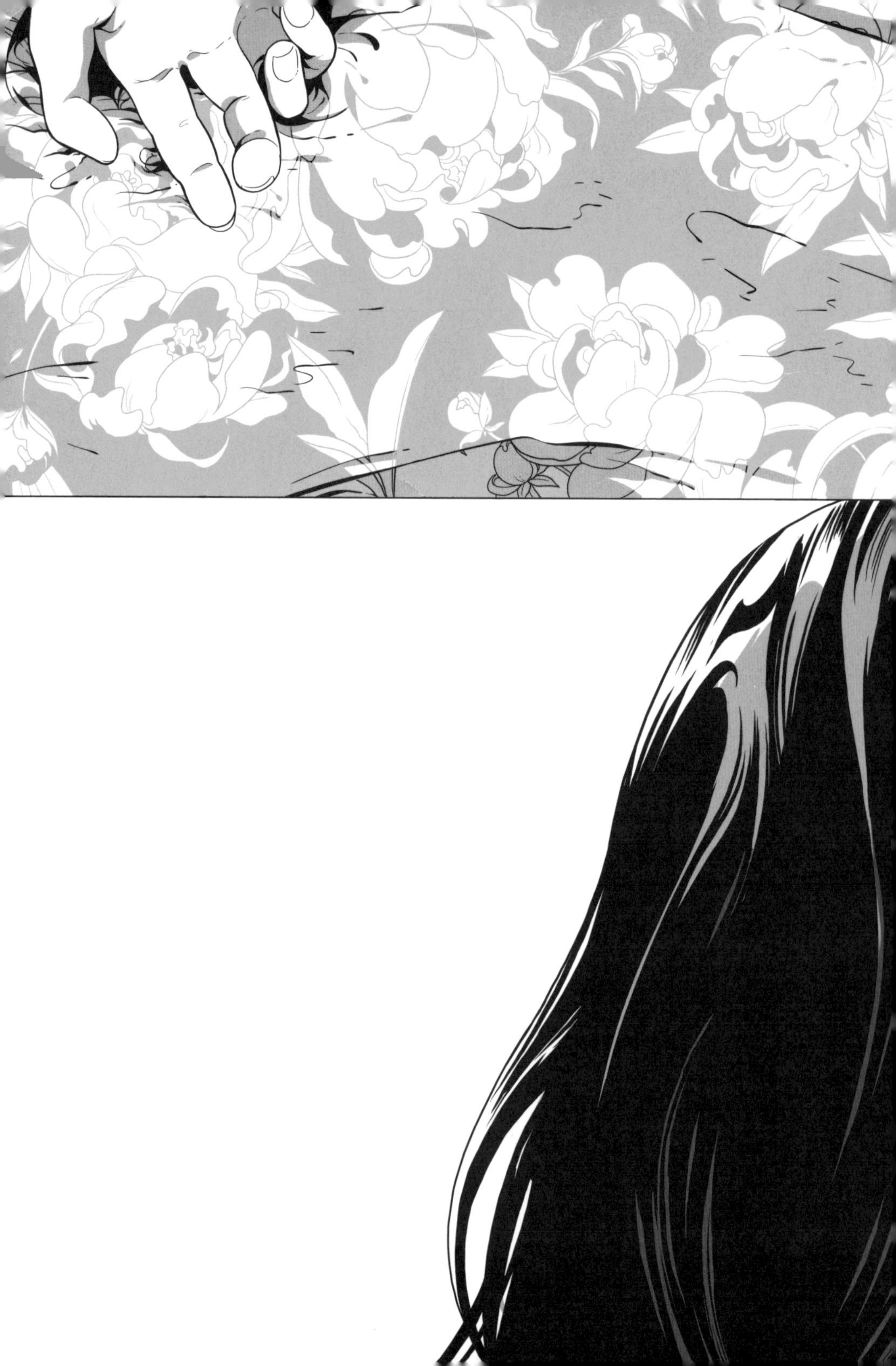

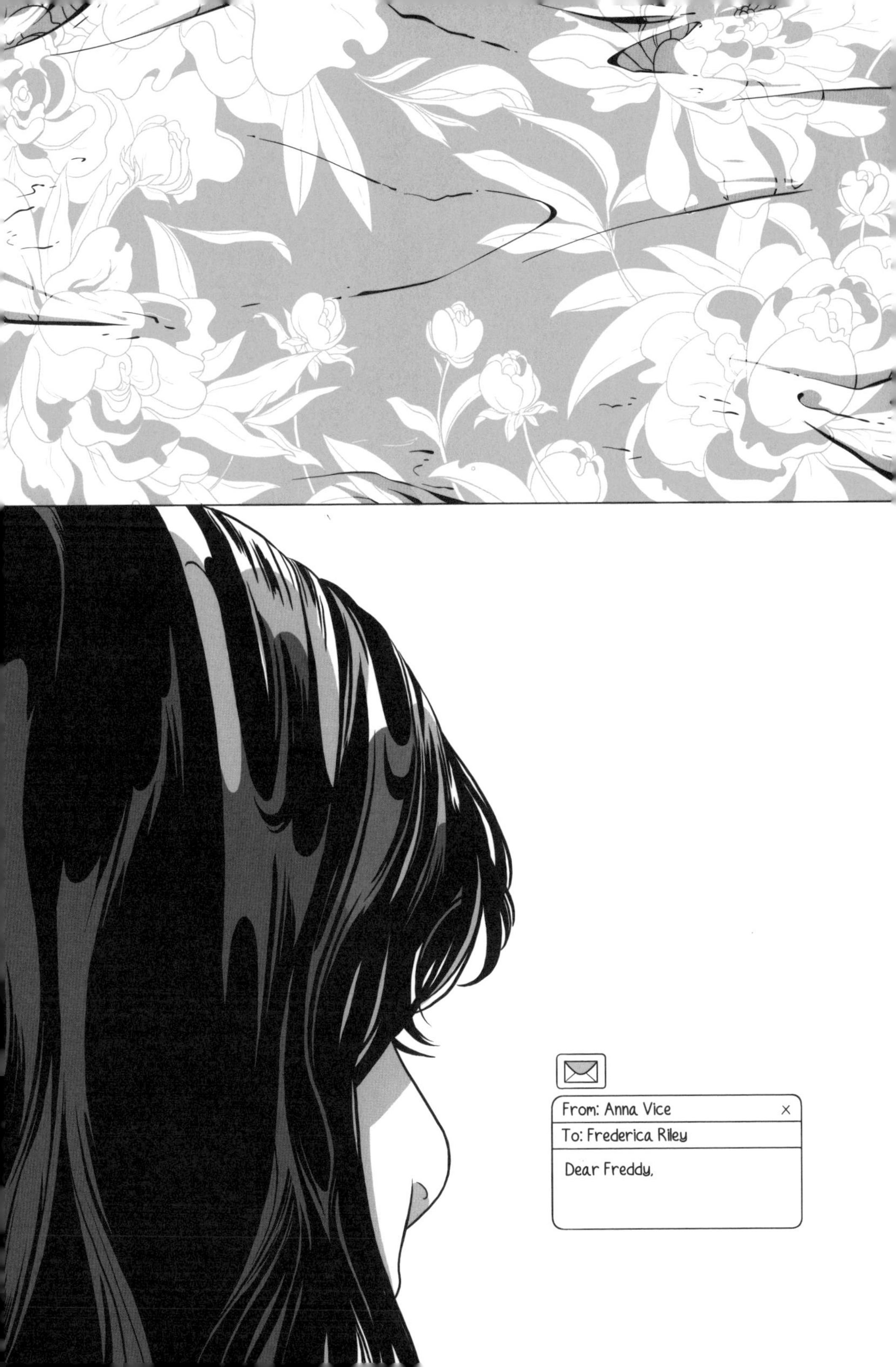
From: Anna Vice
To: Frederica Riley
Dear Freddy,

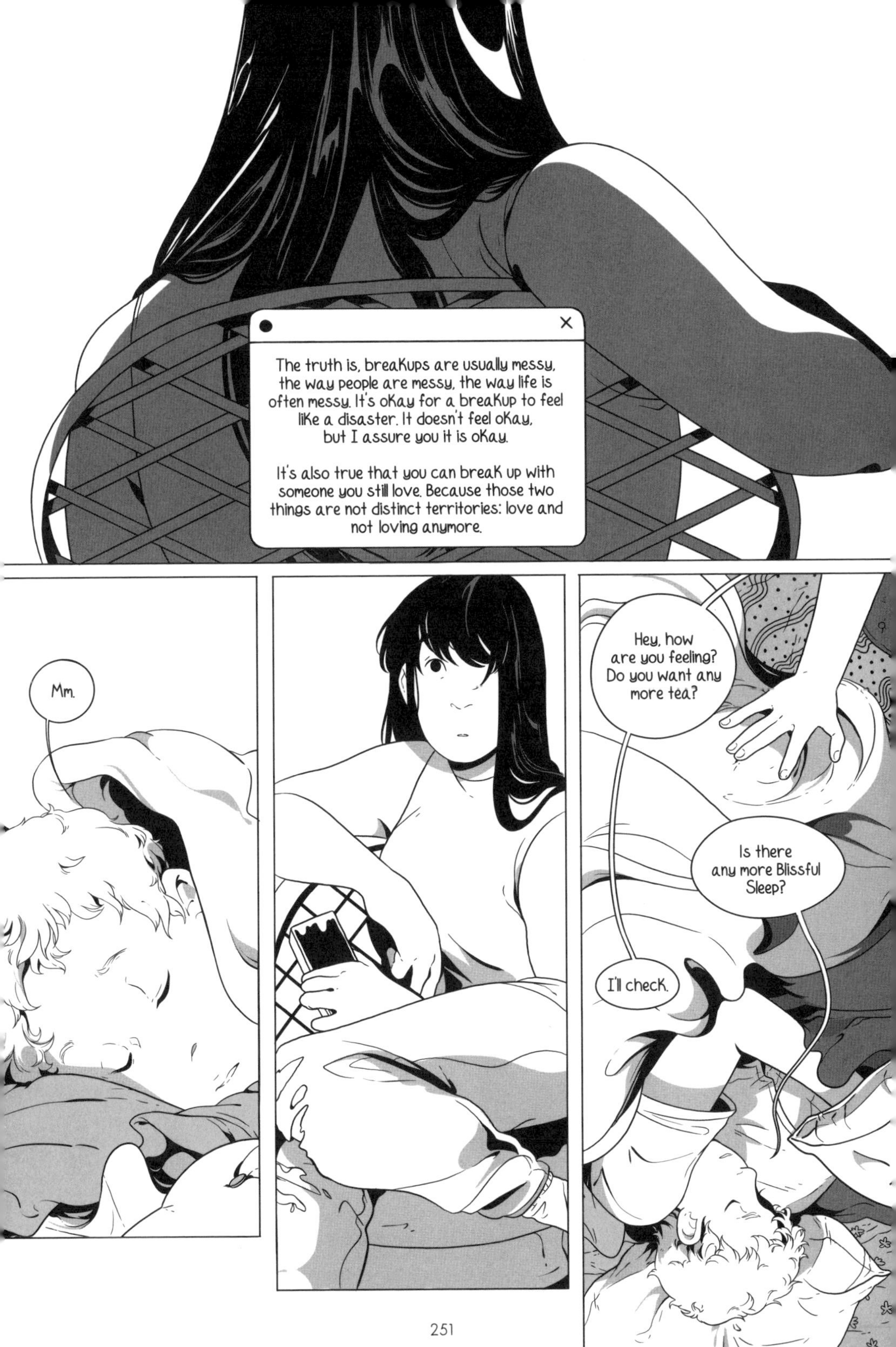
The truth is, breakups are usually messy, the way people are messy, the way life is often messy. It's okay for a breakup to feel like a disaster. It doesn't feel okay, but I assure you it is okay.
It's also true that you can break up with someone you still love. Because those two things are not distinct territories: love and not loving anymore.
Mm.
Hey, how are you feeling? Do you want any more tea?
Is there any more Blissful Sleep?
I'll check.

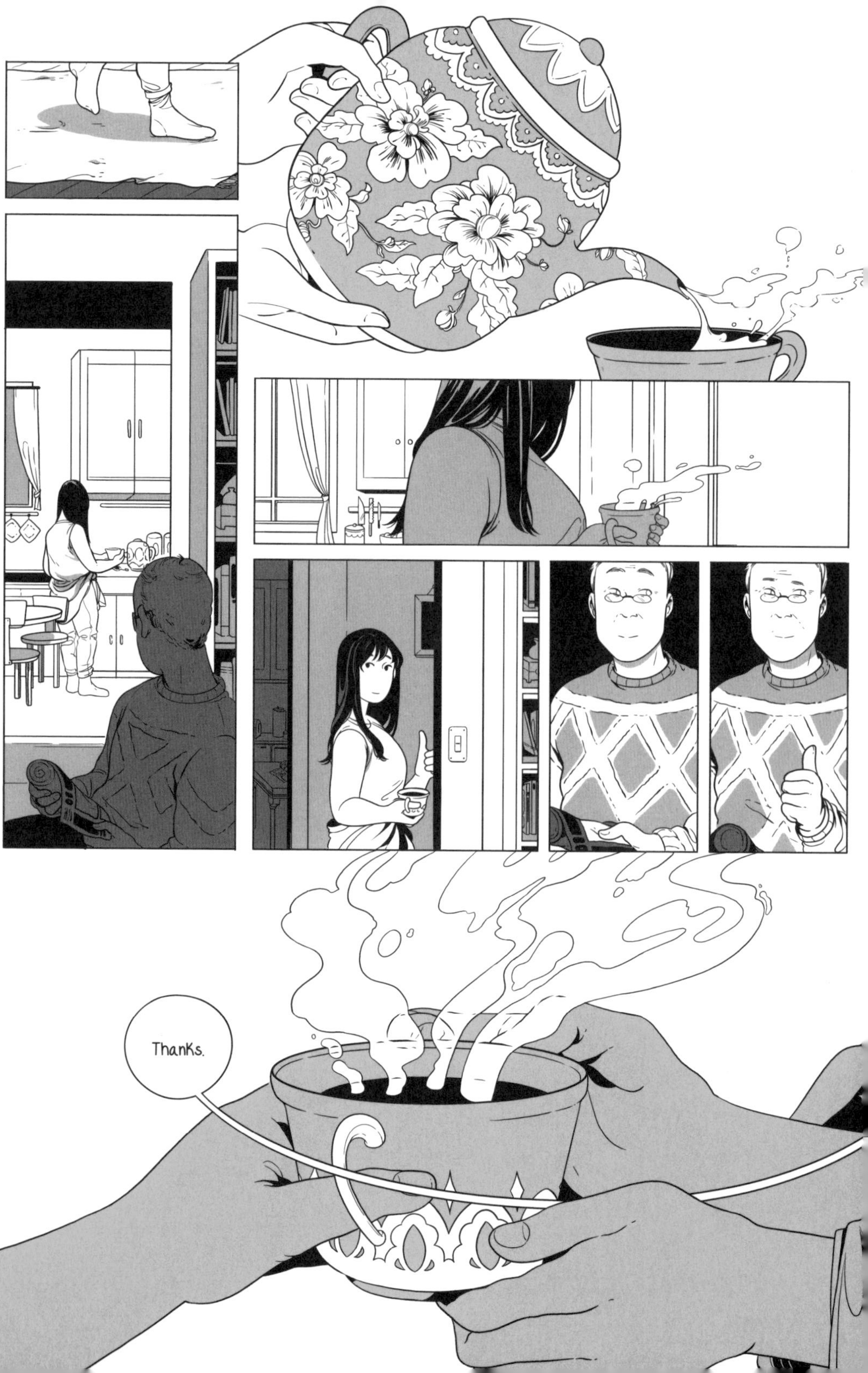
Thanks.

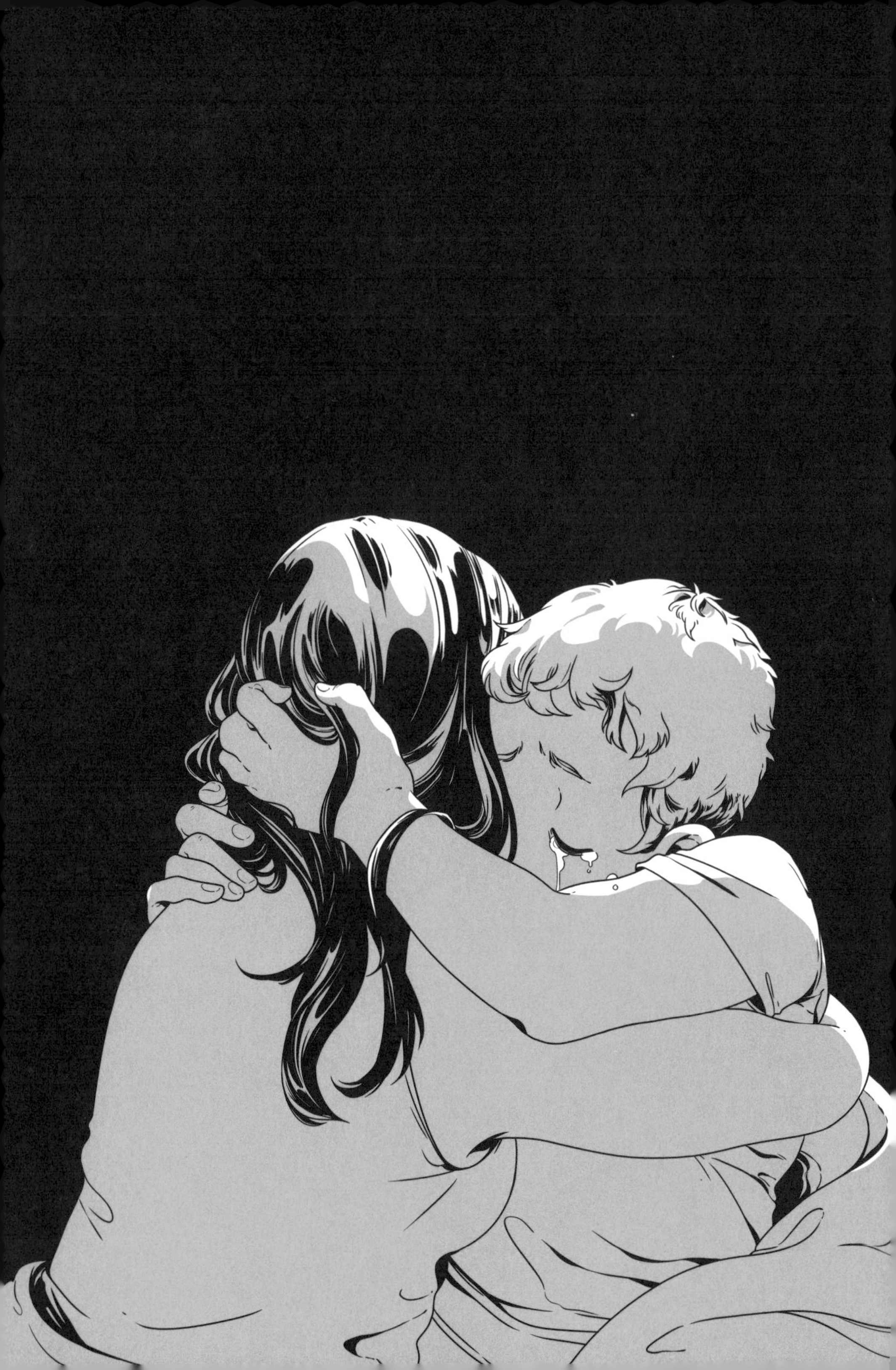

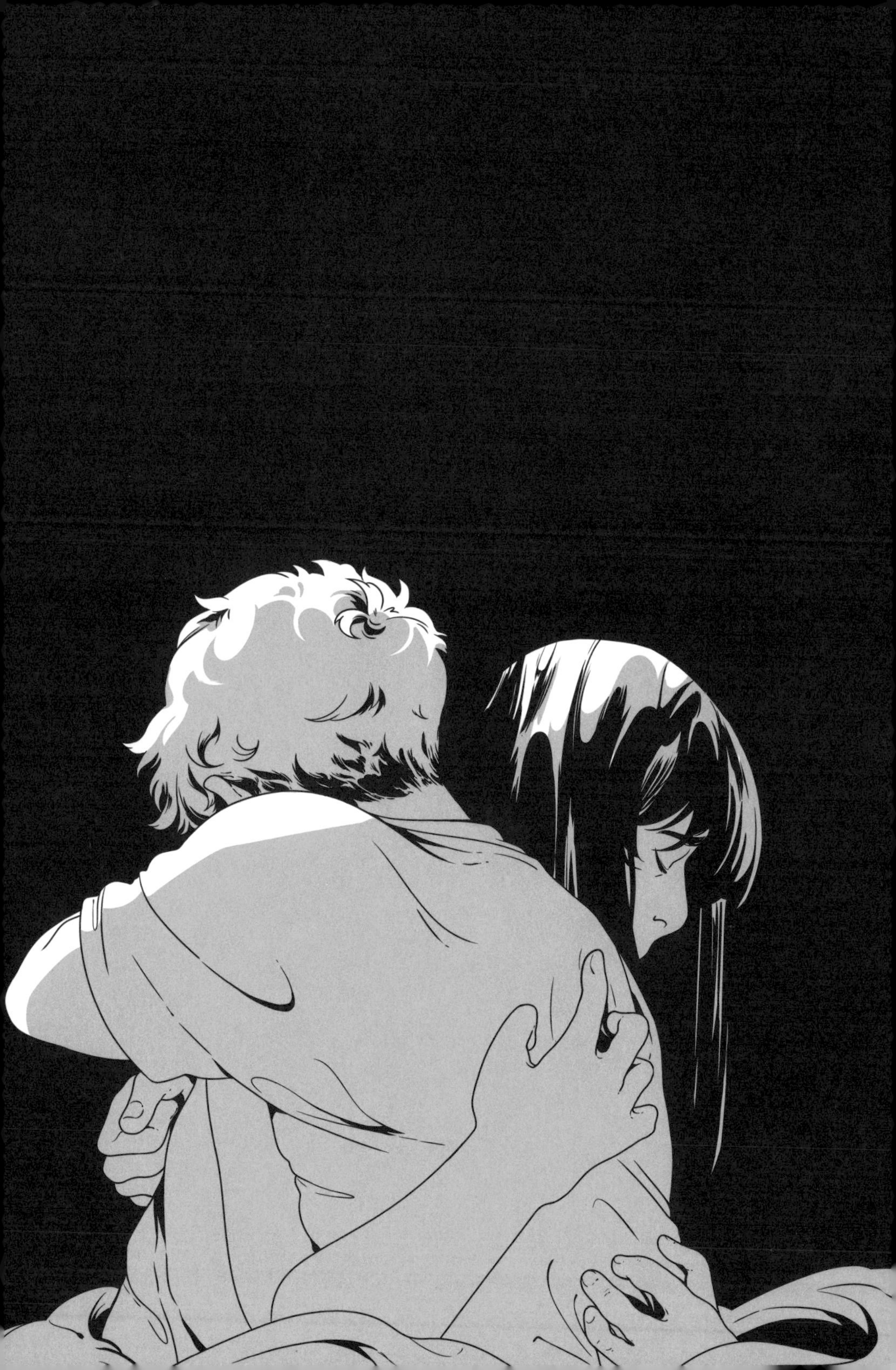

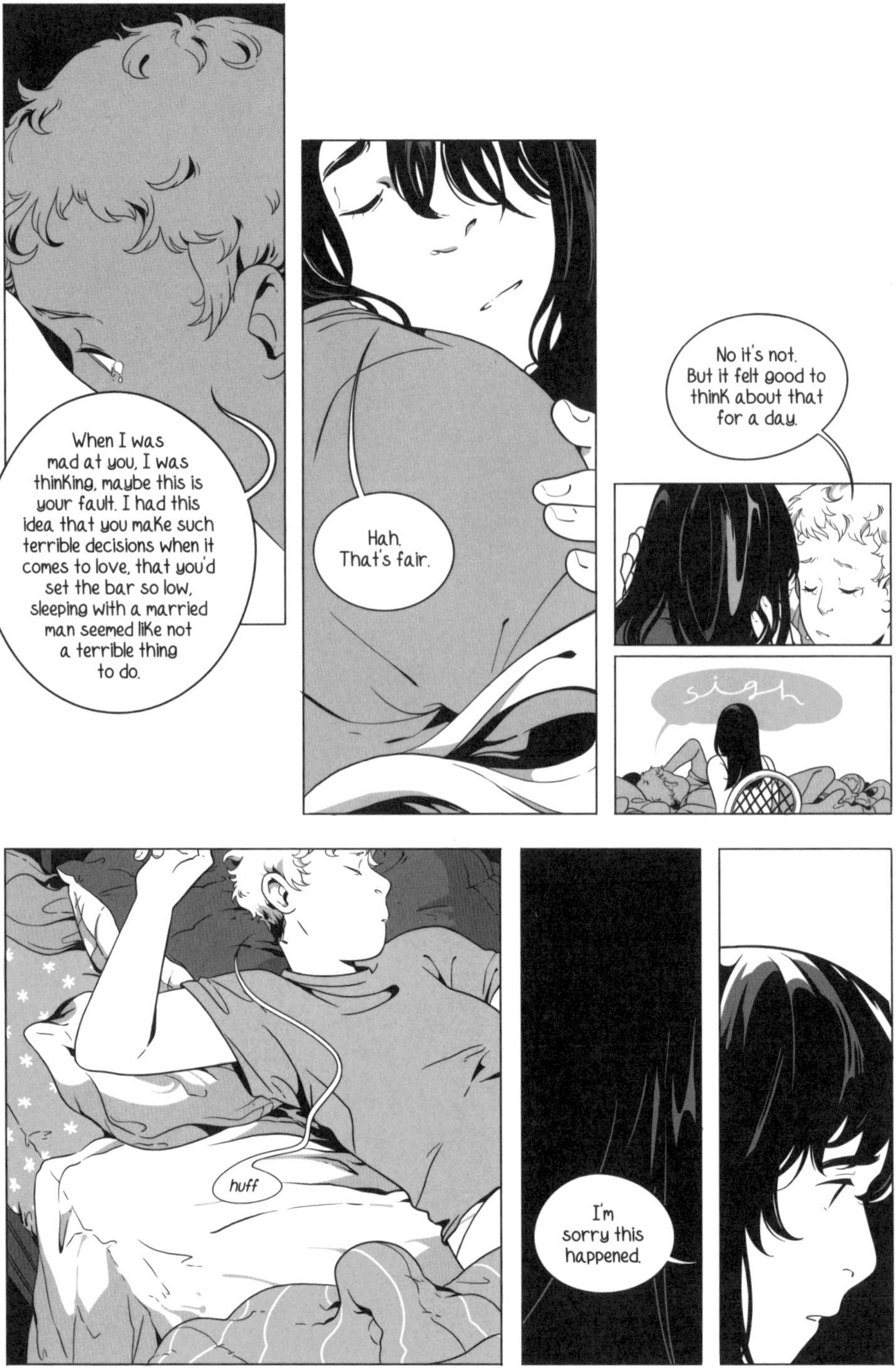
When I was mad at you, I was thinking, maybe this is your fault. I had this idea that you make such terrible decisions when it comes to love, that you'd set the bar so low, sleeping with a married man seemed like not a terrible thing to do.
Hah. That's fair.
No it's not. But it felt good to think about that for a day.
sigh
huff
I'm sorry this happened.

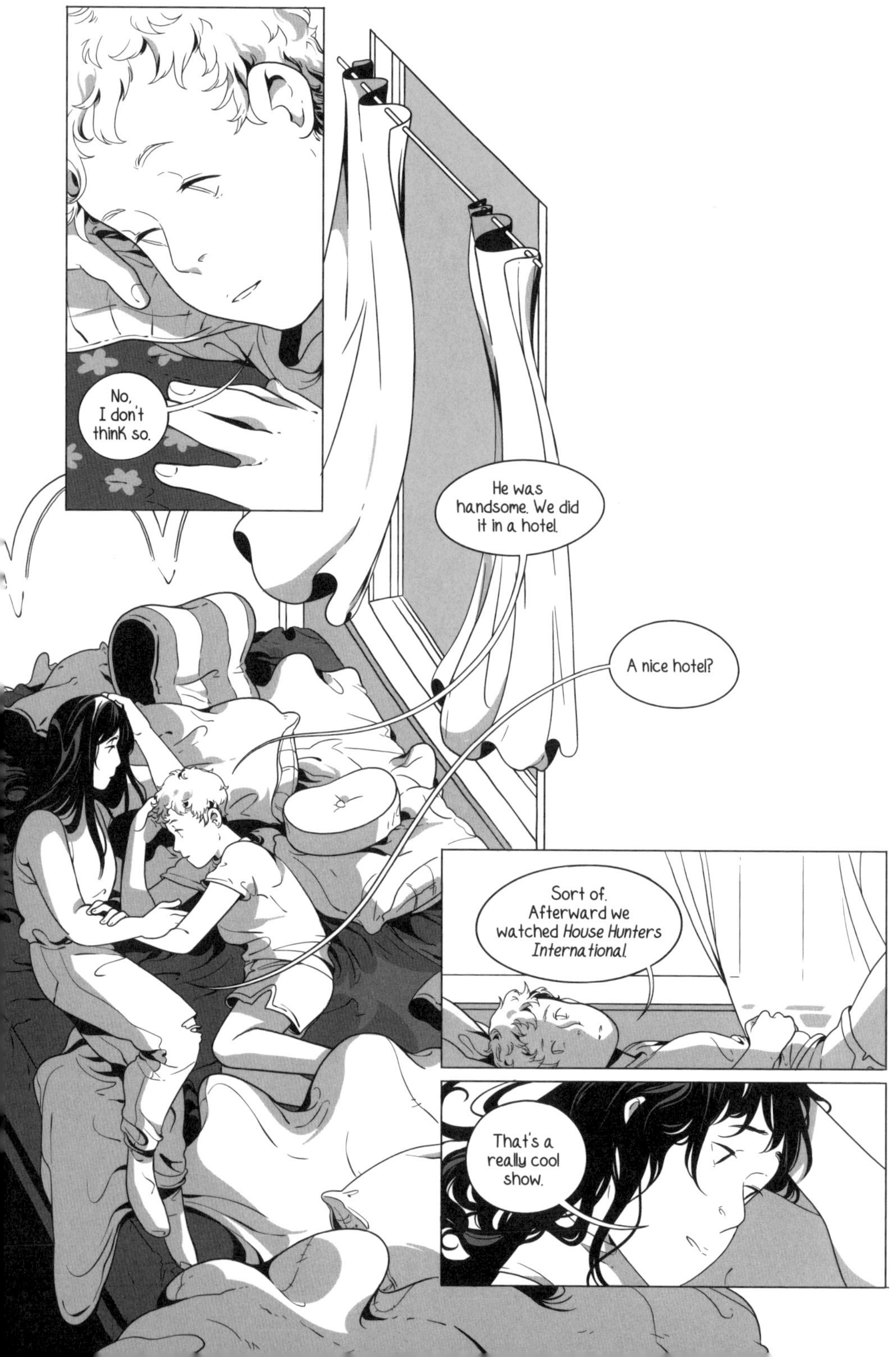
No, I don't think so.
He was handsome. We did it in a hotel.
A nice hotel?
Sort of. Afterward we watched *House Hunters International*.
That's a really cool show.

259

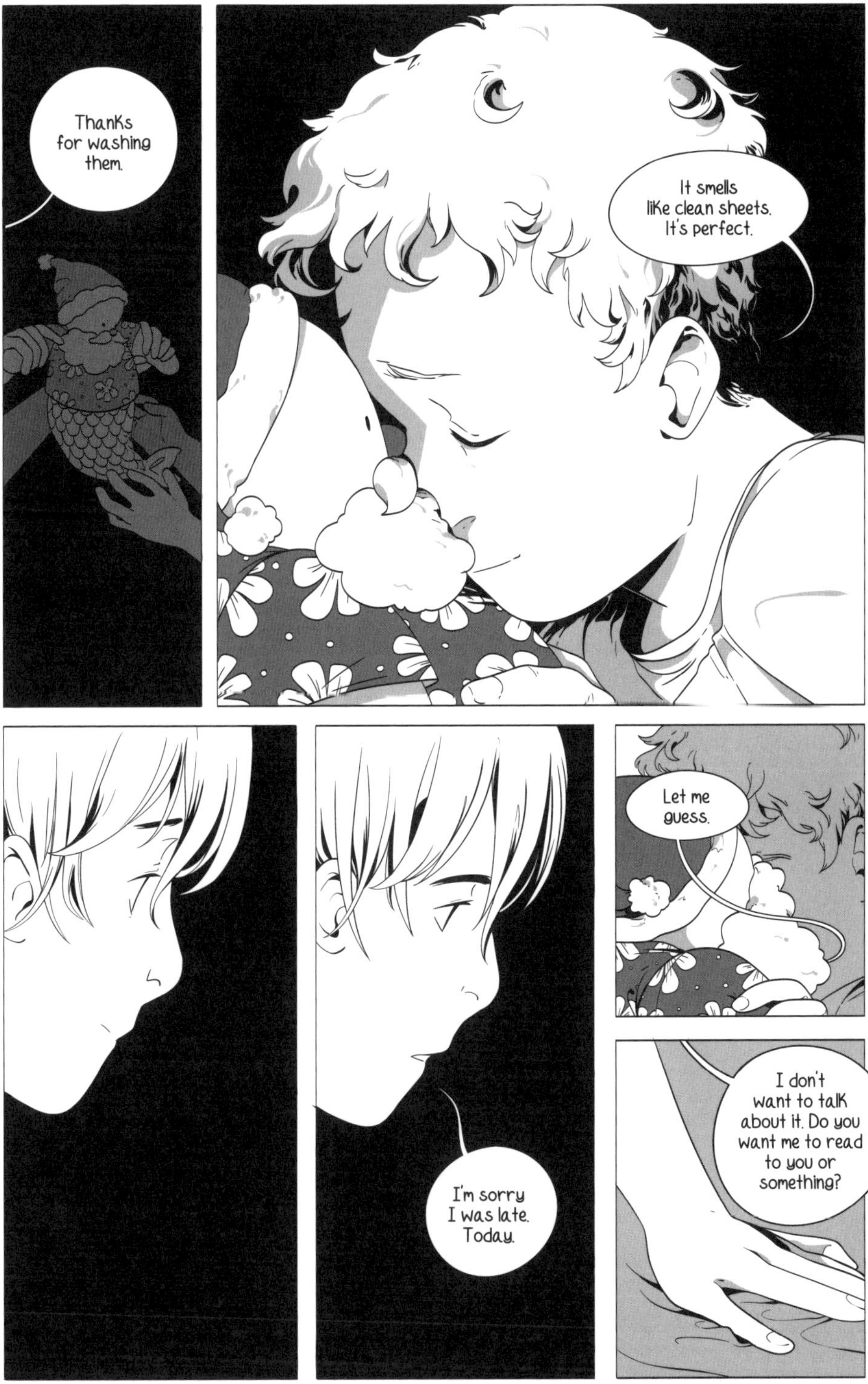
Thanks for washing them.
It smells like clean sheets. It's perfect.
Let me guess.
I'm sorry I was late. Today.
I don't want to talk about it. Do you want me to read to you or something?

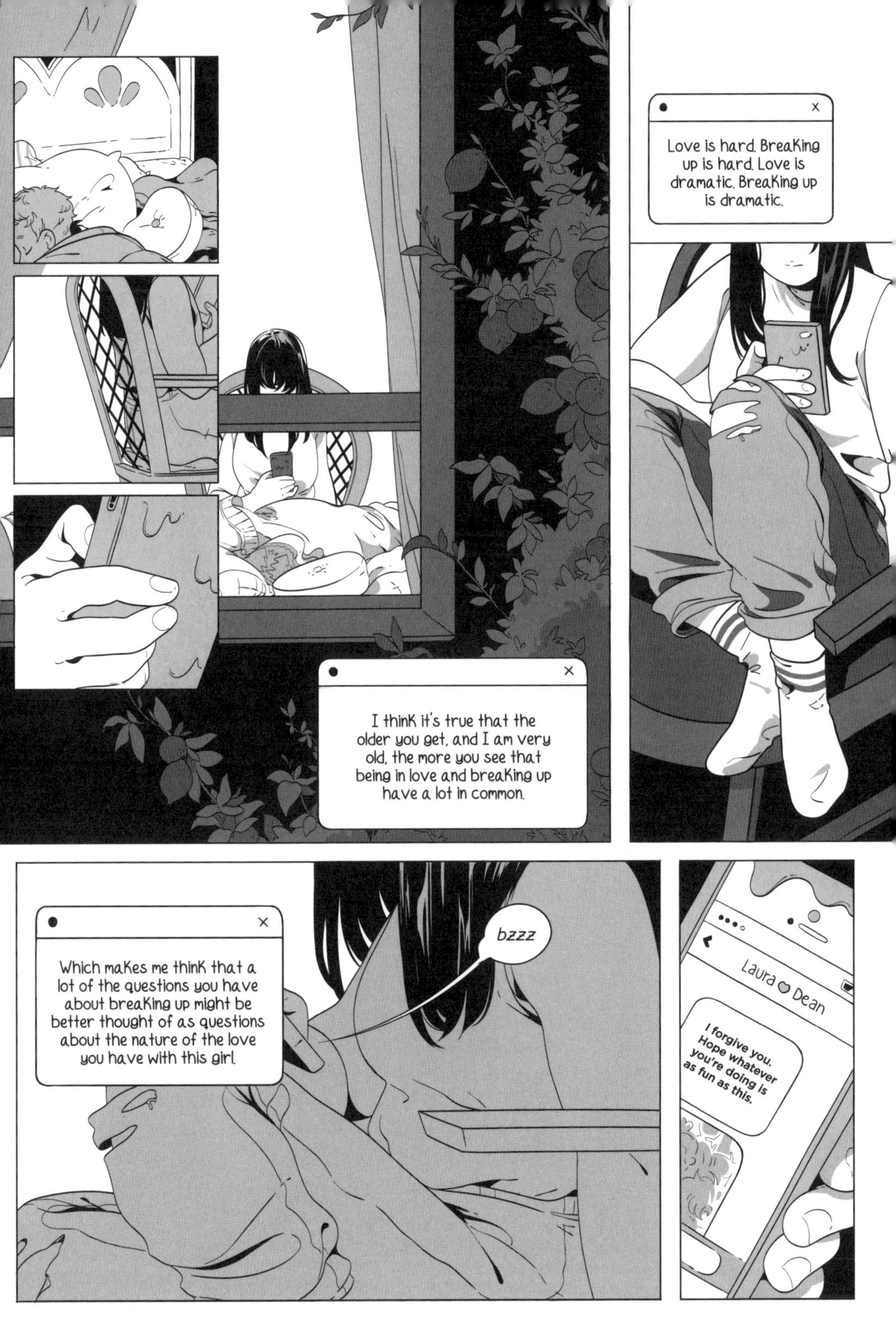
Love is hard. Breaking up is hard. Love is dramatic. Breaking up is dramatic.
I think it's true that the older you get, and I am very old, the more you see that being in love and breaking up have a lot in common.
Which makes me think that a lot of the questions you have about breaking up might be better thought of as questions about the nature of the love you have with this girl.
bzzz
Laura Dean
I forgive you. Hope whatever you're doing is as fun as this.

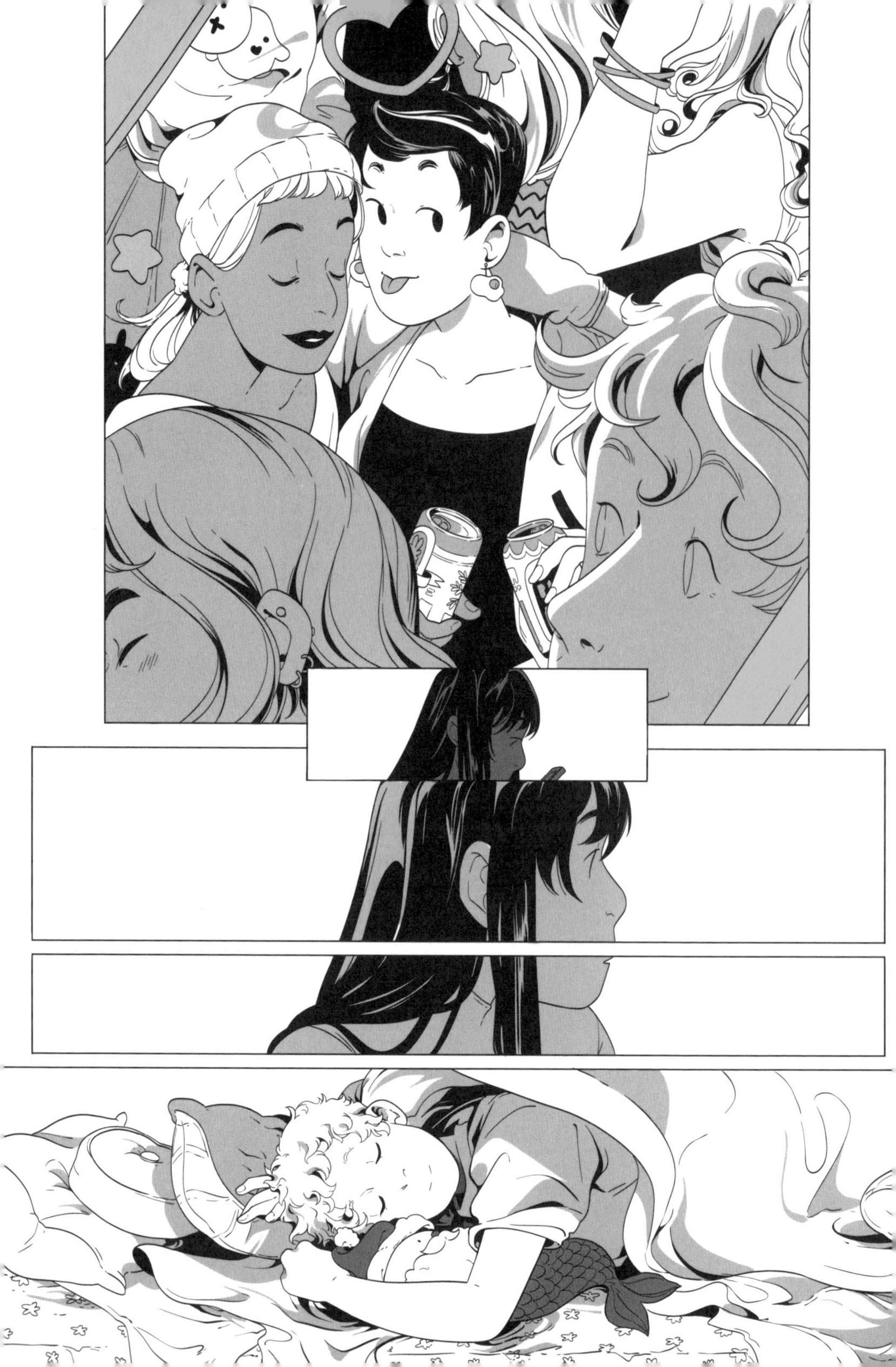

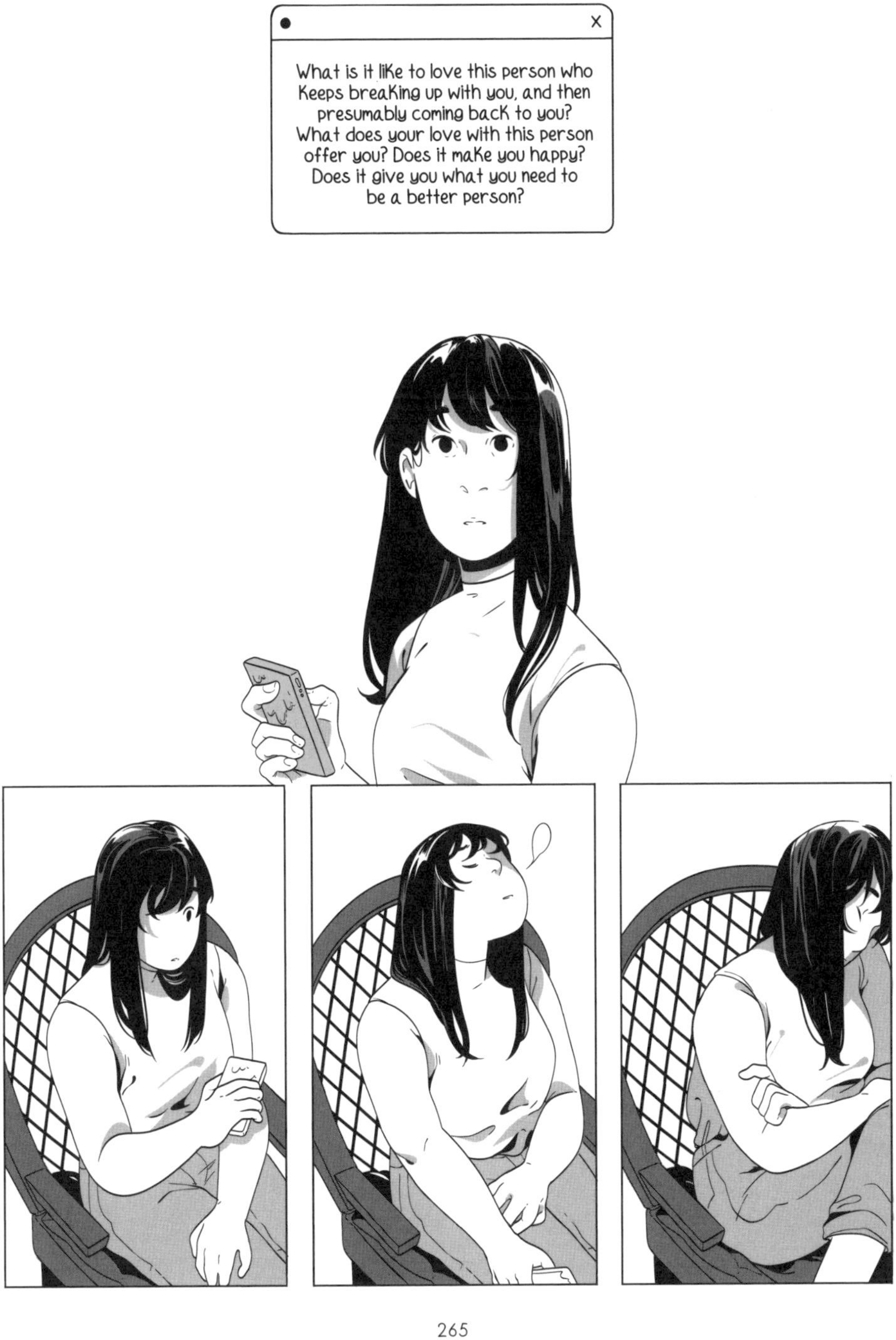
What is it like to love this person who Keeps breaking up with you, and then presumably coming back to you? What does your love with this person offer you? Does it make you happy? Does it give you what you need to be a better person?

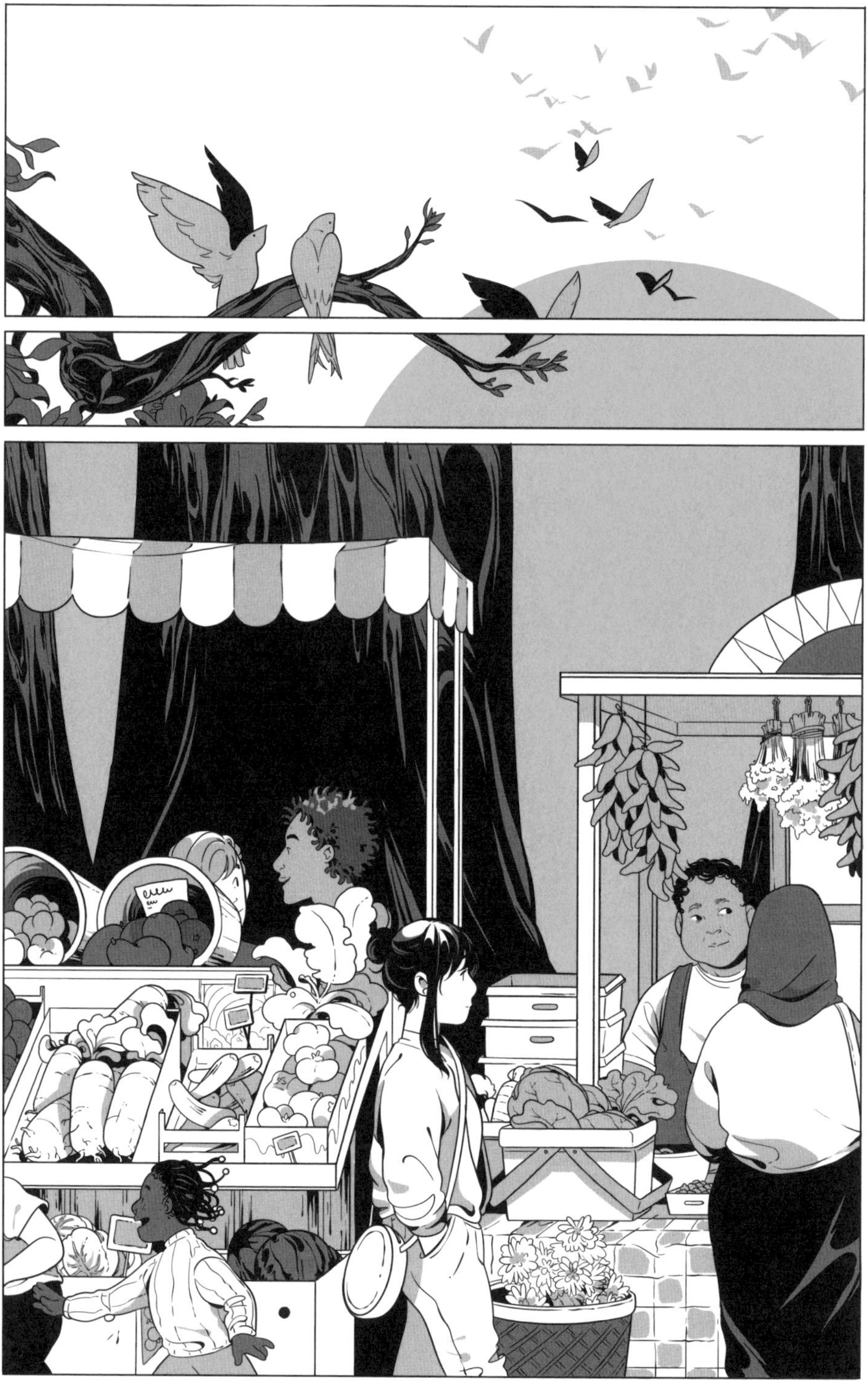

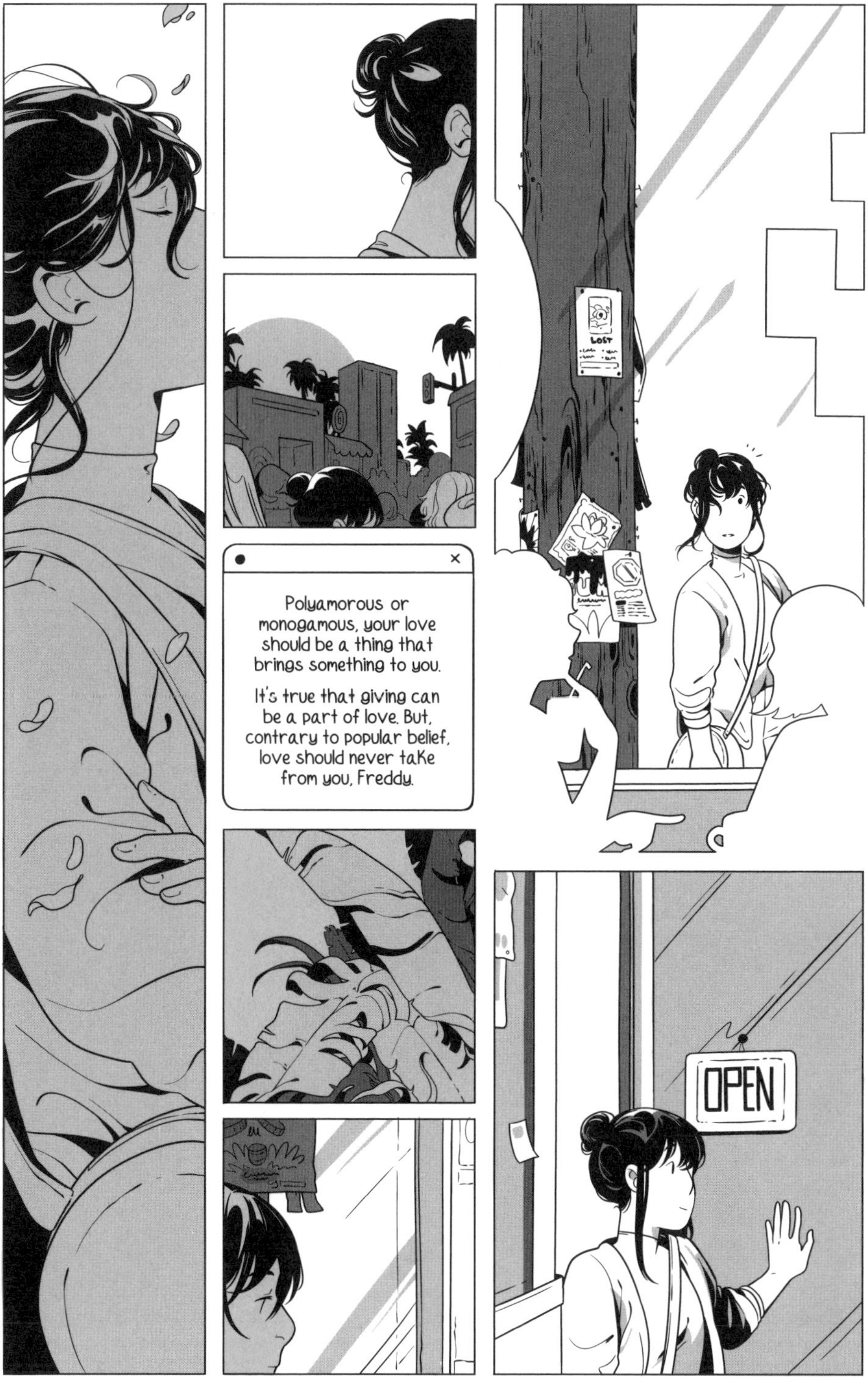
Polyamorous or monogamous, your love should be a thing that brings something to you.
It's true that giving can be a part of love. But, contrary to popular belief, love should never take from you, Freddy.
LOST
OPEN

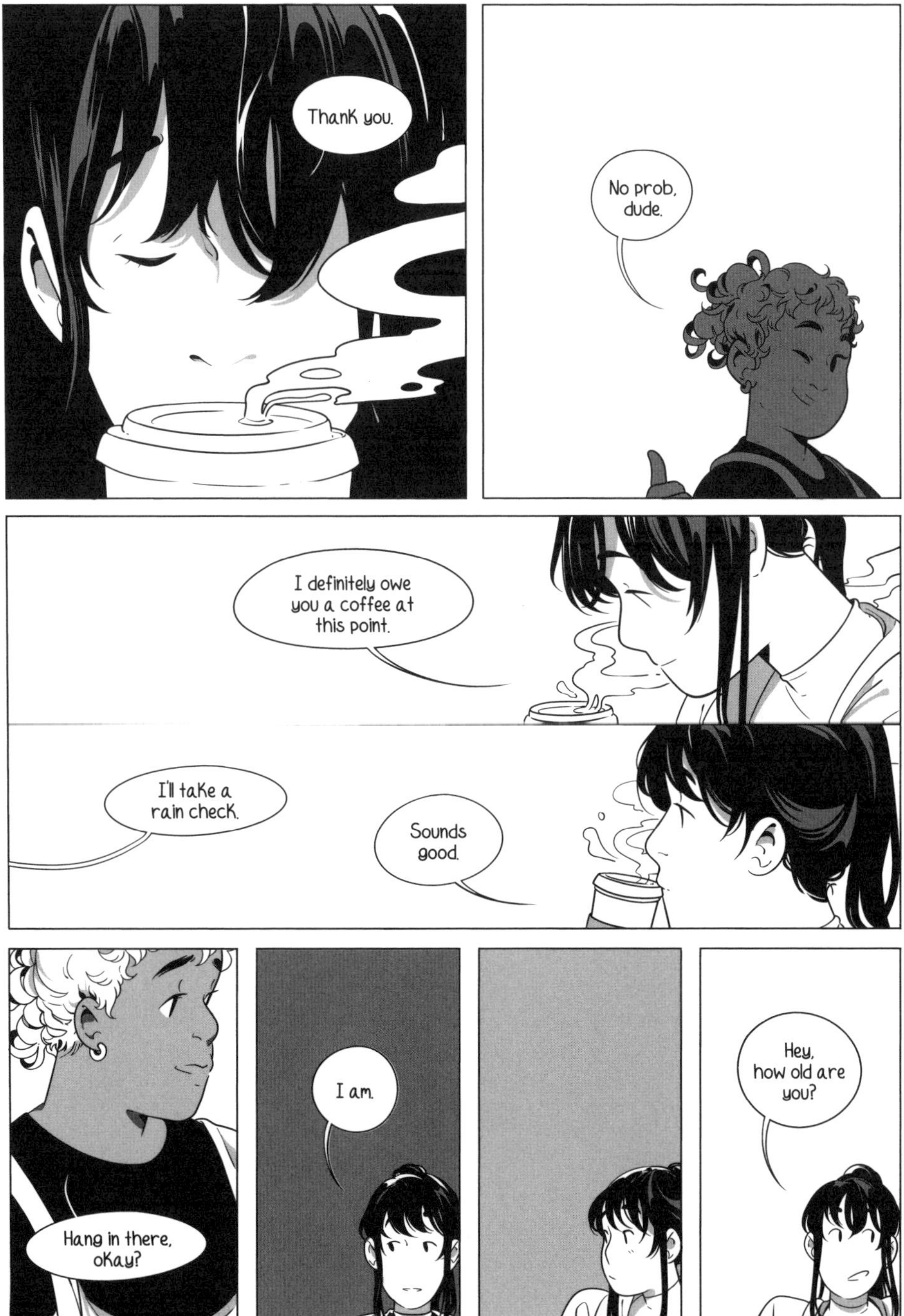
Thank you.
No prob, dude.
I definitely owe you a coffee at this point.
I'll take a rain check.
Sounds good.
Hang in there, okay?
I am.
Hey, how old are you?

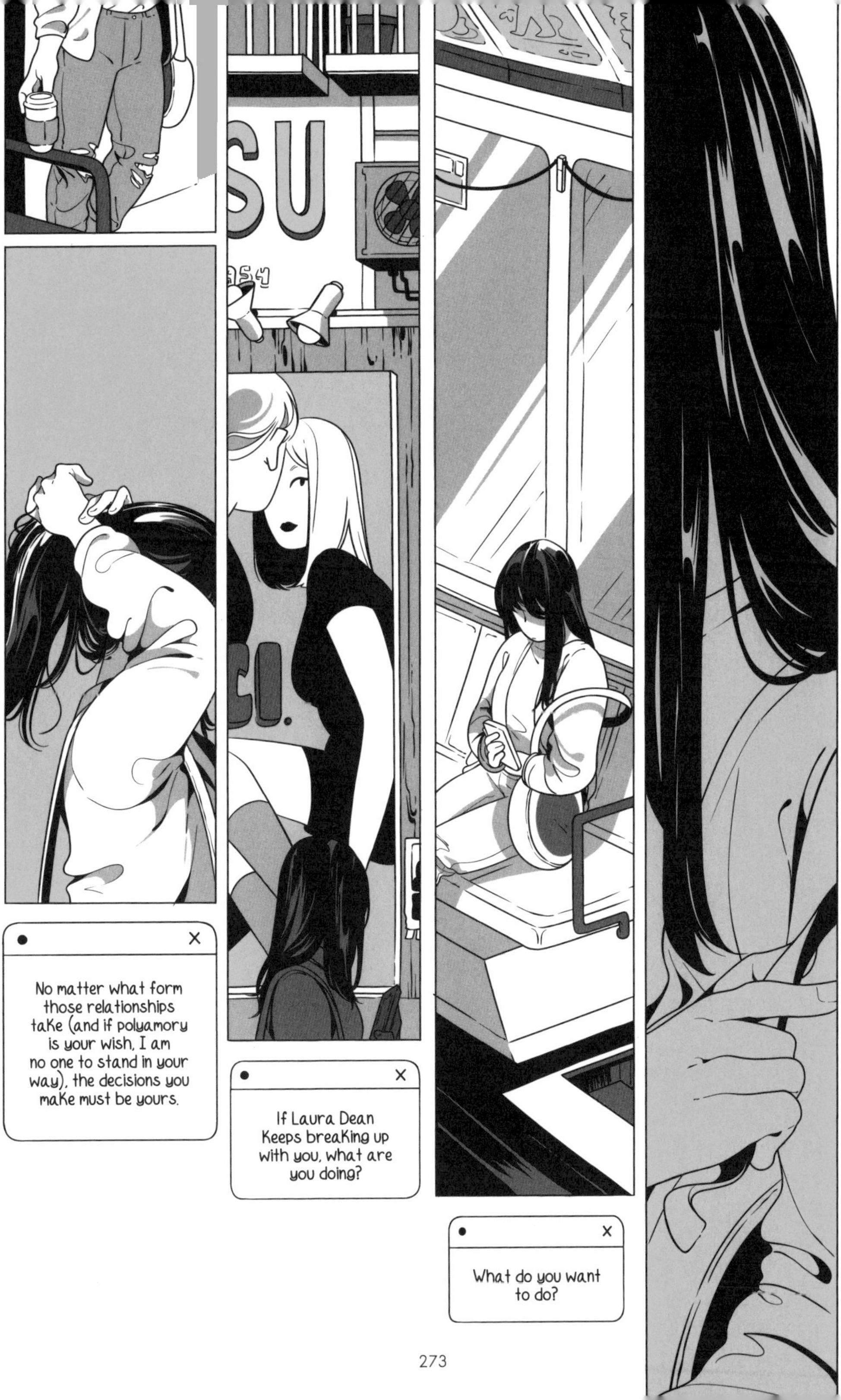

No matter what form those relationships take (and if polyamory is your wish, I am no one to stand in your way), the decisions you make must be yours.
If Laura Dean Keeps breaking up with you, what are you doing?
What do you want to do?

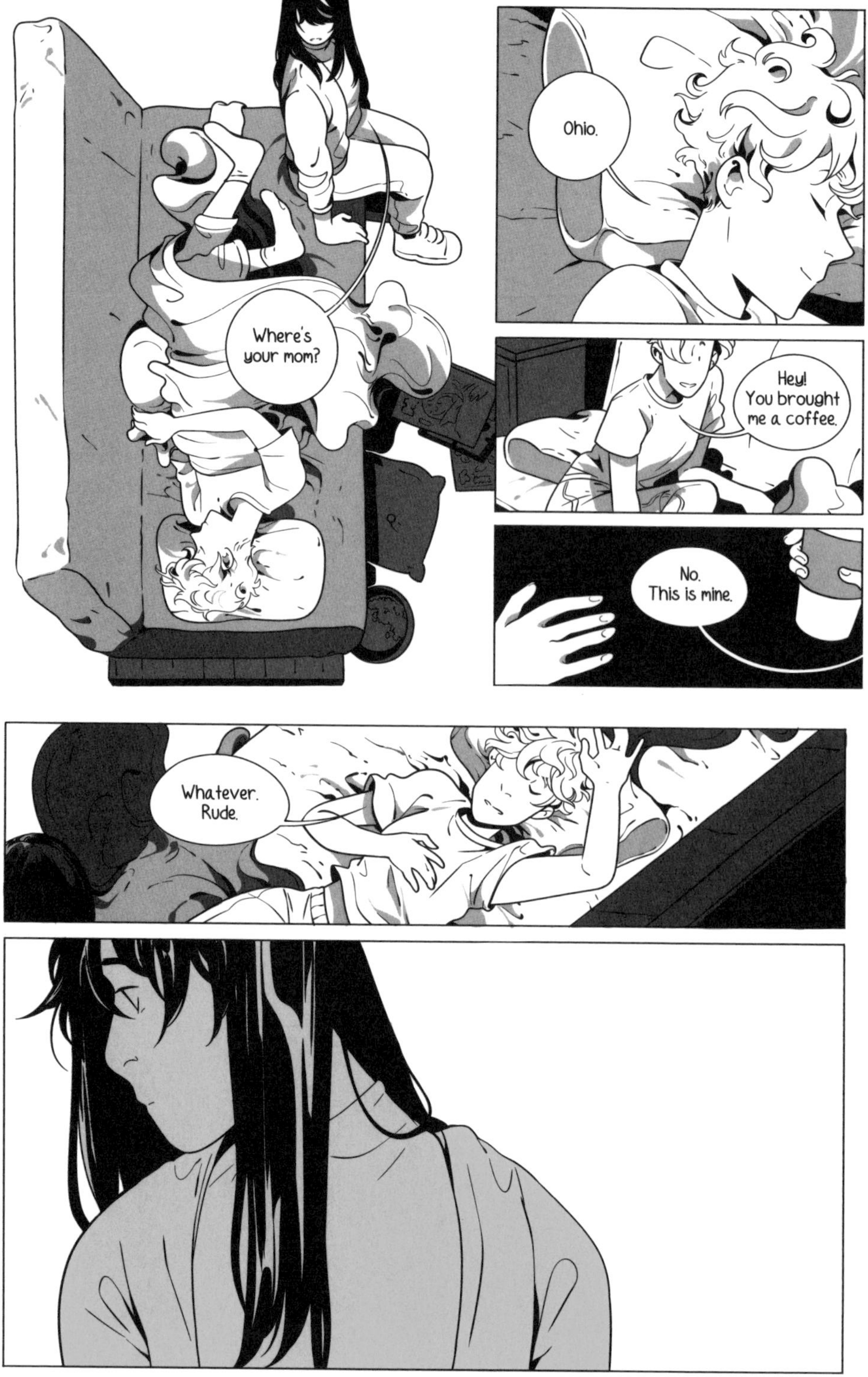
Where's your mom?
Ohio.
Hey! You brought me a coffee.
No. This is mine.
Whatever. Rude.

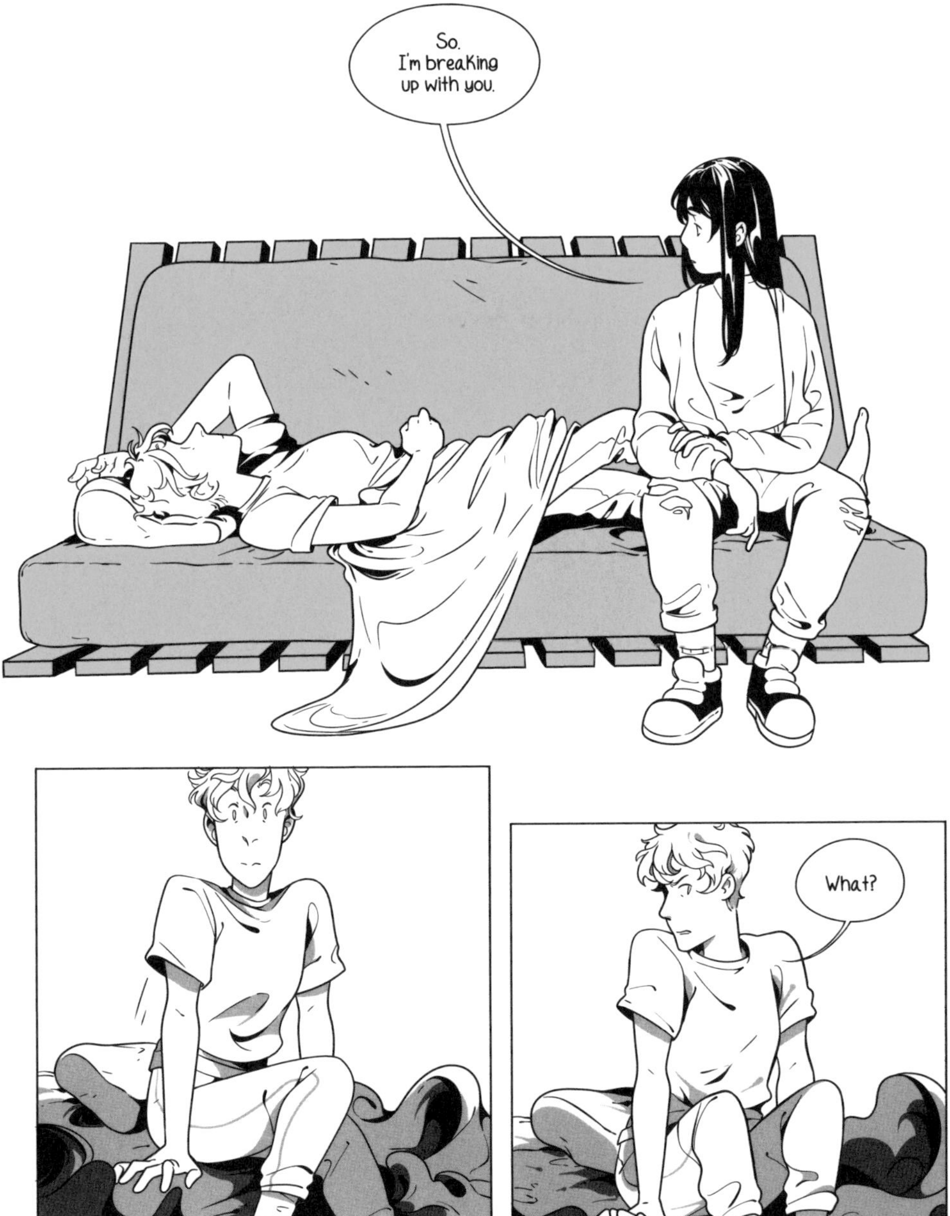
So.
I'm breaking
up with you.
What?

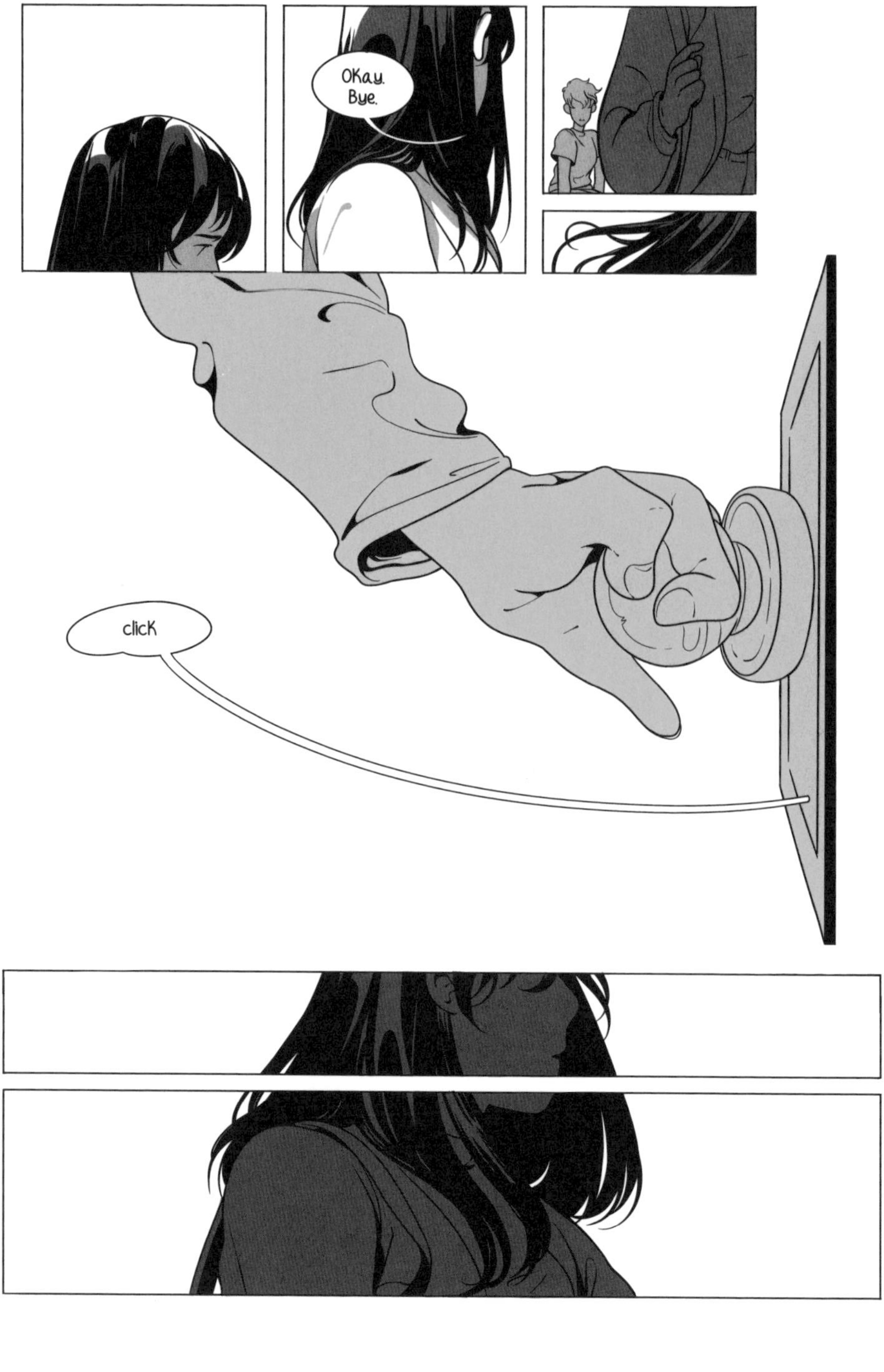
OKay.
Bye.
click

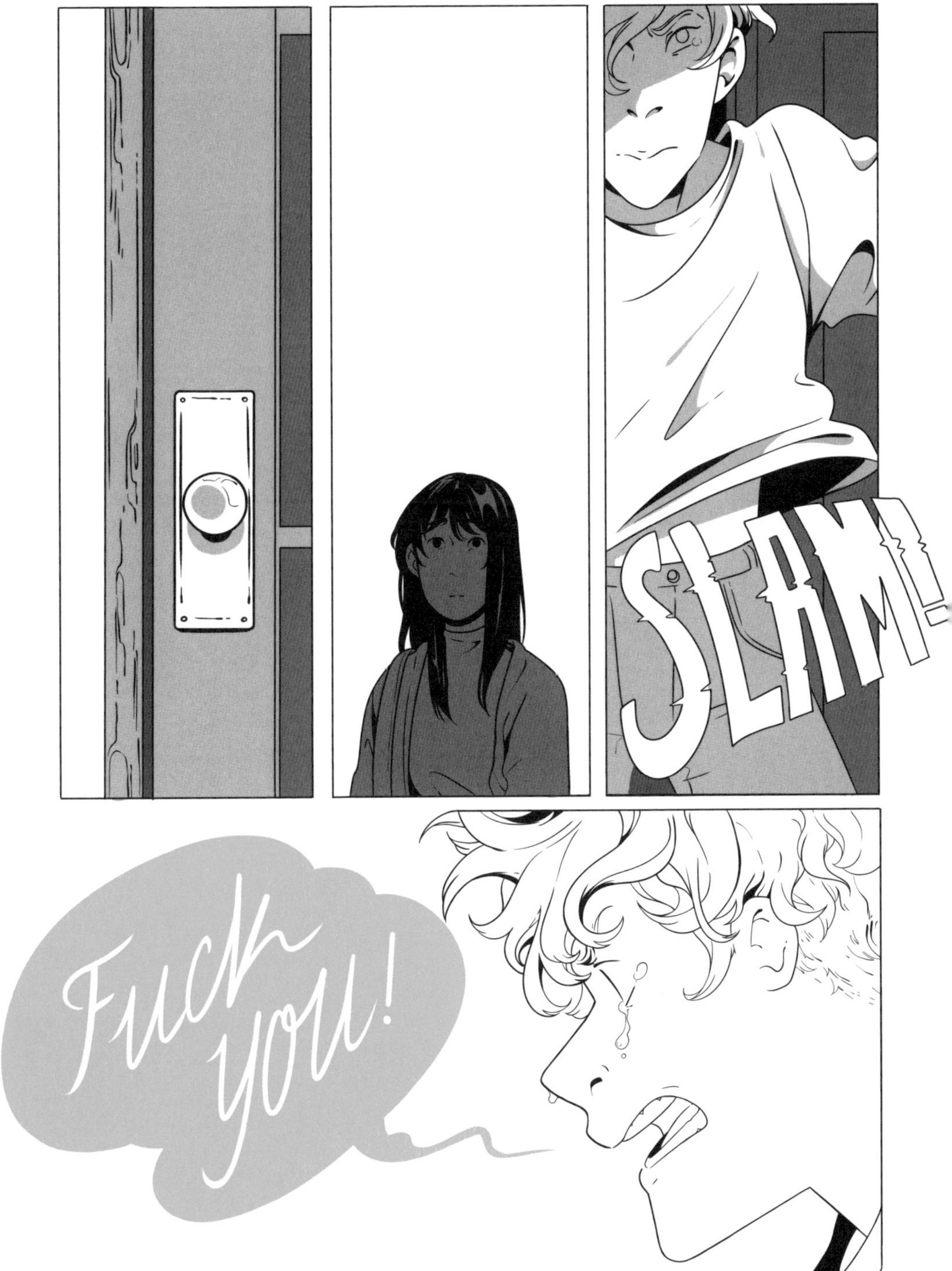
SLAM!
Fuck you!

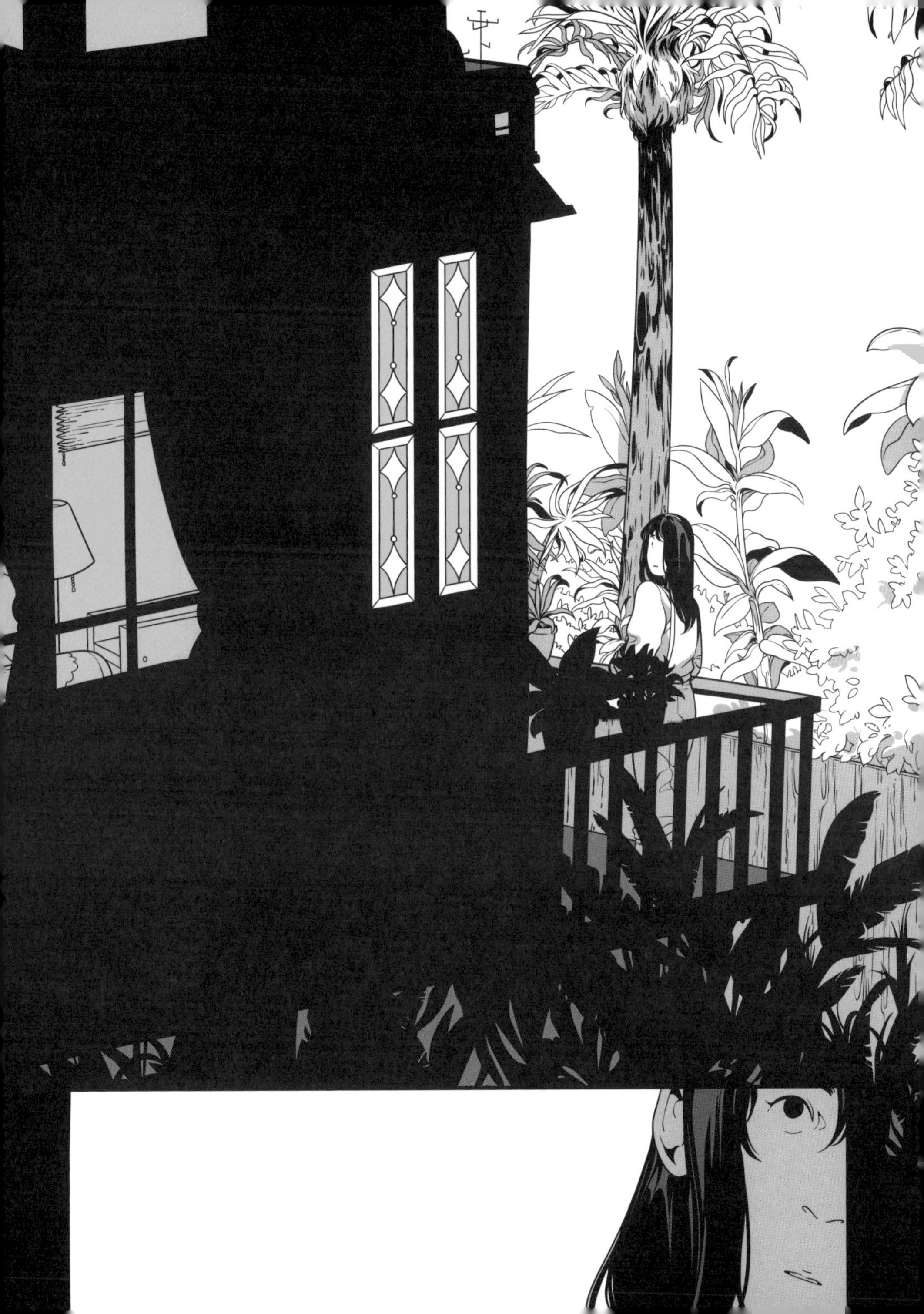

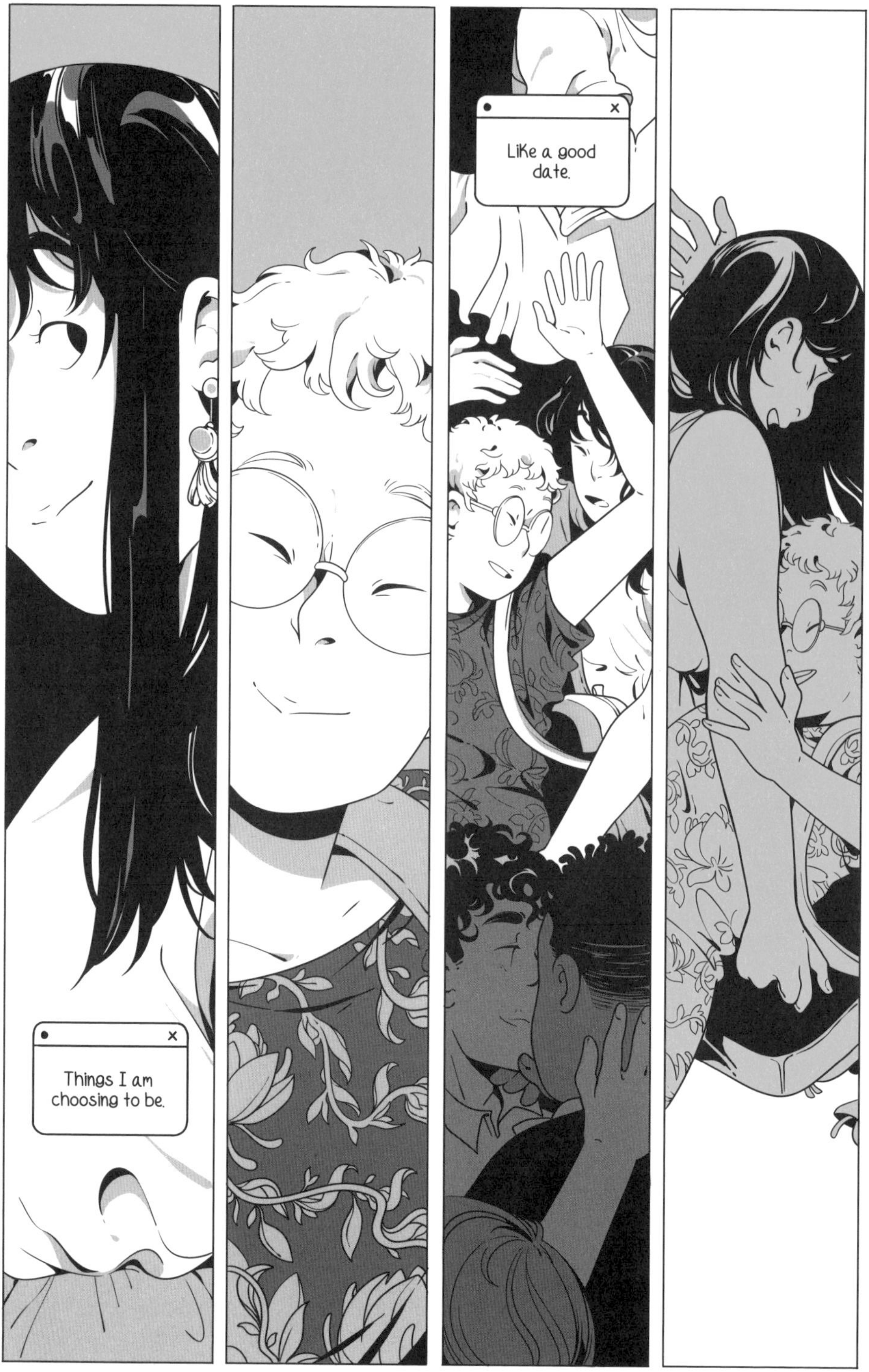
Things I am choosing to be.
Like a good date.

A better friend.

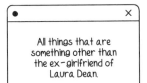

All things that are
something other than
the ex-girlfriend of
Laura Dean.

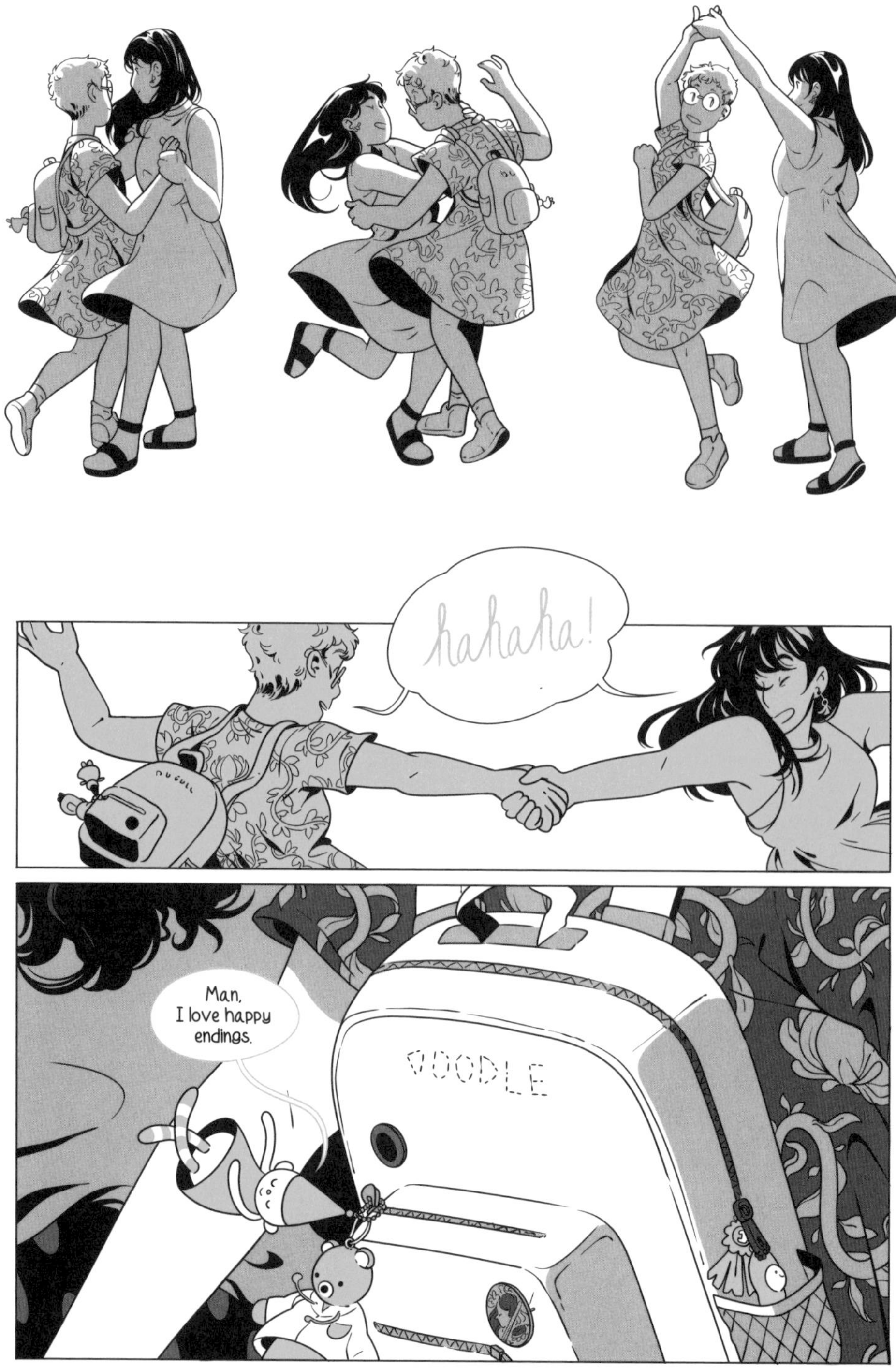
hahaha!
Man, I love happy endings.

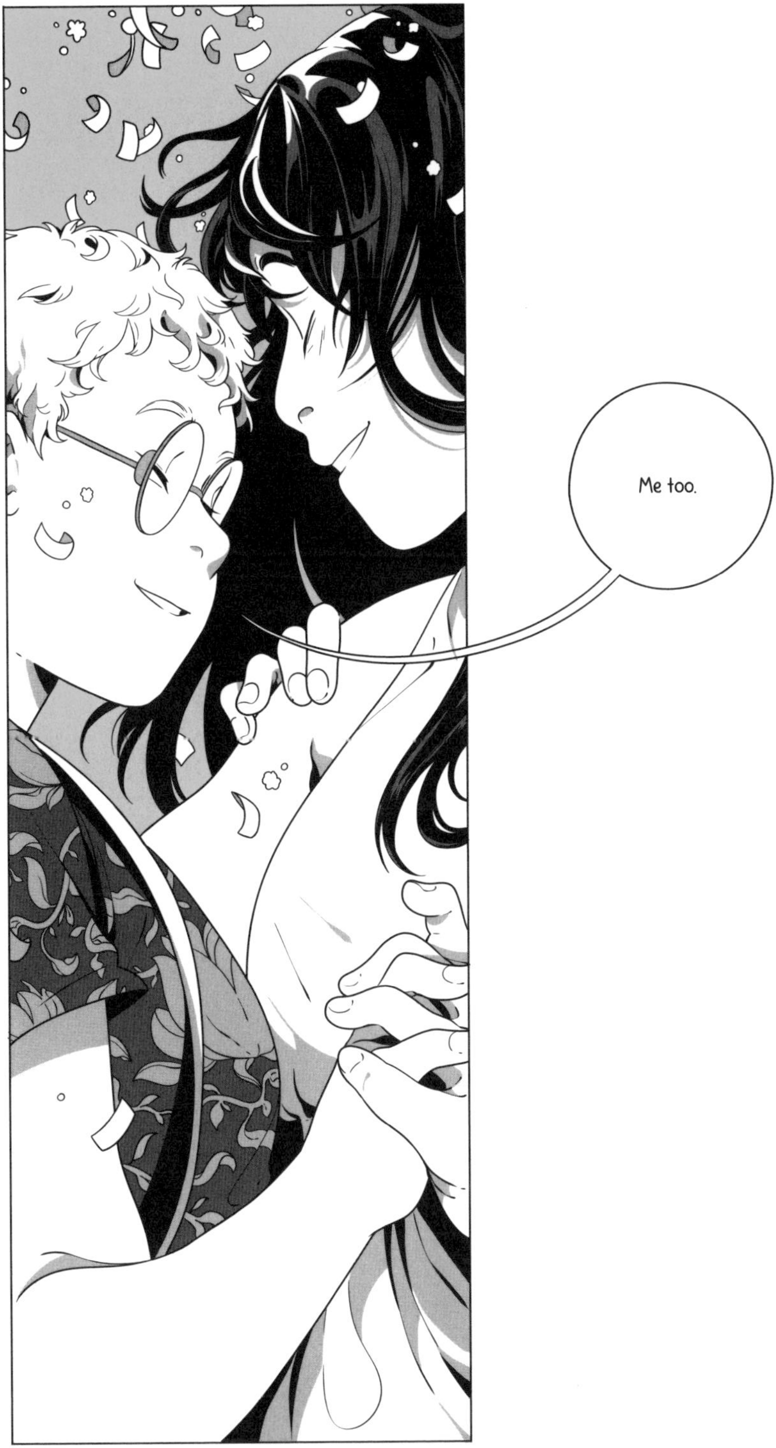
Me too.

ACKNOWLEDGMENTS

Thank you to my agent, Charlotte Sheedy, for her wisdom and guidance. To the many people who read this book, as a manuscript and as an almost fully realized graphic novel, including my editors Calista Brill, Whitney Taylor, Carol Burrell, as well as Kate Schatz, Kim Trusty and Cory Silverberg, thank you for your insight. Thank you to the hard workers at First Second, including Kiara Valdez and Andrew Arnold, who make these books happen in a multitude of unseen but very important ways.

Thank you to all the librarians and educators who I have spoken to over the years at countless conferences for all your support.

Thank you, Rosemary Valero-O'Connell, for working with me and making this book the visual dream that it is. You are so ridiculously talented. You are awesome.

Thank you to my amazing, smart, funny, girlfriend, Heather Gold, my most honest reader, who gives me heart and soul, my real deal love story.

— Mariko Tamaki

Thank you to Charlie Olsen, my incomparable agent, and to Calista Brill, Mark Siegel, Kiara Valdez, Whit Taylor, Andrew Arnold, and everyone else at First Second who worked tirelessly to help bring this book into the world. I will never be able to thank you all enough for the faith you've shown in me, and for the hand you've all played in making my wildest dreams come true. You've changed my life forever.

Thank you to Mariko, whose work lit a fire in my heart when I was a teenager, whose books made me want to throw myself into comics and never look back. You've been a lighthouse to me, and I don't think I'll ever stop having to pinch myself when I remember I got to help you tell this story.

Thank you to Ryan, Maddi, Chase, John, Madeline, Leigh, Lia, Jess, Brando, Spencer, Calvin, Maya, Sage, Corvin, Liz, Andrew, Lizzi, Jack, Chan, Luna, Sawyer, Andy, Mar, Sunmi, Paloma, Kate, Laura, E, Ann, Ashanti, Noella, Sarah, Han, Hannah, Carta, Rii, Carey, Zach, Bryce, Mey, and everyone else who has celebrated with me and encouraged me, who at some point throughout this journey gave me the resolve I needed to take the next step forward.

Thank you to Bob, Zak, Caitlin, and Anders, my mentors, for your guidance, your challenges, and your eternal patience.

Thank you most of all to my mom and my dads, my first and truest cheerleaders, whose unwavering and unflinching love and support keeps my feet on the ground and my eyes unclouded. *Todo lo que soy es gracias a vosotros, y os quiero mil veces más de lo que jamás podre expresar.*

— Rosemary Valero-O'Connell

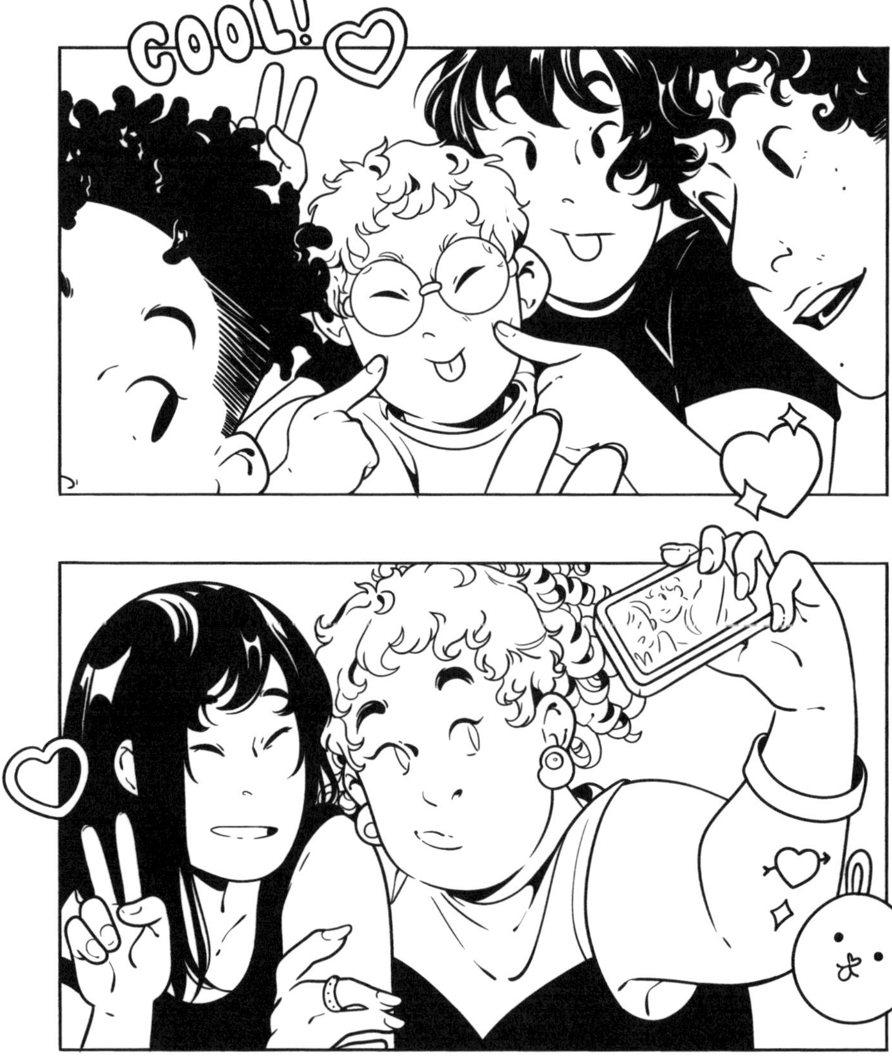
COOL!

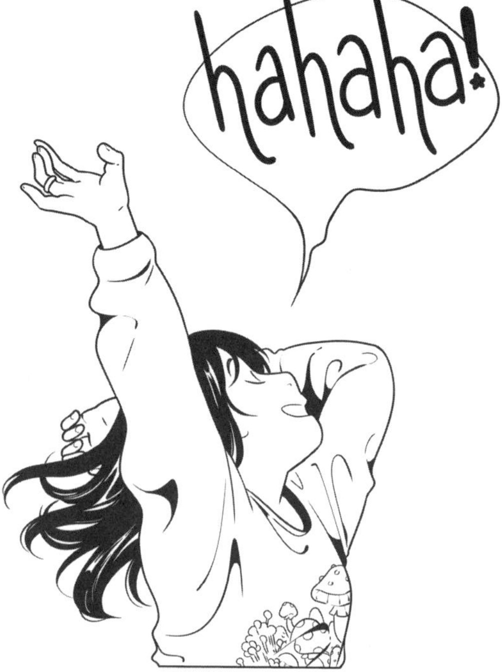
hahaha!

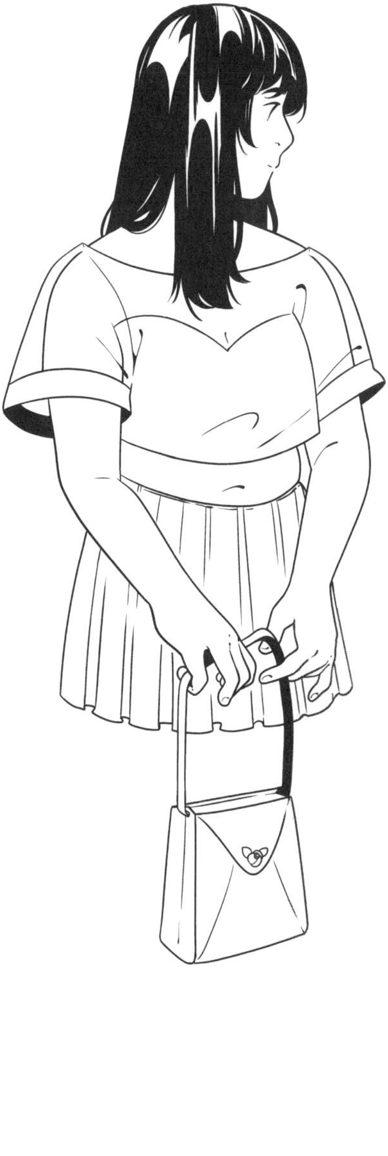

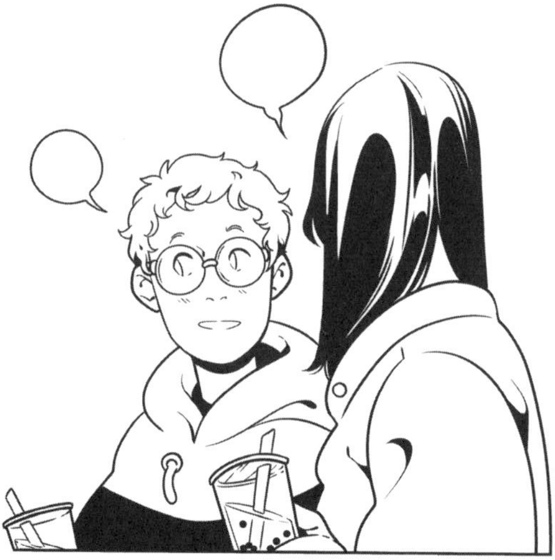

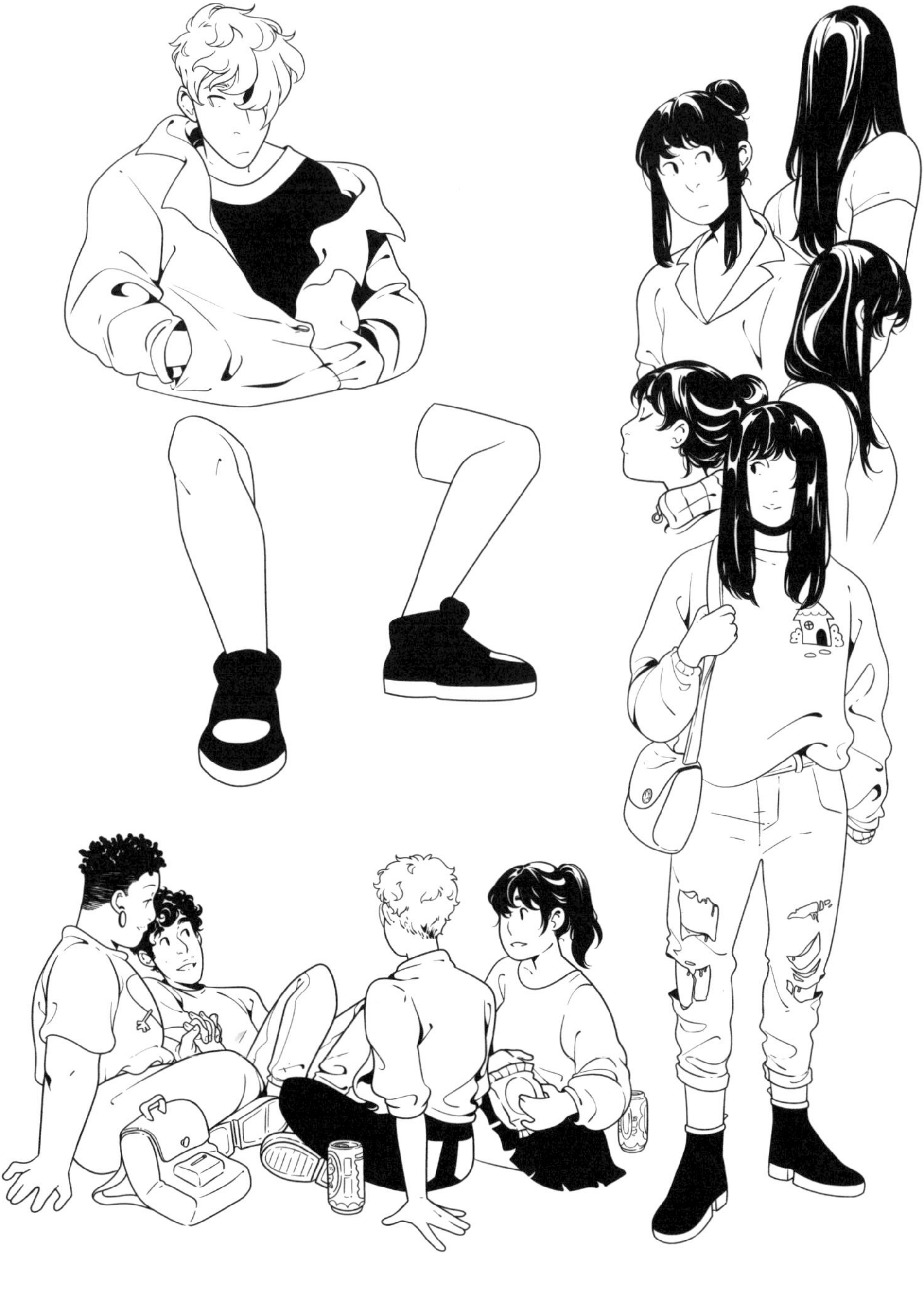

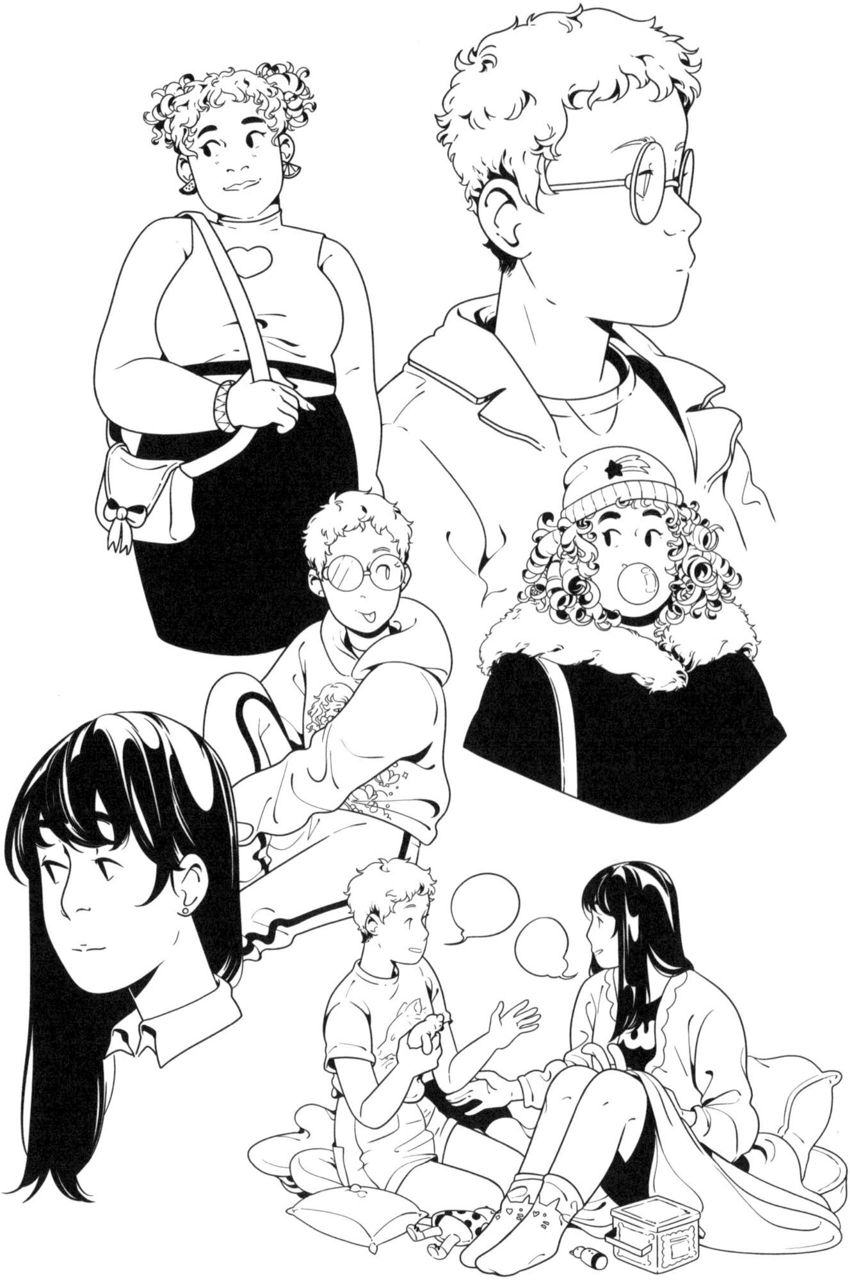

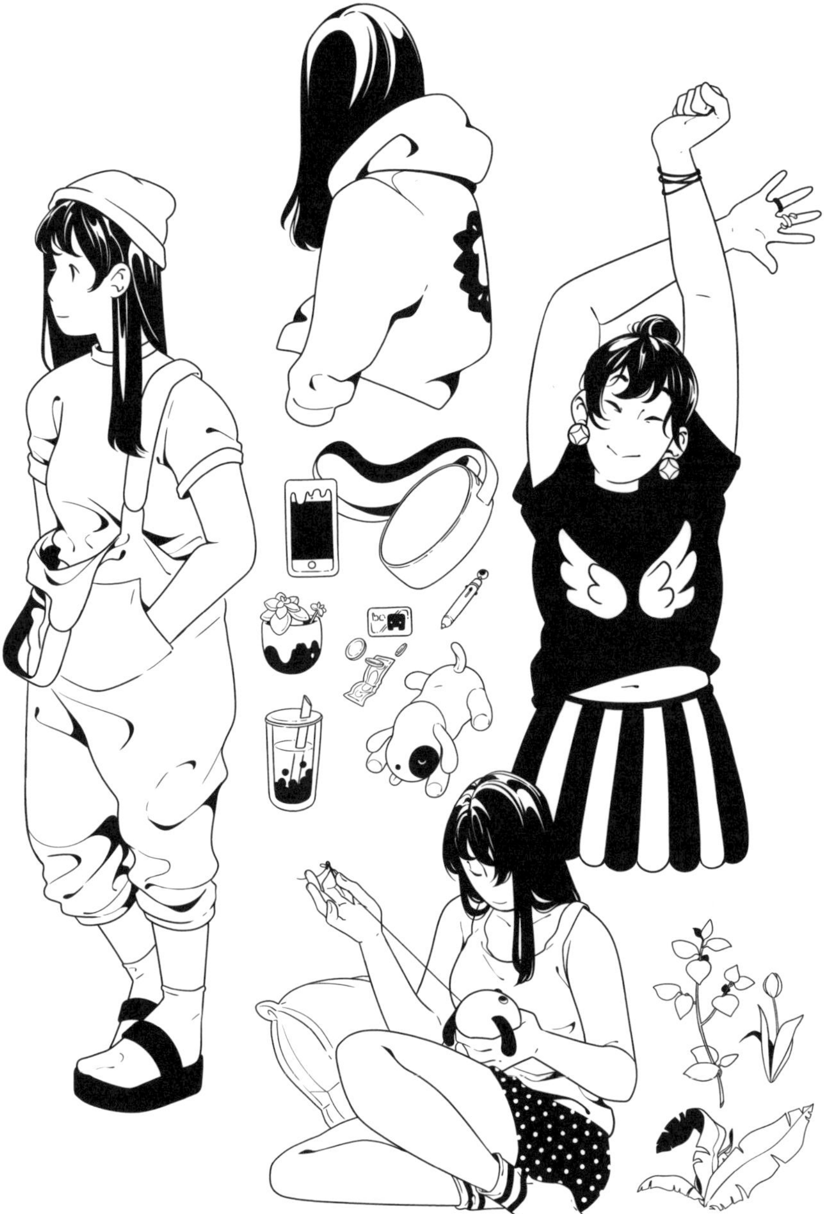

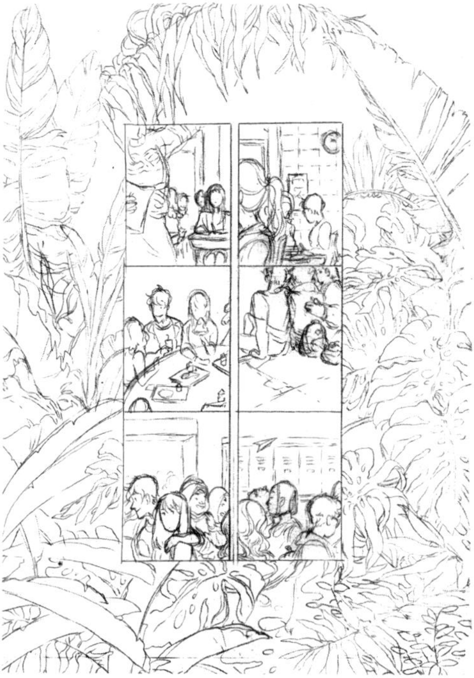

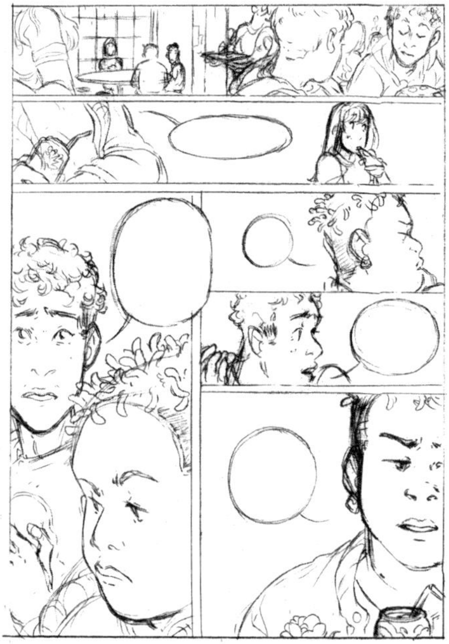

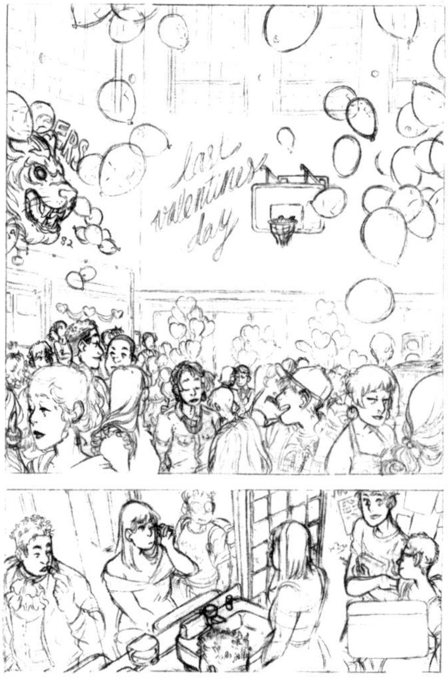
last valentines day
82

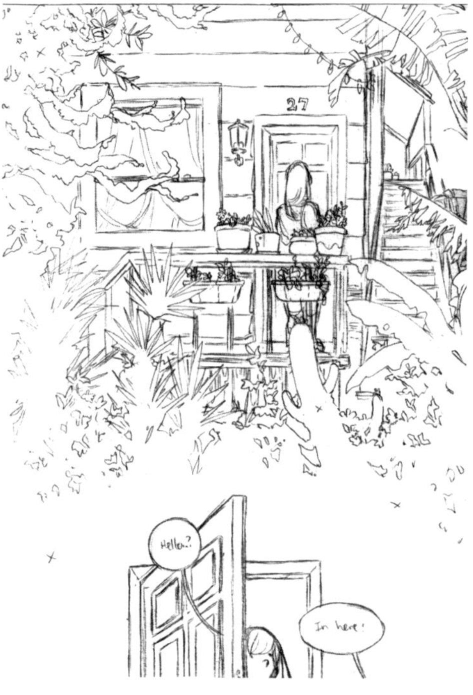
27
Hello?
In here!

First Second

Text copyright © 2019 by Mariko Tamaki
Illustrations copyright © 2019 by Rosemary Valero-O'Connell

Published by First Second
First Second is an imprint of Roaring Brook Press,
a division of Holtzbrinck Publishing Holdings Limited Partnership
120 Broadway, New York, NY 10271
All rights reserved

Library of Congress Control Number: 2018944904

Paperback ISBN: 978-1-62672-259-0
Hardcover ISBN: 978-1-250-31284-6

Our books may be purchased in bulk for promotional, educational, or business use. Please
contact your local bookseller or the Macmillan Corporate and Premium Sales Department
at (800) 221-7945 ext. 5442 or by email at MacmillanSpecialMarkets@macmillan.com.

First edition, 2019

Edited by Calista Brill and Whit Taylor
Book design by Chris Dickey and Molly Johanson

Penciled with Bristol and graphite, inked and colored in Photoshop with a Cintiq 21UX and a Surface Pro.
Printed in the United States of America by Worzalla, Stevens Point, Wisconsin

Paperback: 10 9 8 7 6 5 4 3
Hardcover: 10 9 8 7 6 5 4 3 2 1